YOU'RE NOT WORTH MY TEARS

BY:
CHENELL PARKER

OTHER TITLES BY CHENELL PARKER

Chapter 1

"No, don't park that close. He might see us. It's still daylight!" Royce yelled to her cousin Uri.

"I don't give a fuck if he sees us or not. He better pray that I don't get out of this car and use my Taser on his dog ass," Uri argued.

Uri and her cousin Royce were best friends, so she didn't think twice when her cousin called and asked her to accompany her to do some investigating. Royce didn't want her car to be seen, so Uri drove hers instead. She was ready to knock on the hotel room's door and pull her cousin's husband, Jax, out by the balls if she had to. Uri was especially pissed because her cousin had a heart of gold. Royce would give the shirt off her back to someone in need and she didn't deserve the treatment that she got from her husband.

At twenty-nine years old, Uri was only two years older than her cousin. They were both an only child, but Royce had it a little better than Uri did, being that she grew up in a loving two-parent home. She always had the best of everything. Thanks to Royce's parents, Sondra and Patrick, so did Uri. Her mother's sister and her husband had been a blessing to her for as long she could remember. Uri went to the best schools and wore the same fancy clothes as her cousin. There was no need for jealousy between the two of them because they always had the finest. Uri's living conditions weren't as luxurious, but it wasn't the slums either. She and her mother lived in a nicely furnished upscale three-bedroom condo, courtesy of her favorite aunt and uncle. Uri's mother, Lydia, was fifteen years younger than Royce's mother and Sondra treated her as if she were her child. She paid all of Lydia's bills because she could never hold down a job for too long without being fired or quitting. Uri didn't understand her mother's ungratefulness towards her aunt, but she loved her all the same. Lydia was a single mother and she did the best that she could. Uri never went without and her aunt and uncle made sure of it. Lydia drank more than she should have, but she was a wonderful grandmother to Uri's two kids.

"If I didn't want to ruin my career and reputation, I would go knock on that door and drag his ass out of there," Royce threatened angrily.

Royce was an elementary school teacher, so she had to be careful with how she carried herself. Her father was the vice president of their local newspaper company, where Uri also worked as a manager. Royce's mother used to be a teacher as well, but she was now the assistant principal of the school where she taught. They would die if she ever did anything to embarrass them or bring shame to the Davenport or Calloway family names. Her father, not so much, but her mother lived for the public's opinion. She wanted her family to be perfect in every way, which was why divorce was out of the question for her. Not only that, but Jax's mother was the principal at the school and everyone knew that Sondra was next in line for the position if she were to ever leave. Jax's father was the director of education at the school board office and Sondra loved to throw that in people's faces. Jax was the school's athletic director, but he taught boys and girls track at another local high school as well. He was even worse than her mother. He loved to put on airs like they had a blemish free marriage and Royce was dumb enough to always play along.

"I understand what you're saying cousin, but fuck that. You and Jax have only been married for two years and I've lost count of how many times he's cheated. I know you believe that a lot of it is hearsay, but you know damn well that nigga ain't right. You're seeing this shit with your own eyes now. This ain't no rumors You gotta stop sweeping shit under the rug and let that nigga know what's up. He thinks he's getting away with it because you never confront his ass. He's supposed to be at the gym, but he's at a hotel room in broad daylight instead. That's some straight disrespectful bullshit," Uri fumed.

"I know that Uri, but I never had any real proof before now. I still feel weird about saying anything though. I know that I'm wrong for tracking his phone, but my gut told me that something wasn't right. If I leave his ass now, he won't be able to say shit," Royce replied.

"You ain't going nowhere and you know it. Your mama would die if you got a divorce," Uri reminded her.

"I'm really starting to not care about her feelings or what she has to say. I'm the one that's going through this bullshit, not her. My daddy is a great husband, so she doesn't know how I feel. We're still newlyweds and there ain't a damn thing for me to smile about," Royce said as she wiped the few tears that fell from her eyes.

"Stop crying over that nigga. He's not even worth your tears. Fuck him!" Uri yelled, getting angry all over again.

She hated to see her cousin hurting over a man who stood before God and promised to love and cherish her. Jax wasn't shit and she hated everything about his dog ass. She knew he wasn't the one when he and her cousin first started dating three years prior. Jax was already divorced with two kids and she didn't think he was right for Royce. He always claimed that he and his first wife had a mutual split, but Uri found that very hard to believe. He probably did her the same way he was doing her cousin and she probably got fed up. He treated Royce like a queen, but he just couldn't seem to remain faithful.

"Look," Royce said as she pointed to a car that pulled up right alongside of her husband's brand-new silver Land Rover.

It was an older model midnight blue Maxima with dark tinted windows. The lipstick print sticker on the back window let them know that it had to be a female driver.

"Let's see who this bitch is," Uri said as she tapped on her steering wheel anxiously.

They waited for the driver to get out, but they never did. A few minutes went by before Jax walked out of the hotel room and opened the driver's side door. When he helped a woman out and wrapped his arms around her, Uri was ready to get out and start swinging. Her blood pressure rose to a deadly level as she watched her cousin's husband palm the woman's ass and plant a sloppy kiss on her lips. She looked over at Royce and she seemed to be in another world as she watched everything unfold. When she saw the tears cascading down her cousin's eyes again, Uri was ready for war.

"I can't believe this shit. He divorced her, only to cheat on me with the same bitch," Royce said angrily.

"Who is that?" Uri questioned.

"That's his ex-wife, Sienna," Royce replied.

"Are you fucking kidding me? He's cheating on you with his ex-wife? What kind of Jerry Springer shit is that?" Uri yelled.

"He makes me think that they don't get along, but that's an obvious lie. Now I know why she's been calling a lot more lately for the past few months," Royce said.

"And you were okay with that?" Uri questioned.

"They have kids together Uri. What was I supposed to do? I can't tell the mother of his kids not to call him anymore," Royce argued.

"That's true, but I thought you said that she had a boyfriend," Uri noted.

"She does have a boyfriend that she lives with. Jax is always asking his kids if her man treats them well and stuff like that. They've been living together for over a year now," Royce replied.

"So, he's married and she lives with her man. They're divorced, but fucking around again behind both of y'all backs," Uri said, just to be sure that she understood the scenario.

She'd heard all about Jax's ex-wife, but she had never seen the other woman before. Sienna had never given her cousin any problems, so she didn't have a reason to.

"That's what it looks like to me," Royce acknowledged.

"Okay, so now what? You wanna go in there and drag that bitch out or what?" Uri questioned, ready to put in work.

"Nope. I'm gonna sit right here and wait it out," Royce replied.

"Oh no, bitch. I'm not about to sit out here and wait while your man is in there fucking his ex-wife. If we're not gonna do anything, then we can go," Uri fussed.

"We are gonna do something. I want to follow that bitch home to see exactly where she lives. Her man is gonna get an ear full when I finish telling him everything. My home won't be the only one that's unhappy," Royce replied.

"That's what the fuck I'm talking about. It's time for you get a backbone cousin. I love you, but you're entirely too nice at times," Uri noted.

Before her ex got killed in a motorcycle accident three years before, Uri went through the exact same thing with him. Unlike her favorite cousin, she was not the type to let shit fly so easily. She didn't believe in getting mad, she liked to get even instead. That was exactly why her second child's paternity was in question for a while. Uri had two daughters, but only her first was for her deceased ex. He was hurt when he found out that she'd cheated and made a baby with someone else, but he loved her enough to stay and make it work. Unfortunately, he lost his life a few months later. Uri ended up marrying Ashton, the father of her second child, and they were happy and content. She wanted the same for her cousin, but Royce had to want that for herself as well. She was so worried about embarrassing her mother that she was making herself miserable in the process.

"I can see that being nice gets me nowhere. He wants to be married to a bitch, so now he is," Royce said as she kept her eyes fixed on the hotel room that her husband and his ex-wife walked into.

***

"Shit," Jax hissed as he watched his dick appear and then disappear down Sienna's throat.

He had a firm grip on her ponytail, making sure she took in all of him. His cell phone sat in plain view, recording everything that went down. He couldn't wait to upload the footage and add it to his growing personal collection. Jax loved to go back and look at himself on camera with other women. The rush that he got was one that he could never describe.

Sienna looked in his eyes as saliva trickled down the sides of her mouth down to her neck. She had always been a freak and Jax never could get enough of her. She could run circles around Royce when it came to creativity, but Jax hadn't met a woman yet who could outdo his wife when it came to oral. Royce was a pro at fellatio and there was no comparison.

"Damn girl," Jax moaned as he felt his nut building and ready to be released.

At thirty years old, Jax felt like he had the life that most men only dreamed of. He had a beautiful wife at home and a few other women at his beck and call, including his ex. He and Sienna were the same age, but she was as dumb as they came. Jax sold her so many dreams and she fell for every lie that he'd ever told.

"What are you doing?" Sienna asked when Jax pulled his pants up after he came.

She was ready for round three, but he must have had other plans. He was always rushing home to his wife and that pissed her off every time.

"I gotta go. My wife is probably on her way home from the mall by now. I can't be out too late," Jax said as he continued to get dressed.

"Late? It's still daylight and we've only been here for an hour," Sienna complained.

"It's been over an hour, but what's your point? It doesn't take that long to fuck," Jax replied.

"You know what I mean Jaxon. You usually stay and chill for a while. What's the rush?" Sienna asked.

"I just told you. My wife thinks I'm at the gym. My workouts only last about two hours at the most. I can't be out too long without her getting suspicious," he replied.

He was only free for a few hours on the weekends and it was mostly early in the day. He and his wife usually did something together on the weekends at night.

"This shit is getting real old Jax. You swore to me that things were going to be different, but I don't see it. She gets all your time and attention, and I get whatever is left over," Sienna argued, as she too proceeded to get dressed.

"She's supposed to get all my time and attention. She's my wife," he replied while looking at her like she was crazy.

"Yeah and so was I," Sienna snapped.

"Was, Sienna, we're divorced now, remember?" Jax reminded her.

"Yeah, because you claimed that you weren't ready to be married. You cheated on me throughout the entire marriage and then divorced me like I was the one who did something wrong," Sienna said as she choked back tears.

"Here we go with this shit again," Jax sighed in aggravation.

"You damn right. You made it seem like our marriage was a hindrance, but you wasted no time putting a ring on that bitch's finger," Sienna snapped.

"Make that your last time disrespecting my wife. You always bring that divorce shit up, but that never stopped you from laying down with me again, did it? Besides, what happened to your man who you claimed to be so in love with? You didn't want to be bothered for months when things with y'all were going good. Now that he's doing you dirty, you want to run to me and expect me to ruin my marriage for your ass. I don't think so," Jax rambled in disgust.

Sienna had issues that went back as far as her childhood. She came from a broken home and she didn't want that for herself or her kids. Her mother had four kids by four different men and none of them loved her enough to marry her. Three of them had wives at home already. Sienna wanted better for herself. When she and Jax started a family and got married, that was the happiest time of her life. Unfortunately, her fantasy life didn't last very long because he couldn't keep his dick in his pants. Jax was a self-proclaimed sex addict who didn't know how to be faithful. He fucked every woman that he encountered, including some of the women at the school where he worked. That was also where he met his new wife, Royce, who taught second grade there. Sienna didn't care about Royce in the beginning because she assumed the relationship wouldn't go anywhere. She didn't think things with Royce and Jax would get that serious, but she was mistaken. She was devastated when she found out that they got married, especially since Jax didn't bother telling her about it. His own kids weren't even there to see him give another woman the Davenport last name.

Even still, Sienna was okay because she had a man at home whom she loved unconditionally. That was until she found out that he was no better than her ex-husband. A quick glance through his phone proved that he was just as big a man whore as Jax was. He didn't even try to deny his wrong doings when Sienna confronted him about it. He was brutally honest and answered every question that she asked him. Sienna was heartbroken, and it didn't take long before Jax had sweet talked his way back into her life and her bed once again. She had gone from being the wife and mother of his kids, to the side chick who always came last.

As much as she hated to admit it, Jax loved his new wife way more than he ever loved her. Royce came from a background similar to his own, so Sienna was sure that was the reason why. Her ex in-laws tolerated her because of the kids, but they genuinely loved Royce. She was beautiful and she had the kind of education that fit right in with their perfect lifestyle. Sienna's boyfriend's family didn't care for her too much either. They called her a readymade family since she was divorced with two kids. Sienna tried to be a good girlfriend to him, but he still had a wandering eye. His infidelity was what led her back into the arms of her first love once again.

Meeting Jax in her first year of college was a dream come true for Sienna. He was already a junior, but they clicked instantly and became inseparable. They were the same age, but she didn't go to college right away like he did because she wasn't as fortunate. When she completed her freshmen year and found out that she was pregnant, dropping out of school for a while seemed like the best thing to do. Jax was excited about having his first son and he promised to take care of her. They ended up getting married before their baby was born and Sienna couldn't be happier. Even after she found out that he'd cheated on her only two weeks after they exchanged vows, she still stayed by her husband's side.

By the time their daughter came two years later, Sienna had mastered the role of house wife and college was the furthest thing from her mind. Things went from bad to worse with her marriage. Jax was a straight up dog and he always made excuses for his actions. Not only did he believe that he was a sex addict, he had his entire family believing it too. He claimed he was getting help for his problem, but Sienna knew that was a lie. He had women confronting her all the time and one even accused him of rape. He claimed he broke it off with her and she only said that to get back at him. Then, if that wasn't bad enough, Jax woke up one morning and decided that a wife was no longer what he wanted. He claimed that he wasn't marriage material and had his lawyer draw up divorce papers the very next day.

All Sienna ever wanted was a stable home life, unlike the one that she grew up in. Sadly, none of the two men that she had in her life seemed capable of providing it for her. She would have preferred Jax since they shared children, but he was too caught up with his new wife to even care. Dropping out of college was a decision that she lived to regret, since she couldn't find a decent job to save her

[12]

life. Her best friend, Yada, taught her how to mix drinks, so bartending was the only job that she was qualified for.

"When am I gonna see you again?" Sienna asked once she and Jax were both dressed.

"I can't make you no promises. I'm not trying to have my wife getting suspicious," Jax replied, making her angry.

"Since when did you become so considerate? You never even bothered to come home some nights when we were married," Sienna noted.

"It's not even that serious with me no more. I'm not trying to lose my wife by being careless like that," Jax replied.

"You sound like a damn fool. What do you think will happen if she finds out that you're cheating?" Sienna asked with a smirk.

"She won't find out. Don't fuck with me, Sienna. Problems with me is not what you want and you know it," Jax warned with an angry glare.

Nothing was off limits with his ex-wife, but he would kill her if she told Royce anything about their dealings. Although his actions didn't show it, Jax loved Royce more than he'd ever loved any other woman, including Sienna. Not only was Royce beautiful inside and out, but she was a go getter. She had her Bachelors degree in education just like him and she was fluent in three different languages. Royce already had a beautiful home when they met, so Jax moved in with her when they got married. He and Sienna had two kids, but he was ready to start a family with his wife. His parents loved her and her family adored him just the same. They were perfect together and nobody was going to ruin his happy home, especially his bitter ex-wife.

"What can she do for you that I haven't done already? I've already given you a son and daughter, so what else is left?" Sienna questioned.

There was no doubt in her mind that Jax loved his wife, but he didn't love her enough to be faithful. Sienna couldn't even lie; Royce was beautiful, but so was she. They both had a medium brown complexion, but Sienna was more on the slim side, with Royce being a little shapelier. Sienna preferred to wear her shoulder-length hair in a roller wrap, while Royce opted for a longer sew-in. Aside from having a degree and career, she didn't see what Jax loved about her so much. His family loved her for that reason alone and maybe Jax did too. Sienna regretted dropping out of college to have a family, especially since her family was no longer together. Her new man didn't seem like marriage was nowhere on his mind. He made sure to change the subject every time she even mentioned it. After two years of dating and one year of living together, he still wasn't ready to commit like she wanted him to.

"She's my wife. End of discussion," Jax said as he grabbed his keys and walked out of the room.

Sienna checked her appearance in the mirror and made sure she didn't look too bad before going home to her man. He probably wasn't there yet since it was so early, but she just had to play it safe. Lately, he'd been coming in later and later, and she was tired of asking questions that he never answered. She was aggravated, but that was her own fault. She shouldn't have started up the affair with her ex-husband, but she did it anyway.

After gathering her belongings, Sienna headed for the door. Her kids were at her best friend's house, but she wanted to go freshen up before she got them. Yada always gave her good advice and she needed to talk to her about her dilemma while she was there. After getting into her car, Sienna turned her music up and pulled away from the hotel, never noticing that she was being followed the entire time.

Chapter 2

Jax blew out a breath of frustration as he listened to a conversation that he was tired of hearing. He shifted the phone from one ear to the other as he drove towards his house. When he finally got tired of being nagged, he stopped her mid-sentence to say what he had to say.

"Look, I'm married. You knew that shit when you first met me and nothing has changed since then. If you expect me to ignore my wife while in your presence, then you got me fucked up," Jax said honestly.

"I never asked you to ignore your wife, but all the extra affection ain't even necessary. It's like you know I be watching when you do the shit," Angelique replied.

"The fuck you mean? That's my wife. If I wanna hug and kiss on her all day, that's exactly what the fuck I'm gonna do. If you feel some kind of way about that, then I don't know what to tell you!" Jax yelled.

A lot of employees retired from the school where Jax and Royce worked, so they had a lot of new staff members to come on over the past two years. Angelique was one of them who had been working in the cafeteria for the past six months. Jax made a move on her after the first week and he was upfront about his marriage. She started out being cool at first but, after a few months of messing around, she was starting to be a pain in his ass. He picked up his and Royce's lunch every day and they always sat in the cafeteria and ate during their break time. He was very affectionate with his wife, so it was nothing for him to hug or kiss her whenever they were together. Nobody told Angelique's dumb ass to sit and watch, but that's exactly what she always did. Then, she would call him with an attitude and say that she felt disrespected. He was tired of having the same conversation with her and he was over it already.

"Just be mindful when you know I'm around. That's all I'm asking," Angelique had the nerve to say.

"Wow," Jax said as he laughed sarcastically. "This is getting to be a bit too much for me. I'm not about to watch what I say or do with my own wife. Maybe we need to just end this before things get too far out of hand."

"Yeah, maybe we should. I told you when we first met that I was a jealous lover. You claimed that you could handle it but, obviously, you can't," Angelique snapped.

"Nah, I can't deal. I draw the line when it comes to my wife," he noted.

"Whatever," Angelique replied with her usual nasty attitude.

"But, it's all good. We can still be friends. We'll just do it without the added benefits," Jax said, right before he hung up the phone like the problem was easily solved.

In his eyes, it was solved. He didn't give a damn about how Angelique felt. She could and would be replaced before the end of the week. She was an anything goes kind of freak, so Jax would miss her. Still, Angelique, Sienna, or none of the other women that he dealt with could compare to his wife. He didn't always do right by Royce, but he loved her more than he could ever put into words.

Royce was the true definition of a lady at all times. She had a pretty face, small waist, and a degree to go with it all. She was every man's fantasy and he had her all to himself. Any other man would have been satisfied with just her, but not Jax. His sexual appetite was insatiable, and he seriously doubted if one woman would ever be able to quench his sexual thirst. Royce was good in the bedroom, but she stuck to the basics. She was adamant about them using condoms, but he liked to feel the real thing. A few times she let him hit it raw, but it wasn't enough for his liking. Their sex life wasn't boring, but Jax needed a little more.

Sienna tried her best to make him happy sexually, but their union would have never worked. His parents had an image to uphold and Sienna didn't make the cut. Royce, on the other hand, fit the bill perfectly. She came from an upper class two-parent home and she was an educator, just like them. When she and Jax first started dating, his mother was ready to plan a lavish wedding soon after, unlike the court house marriage that he was forced into with Sienna. They were so disappointed in Jax when Sienna got pregnant. To save face, they made him marry her while she was still expecting, to seem like he was doing the right thing. He was against it from the start, but he had no choice. He and his brothers and sister rarely disobeyed their parents, especially their father, Silas. Even their mother knew better than to go up against the patriarch of their family. Silas was a modern-day tyrant who didn't mind using physical force on anyone who lived under his roof. "Behave like a child and get treated like one," was his father's favorite quote and Jax hated it.

Silas knew that Jax never loved Sienna, which was why he filed for divorce as soon as his daughter turned a year old. His father gave him his blessing, since he stayed married to her for well over a year. His mother, Elena, frowned upon divorce, but she made an exception for Jax. The Davenport name was at stake and Sienna was beneath them, as she often reminded her son. She didn't fit or belong in their family. The kids were a part of Jax, so they were the only exception.

Jax smiled when he pulled up into their driveway and saw Royce's copper colored Jaguar SUV parked in her usual spot. It was his gift to her for their second anniversary, but Royce kept her Mercedes that she had when they first met. She loved that car and didn't want to part with it. Although the house belonged to his wife before the marriage, Jax spent thousands of dollars on renovations and upgrades. Royce had a basement that she hated, so he had it fixed up and turned into his personal man cave. Whenever his brothers or one of his friends came over, that was where they usually hung out.

After grabbing his gym bag from the back seat, Jax got out of the car and headed inside. He had his workout clothes on, even though he'd never stepped foot in the gym that day. That was always the lie that he used, so he had to play the part accordingly.

"Royce!" Jax yelled when he walked into the house. "Where are you, baby?"

The house was still and quiet, letting him know that his wife wasn't home. Royce hung out with her friends or cousin Uri a lot, so that was no surprise. Jax was happy that she wasn't there because it gave him some time to shower and get his mind right. Lately, creeping around on Royce was becoming more and more stressful. Women were too emotional and got attached too fast. He enjoyed having a few women on his team, but none of them were worth losing his wife over. Jax prided himself on being careful, but bitter bitches still went back and reported things to his wife. He always denied everything, and Royce never did have any proof. It was all hearsay and that was always his defense. He would lie until he was blue in the face before he let Royce leave him. His mother-in-law was always on his side so that helped a lot. It was crazy because his wife satisfied him sexually every time. The thrill of being with different women just excited Jax on another level.

After taking a nice hot shower, Jax grabbed his phone to call his wife. It was still early and he wanted to spend some time with her. Taking Royce out for dinner and a little shopping seemed like a great idea. Royce was so up to date on fashion that Jax never even purchased a t-shirt if his wife wasn't with him. She'd upgraded his entire wardrobe and he loved his new look. When Royce's voicemail picked up, Jax temporarily abandoned the idea of them doing something together. The weekends were their only days off, but Royce sometimes made plans without him. That was cool because he often did the same.

He left his wife a message and walked downstairs to his man cave. After locking the door, he grabbed his phone and added the video of him and Sienna to his computer after he watched it first. Unfortunately, he had recorded their argument too, but that was cool. Once that was done, Jax logged on to his favorite porn site. He was sure that Royce would be livid if she knew about his undisclosed addiction, which was why he always paid his monthly subscription fees with his credit union debit card. That was also the card that he used to rent rooms whenever he wanted to do his dirt. He had the account long before he married Royce and he got his banking statements online. Jax had purchased a cheap laptop from Walmart and that was what he used whenever he wanted to indulge. Having other women came in handy for that too. He loved to try new things with his side chicks that he would never dream about doing with his wife. Of course, he recorded the acts to go back and view later and none of them ever knew. He had an addiction to sex and he wasn't sure how to fix it. He told Royce all about his deep dark secret, but she didn't know how bad off he really was.

***

Caleb and Brian sat at the table listening to Bryce fussing at them over the phone. They were at their favorite sports bars enjoying a beer when Bryce called, going off on them. Jaden had just left to go home to his wife and kids, but Caleb and Brian didn't have that to worry about. They were both single and kid free. Although Caleb had a girlfriend, he wasn't married to anyone.

"Alright bruh," Caleb said, trying to rush his older brother off the phone.

Bryce was the oldest of the four boys and one girl, and he took his job seriously. He was always calling his younger brothers, fussing about one thing or the other. Their sister Brooklyn was married with kids of her own, so he let her be. Even Jaden often escaped his wrath because he'd calmed down since he'd gotten married. Brian and Caleb were often his targets because they were reckless and didn't care. Caleb didn't have to see him daily like his other brothers because he didn't work in the shop with him. Jaden and Brian were both barbers in Bryce's tattoo shop, but Caleb was a certified electrician like their father. He'd recently become a regional supervisor, which meant that he got paid more money for little to no work. He basically rode around all day checking up on other employees, but he rarely did that either.

"Don't try to brush me off nigga. If y'all ain't with the shit, just let me know. That's fucked up that Jaden looked out for us and y'all are slacking like this," Bryce argued.

Jaden's wife, Kia's, stepfather put him on with the real estate business. Rob owned several houses, but he was tired and ready to be done with it. He'd recently gotten married to Kia's mother, Mo, and they were trying to enjoy their grandkids. Rob was a pro at fix and flip, where he purchased properties that needed repair and fixed them up before selling them for profit. Being the close family that they were, Jaden wasted no time pulling his brothers into the business to make money with him. His brother-in-law, Dominic, wasn't interested, and neither was his wife's sister's husband, Tigga. They both made decent money with their own businesses and they didn't have the time to devote to anything else. Jaden and Bryce were both naturals when it came to locating properties, but Brian and Caleb didn't care. All four men put up equal amounts of money for the purchase and renovations and they split the profits four ways once the property sold. Brian and Caleb only wanted to collect. They didn't have time for the other small details.

"I said alright man. I know we've been slacking, but we're gonna do better," Caleb swore.

"That goes for you too, Brian. Stop chasing after these random hoes and get your shit together. You do have a baby on the way, just in case you forgot," Bryce reminded him.

"That ain't my damn baby. I don't know why everybody keeps saying that shit," Brian snapped angrily.

"Yeah, well, tell that to mama nigga," Bryce replied.

"How the fuck can mama tell me if somebody is carrying my baby or not? It ain't like she was in the room when we were fucking!" Brian yelled.

"Talk all that shit to me, but I bet you won't say it to mama," Bryce laughed, making Brian shut up.

He played crazy, but he was no fool. Their mother, Pam, wasn't nothing nice and they knew not to play with her. She was a nurse, so she always threatened to whip their asses and patch them up once she was done. And if she didn't knock them on their asses, their father, Bryce Sr., would do it for her.

"Anything else Bryce?" Caleb asked as he gulped down some of his beer and belched.

"Nigga, I know your stupid ass ain't drinking and you drove there. You must have forgotten about the last time you drove after getting drunk," Bryce fussed.

"I'm drinking water bruh," Caleb lied with a frown.

"Yeah okay. Don't be stupid," Bryce warned.

"Alright bruh. Are we good now or is there anything else?" Caleb asked.

"Yeah, we're good for now. Handle y'all business and we won't have to keep having these same conversations. I don't like fussing, just like y'all don't like hearing it. And while I got y'all on the line, make sure y'all are on time for Pops' party next week. Brook already told everybody what they need to bring," Bryce replied.

"Alright man," Brian said, ready for him to hang up.

They had lots of respect for their older brother, but Bryce acted as if they weren't grown men sometimes. Caleb shook his head and sighed when they finally got him off the phone.

"That nigga is disgusting as fuck," Caleb complained.

"Yeah, but we already knew that when we agreed to do this shit. But when I get back to my car, I need to swing by and talk to mama," Brian replied.

"Man, let that shit go. You already know how mama is. She got it in her head that Shanti's baby is yours and nothing but a blood test will change that," Brian replied.

"That's the part that confuses me though. When Mya was claiming to be pregnant, mama was the first one to say that I wasn't the father. I guess since she likes Shanti, it's cool if she's the baby's mama," Brian fussed.

"Man, Mya is a stripper who everybody calls Shaky. You should be happy that she got an abortion. The fuck you want her to be your baby mama for anyway?" Caleb questioned as he sipped from his bottle.

"I don't want nobody to be my baby mama. I'm not even ready for kids yet," Brian replied.

"Well, you should have thought about that shit before you started going in them hoes raw. And, honestly, I think that's your baby too. Shanti ain't even like that. She's been coming around for years and she's always carried herself like a lady," Caleb noted.

"I can't dispute that, but I wasn't the only nigga that she was fucking at the time. She had mad niggas calling her phone and shit. I don't know why she ain't trying to blame one of them other niggas that she was fucking with," Brian frowned.

Ashanti was one of Jaden's sister-in-law, Keller's, friends who they were all cool with. Whenever Keller took some time off from doing nails at the shop, Shanti was who she referred her customers to. Since Keller was now a wife with four kids and two step kids, she and her husband, Tigga, decided that she would be a stay at home mother. Shanti worked at a shop nearby, but it was nothing for Bryce to rent out the vacant space to her. She and Brian always flirted with each other whenever she came to the shop for Keller, but things really heated up when she started to work there permanently. She and Brian hung out all the time and he had started falling for her. That was until he found out that she was entertaining him and a few other niggas on the side. Brian had his share of women too, but he was pissed to know that she was doing the same. He put Shanti on a pedestal and she fucked up that perfect image.

When she came to him claiming to be pregnant, Brian wasn't trying to hear it. He knew that he wasn't the only man in her life and he wasn't taking that charge. Unfortunately, his mother, sister, and Keller thought otherwise. They didn't view Shanti as the hoe he tried to make her out to be and they all believed that he was the baby's father. Shanti was four months into her pregnancy and his mother had accompanied her to every doctor's visit so far. Brian questioned the paternity, but he made it his business to be there for her as well. He didn't want the baby to end up being his and miss out on being there for everything. To make matters worse, Shanti was having a girl. Brian was scared to death of karma coming back to him through his daughter.

"Maybe she's sure about you being the father. You ever thought about that?" Caleb asked, interrupting his brother's thoughts.

"I guess a blood test will have to determine that," Brian shrugged as he downed the rest of his beer.

"I guess so. But, aye, I didn't wanna say shit to Bryce, but I've been looking at a few properties. I got a few prospects, but one of them I'm thinking about keeping for myself," Caleb noted.

"Are you thinking about moving ole girl in with you?" Brian asked with a smirk.

"Fuck no! Moving in with her was the dumbest decision that I've ever made. And Bryce is right, we all make too much money to keep paying rent. I'm about to be like y'all and become a home owner," Caleb replied.

He was the only one of the siblings who didn't own a home, but he was ready to change that.

"I'm happy that I made that move when I did. I was paying more for rent than I'm paying on my house note. I just need to take some time out to decorate and shit. If Shanti's baby is mine, I have to make it comfortable for them too," Brian countered.

Besides a living room and bedroom set, he didn't have anything else in his three-bedroom home. He had been there over a year and never took the time to fully furnish the place.

"Them? So, what, you trying to be with Shanti if the baby is yours?" Caleb asked with a smirk.

It was no secret that Brian and Shanti were still fucking. They tried to play it off, but it wasn't hard to figure out. Brian wanted to be with her, but his pride was the only thing stopping him. Shanti was always at his house, but he used her pregnancy as an excuse for the times that he catered to her. He did things for her like a man in love, but he got mad whenever they called him out on it. Brian even paid her rent faithfully every month, but he didn't think they knew about that either.

"Hell no but, if we share a child, I have to make sure that she's straight. You know mama and daddy don't play that shit," Brian reminded him.

"I know but, aside from that, I think you and Shanti would be good together. I don't know why y'all broke up the first time around," Caleb said.

"Man, you know how I felt about Ashanti, but I don't have time for all the games. She got niggas calling her phone and popping up at the shop and shit. I'll fuck around and go to jail messing with her ass." Brian frowned at the thought of it all.

"But, that's the same shit that you used to do to her. What's the difference?" Caleb questioned.

"She's a female bruh. Shit is different with women," Brian noted.

"That's bullshit, and you know it. You were pissed because Shanti played the same game as you and your ass couldn't handle it. You fucked with other broads all the time and you hated to think that she was doing the same thing," Caleb said, calling him out.

"I don't wanna talk about this shit no more. I'm getting mad all over again. Let's roll. I need to get to my car, so I can make some moves," Brian said in aggravation.

Caleb chuckled at his brother because he knew him so well. Brian hated to be wrong about anything and he always ended the conversation if it didn't go his way. He tried hard to fight it, but he had fallen in love with Shanti and it killed him to admit it. Shanti's nonchalant attitude bothered Brian the most because she didn't seem fazed by anything. Brian wanted her to fawn over him like other women did, but she wasn't the one. Even when he denied being the father of her child, Shanti held her head high and kept it pushing. She never asked him to accompany her to her appointments, but she didn't try to stop him when he did. She wasn't playing Brian's game and that killed him the most.

After downing the last of his drink, Caleb stood up and followed his brother outside. Brian's car was parked at his apartments, since Caleb offered to drive. It was way too early for him to go home, but he had to bring his brother to his ride. The sun had just started to set, so Caleb had a while before he would be going inside, if he went inside at all. He couldn't say too much about Brian because he wasn't considered the model boyfriend either. He cheated often, so he wasn't trying to judge his brother. It wasn't that he didn't want a steady relationship. He just didn't want it with the person that he was with.

"The fuck is that?" Caleb asked out loud when he pulled up and saw an unfamiliar car parked in his second parking spot.

He and his girlfriend both had cars, but that car didn't belong to either of them. Brian's car was parked in another vacant spot that was used for visitors. The windows on the Acura were darkly tinted, making it hard for him to see inside.

"I hope you got your heat on you because mine is in my car," Brian said as he too spied the suspicious looking vehicle.

"You already know I'm prepared," Caleb said as he reached under his seat and put his gun on his lap.

He parked in his assigned spot as he and Brian both got out of the car. He was ready to start shooting when both doors to the other car opened simultaneously. Both men visibly relaxed when they saw two women exit the car and walk towards them.

"Damn! I'll take either one of their fine asses. You know them?" Brian asked his brother as he looked at the women who closely resembled each other.

"Never seen them before in my life," Caleb replied, as the two ladies approached and stood not too far away from them.

They were both beautiful, but one captured his attention more than the other. She looked like a younger, caramel colored Dorothy Dandridge with long hair that he wasn't sure was all hers. She was fine as fuck, so it didn't even matter. He was ready to start flirting until his crush opened her mouth and pissed him off.

"Which one of you is Caleb?" she asked with an attitude.

"I'm Caleb and you are?" He asked, matching her hostile tone.

"Who I am doesn't matter, but we have a situation," she flippantly replied.

"You can have that one. Her attitude is fucked up," Brian said with a frown.

"This doesn't sound like a social visit, so what is it that I can do for you?" Caleb inquired.

"What you can do is keep your bitch here with you and away from my husband. If he still wanted to be married to her, he would have never divorced her ass," the woman snapped.

"Bitch-" Caleb started, before the other woman cut him off.

"Disrespecting my cousin is what you're not gonna do. Her name is Royce and I'm Uri, if you want to address us," Uri spoke up.

"I give zero fucks about your names or the bullshit that your homegirl is spitting. What I do care about is the fact that y'all were bold enough to bring y'all grown asses to my house with all this childish ass drama," Caleb barked.

"We're not the ones starting the drama, your girlfriend is," Royce interjected.

"Fuck that bitch too!" Caleb yelled, losing his patience with each word that came out of her mouth.

"The fuck you over here telling my brother for? Shouldn't you be having this conversation with your husband?" Brian questioned.

"She's gonna deal with him too," Uri noted.

"Who are you supposed to be, her spokeswoman? I don't give a fuck about your husband or Sienna. He can fuck her six ways from Sunday in your bed and I still wouldn't care. What y'all need to do is move that car out of my parking spot before I have NOPD come tow that bitch away. Silly grown ass women on that dumb shit," Caleb replied angrily.

"Fuck you!" Royce snapped as she turned and walked away, with Uri following right behind her.

"Nah, go fuck your husband and maybe he wouldn't have to get it from my bitch," Caleb replied.

[25]

"The fuck just happened here?" Brian questioned as he watched the women get into their car and speed away.

"I don't know, but I don't have time for that dumb shit," Caleb replied.

"I guess Sienna is on some foul shit huh," Brian remarked.

"Man, fuck Sienna! I can't wait to get my own house and get away from her disgusting ass," Caleb noted.

He liked Sienna in the beginning, but she quickly became another problem that he didn't need. Caleb didn't have any kids of his own and she was trying to force him into the stepfather role with hers. His parents didn't agree with his decision to be with her, but he was a grown man. Sienna was married and divorced at a young age, and Caleb's mother didn't want that for him. She wanted him to start a family of his own with someone who had more to offer. Sienna was a college dropout who bartended for a living, while Caleb took home six figures a year from his job as an electrician. He had just been promoted to supervisor of his division and his pay rate got a generous increase.

"Who is ole girl's husband?" Brian asked, shaking Caleb away from his thoughts.

"I guess she's married to Sienna's ex-husband, Jax. Sienna stupid as fuck if she's messing with that nigga again. He did her dirty, then divorced her. A bitch is really dumb to go from being the wife to the side chick," Caleb said as he and his brother laughed.

"Damn bruh, you got more shit going on than I do. You got your main bitch sneaking with her ex-husband. Then, you got your probation officer blackmailing you for the dick," Brian commented with a chuckle.

Caleb was arrested for driving under the influence a few months prior and he was put on five years' probation. He smoked occasionally, but he loved to have a drink or two on his off days. Being on probation, he was prohibited from doing either. He made the mistake of failing a drug test and his probation officer had been on his ass ever since then. Instead of sending him to jail like the law required her to, she held it over his head. She didn't bother with the normal monthly visits. Caleb had to see her every week and every week she wanted the dick. If he refused, she always threatened to have him locked up.

"Man, fuck all them hoes. I don't even want a girl after all this shit. I'm thinking about packing up and moving back in with mama until I find a permanent spot of my own," Caleb said in frustration.

He knew that he had a lot going on in his life, but to hear Brian say it had him even more aggravated. He looked at how happy his other two brothers and sister were with their families and he wanted that for himself. Sadly, with the way things were going, he wasn't sure if he ever would.

"If that's what you feel is best, then do you. I'm tired of all the dumb shit too. It's like a nigga can't catch a break," Brian replied.

He stayed out front and talked with Caleb for a while, until he got a call from one of his boys who needed a haircut. Brian was off on Sundays, but he doubled his fee if somebody wanted him to work. It wasn't like he had a woman to go home to, so he could make his money any time.

"Money calls, so I'm out," Brian said before giving his brother a fist pound and walking over to his car. Caleb disappeared into his apartment, right as Brian pulled out of the complex.

Chapter 3

"Sit up straight and stop slouching Royce. A real lady has perfect posture at all times," Sondra said as she looked over at her daughter.

"We're not out in the public mother. Can I just be normal for once in my life?" Royce snapped angrily.

"You better watch your damn tone. I don't know what's gotten into you lately," Sondra replied.

"Leave her alone Sondra. Damn, just let the girl breath for a change," Patrick said, defending his daughter.

"Don't you dare take up for her when she's talking to me like that," Sondra said angrily.

Royce wasn't in the mood to go through the motions, so she sat up straight and continued to play around with the yogurt that she was supposed to be eating. She would usually spend the weekends with her husband, but she had been avoiding him as much as she could lately. Two weeks had passed since she'd seen him at the hotel with his ex-wife, but she hadn't worked up the courage to confront him yet. Uri was pissed at her for backing down yet again, but Royce hated confrontations. Even the situation with Sienna's boyfriend went all wrong. He was an arrogant, disrespectful bastard and Royce could see why Sienna was cheating on him. She just wished that she was cheating with someone else other than her husband.

"Where is Jax? He usually comes over with you when you visit," Pat asked his daughter once he was done reading over some of his work emails.

"Honestly daddy, I don't know where he is, and I don't care," Royce replied, making her mother stop and turn to face her.

"What the hell is that supposed to mean?" Sondra questioned.

"It means just what I said. I didn't tell him where I was going, and I didn't feel the need to," Royce answered.

"Is everything okay baby? Are you and Jax having problems?" Pat asked.

"The only problem is my husband who can't seem to remain faithful," Royce replied.

"Here we go with this again. You need to stop listening to all that negativity about your husband. People are envious Royce. You and Jax are young and in love with great careers and people are jealous. They'll say anything to make you as miserable as they are," Sondra said.

It took everything in Royce not to jump up from the table and wrap her hands around her mother's neck. She was never able to talk to her about her marriage and, most times, she really needed to. Sondra was team Jax all the way and Royce didn't stand a chance. She tried talking to her about some of the stories that she'd heard in the past, but that was a dead end. Sondra told Jax everything and he was quick to deny it all, calling it gossip and rumors. She believed whatever her son-in-law said without even trying to be there for her one and only daughter.

Sondra lived to please others, especially the Davenport family. Jax's mother, Elena, was the true illustration of snobbish and Sondra quickly followed her lead. Sondra always did care about what others said and things only got worse about eight years prior when she met Elena. Her entire view on life changed and she took on a personality liken to the other woman. Elena's husband was a proud member of the Zulu Social Aid and Pleasure Club, so Sondra just had to walk in her shadow. She too made sure that her husband joined the all-male club that mostly catered to affluent blacks, even though she hated Mardi Gras and everything that it stood for. The Zulu Club did a lot for the community, but they were all a bunch of show offs in Royce's opinion. It was almost like a contest to see who had more money than the other. Each year, they crowned a king and both women longed for that title for their spouses. The king got to choose his queen and that was what both women wanted the most. They also had a Zulu parade that rolled every year for Mardi Gras and they tried to outdo each other each year for that as well. Both families had money and that was the only thing that tied them together. That and the fact that their kids were married now. A situation that Royce couldn't wait to get out of.

"It's nothing daddy. Everything is okay," Royce said after a long pause. She didn't even waste her time trying to tell them about what she had seen. Her mother wouldn't have believed her anyway.

"You know you can talk to us about anything Royce. I know that you confide in Uri a lot, but we're here too," Pat assured her.

"I know daddy and I appreciate you," Royce said, purposely leaving her mother out of the equation.

She was much closer with her father and Sondra knew it. She'd pushed Royce away a long time ago when she started trying to walk in Elena Davenport's expensive shoes.

"What do you have planned for the day?" Royce's father asked.

"Not much, but I'm going to a party at my friend's house," Royce replied.

"And where is your husband going to be while you're out partying?" Elena questioned.

"Jaxon is a grown man. I'm sure he'll find something or someone to get into," Royce said as she stood to her feet.

"You better get your act together before you lose a good man. I'm sure a lot of women will be happy if that happens," Elena noted.

"A lot of women are happy now and we're still together. And just in case you didn't notice, I'm just as much of a prize as Jax is. He should be more concerned about losing me," Royce snapped as she headed for the door.

"Don't forget that you and I are having brunch with Elena tomorrow. Don't embarrass me by being late!" Sondra yelled after her daughter.

Royce shook her head in disgust as she got into her car. Elena's life wasn't as perfect as Sondra thought it was. Jax told her some stories about his parents that left her with her mouth wide open in shock. As soon as Royce backed out of the driveway, Uri was ringing her phone.

"Yes Uri," Royce snapped unintentionally as she drove to her destination.

"Uh-uh bitch. What's wrong with you?" Uri quizzed.

"I'm sorry cousin, but your auntie makes me sick to my stomach," Royce replied.

"Girl, you know how your mama is. She's all about appearances. My mama gets on my nerves too, but I'll take her ratchet ways any day over that shit," Uri said honestly.

"She talks like Jax is more than what his dog ass is. She be pissing me off with that shit," Royce complained.

"Oh, Royce please. You ain't no better. You be knowing shit that he does, and you refuse to confront him about it. Say what you want, but you care about appearances just as much as Auntie Sondra does. Ain't no way in hell you should have let Jax get away with that shit that we saw. That wasn't hearsay. You saw that shit with your own eyes. You gon' fuck around and catch something that you can't get rid of from your own damn husband," Uri fussed.

"That'll never happen. That's exactly why I make his ass strap up," Royce noted.

"You're missing my entire point Royce. That's your husband. You should be able to have unprotected sex with him if you want to. That's some straight bullshit."

"I know Uri, but you know my life. You know what kind of background Jax and I come from. Appearances mean a lot to both of us and our families," Royce admitted.

"I don't give a damn Royce. It was crazy for you to confront another man and not confront your own husband. What sense did that make?" Uri asked.

"I'm barely speaking to his ass and I don't plan to start," Royce fumed.

"That's stupid, especially since he doesn't know why you're not speaking to him. He's gonna keep on doing the shit because you never do anything about it. That nigga Ronald tried that cheating with different bitches shit with me. I got his mind right real quick. God bless his soul, but he went to his grave knowing that I wasn't the bitch for him to play with," Uri ranted.

"So, what are you saying, that I should cheat on my husband?" Royce asked.

"I'm not telling you to do anything. But, it seems like you're the only one married if you ask me," Uri replied.

"I gotta go Uri. I just pulled up to the house," Royce said, feeling a little down.

"You know I love you, cousin. I would never say or do anything to hurt your feelings. You have a good heart

Royce and you deserve to be happy. I want that for you more than anything."

"I know you do and I appreciate you for always being here for me," Royce replied.

"That's what family is for. But, enjoy the party and tell everyone that I said hello," Uri said before they disconnected.

Royce grabbed the greeting card that held a gift card inside and exited her car. She heard loud music coming from the backyard of her friend's house and chlorine from the in-ground pool could be smelled in the air the closer she got to the entrance. Royce was a little nervous once she entered the yard and saw all the people who were in attendance. She looked around for her friend or any of the other faces that she was familiar with.

"Hey girl. I'm happy you could make it," a familiar voice said from behind her.

"Hey, I was just looking around for you," Royce replied as she gave her a hug.

"We're sitting right over there," she said as she pointed to their table. "My cousin spotted you when you walked in."

"Here, I got your dad a card. I know you said that he likes to bowl, so I got a gift card to the pro shop. They sell everything for every sport in there," Royce said as she followed her over to her table.

"Thanks girl, he's gonna love it. Everybody, this is my friend Royce. I know most of y'all have already met her," Brooklyn said to everyone who was seated at the table.

"Hi," Royce said as she waved and smiled at everyone.

She knew most of the people in attendance, but a few faces were unfamiliar. Royce had hung out with Co-Co, Candace, Kia, and Keller before and she genuinely liked them all. They kept her laughing and they weren't stuck up like some of her other friends. Just like her, Brooklyn was also a teacher. They'd met the year before when they attended the same teacher's conference and they clicked immediately. Brooklyn was married as well with three kids, unlike Royce who still didn't have any. In fact, all the women had one child or more, making Royce long for one of her own. Her husband already had two, but it just wasn't the same.

[33]

"Hey Royce. Sit down and help yourself to some of this seafood and liquor," Co-Co said as he pulled out a chair for her.

"Thanks, but I don't drink," Royce replied.

"Girl, let me mix you up some of this apple crown and Sprite. I guarantee you'll love the taste of that. Sit down boo, I got you," Co-Co ordered.

Royce did what she was told and immediately fell into a comfortable routine with Brooklyn and her family. They always made her feel welcome and she appreciated that. A man, who Brooklyn identified as her uncle Shaq, kept the seafood and drinks coming to their table every time it looked like they were getting low. They treated Royce like family, even though that was her first time seeing most of them. Aside from the people who she'd hung out with before, the only other person that Royce had met was Brooklyn's husband, Dominic. Royce was just about to ask Brooklyn where he was when she saw him walking into the yard, carrying cases of beer. Three other men followed behind him, but Royce had her angry glare focused on one.

"Brooklyn, please don't tell me that your husband is related to that disrespectful bastard," Royce said as she scowled at one of the men who was with Brooklyn's husband Dominic.

"Which one?" Brook asked as she looked over at all the men.

"I'm talking about the one with the white Gucci t-shirt on. I'm sorry if he's related to your husband, but I hate his arrogant ass," Royce fumed.

"Bitch, I almost choked on my wine cooler. She's talking about Caleb," Co-Co laughed.

"How do y'all know him?" Royce asked.

"That's my brother," Brooklyn smirked. She joined in on the laughter when she saw the horrified look on Royce's face.

"Oh shit. I'm sorry Brooklyn. I didn't mean any harm, but my feelings are still the same," Royce admitted.

"Girl, I'm not worried about that," Brooklyn said, waving her off. "But, what did he do to you like that?"

"It's a long story that I'll have to tell you about later. I was enjoying myself at first, but I'm ready to leave now. I don't want to be anywhere around his ass. I'm sorry Brook, but I'm about to go," Royce said while cleaning and sanitizing her hands.

"Oh no, bitch. You ain't going nowhere until we find out what's going on. I need some entertainment and you and Caleb are about to provide it. Caleb!" Co-Co yelled to his cousin.

"Why did you do that Co-Co? She obviously doesn't want to see him. You always do the most," Candace said, fussing at her brother.

"Too late now. He's on his way over," Co-Co said as he clapped his hands dramatically.

"And I'm leaving," Royce said as she grabbed her purse from the back of the chair that she was sitting in.

"Wait Royce, let me walk you out," Brook said as she too stood up from her chair.

"You know her, Brook?" Caleb asked as soon as he walked up and saw his sister standing next to the woman who he'd often thought about since their first encounter.

Caleb wasn't a cold-hearted person and he really did feel bad about how he'd talked to Royce when they first met. She was dead wrong for approaching him on some dumb shit, but he could have handled it better. He never even confronted Sienna about what he'd heard and he didn't plan to. She was a non-factor and he was in the process of moving back in with his parents until he got ready to buy a house of his own. He was tired of renting, when he could pay less to own a home. Sienna couldn't afford to pay the bills on her own, but that was her problem.

"I have a name," Royce snapped with a frown. "Come on Brooklyn."

"Hold up," Caleb said as he gently touched her arm.

"Don't touch me!" Royce yelled as she pulled her arm away.

"Damn, I'm sorry baby. I didn't mean any harm," Caleb said as he raised his hands in mock surrender.

"And I'm not your baby," Royce corrected.

"Look, I know that I owe you an apology and I'm man enough to give you one. I have women in my family who I respect and I want other people to respect them too. I'm sorry for how I talked to you, but you have to take some of the blame too. That's a dangerous game that you and your girl played. Y'all can't just be rolling up on people that y'all don't know on some rowdy shit. Your husband or Sienna ain't even worth all that," Caleb replied.

Royce's attitude shifted a little once she realized just how right Caleb was. She and Uri had no business going to confront a man that neither of them knew. She was upset with him, when she should have been pissed at her husband instead, just like her cousin said. The way he came off just had her heated, but she started the madness when she showed up to his house.

"I guess I owe you an apology too. It wasn't my intentions to come at you like that, but I was upset," Royce admitted.

"What am I missing here? How do y'all know each other?" Brooklyn questioned.

Before either of them had a chance to answer, Brian walked up and started going off.

"The fuck is she doing here? You and your girl better not be coming to my sister's house with that dumb shit," Brian argued as soon as he saw Royce standing there.

"What dumb shit? That's my friend," Brooklyn interjected. "How do you know them Royce?"

Everyone sat there and listened as Royce, Brian, and Caleb told them about their first encounter. It was funny when they talked about it now, but there was no reason to smile when it first went down.

"What kind of daytime talk show shit is that? You're married to Sienna's ex-husband, but they're still messing around. They should have just stayed together," Co-Co noted, surprised by the newfound information.

"That's the same thing I said." Royce shrugged.

"What did he say when you confronted him?" Brooklyn asked.

"I never said anything to him, but I'm sure he knows that something is wrong. I've been avoiding him for two weeks now," Royce replied.

"You're better than me, honey. I wish Tigga would play with me with his ex and I don't say nothing about it," Keller spoke up.

"Bitch, please. Tigga's ex don't even do dick no more, so you're good. But, I always did tell Caleb that I didn't like Sienna's sneaky ass. You can't trust a bitch who still slick her hair down with grease and water. She'll do anything without thinking twice," Co-Co said as he sipped on his wine cooler.

"Forget all that. What's up with our card game?" Caleb asked as he looked around.

"I'm ready, but I need a partner since Dwight is at work," Co-Co replied.

"You wanna play some spades?" Caleb asked while looking over at Royce.

"No, I don't really know how to play," Royce said, feeling slightly embarrassed by her admission.

She'd never really played cards before and she was horrible at it the few times that she tried. Royce was sheltered and that was the main reason why it was so easy for Jax to do what he did to her.

"It's cool. Have a seat and let me teach you," Caleb replied while pulling out a chair for her.

It had been a while since Royce had as much fun as she did at Brooklyn's house. They played cards for hours and Royce even got in on a few games. Caleb was patient as he showed her the rules of the game. They all said that Royce was a natural when they started playing pitty pat and she took all their money. Thanks to Co-Co and his bartending skills, she was now in love with crown apple mixed with Sprite too. She was being introduced to a whole new world and she had no complaints. Brooklyn and her family made Royce see just how boring and uneventful her life with Jaxon really was. Royce was ready to kill Caleb a few weeks ago, but he turned out to be cool. They ended up exchanging numbers before she left and he called her the very same night. Jax was in bed asleep while Royce sat in the living room, whispering on the phone with another man.

Chapter 4

"Shit!" Royce hissed as she jumped up from the sofa and looked at her huge walk clock. Her mother was going to kill her because there was no way that she would make it to brunch on time. She still had to shower, do her hair, and find something to wear. Sondra had called her four times already and she didn't answer once. She didn't realize that she had fallen asleep on the sofa until the vibration of her phone woke her up. She talked to Caleb all night until she could no longer fight her sleep. Thanks to her drinking four cups of liquor, she now had a headache that she needed to get rid of too.

"Are you okay? Your mother said that she's been trying to reach you," Jax said when he walked into the living room and saw his wife standing there looking at her phone.

"I'm fine," Royce replied while walking away to their bedroom.

"Why did you sleep on the sofa?" he asked while following behind her.

"I wanted to watch tv and I didn't want to wake you," Royce lied as she gathered some underwear to go take a shower.

"I don't know what I did, but I wish you would talk to me. You're driving me crazy with this silent treatment shit. I can't fix the problem if I don't know what it is," Jax said while looking at her.

Royce wanted to tell him that nothing was wrong, but she was tired of masking her feelings. Uri was right. Jax thought he was getting away with doing her wrong because she never confronted him. She shouldn't have felt comfortable confronting another man and not her own husband.

"Unless you can keep your dick at home where it belongs, there is no problem to fix," Royce snapped as she stripped down out of her clothes.

"Here we go with this shit again. Which one of those miserable bitches did you let get in your ear this time?" Jax asked as he admired her naked frame. Royce was almost perfect to him, but he still didn't do right by her.

"I saw the shit with my own eyes, so don't even try it Jaxon," Royce noted.

"Exactly what do you think you saw Royce?" Jax smirked sarcastically.

"I don't think, I know that I saw your ex-wife pull up to a hotel and park right next to your truck. I also know that you came out and greeted her with a kiss before disappearing inside for over an hour," Royce said, removing the stupid looking smirk from his face.

"It wasn't even like that Royce. Her and my kids have nowhere to stay right now. Her boyfriend is moving out of the house and she can't afford to pay all the bills by herself," Jax replied, repeating what Sienna had told him only two days before.

He didn't have a defense for what his wife had seen, so he thought of the first thing that came to mind. He was curious as to how she had seen anything at all. He was slipping big time for that to happen. Jax usually prided himself on being extra careful, but he obviously wasn't.

"And what does that have to do with you meeting her in a hotel room, when you were supposed to be at the gym?" Royce questioned.

"I have to make sure that my kids have somewhere to stay Royce. That hotel room might be their home until Sienna can get something permanent," Jax answered.

"Yeah, and I guess y'all had to do a trial run on the bed to make sure it was comfortable enough. There is no lie that you can tell to get yourself out of this one. The ass grabbing and kissing was all the proof that I needed to see," Royce said as she walked away to their master bathroom.

Jaxon's heart was beating a mile a minute as he followed behind her and watched her start the shower water. His excuse for meeting his ex-wife was lame as hell, but he didn't have a defense for the display of affection that his wife had witnessed.

"I'm sorry about that baby, but she was upset. She had been crying about not having a place to live and I was only trying to comfort her," Jax said, not even believing his own story.

"Okay, well, now I'm upset. The only difference is, I refuse to cry anymore. You're not even worth my tears. Continue to offer comfort to your ex-wife while losing your present wife in the process," Royce threatened as she closed the glass shower door and tuned him out.

Jax was begging and pleading for her to hear him out, but she was done talking. He felt like he was drowning in his lies, but he needed a lifeline. He could see that Royce was getting fed up and he needed to get the situation under control. Jax knew that a romantic gesture probably wouldn't be well received, so he wasn't going to bother. He walked out of the bathroom and made a call to the only person who he felt would be able to help him.

***

Royce valet parked her car and rushed inside of The Southern Yacht Club where she and her mother were meeting Elena for brunch. She was almost an hour late and she knew that Sondra was going to have a fit. She talked on the phone with Caleb the entire ride over and he was begging to see her again. Royce was battling with herself, but she really did want to see him too. Jax was doing him and she saw no reason why she couldn't do the same. Unlike her husband, Royce had a conscience and it bothered her every time she did something wrong.

"Sorry I'm late," Royce said as she walked up to her mother's table and took her seat.

"You're actually right on time. I purposely gave you an earlier time because I knew that you were going to be late. I'm just happy that Elena is not here yet," Sondra replied as she sipped on her lemon water.

"So what if she was. Elena is not the FLOTUS, just in case you didn't know. She got more issues than both of us combined, but I bet she won't tell you that," Royce flippantly replied.

"I don't know what's gotten into you, but your attitude needs adjusting. You've been in a foul mood lately, snapping on your husband for no good reason. Poor Jaxon was almost in tears when he called me," Sondra noted.

"Fuck Jaxon!" Royce spat angrily.

[41]

She was tired of being made out to be the bad person, when her husband was in the wrong. Jax was just like a spoiled child. He always ran to her mother with some bullshit whenever things didn't go his way. He was busted and he didn't have a defense. Royce needed her mother's support more than anything, but Sondra was never on her side. She took whatever story Jax told her and ran with it. Royce was getting fed up with her mother and she had started lashing out more. She tried her best to respect her but, sometimes, it was easier said than done.

"You better watch your mouth! What the hell is wrong with you? You're starting to act just like your cousin Uri," Sondra replied as she looked around to make sure nobody heard her daughter's sudden outburst.

"Maybe I need to act more like Uri, so I wouldn't get messed over all the time. And I'm not the one with the problem, Jaxon is. Since he wants to call and tell you everything, did he tell you why I snapped on him? Did he tell you that he was in a hotel room with his ex-wife for over an hour? And that wasn't a rumor. I saw it with my own eyes," Royce noted.

"Oh, Royce please. They have kids together and she needs a place to stay. No man in his right mind is gonna let his kids and their mother suffer. You knew that Jaxon had kids when y'all met. Don't start being selfish now," Sondra fussed.

"Selfish?" Royce repeated "I've never been a selfish person, but I'm tired of being a fool. You want me to turn the blind eye to what he's doing just to save face and I'm not the one. I've done that long enough and I'm tired."

"Stop being so naïve Royce. What man doesn't cheat? Sometimes the stress of life gets to them and they crave something different. Your father is not as perfect as you think he is, but I would never dream of leaving him. Jax is just being a man, like so many others. It's in their DNA," Sondra said dismissively.

"Wow, great advice mom," Royce said sarcastically as she rolled her eyes.

She couldn't believe what she was hearing, but she shouldn't have been surprised. Jax could have fucked another woman in their bed and Sondra would have told her to go to another room until he was finished. Royce had never known her father to step out of his marriage, but the way her mother talked made it seem like he did. Her parents' marriage seemed perfect to her, minus an occasional lovers' quarrel. It was nothing that wasn't resolved at the end of the day though.

"Well, you and a lot of other women might be okay with it, but I can't deal. That's y'all old school wives who let your husbands cheat and pretend like y'all don't know. Unlike you, I'm not opposed to divorce," Royce said, making her mother choke on her water.

"You must be out of your mind. Where else are you gonna find a well-educated black man with wealth and stability like Jaxon Davenport?" Sondra asked.

"Well, since I'm a well-educated black woman with her own money, I won't have to look far. He'll find me if it's meant to be. I'd rather be single forever before I let a man continue to walk all over me. I'm tired of pretending to be happy when I'm miserable," Royce said, trying hard to hold back her tears.

"Royce, please, don't make a permanent decision while acting on temporary emotions. No marriage is perfect, but yours is damn near close to it. Maybe you and Jax just need a vacation. Book a trip somewhere and put it on my black card," Sondra suggested.

"I'm not interested," Royce replied with a wave of her hand.

"I'm only trying to help here Royce," Sondra pointed out.

"No, you're trying to save face, just like always," Royce countered, right as Elena glided into the building.

Elena wore a long flowing white dress with gold heels and the matching clutch. Her silky, black, shoulder-length hair was pulled into a tight bun with a flower adorning it. Her cinnamon colored skin was flawless with just a light coating of makeup to enhance her natural beauty.

"Sorry I'm late ladies. I had the hardest time trying to figure out what I wanted to wear," Elena said when she walked over to their table.

"It's okay, and you look beautiful by the way," Sondra said as she smiled at the woman who she so desperately wanted to be like.

They blew air kisses at each other, as Royce looked at her mother like she was crazy. A minute ago, Sondra was ready to jump down her throat for being late, but the great Elena Davenport could no wrong in her eyes.

[43]

"Thanks darling. And how is my beautiful daughter doing this morning?" Elena asked, as Royce stood up to hug her.

Elena and her husband had three sons and one daughter. She always referred to Royce as her second daughter and that's how she felt about her. She had two other daughters-in-law, but Royce was her favorite. She was the only one with a college degree and career, while the other two were stay at home moms. Her daughter's husband was the son of a prominent judge, so he had Elena's vote from day one.

"I'm good Elena. How are you?" Royce asked with a smile.

"I couldn't be better," Elena replied as she took her seat.

She winced in pain when she sat down, but she quickly masked it with her signature smile. Sondra saw the pained expression on her face and so did Royce.

"Are you okay Elena?" Sondra asked, kissing ass like always.

"I'm fine honey. These old knees just don't bend the way they used to," Elena smiled awkwardly.

"I bet they don't," Royce mumbled to herself.

"So, how have you and my son been doing?" Elena asked as she summoned the waiter and placed her drink order.

"Better than ever from what I've been hearing," Sondra interjected, making her daughter look at her and frown.

"I don't know where my mother has been getting her info from, but things are not that great with us," Royce said, to Sondra's dismay.

She could have slapped her daughter silly for divulging that kind of information to Elena. Royce was making a big deal out of nothing and Sondra wanted her to stop it.

"It's nothing Elena. Royce is just upset about his interactions with his ex-wife. I tried explaining to her that he's only trying to help them find a place to live," Sondra spoke up again.

"I can talk for myself and that is not why I'm upset," Royce snapped.

"What's wrong Royce? Does Silas and I need to have a talk with our son?" Elena asked her.

[44]

Sondra looked at her daughter, pleading with her eyes for Royce not to embarrass her. Things with her and Jax weren't all that bad for her to be acting that way.

"No, it's nothing that we can't handle," Royce replied, making her mother visibly relax.

"Good, and don't worry about Sienna. My husband and I will take care of her dilemma. She better thank God that she has two of my grandbabies. Her ghetto ass would be living on the streets if she didn't. She's what's wrong with society today. An uneducated black woman with kids that she can't afford to take care of." Elena frowned, like her son wasn't half responsible for the kids in question.

"I agree. Some of these poor kids don't stand a chance," Sondra co-signed.

"That's what disgusts me about my other sons' wives. Lazy women who depend on a man to take care of them repulse me. They don't deserve to be treated equally, since they don't contribute to the household. And they know better than to call and complain to me. I don't want to hear it. They might as well be a child in the home since they have to be cared for like one. Like my husband always says, behave like a child and get treated like one," Elena replied, sounding like her male chauvinist husband.

"I know that's right," Sondra agreed.

Royce had heard enough and she was done listening to their stupidity. Sondra was horrified when she pulled out her phone and started texting, but she didn't give a damn. Caleb had asked if he could see her when she left from brunch and she was trying to confirm the location. Royce jumped slightly when Sondra kicked her under the table, signaling her to put her phone away. Sondra jumped a short time later, shocked that Royce had kicked her right back. The defiant look on her daughters' face was one that Sondra had never seen before. She didn't like the change that she was seeing in Royce and she knew that her niece probably had a lot to do with it. Uri was a firecracker like her mother, but Royce had always been so reserved. She made a mental note to have a talk with Royce later to see what was going on with her.

Whatever it was, she needed to get over it and move on. Sondra had too much to lose if she didn't. Elena was in a great position to get a promotion working alongside her husband at the school board office. Sondra was her first choice to take over as principal when she did. Nothing or no one was going to stand in the way of that, including her spoiled, selfish, ungrateful daughter.

Chapter 5

66 I get what y'all are saying, but the shit ain't that easy. She signed a lease and I can't just break it like that," Bryce reasoned as he argued with his cousins and brother.

They were at Jaden and Kia's house discussing Shanti's baby shower, but they used that as an opportunity to voice their concerns about the shop. Bryce worked at night, while Co-Co ran things in the daytime. Everything was cool for a while, but they all seemed to have a problem with the new stylist, Cookie. Bryce rarely saw her, so he didn't know much about her personality.

"Man, tell that bitch that her contract is up," Brian replied.

"She just signed the shit three months ago, and it's for eighteen months," Bryce argued.

"You shut up Brian! It's your fault that the messy bitch is there!" Co-Co yelled.

"How is it my fault? I didn't tell her that we had a booth for rent," Brian challenged.

"No, but you told that bitch Shaky, and you know that Cookie is her best friend," Co-Co noted.

Cookie was a stylist who Bryce let work in the shop a few months ago. She was the best friend of Brian's ex, Mya, and she also worked at the club with her. Mya was a stripper, but Cookie worked as a topless bartender. She was okay when she first started working there, but things quickly went downhill soon after. She kept up too much mess at the shop, being that Brian and Shanti both worked there. Mya was crazy in love with Brian and she hated that Shanti was having his baby. He paid for her to get an abortion and she felt like Shanti should have done the same. Brian was able to manipulate her to do whatever he said, but Shanti wasn't the one. She was determined to have her baby with or without Brian's help.

"What's your problem with her, Co-Co? From what I hear, she likes you more than anybody else," Bryce acknowledged.

"Baby, I'm Co-Co, everybody likes me. That bitch just gets under my skin sometimes," Co-Co replied.

"You sure that it's not jealousy that's making you feel like that. Ole girl be having mad clients coming up in there to see her," Bryce smirked, knowing that he was about to get his cousin hyped up.

"Jealously!" Co-Co yelled. "What the fuck is there to be jealous of? I sat there and watched her take out a quick weave and put perm on top of hair glue. Bitch should have just taken a razor and shaved her client's head. You better make her ass sign a disclaimer before one of those customers sue you and be owning your shop. Our shop is a business, not a popularity contest."

"That bitch can't do no hair. All her customers are strippers from the club where she works," Candace chimed in.

"Exactly!" Co-Co agreed. "Bitch need to put an Amber alert out on her missing edges."

"I get what y'all are saying, but my hands are tied. She can't break the lease and neither can I," Bryce said with finality.

"I thought we were supposed to be discussing the baby shower. The fuck are we talking about the shop for?" Jaden questioned.

"Me too. That's why I came over here," Caleb spoke up.

"Yeah, let's finalize these plans, so I can get back home to my husband and kids. It's Sunday and I need to cook and iron for tomorrow," Brooklyn replied.

She once again started talking about the baby shower that she and her mother were throwing for Shanti. Everyone was helping financially, but Brian put up the most. They decided on pink and gray for the colors, since Shanti didn't want a theme.

"Man, I already spent close to two thousand dollars for all this shit. What do you need money for now?" Brian asked, when Brooklyn told him that she needed an additional three hundred dollars.

"I don't know, but mama said to get the money from you for something that she needed to order. Don't kill the messenger," Brooklyn replied.

"Nigga, that's your baby. You're supposed to put up more than everybody else. We did our part as the uncles and auntie," Jaden informed him.

"And you know that Shanti don't really have a big family. It's just her and her three older brothers and they be in the streets more than anything. Her auntie Karen is helping out too though," Kia spoke up.

"Man, I swear, if this ain't my baby, I'm taking her ass to court and sue for all my money back. This is exactly why I didn't want kids. This shit is too damn expensive," Brian fussed as he dug into his pockets and gave Brooklyn the money.

"Strap up then nigga," Bryce replied as he stood up and headed for the door.

Before he had a chance to walk out, Jaylynn and her little brother were walking in. Lil Jaden, or Juice, as they called him, ran straight to his father and showed him the game that Jaylynn had just took him to purchase. He was only three years old, but he was bad as hell thanks to Jaden. He was a game head just like his other boy cousins. Jaylynn was sixteen and her parents had purchased her a car for her birthday. Her little brother ran her like crazy, but she didn't mind. She had him just as spoiled as their parents did.

"Hey everybody," Jaylynn spoke when she walked into the house.

Everyone spoke back, except for Co-Co. He gave her the evil eye as he got up and followed her into the kitchen. As soon as the coast was clear, he started going off just like she knew he would.

"Come here you lil sneaky bitch," Co-Co whispered as he grabbed her up by the collar of her shirt.

"I'm sorry Co-Co. I was scared, and I didn't know what else to say," Jaylynn hurriedly explained.

"That's bullshit and you know it. I told you before not to put me and Sweets in the middle of you and Hayden's mess. If your daddy doesn't want you to have a boyfriend, then you need to respect his wishes. The only reason I went along with the shit is because I didn't want Jaden to murder my best friend's nephew," Co-Co replied.

It was purely coincidental that the little boy who Jaylynn met at Tessa and Ryan's wedding was Sweets'

[49]

nephew. Sweets' oldest sister, Mona, had four boys and Hayden was her youngest at eighteen years old. Co-Co had never really met any of Sweets' family members because he never went to any of their family gatherings. Sweets had a big family just like him and they were close. Hayden and his father were both customers at Ryan's barber shop, so that explained why they were at the wedding. He and Jaylynn exchanged numbers and had been in contact with each other ever since. Jaden didn't approve of her having a boyfriend, so she and Hayden started sneaking around to see each other. Co-Co and Sweets were often thrown in the middle, since the two youngsters always lied and said that they were at one of their houses. Usually, Jaylynn would lie and say that she was at volleyball practice when she wanted to spend time with Hayden. Even though she'd quit the team after only one week, her parents didn't need to know that. Since it was a weekend and there was no practice, she had to make up something else.

"It was just a little white lie," Jaylynn sassed.

"I'm colorblind to lies when they involve me, honey. Jaden and Kia need to put your hot ass on some birth control pills," Co-Co replied.

"I don't know why. It's not like I'm having sex." Jaylynn frowned.

"Bitch, please. Your auntie said the same thing until we walked down on her sneaky ass right in the act. Your ass and hips ain't spreading like that for nothing," Co-Co said.

"But, I'm sixteen years old. This is the age when I'm supposed to start dating. My daddy needs to calm down," Jaylynn pouted.

"I'm sorry Jay, but that's not my decision to make. You need to sit down and have a talk with your father. You're only making shit worse by lying and sneaking around. I went through this same shit with your auntie Brooklyn, but I'm getting too old for it now. The next time you lie on me, I'm telling your daddy and you can deal with it from there," Co-Co said with finality as he walked away and rejoined everyone else in the front room.

Jaylynn just stood there and stared off into space for a while. She loved her father with all her heart, but Jaden could be a little unreasonable at times. He was too overprotective and that drove her crazy. Even her mother agreed to let her start dating, but Jaden wasn't having it. Kia tried several times to talk some sense into him, but he wasn't budging. Hayden was Jaylynn's first boyfriend and she wasn't going to stop seeing him. She just had to come up with more creative ways to sneak around to be with him.

"Alright, it's time for me to get out of here," Brooklyn said as she stood to her feet and stretched.

"Aye Brook, let me talk to you for a second," Caleb said while following his sister out to her car.

"What's up?" Brooklyn asked.

"Call Royce for me. I don't want to call her at a bad time," Caleb replied.

"Hell no, Caleb. Don't put me in the middle of that mess. That girl is married," Brooklyn said.

"You really kill me with that bullshit. Stop trying to act brand new all the time. Dominic had a fiancée and a wife when you got pregnant the first two times," Caleb reminded her.

"Boy bye. That was years ago. Y'all always trying to bring up old shit just to prove a point," Brooklyn fussed.

"Sometimes you need your memory jogged, just so you don't forget," Caleb chuckled.

"Whatever," Brooklyn said as she dialed Royce's number and waited for her to pick up.

"Hey girl," Royce said when she answered the phone.

"Hey boo. Can you talk?" Brooklyn asked her.

"Yeah, I'm in my car on my way back home from the nail salon," Royce replied.

"Oh, well, Caleb is standing here. He wanted me to call and make sure that you could talk," Brooklyn replied, making the other woman smile and blush.

"Okay, tell him that I'm calling him now," Royce said before hanging up.

"She's about to call you," Brooklyn repeated to her brother.

"Good looking out sis," Caleb said as he watched her get into her car and pull off.

He smiled like a kid at Christmas when his phone started ringing a few seconds later.

"How can I help you?" Royce asked when he answered the phone.

"I'm trying to see you," Caleb said, getting straight to the point.

"When and where?" Royce asked eagerly.

"Right now. Come park your car at my brother's house and ride with me," Caleb suggested.

"Will your brother be okay with me doing that?" Royce questioned.

"Yeah, he won't mind," Caleb answered.

"Okay, text me the address," Royce said.

"It's coming to you now. I'm outside, so I'll see you soon," Caleb said before they disconnected.

Royce was too excited as she entered the address in her GPS and followed the directions to her destination. She had been talking to Caleb every day since they met, but their schedules didn't always permit them to see one another. Caleb had moved out of the house with Sienna and back in with his parents. He was trying hard to find him a home to purchase, but he hadn't had any luck with that yet. Jax had been on Royce's back hard, trying to get her to forgive him. She probably would have done it by now, but her interactions with Caleb was making it hard. That and the fact that Jax was still being a dog. A few women at the school were whispering about him and one of the cafeteria ladies. Royce knew that it had to be true because the same woman in question threw her shade whenever they saw each other. They didn't know each other well, so there was no reason for her ongoing attitude. Royce didn't even waste her time trying to confront him because it was a waste. Jax was a compulsive liar and nothing that came out of his mouth was true. It was all good with her though. Royce was ready to start playing the same game that her husband had mastered. He wasn't the only one who could be married and have a little fun on the side.

Chapter 6

66You better hide by your daddy. Bad ass lil bastard," Co-Co said while looking at Juice.

He was wedged into a small little area under Jaden's work station while his father was cutting hair. He was scared to death to move because Co-Co was after him. Between Jaylynn calling him all day and Juice being his usual bad self, he was drained. He wished to the heavens above that Jaden and Kia never reproduced again. He didn't even know what Jaylynn wanted and he didn't care. He was done lying for her sneaky ass.

"What that lil bad ass nigga did to you?" Brian asked.

"Nothing," Jaden laughed.

"I don't see nothing funny about you raising a juvenile delinquent. What kind of child gets suspended from daycare?" Co-Co asked.

"I'm not in daycare!" Juice yelled from his makeshift hiding place.

"Lil boy, please. Pre-K three ain't nothing but a nursery for bad kids," Co-Co replied.

"What happened?" Brian asked again.

"I got some gumbo from the corner store for lunch, but I put it in the break room. I didn't even think to move my shit when Jaden sat his bad ass in there to eat. I went to go warm my shit a few minutes later and almost died," Co-Co said as he frowned at the memory.

"Stop being so damn dramatic all the time. The shit wasn't even that bad," Jaden replied.

"You can't be serious. That bastard dumped the whole container of salt in my food. He's trying to run my pressure up and kill me!" Co-Co yelled.

"I made a mistake," Juice swore.

"Yeah, well, it won't be a mistake when I burn your bad ass with these curlers," Co-Co threatened as he held the flat iron up for Juice to see.

"Daddy, don't let him burn me," Juice said to Jaden, making everybody laugh.

"He's not gonna burn you," Jaden assured him as he continued to cut his client's hair.

"You better stay right there until it's time for you to go home," Co-Co warned him.

"Man, I'm hungry again," Juice whined, even though he'd just eaten not too long ago.

When the door chimed, everyone looked up just in time to see Shanti walking through the front door. Brian's smile quickly faded as he watched one of her ex niggas carrying her work bag inside for her. Cookie had a smirk on her face as she watched Brian to gauge his reaction. She couldn't stand Brian most of the time for how he treated her girl. Her best friend, Shaky, was in love with Brain and he was in love with someone else. Cookie was a newly licensed hair stylist, but working in Bryce's shop was not what she had in mind for her first job. Since Shaky begged her to do it, she took one for the team and applied for the job. She was happy that she did because they kept her entertained with all the daily drama that went on. That and the fact that she could report Brian's every move to Shaky was a plus. Shaky was hurt that he begged her to get an abortion, but let Shanti have her baby.

"Good evening," Shanti spoke as she made her way to her work station.

She had just entered her fifth month of pregnancy, and Brian had accompanied her to the clinic earlier that morning. She told Brian that she was coming in late, but he didn't know that her hooking up with her ex was the reason why. That was exactly why he was having doubts about the paternity of her baby. Shanti stayed in some different nigga's face every other day.

"Hey girl. What you got to eat?" Candace asked when she saw her sit a plate down on her table.

"That's a shrimp and fish plate, but I wanted pizza," Shanti replied while looking at her ex, Kerry.

"Don't even play me like that. I told you that I would order you a pizza if you wanted me to. I know you and lil mama gotta eat," Kerry said, referring to her and the baby.

"No, I'm good. I appreciate what you got for me," Shanti replied.

Brian was on fire as he watched Shanti walk Kerry to the door and stand outside and talk to him. He was in his feelings, but he tried hard to play it off. He couldn't let Shanti know that she had him bothered like that.

"Order some pizza for me, Co-Co," Brian requested.

"Are you paying for it?" Co-Co questioned.

"I wouldn't have told you to order it if I wasn't. And make sure one of them got everything on it," Brian replied, knowing what Shanti liked.

"Give me your card," Co-Co demanded as he pulled up the pizza app on his phone.

"Here Juice, you can have this," Brian said as he handed his nephew the plate that Shanti had just sat down on her desk.

"No man, don't give him that girl's food," Jaden fussed.

"Man, fuck that food and the nigga that paid for it. Eat it Juice," Brian ordered.

He didn't have to tell his nephew twice. Juice opened the plate and stuffed a handful of fries into his mouth. Jaden handed him a bottle of water, since it seemed that he would be down there for a while. Co-Co had him scared to death, but that was nothing new. Juice was always doing something to piss his older cousin off and Co-Co was always after him.

"Shanti gon' kick your ass Brian," Candace laughed.

"She didn't want that shit anyway. Her pizza will be here soon," Brian replied, right as Shanti walked back inside.

"That's right cousin. Make sure your baby eats," Co-Co said while looking at Cookie.

She had some lady in her chair, fucking up her haircut. Co-Co wanted to laugh at what he was seeing, but he just shook his head in pity instead.

"Where's my food?" Shanti asked as she looked around on her work table.

"Right here!" Juice yelled from under his father's work station.

"Boy, I know you're not eating my damn food," Shanti fumed.

"My uncle Brian gave it to me," Juice revealed.

"Lil bad ass is always snitching," Co-Co laughed.

[55]

"I ordered you a pizza," Brian said while looking at Shanti.

"Are you serious Brian? I'm hungry right now," Shanti fussed while storming off to the break room.

Brian jumped up and followed behind her, as everyone else looked on in amusement. Cookie rolled her eyes in disgust as she refocused her attention on her client.

"The fuck you got an attitude for? I just said that I ordered you a pizza!" Brian yelled as soon as he and Shanti were alone.

"Who the fuck is you yelling at, nigga? I'm not Shaky or none of them other hoes that you play that shit with. I don't care that you ordered a pizza. I'm hungry right now," Shanti said as she sat down in the chair.

Brian opened the fridge in the break room and took out a bag with a Styrofoam container inside. He took the plate out and handed it to Shanti along with a fork. Her frown was quickly replaced with a smile when she saw the Chantilly berry cake that was inside.

"Greedy ass," Brian laughed as he watched her stuff her face.

"Whatever," Shanti said with a mouth full of dessert.

"You thought about what I said earlier?" Brian asked while sitting down next to her.

"I'm not doing this with you, Brian. One minute my baby is yours and the next minute she's not. I'm not naming my baby after a nigga who's having doubts about her even being his," Shanti replied.

"That's your fault though, Shanti. Shit was all good with us until you started fucking with a bunch of other niggas. How do you think that shit made me feel?" Brian asked, trying not to sound as bothered as he was.

"Probably the same way I felt when you were fucking with a bunch of different hoes. I don't have to try to convince you that this is your baby. I'll let the paternity test prove it. I can talk to a million different men, but that doesn't mean that I was fucking them. I know who I was with when I got pregnant and I don't have any doubts," Shanti noted.

"Man Shanti, I swear, I really want to believe you, but I don't want my feelings to get hurt if this is not my baby. I already feel like I'm attached to her and that shit is gon' kill me," Brian said honestly.

"I really don't care if you believe me or not. I just told you that I'm not trying to convince you one way or the other. Only hoes who have doubts do shit like that. The test will do all the talking for me. I told you that we could have done the test before the baby even came," Shanti reminded him.

"I don't want to do it like that. I can wait," Brian replied.

Truthfully, he was scared to death of finding out the truth. Waiting until the baby came gave him a little time to get his emotions in check. As crazy as it may have sounded, he wanted Shanti, even if the baby wasn't biologically his. He would never say that out loud to her or anyone else though.

"Okay, well, stop stressing about if you're the father or not." Shanti shrugged.

"What about her name? Did you think about the ones I told you I liked?" Brian asked as he caressed her stomach.

He tried to act unaffected by Shanti, but it was too hard. He was in love with her, no matter how hard he tried to fight it. He was scared to be a father, but there were many nights that he prayed for Shanti's baby to be his. Starting a family with Shanti was a good look, in his opinion. Brian was getting older and he was ready to settle down. He just hoped that Shanti was ready to do the same. Four more months and a paternity test was all that stood in the way of him finding out if his dream would become a reality.

"I like Brielle, but I'm not giving her a name until after the test is done," Shanti said, pulling Brian away from his thoughts.

"Why is that? I thought you were so sure that she was mine," Brian said, looking at her sideways.

"It has nothing to do with me being sure. I never had my father's name on my birth certificate and I don't want that to happen with my baby. The test is being done in the hospital and I'm paying a grip to get the results back in forty-eight hours. That way, all doubts will be removed and you can sign the birth certificate with no worries," Shanti replied.

"I want her to have my last name too," Brian noted.

"That's cool," Shanti replied in her nonchalant tone that Brian hated.

[57]

"Come spend the night with me," Brian requested as he kissed her neck.

"Okay," Shanti agreed without putting up much of a fight.

Brian pissed her off more than she cared to admit, but she still loved him. He tried to play hard, but Shanti knew the real him. As much as she hated to admit it, she understood why he had doubts about the paternity of her baby. Most of Shanti's friends were males and she was always accused of them being more. Her mother died twelve years prior when she was only sixteen years old, and her older brothers and aunt Karen took care of her until she could fully take care of herself. Her brothers' friends became Shanti's friends and they looked out for her as if she were their little sister too. None of her boyfriends understood that, and her relationships always ended because of it. Shanti could be called many things, but a hoe was not on that list. That was exactly why she was still sleeping with Brian. She was always horny and she couldn't see herself having sex with just anybody, especially while she was pregnant. He was the father of her child and she wouldn't have it any other way.

"Not just one night Shanti," Brian said after a long pause.

"What do you mean?" Shanti asked, as he continued to shower her face and neck with kisses.

"I don't want you to just spend one night. Bring enough clothes to stay for a few nights," Brian suggested.

"You gotta pick me up then. You know I hate driving with this big ass belly," Shanti replied.

"I guess that's why that lame ass nigga dropped you off." Brian frowned.

"I don't say nothing when your stripper bitch come in here and be all in your face. Give me the same respect," Shanti said.

"Fuck that nigga," Brian spat.

"And fuck that bitch," Shanti retorted.

"See, this is why we can't get along. You always gotta challenge everything I say," Brian fussed.

"You just can't take what you dish out, but you better learn," Shanti replied.

"Give me a kiss," Brian said as he pulled her chair closer to his.

Shanti blushed and puckered up for a kiss. Moments like those made her realize why she had fallen so hard for him in the beginning. Brian had a heart of gold, but he was stubborn and selfish at times. He wanted his woman to wear a halo while he went out and did whatever he wanted to do. That usually worked for him in the past, but Shanti was the exception. She never got mad; she always got even. The difference with her was that she never slept with other people, but Brian didn't know that.

"I hope the food comes before my appointment gets here," Shanti said once they pulled away from their intense lip lock.

"Why didn't you call and tell me what you wanted to eat? I could have had it here already," Brian replied.

"I already had something to eat until you gave my food to Juice," Shanti fussed.

"Fuck that food," Brian spat angrily. "And keep your niggas away from here. This is a place of business."

"I don't tell you nothing when that bald head bitch Shaky comes in here. Make up your mind boo. Either you want me or you don't," Shanti replied.

"Don't do me that Shanti. You know I wanted you, but you play too many games. How you going out to eat with other niggas and shit, when we were supposed to be together?" Brian questioned.

"The same way you took another bitch to the hotel and didn't think I was gonna find out. Don't play with me, Brian. I told you that from day one. I'm not begging you or no other nigga to do right by me. I grew up in a house full of men, so I know the kind of games y'all play. I'm not the one. Don't expect me to sit at home waiting for you to come back. I had a life before you and nothing has changed," Shanti replied.

"See, that's the shit that makes a nigga doubt you. You got me fucked up if you think you gon' have all these different niggas around my daughter. That shit ain't happening," Brian fussed.

"Oh, so she's your daughter again? Your ass is too confused for me," Shanti said as she pulled away from him.

"I really want her to be," Brian said while pulling her up and sitting her on his lap.

He was finally admitting out loud what he'd been thinking all along. Shanti smiled and pulled Brian in for another kiss. He was nervous about the outcome of the

[59]

paternity test, but he had no reason to be. She had no doubts, but she was ready to ease his mind as well. They were so wrapped up in each other that they never even paid attention to someone standing there watching their every move.

"Girl, look at that picture that I just sent you. That nigga plays all kinds of games," Cookie said when she called her best friend on the phone.

She had gone to the bathroom, but she took a few minutes to spy on Shanti and Brian before she went back to the front of the shop. Brian was always talking shit about him and Shanti not being together, but they sure looked mighty close in the break room. She knew that Mya was going to have a fit and she had every right to. Brian had been stringing her along for a while, knowing that he wanted to be with somebody else. Cookie wasn't going to let him play her friend and she didn't care who didn't like it.

"Oh okay, so he wants to keep playing these games I see. Him and that bitch got me fucked up. I'm so sick of this shit," Mya said as she tried to fight back her tears.

Brian was always on some bullshit, and she regretted the day that she fell in love with him. He was constantly lying to her, and she was fed up with it all. To see Shanti sitting on his lap kissing him was like a slap in the face. To see his hand on her very pregnant belly was like a knife being plunged in her heart, especially since he begged her to get rid of her baby. Mya was a fool and listened, but she regretted that as well.

"Don't worry about it friend. You know he'll be back in your face and your bed by the end of the week," Cookie assured her.

"Yeah, I know," Mya replied, knowing that she was going to let him.

That was the problem. Brian always did her dirty and she always forgave him. He would come to the club and watch her dance and have her bent over the trunk of his car a few hours later. Mya knew that she degraded herself to be with him, but her heart wouldn't have it any other way. Brian was always claiming that he was single, but that's not how it looked to her.

"Her baby shower is coming up too. From what I'm hearing, he spent a grip on that shit," Cookie instigated.

"Yeah and I got something for his dog ass too," Mya promised.

"Okay friend, I have a customer coming soon, but I'll see you at the club later," Cookie said before she hung up the phone and walked away.

She was right on time because Brian and Shanti came out of the break room a few minutes later. Cookie was already back at her work station pretending to straighten up. She watched out of the corner of her eyes, as Brian and Shanti smiled at each other as they went their separate ways.

"Somebody's in a better mood. I wonder why," Co-Co instigated as he looked over the different hair colors that he'd purchased for himself.

He never kept his short hair the same color for too long and he was ready to make a change.

"Where is my pizza?" Shanti asked him.

"It should be here any minute," Co-Co replied as he settled on a reddish-pink looking color that he wanted to try.

"Ooh, that's pretty," Cookie complimented as she walked up on him.

"I know honey, but you need to give me some breathing room. I don't like people all up in my personal space like that," Co-Co replied, resisting the urge to tell her to back the fuck up.

"That's gonna look so cute on you. When are you gonna let me do your hair Co-Co?" Cookie asked him as she stepped back a little.

"When pigs fly and drop bacon from the sky," Co-Co replied, as the entire shop erupted in laughter.

Cookie laughed too because she expected a snappy reply. Co-Co was really the only one that she liked in the shop, but she was too dumb to see that the feelings weren't mutual. He was always cracking on the way she did hair, but his comments always went over her head. Co-Co didn't play about his hair and he would never let Cookie lay a finger on him. He loved his edges and Cookie didn't have any. That was a dead giveaway as to what kind of stylist she was. If she couldn't save her own edges, her clients didn't stand a chance.

"The pizza is here!" Juice yelled, still perched in his hiding spot under his father's work station.

"It's about damn time. I'm starving," Shanti replied.

Brian met the delivery man at the door and gave him a tip. He grabbed the pizza boxes from his hand and nodded to Shanti to follow him to the back. Cookie was paying attention to it all and she couldn't wait to report back to her girl. She hated to say it, but Mya was wasting her time with Brian. He was already crazy in love with Shanti. If her baby turned out to be his, the feelings were only going to get deeper.

Chapter 7

Caleb tried, but he just couldn't force himself to enjoy what he was doing at the moment. Mrs. Lockwood, his probation officer, was breaking a sweat as she cupped her breasts and bounced on him like a cowgirl in heat. She was panting and mumbling something that only she understood. She was always careful not to be too loud, since they had about ten other offices in the building with hers. She was the supervisor of the probation department and she had a huge office equipped with a sofa and bathroom at the rear of the building. Her employees were trained not to bother her when she had her *do not disturb* sign on her door, but she never really used it unless Caleb was coming to see her.

Mrs. Lockwood was an attractive woman, but she was also a bitch. She talked to her employees like they were nothing, even though most of them were older than she was. Caleb was assigned to another worker at first, but Mrs. Lockwood quickly fixed that problem. She gave her employee one of her female clients and took Caleb as her own. He soon found out why when he got there one day, and she dropped to her knees and gave him head right there in her office. Caleb was shocked that the prissy, well put together woman went there with him.

After a while, that shock wore off and he got used to their weekly rendezvous. He tried to break it off with her a few times before, but she had him by the balls. She held his freedom in the palm of her hand and there was nothing that he could do about it. Mrs. Lockwood sat on the board of the probation and parole department. She could have ended Caleb's probation altogether because he was a first-time offender. Since she wanted to keep fucking him, he would probably be doing the remaining four years that he had left.

"I'm gonna cum baby. Shit! This feels so good," Mrs. Lockwood moaned as her entire body shook.

She was trying to break Caleb in two with how fast and wild she was moving. He wasn't really into it, but he felt his release building up not too long after. Caleb gripped the pillow on the sofa as he filled up the condom that covered his erection.

"Ugh!" he grunted, right as Mrs. Lockwood came and collapsed on top of him.

"God, that was so good. You just don't know how much I needed that." She smiled as sweat dripped from her body onto his.

"Raise up," Caleb demanded as he tapped her thigh.

"You could at least pretend to be interested Caleb. You barely even touched me," Mrs. Lockwood complained.

"The fuck I need to touch you for? You wanted a nut and you got it," Caleb replied.

"What the hell is going on with you lately? You used to be into it just as much as I was. I guess your bitch at home must be doing her job now," Mrs. Lockwood replied.

"You don't know shit about my personal life so stop fishing. I was never into this shit, but I enjoy my freedom," Caleb said as he stood up and walked over to her bathroom and flushed the condom.

She was always trying to get information out of him about the women in his life or his family. It was bad enough that she knew where he lived and worked. He wasn't about to volunteer anything else.

"I know there must be trouble in paradise. You wouldn't have moved out if everything was all good," she noted.

Caleb had to do an address change and she had been asking questions ever since then.

"How do you know that I was ever living with a woman to begin with? The fuck you worried about me for anyway when you have a husband at home? That nigga need to be dicking you down, so you can stop fucking your clients," Caleb snapped as he used one of her towels to clean himself up.

"Fuck you! Keep disrespecting me and I'll have your ass locked up. Your urine has been dirty since you started coming here. You have no room to talk," she replied while standing and stepping into her dress.

"How would you know? It ain't like you ever test the shit. The first thing you do when I come here is get naked and bust your legs wide open," Caleb said.

"How about we test it now? You know where the cups are. Go take a piss in one of them," she smirked, knowing very well that he wouldn't.

"I'm out. I'll see you in a few weeks," Caleb said as he headed for the door.

"That's what I thought. And you can kill that few weeks nonsense. I'll see you next Friday, just like always!" she yelled to his departing back.

"Stupid ass bitch," Caleb mumbled as he headed to his car.

He was still on the clock at work, but that didn't matter. He was a field supervisor, so he had the freedom to do whatever he wanted to. As soon as he started his car and pulled off, his phone rang, displaying Sienna's number. He had just left one stupid bitch, only to have another one calling him soon after. Caleb couldn't win for loosing. The only bright spot in his life lately had been Royce. She and Caleb talked or texted daily, and he loved when she was able to get away to spend some quality time with him.

"The fuck you want Sienna?" Caleb barked when he answered the phone.

"What's going on with the deposit for the apartment Caleb? I paid half of it and it's not fair for you to keep it all," Sienna replied.

"I'm not trying to keep them lil four hundred dollars man. You can have it all. Call the complex and see what's up with it. They didn't give the shit to me," Caleb swore.

"Are you sure Caleb? It's been weeks and they should have said something by now," Sienna said desperately.

"Man, I don't have a reason to lie to you about that lil money. They probably didn't give you nothing back since your bad ass kids tore their shit up. Blinds hanging off the windows and the carpet is all fucked up," Caleb noted.

"Okay, but I should still get something back once they deduct that," Sienna replied.

"You must really be hurting for money. The fuck you still screwing your ex-husband for, if the nigga ain't doing nothing for you?" Caleb asked.

[65]

"What the hell are you talking about? I was faithful to you, even when you fucked over me with a different bitch every week. The only time I talk to Jaxon is about our kids!" Sienna yelled.

"Yeah okay. I guess y'all rented a room to discuss y'all kids not too long ago," Caleb said, repeating what Royce had told him about them being in a hotel room together.

"That's a lie!" Sienna shouted guiltily.

"The way I see it, you shouldn't be worrying about money or a place to stay. You got two kids for the nigga and you're still fucking him. He should make sure that you're straight in every way. I'm still having a hard time figuring out how you went from being the wife to the side chick," Caleb chuckled.

"What did I ever do to you, Caleb? I was a good girlfriend and I didn't deserve the treatment that I got from you," Sienna said, changing the subject.

"Here we go with this shit again. Stop always trying to play the victim Sienna. Your ass is sneaky, and the shit just caught up with you. I did my part when I was with you, but I'm not obligated to do anything else. We don't have nothing else to talk about, so make this your last time calling me," Caleb replied, right before he hung up the phone.

He dialed Royce's number right after to see if she would be free to hook up with him later that day. He needed to get home to wash the sex off him and, then, he was free for the rest of the day.

"Hold on a sec. Let me step out of my classroom," Royce whispered when she answered the phone for him. Caleb heard her fumbling with the device before she came back to the line.

"What you got going on today?" Caleb asked her.

"Nothing much. I'm attending an event at the Zulu Club next weekend and I need to find me some shoes. Other than that, I'm free. What did you have in mind?" Royce asked.

"You want to go grab something to eat with me when you're done? I can pick you up from your auntie's house again if you want me to," Caleb answered.

Royce had parked her car at her auntie Lydia's house twice before and Caleb would pick her up from over there. Uri's mother was her favorite auntie and she didn't mind at all.

"Okay, we can do that. I already know what kind of shoes I want, so I shouldn't be long," Royce replied.

"You think that fuck boy might get suspicious? I don't want to have y'all getting into it and shit. I know you said that he was questioning you the last time I kept you out too late," Caleb said.

"Fuck Jaxon. He might not even know that I'm gone. Let him find one of his other hoes to keep him company," Royce snapped.

"Damn baby. You been poppin' off at the mouth a lot lately. You might wanna lay off that crown apple for a while," Caleb joked.

He was only playing because he loved the attitude that Royce was starting to embrace. It was Caleb who told her to start saying what was on her mind. Royce was too busy worrying about what other people had to say and she wasn't living her life the way she wanted to. Her cousin Uri kept telling her the same thing and she was finally starting to get it. She was too young to be so serious all the time. She was starting to let loose and have fun for a change.

"I can't, I'm hooked now. Jax looked at me like I was crazy when he saw me drinking it at home. I snapped on his ass when he said something about it," Royce laughed.

"Co-Co turned you out just like he does with everybody else," Caleb said.

"I'm still not much of a drinker, but I like the apple taste," Royce replied.

"Okay, well, I won't hold you. Hit me up when you're on your way to your auntie's house and I'll come get you," Caleb requested.

"Okay, I will. I'll see you later," Royce said as she hung up the phone with a huge smile covering her face.

*** ***

"Fuck Jax!" Lydia spat, as her niece sat on the sofa in her living room and told her all about her rapidly crumbling marriage.

"I feel the same way auntie, but you know how your sister is. I don't even feel like I'm married anymore. It's like Jax and I are roommates trying to keep up a facade for our families. He's barely home and neither am I," Royce admitted.

"Fuck Sondra too!" Lydia yelled as she sipped from her rum and Coke.

Royce never understood the relationship between her mother and her auntie. The rest of the siblings treated Lydia like an outcast, but Sondra was always there for her. She paid all of Lydia's bills and kept money in her pockets.

"She's all about appearances and that's gonna be her downfall. I got pregnant and gave birth to Uri when I was only seventeen years old. You would have thought I had Ebola with the way she kept me hidden from everybody. I just never understood why our mother let her do it. Sondra was the one who raised me, so I could never defy her or go against what she said. My own mama didn't care enough to see what I was going through. My other brothers and sisters didn't give a damn, since I was always labeled the problem child of the family. They were happy when Sondra stepped up and took control. That's exactly why I stay away from everybody, including my own mama," Lydia continued as she stared into space with a blank expression on her face.

"I don't understand that though auntie. You're grandma's youngest child and she was fully capable of taking care of you. Why did she feel the need to let my mother raise you?" Royce asked.

"Oh, that part is simple. Mama was done having kids after she had Sondra. Her first husband had died, and her kids were big enough to do for themselves. Having another baby was nowhere in her plans. She only kept me because she thought that my married daddy would want to be with her when she revealed her pregnancy. Once he packed up his family and moved to North Carolina, she didn't have any more use for me. In fact, she hated the sight of me since I looked so much like him. She always told me that I was a burden, so a burden is what I became." Lydia shrugged.

Royce always wanted to know the details about the rift in her family, but she never mentioned it around her auntie. She asked her mother a few times, but Sondra always brushed her off. She just said that Lydia had always been a handful, but Royce didn't know what she meant. She was happy that her auntie was talking about it because she had a few questions.

"How old were you when you went to live with my mama?" Royce asked.

"Only five years old, but it was off and on. She would take me off of mama's hands whenever I got on her nerves. Your mama met your daddy when I was three and she was eighteen. They got married when she was twenty and I was five. My life has been fucked up ever since. She tried her best to turn me into the perfect little girl, but I guess I had too much of my daddy's evil ways in me. At least that's what my mama always said," Lydia answered as she lit up a cigarette.

"Yeah, I know the feeling of being made to feel like I had to be perfect. All those etiquette classes and debutant balls was a bunch of bullshit for her to brag about," Royce replied.

"I hate that she did that to you and I told her about it every chance I got. She tried to do it to Uri, but I refused to let her. I did all that dumb shit too and look at how far it got me. Kids need to be free to live however they want to, but not in Sondra's eyes. She has to be in control of everything and your pussy ass daddy don't say shit," Lydia spat.

"My daddy is nothing like her. I agree that he can be too passive at times, but he's never tried to run my life," Royce defended.

"Patrick is a good man, but he needs some balls. Your mama is the head bitch and Pat is her little flunky. He pretends to put up a fuss, but he agrees to whatever Sondra says," Lydia noted, making Royce wonder what she was talking about.

Lydia always passed little remarks about Royce's parents around her, but Uri usually shut it down. She didn't appreciate her mother's ungrateful attitude and she didn't want to hear her talking about the two people who gave them both a better life. If it weren't for Sondra and Patrick, Uri knew that she would have had a hard life. They paid her tuition throughout high school and paid for her to go to one of the best colleges. As soon as she graduated, her uncle Patrick got her a job at his company making a nice salary.

"Did something else happen between you and my mother? You know, aside from the fact that she tried to plan out your entire life just like she did mine," Royce chuckled.

"Let's just say that I can't wait for her perfect little world to come crashing down around her. Karma is gonna be a bitch named Lydia," her auntie replied as she puffed on her cigarette.

"Um... okay," Royce said, for lack of anything better to say.

"Who is this person that you come over here to meet up with?" Lydia asked in her raspy smoker's voice.

"His name is Caleb, but we're just friends," Royce hurriedly corrected.

"Uh-huh. If that's the case, why didn't you meet him at your own house or your mama's?" Lydia replied.

"Are you trying to get me killed?" Royce laughed.

"Exactly. He ain't no damn friend, just like I thought. Are you fucking him?" Lydia asked bluntly.

"Oh my God, auntie! No! I'm not having sex with him. I'm not even having sex with my own damn husband right now," Royce admitted.

"Do you kiss him?" Lydia questioned as she looked over at her niece.

"Are you drunk auntie?" Royce questioned.

"Girl please. It's gonna take more than this bottle of rum to get me right. Now, answer my question. Do you kiss your so-called friend?" Lydia repeated.

"It only happened twice," Royce admitted.

"And you like him, don't you?" Lydia asked.

"Yes," Royce admitted again as her cheeks flushed with embarrassment.

"Why are you still with Jax then?" Lydia questioned.

"What do you mean? He's my husband," Royce replied.

"But you're not happy with him, Royce. Why would you want to stay with a man who makes your mama happier than he makes you? You might think what you're doing is innocent, but you're having an affair. Just because y'all ain't fucking don't mean you ain't messing around. Any time feelings are involved, it's cheating. So, now you and Jax are cheating on each other and I just don't understand why y'all are still together," Lydia argued.

"It's complicated auntie," Royce replied, sounding defeated.

"Ain't shit complicated about telling a muthafucker to kick rocks. You know I never did like his sneaky looking ass. With them shifty, wandering eyes," Lydia said.

"You and that mouth," Royce chuckled.

[70]

"I'm serious Royce. I know I be drunk more than I'm sober, but this is only my second drink of the day so far. Stop letting people run your life. Live the way you want to and be happy about it. Your mama got the man she wants and you should be able to do the same. Staying married to Jax is benefiting your mama more than anything. She don't care about him cheating and all that other shit. She wants to keep Elena happy and nothing more."

"I know," Royce agreed, right as Caleb sent a text telling her that he was outside.

"That's your friend?" Lydia asked while making air quotes.

"Yeah, I gotta go. I'll be back to get my car, but I won't knock or anything," Royce replied.

"Okay baby and you remember what I said. From this day forward, start doing what's best for you," Lydia said.

"I will auntie and thanks," Royce said as she kissed her cheek and ran outside to the car where Caleb was waiting.

Chapter 8

"**Y**es baby, just like that," Angelique panted as she held on to the wall with one hand and lifted her shirt with the other.

Her white scrub pants had been taken completely off so they wouldn't get dirty, but she didn't have time to remove the shirt. Angelique had faked a stomachache, just to get away to spend some alone time with Jax. He and Royce must have been having problems because it was their third day meeting up in one of the staff bathrooms in the school that no one really occupied. The toilet was always overflowing and Jax's mother ordered everyone to stay out of there. Just to be on the safe side, Jax hung an *out of order* sign out front and made sure the door was locked.

"Throw that ass back and stop acting scared," Jax grunted as he drilled into her deeper.

He had his phone propped up on a roll of tissue, making sure he captured all the footage.

"Harder baby. Beat this shit up like you always do," Angelique moaned as she threw her leg up on the sink to give him better access.

Jax was moving with the speed of lightening and hitting her spot all at the same time. She kept telling herself that she was done with him, but that feeling never lasted too long. Whenever Jax requested her presence, she was there with no questions asked. Jax was the finest man that she'd ever had the pleasure of meeting, with features almost identical to Derek Luke. Angelique found it easy to get lost in his medium-brown hued hooded eyes that seemed to see right through her. Jax had dark brown skin and a low cut with the prettiest smile that she'd ever seen. His body was nothing short of amazing and he stayed in the gym to keep it that way. Even his wardrobe turned her on. He admitted that his wife was his personal stylists, but she made him look good enough for everybody else.

"I'm about to nut. Come get this shit," Jax demanded as he pulled out of her and watched her drop down to her knees in front of him.

Angelique was a true freak who didn't care about anything else but pleasing him. Jax's dick was already slick with her juices, but Angelique still spit on it before taking him to the back of her throat. Jax fucked her mouth and watched in amusement as she gagged on his girth. Angelique was second in line with oral compared to his wife, but she was getting better. Jax felt his release building up and he braced himself for the explosion. Angelique was preparing herself as well because she knew that Jax wasn't going to pull out. She relaxed her throat, ready for him to spill his seeds, when the bathroom door flew open and Jax's mother stood there with a shocked but angry expression covering her face. The keys that she'd used to open the door fell to the floor as she stood there in awe.

"Shit," Jax hissed as he pushed Angelique away and turned his back to his mother.

He hurriedly fixed his clothes, as Angelique embarrassingly scrambled to find her pants.

"Are you out of your fucking mind Jaxon?" Elena yelled when she finally found her voice to say something.

She was in disbelief when she opened the door and caught her son in the act with one of the cafeteria workers. One of the teachers had complained about students playing and running down the hall in that area, and Elena decided to investigate for herself. The security guard or disciplinarians would have done it for her, but she was happy that she had followed her first mind and checked it out herself. Finding her son with his dick stuffed down a cafeteria worker's throat would have been the talk of the school and she just couldn't have that. Not to mention, someone would have possibly told Royce and that was a disaster within itself.

She heard the heavy breathing and soft moans coming from the bathroom as soon as she opened the door, but she thought it was the students who she was about to catch. The *out of order* sign on the door was what really got her attention because the bathroom had been repaired a few weeks before. The note was handwritten, and Elena knew that she didn't put it there.

"I'm sorry ma," Jax said as he dropped his head in shame.

Once Angelique was dressed, she tried to hurry pass her boss and her lover, but Elena stopped her before she had a chance to get too far.

"You need to clock out and go home for the day. You will not be working in the kitchen around these children's food after what I just saw," Elena fumed.

"Yes ma'am," Angelique mumbled as she hurriedly walked away to do as she was told.

Elena closed the bathroom door and turned her attention back to her man whore of a son.

"Your wife is downstairs teaching her class and you got your dumb ass up here fucking a bottom feeder. In my damn school at that. Are you trying to ruin everything that your father and I have worked so hard to obtain? Are you trying to ruin your marriage Jaxon?" Elena asked him.

"No, but things haven't been good between Royce and me. She barely lets me touch her anymore. I'm a man before anything else and I have needs," Jax replied.

"Your needs almost landed you in jail once before when you couldn't take no for an answer," Elena reminded him.

"That was a lie. I've never forced myself on anyone. I've never had to," Jax assured her.

He hated when his parents reminded him of the incident that happened when he was in college. Jax was a handsome young man and he was popular on his college campus. Just about every girl there wanted him and he tried his best to please them all. One girl wanted more than he was willing to give, and her feelings got hurt when he denied her request. She ended up lying on him saying that he tried to rape her, and his parents paid a lot of money to keep her quiet and out of the spotlight. They made sure to remind him of that every time he did something that they didn't approve of.

"You better get your shit together Jaxon. I will not let you ruin me and your father's reputation. We've worked too hard to get to where we are, and you will not destroy the Davenport name. Do you understand me?" Elena questioned as she looked deep into her son's eyes.

"Yes ma'am," Jax replied obediently.

[75]

"I will not allow you to ruin your marriage over that common gutter trash either. Royce is the best thing that has ever happened to you and you better start acting like it. I don't care what you have to do, but you better make it right with your wife. What if Sondra would have come in here and caught you cheating on her daughter?" Elena inquired.

"I said I'm sorry mother. It won't happen again," Jax promised her as he grabbed his phone.

"You damn right it won't because your little stunt just cost Angelique her job," Elena snapped before she turned and walked away.

***

Angelique was a nervous wreck for the next few days after Elena walked in on her and Jax. The incident happened on Monday and she still hadn't heard anything else about it. It was now Friday, so she felt a little better about everything. Elena could be a bitch at times and everyone in the school could attest to that. Angelique had been doing her job better than ever, in hopes that the entire situation would just blow over. Jax had been staying his distance and he didn't bother answering whenever Angelique called him. He and his wife had lunch in the cafeteria the day before, but Royce didn't look like she wanted to be there. Jax was all smiles as he hugged and kissed her, but she didn't seem to be enjoying it.

"Grab me some plastic bags and ties from the storage cabinet Angelique," her supervisor, Ms. Adams, requested, breaking Angelique out of her daydream.

"Okay," Angelique replied as she walked over and did as she was told.

"I need you to help me bag up these cookies for Mrs. Davenport," Ms. Adams noted.

"What does she need cookies for? Are they having a staff meeting or something?" Angelique inquired nervously.

"No, she's doing snack bags for her classroom," Ms. Adams replied.

"Oh, you mean that Mrs. Davenport," Angelique said with a frown when she realized it was Royce who her supervisor was referring to.

"What is that supposed to mean?" Ms. Adams asked her.

"Nothing, just tell me how many cookies go in each bag," Angelique replied.

"Listen up, lil girl. I don't know what your problem is with Royce, but you better suck that shit up and get over it. Love her or hate her, she's the daughter-in-law of our boss who happens to love her to death," Ms. Adams scolded.

"I don't have a problem with her, but I'm not about to treat her like she's royalty or something. I don't care who she is," Angelique said, right as the phone rang in the kitchen.

Ms. Adams scurried away to go answer it, as Angelique pulled some of the bags and ties from the box. She heard her supervisor on the phone, but she didn't know who she was talking to. Ms. Adams came back in a few minutes later and pulled her apron from her pudgy waist.

"Put three cookies in each bag and make sure there are twenty-seven bags. I have to go up to the office right quick," Ms. Adams said before she quickly disappeared.

Angelique wanted to protest, but she was in enough shit already. She didn't want to do anything else that would have anyone, especially Mrs. Davenport, looking at her sideways. She felt like Royce's maid as she bagged up the cookies that she had requested. It didn't take her long and, about twenty minutes later, she was done and cleaning up her mess. Her supervisor still hadn't returned, but Royce walked in right as she decided to take a break.

"Hey Angelique. Is Ms. Adams here?" Royce asked with a smile.

"Do you see her?" Angelique flippantly replied under her breath.

"Excuse me?" Royce questioned, hearing her loud and clear.

"No, she's not," Angelique answered.

"Do you know when she'll be back?" Royce questioned.

"What is it that you need?" Angelique asked with aggravation in her tone.

"The first thing I need you to do is kill the attitude. There's no need for all that sweetie. Don't be mad at me because you're fucking Jax and still have to catch the bus to work every day. I got a car and a ring and he's not even getting the pussy from me," Royce replied, making Angelique's mouth drop in shock.

She was surprised to hear Royce get rowdy with her because she was always so prim and proper. Not only that, but Angelique was shocked to know that Royce knew about her and her husband messing around. They had been very careful, up until recently when his mother walked down on them. She didn't know if Jax had been talking to anyone, but she hadn't told a soul. Maybe she wasn't doing as good a job of hiding it as she thought she was.

"Don't look so shocked boo. Even if people weren't talking about it, your attitude would have given it away," Royce said, like she was reading her mind.

"I have no idea what you're talking about," Angelique replied.

"I know you feel stupid, so I don't blame you for denying it. Imagine how I feel being married to his sad ass and knowing that he's cheating," Royce spoke up.

"Whatever," Angelique said with a roll of her eyes.

"But, anyway, I need the cookies for my students that Ms. Adams baked. Can you go fetch them for me?" Royce asked.

"I'm not a dog," Angelique snapped.

"I beg to differ, but we can agree to disagree." Royce shrugged as she walked around the long stainless-steel counter and found the cookies herself.

Ms. Adams walked back into the kitchen, right as Royce was walking out.

"I hope that's enough for everybody Mrs. Davenport." She smiled.

"It's more than enough and I really appreciate it. Thank you," Royce replied as she smiled and walked away.

Angelique rolled her eyes at her departing back as she turned her attention towards her supervisor.

"I need to see you in my office," Ms. Adams said with a concerned look on her face.

"Why? What's wrong?" Angelique questioned, hoping that Ms. Adams didn't hear her and Royce's exchange of words.

"It's private," she replied as she walked away towards her office with Angelique's termination papers in her hands.

She didn't know what Angelique had done, but she had to follow the orders that were given to her. Per their boss's instructions, that was Angelique's last day on the job. Ms. Adams hated to do, but that was all a part of her job as head cook in the school's cafeteria.

Chapter 9

Jax looked down at his phone and blew out a breath of frustration. He was in his man cave looking at a video that he'd made of him and one of the ladies at the gym, but he couldn't even enjoy it. Angelique had been calling him non-stop since she got terminated the day before. He couldn't do anything to help her, so he never bothered answering for her. Then, Sienna had been on his back about spending time with his kids, but Jax knew what that was all about. She wanted him to spend some time with her, but he was trying to make things right with his wife. His parents had put Sienna and his kids up in one of their furnished three-bedroom rental properties, but she still wasn't satisfied. She wanted Jax to be up under her all day, but that wasn't happening. He passed through from time to time to drop off money and fuck her and that was all that he had to offer. His wife had already found out about him being at the hotel with her and he didn't want to make matters worse. He didn't want to lose Royce by being so careless, but he felt that she was slipping away. Jax had never questioned his wife's fidelity, but Royce had been moving differently lately. They used to always ride to work together, but she had started taking her own car. Jax thought it was because she was mad at him, but it seemed to be more than that. Royce never went anywhere after work, but she hadn't been coming straight home lately. She always had an excuse as to where she was, and Jax never questioned it. They seemed to be drifting further apart and he didn't know what to do about it.

"Are you almost ready to go baby?" Jax asked when he walked up the stairs and into his bedroom.

Royce was in the mirror applying gloss to her lips, as he openly admired her beauty. Royce looked like a porcelain doll with her beautiful, almond shaped eyes and perfect smile. Her caramel complexion went well with the rust colored, form-fitting halter dress that hugged her curves. Royce's long, jet-black hair cascaded just past her shoulders in loose curls. Her stylist was a pro at making her hair seem like it was her own. She was on the short side, but the strappy heels that she wore gave her a little extra height and put her plump backside on full display.

"Yeah, I'm ready," Royce replied as she grabbed her purse.

"You look beautiful baby," Jax complimented as he snaked his arm around her waist.

"Thanks," Royce replied as she tensed up from his touch.

"What's wrong Royce? I feel like we're drifting further and further apart, and I don't know how to stop it," Jax replied.

"There's nothing that you can do stop it Jax. I'm over all the lying and cheating. Honestly, I'm over this entire marriage," Royce confessed.

"Baby, please don't do this. I'm not doing anything wrong and I wish you would stop letting people get in your head," Jax pleaded.

"Don't talk to me like I'm fucking stupid Jaxon! Stop trying to placate me!" Royce yelled, shocking her husband with her behavior and explicit language.

"I'm not," he replied as he studied her angry face.

"Stop acting like you didn't cheat for damn near our entire marriage. That playing dumb routine is old. I was a damn fool for staying with your ass as long as I did. I'm tired of playing this game and worrying about what people will say. You want the marriage to work, but you can't even admit to your wrongdoings," Royce continued.

"I know that I have to do better and I promise you that I will. Just give me a chance to get it right," Jax begged, as she rolled her eyes to the ceiling.

Royce was different, but he didn't know what brought about the change. She was never one to initiate an argument and she was non-confrontational most of the time. A few kind words and a kiss were usually enough to calm her down and end whatever dispute they were having. The look that was in her eyes now was telling Jax not to even try it. She had gotten a backbone from somewhere, and he had a feeling that Uri was the person who was responsible for it.

"Let's go before I change my mind about going to this bullshit," Royce snapped, surprising him once again.

Jax was quiet as they exited the house and made their way over to the club. Royce ignored him and played on her phone the entire time. There was so much that he wanted to say, but he didn't want to piss her off again. Lately, everything that he said or did was met with disapproval. It was best for him to remain quiet and let her talk whenever she felt like it.

Once they arrived at the club, Jax opened her door and waited for her to get out. He reached for her hand and Royce looked at him like he was crazy.

"Things are getting too far out of hand and we need to get control of it. We can't go on like this and run the risk of people seeing us at odds with each other. Our parents would have a fit if we embarrassed them. We have to have a serious talk when we get home tonight Royce," Jax said, right before they entered the building.

"Fuck you. Go talk to one of your hoes. I'm going to the bar," Royce said as she sashayed away to where a makeshift bar had been set up.

Jax saw his parents and hers at a table in the middle of the floor, but he couldn't walk over to them without his wife on his arm. His sister, Ashely, and her husband, Broderick, were there as well and he needed Royce to act like she had some common sense.

"When did you start drinking like this?" Jax asked, low enough for only his wife to hear.

"Around the same time that you started fucking your ex-wife again," Royce replied as she ordered her favorite apple drink with Sprite.

"Royce, baby, please don't do this. Let's just get through the night and I promise you that we'll talk about this when we get home. I'll do whatever you want me to do. Counseling, whatever you want," Jax swore.

"Jax, please. You're a sex addict, remember? No counselor in the world can make you stop slanging dick all over New Orleans boo," Royce chuckled sarcastically.

"What the fuck is wrong with you, Royce? This is not even you right now," Jax fumed as he walked up on her.

It looked as if he was about to kiss her to anyone else, but Royce's eyes dared him to even try.

"I wish you would try to put your nasty ass lips on me," Royce warned.

"Can we just please act civilized in the presence of our parents? You can curse me out all you want to once we get home," Jax replied.

"That's fine with me. I'm a pro at pretending to be happy." Royce shrugged.

Jax was happy that she didn't protest when he grabbed her hand. He plastered a smile on his face, as they walked over and greeted everyone.

"Royce, you look lovely as always," Silas, Jax's father, said as he stood to greet her with a kiss.

He looked at his son with a scowl before returning his attention back to his daughter-in-law. Jax knew that his mother had probably told him what happened, and it was only a matter of time before Silas requested his presence at their family home.

"Thank you." Royce smiled, as Jaxon pulled out her chair for her to sit down.

"I love that dress," Ashley said, as she too smiled at her favorite sister-in-law.

"Thanks, and I love yours as well," Royce replied robotically.

Jax visibly relaxed when he saw that the old Royce was back and in attendance, the one who played the game and always knew exactly what to say.

"What is that you're drinking?" Sondra asked as soon as she saw the glass in Royce's hand.

"Ladies don't drink in public Royce. You do remember that, right?" Silas asked as he sipped from his own glass filled with brown liquid.

Royce wanted to tell him to kiss her ass, but she only smiled and continued to sip. Silas was a trip. He would drink until the bottle was empty, but he always had something to say about somebody else. His views on women's etiquette were old fashioned and ridiculous. Silas was still stuck back in the day before women could vote and make their own money. He had Royce fucked up though. She was not Elena and he needed to know that.

"Let her be honey. It's probably just some champagne," Elena chuckled as she defended Royce.

She winced in pain when her husband grabbed and squeezed her leg underneath the table. She was only trying to come to Royce's defense, but she had angered Silas in the process. He gave her a look that let her know that he was not pleased with her comment and Elena regretted saying anything.

"I'm sure she's not drinking the hard stuff." Broderick smiled, along with his wife.

"Anything is hard to someone who doesn't drink at all." Sondra frowned, prompting her husband to lightly stroke her hand.

She got the hint and decided to leave her daughter alone. Royce had been acting crazy lately and she didn't want to start an argument and be embarrassed. She was happy to see that Royce and her husband were in a good place. They held hands and whispered in each other's ear throughout the night. No one would have ever known that Royce was actually cursing him out for touching her. Sondra wanted to scream when Royce made a few more trips to the bar, but she was satisfied knowing that Jax was with her each time.

Hours had gone by and the event was better than they expected it to be. They were in for a terrific Mardi Gras season, but she wasn't looking forward to it. Sondra hated the overcrowded holiday and she always did. She only wanted her husband to become a member of the club because it scored her a few extra points with Elena. She could do without all the extra, but it had to be done.

"I'll be right back," Royce said as she got up and headed to the bar once again.

She almost fell and Jax had to help her stand. Sondra was trying to keep her cool, but she had lost count of how many drinks her daughter had consumed. When she saw the look that Elena and her husband gave each other, she was mortified. Sondra excused herself from the table and decided to put an end to her daughter's irrational behavior. Jax didn't accompany her that time and her mother was happy that they were alone.

"What the hell is wrong with you, Royce?" Sondra sneered as she stood in the beverage line behind her daughter.

"What the hell is wrong with you, mother?" Royce mocked, as her words slightly slurred.

"Oh, my God. Are you drunk?" Sondra asked her.

"Two or three more apple crowns and I will be," Royce snickered.

"You're drinking Crown Royal?" Sondra questioned in shock.

"That's the only way that I was able to get through this bullshit ass night with y'all," Royce laughed.

"You need to sit down and drink some water," Sondra said as she grabbed her arm.

"I'll sit down, but only with my apple crown. Oh shit, that rhymes, don't it? I can be a teacher and a rapper too," Royce slurred as she snickered at her own joke.

"Royce, sweetheart, please, just sit down for a minute and let me get you some ice water," Sondra begged as she motioned for Jax to come over.

"Are you embarrassed mother? Huh? Are you ashamed of your perfect little daughter?" Royce asked as she ordered two more drinks.

"Don't you dare drink another one," Sondra ordered sternly.

"I'm not gonna drink another one. I'm gonna drink another two," Royce laughed as she gulped the contents in one of the glasses.

"What's wrong?" Jax asked when he rushed over.

"Your wife is drunk is what's wrong. Did you know that she was drinking Crown Royal?" Sondra questioned.

"Shit," Jax hissed as he wrapped his arm around his wife's waist.

He looked around to make sure no one was looking as he sat her down at an empty table nearby. Sondra saw Elena headed their way and she wanted to sink into the hardwood floors.

"You wanna play cards Jax? I got a bunch of singles in my purse," Royce said.

"No baby. You don't even know how to play cards," Jax replied as he wiped her face with the paper towel that he had just picked up.

"Nigga what! I'm a beast at cards now. I bet I'll take everybody's money in here," Royce said, talking loudly.

"Oh God. Is she drunk? Your father is going to die," Elena said as soon as she got closer to them.

"I need to get her out of here without making a scene," Jax noted.

"Let me distract your father so you can go," Elena said as she walked away.

[86]

She was happy when one of the club's presidents stopped her because he was the perfect decoy. He started talking to her about some fundraising ideas that they could do at her school, as she walked him over to her husband. Silas wasted no time joining in on the conversation, as Jax and Sondra tried to get Royce out of the building. Silas kept his poker face on, but he'd seen the entire scenario unfold from the corner of his eye. Elena was scared to death when he looked up at the door and saw his son almost dragging his drunk wife outside. He looked at her and scowled before turning his attention back to his conversation.

"Go get the car and I'll stay here with her," Sondra said to Jax.

There was a chair out front that he sat Royce in before he ran up the street to get his car. Sondra tried to make her drink some water, but Royce kept slapping her hand away. Thanks to her daughter, she was ready for her husband to terminate his membership at the club and put in her resignation letter at the school. She was beyond embarrassed and she would never be able to live it down.

"Come on baby," Jax said when he got back and helped Royce stand to her feet.

He had his car double parked with the engine running and both doors open. Royce stood to her feet, but her legs felt like noodles. She almost hit the ground, but Jax caught her before she went down.

"What has been going on with her lately? Does she drink like this at home? This is so unlike Royce," Sondra said.

"I saw her drink once, but she snapped on me when I asked her about it. I don't know what's been up with her lately," Jax replied.

"I'm gonna throw up," Royce said as she tried to pull away from her husband.

"Shit," Jax hissed as he held her up and watched her paint the concrete with all the food and liquor that she had consumed that day.

"Oh, my God. I'm so ashamed right now," Sondra said as she looked around to see if they were being watched.

She was thankful that they were out there alone, but she dreaded having to go back inside. She was prepared to tell everyone that Royce wasn't feeling well, but she was sure that they already knew the truth.

"Here baby, drink some water," Jax said as he helped Royce drink the water that her mother had in her hand.

Royce gulped down half the bottle before he walked her to the car and strapped her inside.

"You tell her that I am very pissed off and we are definitely going to have a talk about her behavior tonight," Sondra said as she hugged Jax.

"I will," Jax replied, right before he got into the car and pulled off.

"I'm so hot," Royce said as she moved around in her seat.

"I have the air on high baby. That's just the alcohol making you feel like that. Drink some more water," Jax suggested.

"Fuck me, baby. I'm tired of us just kissing," Royce said as she lifted her dress up around her waist.

Jax didn't know what she meant by that because they hadn't kissed in a while. His eyes bugged slightly as he watched his wife trying to wiggle out of her thong. He didn't know she meant that kind of hot, but he wasn't complaining. Royce always said that he was a dirty nigga and she refused to have sex with him anymore. He didn't care that she was drunk. He was ready to break her sexy ass in two and take full advantage.

"Royce, baby, calm down. I can't do nothing while I'm driving. Let me get us home first," Jax said when Royce reached over and started feeling him up.

She was trying to climb over to his side, but he used his arm to stop her. She was not herself, but Jax didn't care. He would take her any way that he could get her. There was no telling if or when he would have another chance. As soon as they pulled up to the house, Jax picked Royce up and carried her inside. She was kissing him all over his face and neck, making him hard as a brick.

"Don't hold back baby. I want you to do everything that you said you were gonna do to me," Royce panted as she ripped his shirt open, popping all the buttons.

"What?" Jax asked as he looked at her strangely.

Royce was saying some off the wall shit, making him wonder if she thought that he was someone else. His insecurities quickly went away when she pulled her dress off and laid back on the sofa. Jax was frozen in place as he watched Royce slip a finger inside of her wet box and move it around seductively. She had liquid courage, and he wanted her to get drunk more often.

"Come on baby. Come taste it," Royce begged as she closed her eyes and moaned.

"Damn," Jax mumbled as he licked his lips with anticipation.

She only had to say it once before he rushed over and buried his entire face in between her legs.

"Yes baby, just like that," Royce coached as she arched her back and rotated her hips.

She was humping his face like a dog in heat and that only turned him on more. Her moans of pleasure were like motivation for Jax. He licked Royce's freshly waxed bottom lips and all around her clit. He opened her legs wider for better access, as he sucked and slurped her middle like she was his favorite dessert.

"Shit baby, you taste so damn good," Jax mumbled as he continued to give Royce oral pleasure like she'd never had before.

When he felt her body tense up, he started moving his tongue faster until she erupted like a volcano. Jax didn't even wait for her to recover. He pulled off his pants and boxers and hurriedly plunged into her tight wetness.

"Ugh," Royce moaned as she wrapped her legs around her husband's waist.

Jax was in heaven as he closed his eyes and enjoyed his wife. He started out slow, but Royce was begging him to fuck her harder. After a while, he had Royce in every position imaginable as they made their way through the entire house. They hadn't had sex in a while and Jax was enjoying every minute of it. They hadn't gone at it that long since they were newlyweds, but he had no complaints. For the first time in a while, Jax and Royce went to sleep wrapped up in each other's arms. He was content until he got up the next morning to a text from his father demanding that he come to see him.

Chapter 10

It was after one that afternoon when the ringing of Royce's phone woke her up. Her head was pounding, and her entire body was aching. She was butt ass naked in bed alone and she didn't know where Jax was.

"Yes," Royce mumbled groggily when she answered the phone.

"Where is Royce?" Uri asked with attitude dripping from her tone.

"This is me, Uri," Royce replied.

"Bitch, you sounded just like Jax. What the hell is wrong with you?" Uri questioned.

"I feel like I'm dying," Royce answered.

"What's wrong Royce? You have a cold or something?" Uri asked.

"A hangover is more like it," Royce revealed.

"What!" Uri yelled. "Are you serious?"

"My mama is probably pacing the floor smoking a pack of cigarettes by now," Royce chuckled as she slowly sat up in her bed.

"Auntie Sondra doesn't even smoke, so it must be really bad. What happened?" Uri asked.

She listened intently as her cousin told her everything that had taken place the night before. Uri thought it was hilarious that her cousin not only got drunk in front of her parents, but she did it in front of her in-laws too. Royce was groomed to always be perfect, so it was good that she let her hair down and had fun for once in her life. She was too young to be so serious all the time.

"Bitch, I'm so weak. I know your mama wanted to die," Uri said as she doubled over with laughter.

"I don't give a damn, but that's not the worst part," Royce replied.

"Oh Lord. What else happened?" Uri inquired.

"I had sex with Jax last night," Royce confessed.

"Um, that is your husband Royce. He got community dick, but you still got papers on it," Uri laughed.

"I know, but I didn't want to sleep with him. I feel like I cheated on Caleb, but I swear that's who was on my mind the entire time. I hope his ass enjoyed it because I'm never doing it again. And I'm done with the drinking too. I can't be feeling like this," Royce said as she held her pounding head.

"Well, I think you went too far with the drinking, being that you're still a beginner, but I'm happy that you stepped outside of your comfort zone. There's nothing wrong with sipping every now and then, but you need to take it slow. And as far as you and Caleb, that's a conversation that I'm gonna stay away from," Uri replied.

"Why Uri? I need some advice. I think I'm falling in love with another man and I'm still married," Royce whined.

"I don't think you want my advice so don't ask," Uri cautioned.

"If I didn't want it, I wouldn't have asked," Royce snapped.

"Royce, listen, you already know what's up with me. I'm the wrong bitch for a nigga to play with because catch back is my middle name. As much as I want to tell you to play the same game that Jaxon is playing, it's not my place to say. I just want you to finally be happy for once in your life. If that means leaving Jax and moving on, then so be it," Uri replied.

"Thanks for nothing Uri," Royce said sarcastically.

"That's your whole problem now. You always want people to tell you what to do. You need to do what you want to do and fuck whoever got a problem with it," Uri fussed.

"I guess that's why I got a hangover now. From doing what I wanted to do," Royce laughed.

"Yeah, but I bet it felt good doing it and not worrying about what nobody had to say. That should be how it is every day," Uri said.

"Yeah, it did feel good, even though I'll probably be hearing my mama's mouth soon," Royce noted.

"You're a grown ass woman Royce. Who cares what your mama has to say. Auntie Sondra needs to stop all that stupid shit," Uri argued.

"I'm at the point where I don't even care anymore. It is what it is." Royce shrugged.

"You should have been at that point. But, anyway, what do you have planned for today? My hubby and kids are going to his nephew's party, so I'm free all day," Uri said.

"I need to find a gift for Shanti's baby shower week after next. You're still coming with me, right?" Royce questioned.

"I forgot all about that but, yeah, I'm still coming. I guess I need to roll with you and find me a gift too," Uri replied.

"Okay, let me get up and get myself together. I need to take something for this headache," Royce said as she threw her legs on the side of the bed.

She felt a little dizzy, so she wanted to sit there for a while and not move too fast. She needed to put something on her stomach because taking medicine while it was empty would only make things worse.

"I guess I can drive, since you're hungover and stuff," Uri snickered.

"That's why I love you. And lunch is on me. I'm about to hop in the shower, so you can be on your way," Royce replied, right before they disconnected.

She looked down at her phone and read the text messages from her mother and frowned. Sondra was telling her how disappointed she was in her, as if Royce gave a damn. She was tired of trying to please everybody and she vowed that she was going to stop. She couldn't even be herself around the people who were supposed to love her, and that was miserable. That was exactly why she loved being around Caleb and his family because they were down to earth and didn't judge. She had two missed calls from him too, but she decided to get ready before she called him back. There was also a text from Jax telling her how happy he was that they were working on their marriage, but he was sadly mistaken. Whatever Royce said or did was because of the liquor and nothing had changed. He said that he was on his way to his parents' house and he wanted to spend some time with her when he got back. Royce jumped up and rummaged through her closet to find something to wear. Her head was still spinning, but she wanted to be long gone before Jaxon retuned. She was sure that his parents were upset about her behavior the night before, but she didn't care. They could kiss her ass, right along with her mother and their son.

***

Jax sat in front of his parents' house trying to buy himself some time. He knew that he was about to get an ear full and he wasn't prepared to hear it. He was a grown ass man, but his father didn't care about that. When he talked, he expected his kids and his wife to listen and obey. Silas was once a teacher and principal and he ran his house like he used to run the school. It was hell growing up under his roof, but there was nothing that Jax or his siblings could have done about it. He made the rules and they had to follow them, no matter how old they were. The thought of being cut out of the family's inheritance always kept them in line, if nothing else. That and the fact that his father held his job in the palm of his hands was enough to make Jax do right.

After stalling long enough, Jax got out of the car and walked into the two-story ranch style home that he grew up in. His mother was the first person that he saw when he walked into the kitchen.

"Hey," Jax spoke when they locked eyes.

"Hey? Are you a horse Jaxon?" Elena asked him.

"No, I mean hello," he said as he corrected himself.

"That's better," Elena said as she gave him her cheek to kiss.

To everyone else, Elena Davenport was a role model, someone that they admired and could look up to. To Jax and his siblings, she was nothing more than a weak woman who put on airs for the people around her. She hid her pain very well behind a million-dollar smile and a bunch of expensive cosmetics. He never understood how his mother prided herself on empowering other women and she needed someone to empower her.

"I guess I don't have to ask what I'm here for," Jax said as he looked over at her.

"Yeah, well, I don't have to tell you that your father is pissed. What the hell was Royce thinking? He already

[94]

frowns down on women drinking in public. She went to the extreme when she got drunk," Elena replied while shaking her head.

"What about that other thing? Does he know about that too?" Jax asked, speaking of her walking in on him and Angelique.

"I had to tell him, Jaxon. You know what would have happened if he would have found out on his own," Elena replied, with a fear in her eyes that was all too familiar.

"I'll go see him in a minute, but how have you been ma? Are you okay?" Jax asked out of concern.

"Of course, baby, I couldn't be better," Elena answered, flashing her award-winning smile.

"Come on ma, this is me that you're talking to. You don't have to pretend or put on a show. Are you really okay? How are your knees? Are they still bothering you?" Jax asked her.

"I'm fine honey. It's nothing that a few aspirin won't help. Don't worry about me. Go talk to your father. I'm making club sandwiches. I'll bring you one in a minute," Elena replied.

Jax shook his head in pity and made his way down the hall to his father's favorite part of the house. The sitting area was huge, and Silas loved to relax in there. He had a huge seventy-inch television mounted on the wall and he dared anyone to touch it. He had a specially made chair with a table connected to it, and no one dared to sit there either. He had rules, and everyone knew to follow them or face his wrath.

Jax knocked on the door and waited until he was granted entry a few seconds later. He spoke to his father, but Silas never took his eyes off the tv screen. Jax knew that he saw him standing there, but he never acknowledged him. That was just his normal controlling way. No one made a move until he said so. Silas waited until he was good and ready before he gave his son some attention and acknowledged his presence.

"Sit down," he demanded in his deep, domineering voice.

Jax did as he was told, feeling more like a little boy instead of the grown man that he was. He hated when Silas took his time and prolonged a situation. He always had to let everyone know that he was in charge and he wouldn't be rushed. Jax was ready to tell him to hurry the fuck up, but his mother opened the door and walked in before he could make such a stupid move. Jax watched as Elena set up her husband's food and drink on the table that was connected to his chair exactly how he liked it. Silas nodded his head in approval, and Elena scurried away like the obedient wife that she was trained to be. She came back in a few minutes later and sat a plate and a glass of lemonade in front of Jax.

"Bring that back to the kitchen. You know I don't allow them to eat in here," Silas bellowed.

"You made that rule when they were kids, honey. He's thirty years old now. I'm sure he won't waste anything," Elena softly replied.

Jax saw the veins pop out of his father's forehead, as he contorted his face into an angry scowl.

"Did I ask you to tell me his age?" Silas barked.

"No," Elena mumbled meekly.

"What did I tell you to do?" Silas questioned angrily.

"I'm sorry," Elena apologized as she grabbed the plate and glass from the table.

"Put it down and answer my question. What did I tell you to do with the food?" Silas asked as he stood up from his chair and walked over to his wife.

"You told me to bring it back to the kitchen," Elena said as she sat the dishes back on the table.

"Do you have a problem following directions Elena?" Silas questioned.

"No," Elena mumbled, her voice quivering with fear.

"I think you do. I think you've been forgetting your place lately. You talk out of turn and you seem to have forgotten who the head of this household is," Silas accused.

"No, I haven't forgotten who's the head. I'm sorry," Elena apologized again.

"Are you a child, Elena?" Silas asked, as Jaxon dropped his head in anger and hurt. He knew what was coming next and he hated that he was there to witness it.

"No, I'm not a child," Elena spoke up.

"Then, why are you behaving like one?" Silas asked.

"I'm not," Elena denied as warm tears cascaded down her cheeks.

"Behave like a child and get treated like one," Silas said, making Jax cringe with hate at his favorite mantra.

"Dad-" Jax said before his mother stopped him.

[96]

"No Jaxon, it's okay," Elena cried softly.

He wanted to snap when his father grabbed his mother by her shoulders and shoved her into the corner.

"On your knees," Silas ordered his wife as if she were one of her students.

"This is some bullshit!" Jax yelled as he jumped up from his chair.

"Sit your ass down boy! How can you run to someone else's rescue when you don't even have your own house in order? Maybe you should have disciplined your own wife and she wouldn't be behaving like a drunken whore," Silas bellowed.

"Stop it Jaxon. I'm fine," Elena said while pleading with her eyes.

Jax knew how powerful his father was. Silas had pull all over New Orleans and other areas of Louisiana. Silas' father was a former politician and some of his brothers still were into politics. The clout that he held at the school board administration office was the reason why Elena and Jax had their positions and their pay at the school. He was a strict disciplinarian, just like his father and grandfather. He ruled his house with an iron fist and they all knew that. Jaxon didn't care about the harsh punishments that he and his siblings received. He just hated that his mother got the same treatment. Jax remembered being made to kneel in the corner for hours at a time. Sadly, his mother would be right there next to him sometimes. Elena was too weak to speak up for herself and she never spoke up for them either. Jax hated his father, but he'd never expressed that to anyone but Royce. He often vented to his wife about his less than perfect childhood because he couldn't talk to anyone else. Royce was shocked to know what Elena was enduring at home because she seemed so well put together on the job and in person. She seemed confident and happy, but that was obviously a front. Elena was always complaining about her knees aching and Royce now knew why.

"Let me tell you something boy," Silas said, breaking Jax away from his thoughts, "I don't know what the hell you have going on under your roof, but you better get that shit in order."

"My house is in order," Jax replied.

"Bullshit!" Silas roared. "Your wife was an embarrassment to the Davenport name last night and you aren't any better. I don't even know why I'm surprised by anything that you do."

"What is that supposed to mean?" Jaxon asked.

"First, you went and knocked up that gutter rat Sienna, not once but twice. That was after we paid thousands of dollars to make the rape allegations against you go away. We finally managed to get you out of all that mess, only for your mother to catch you in the bathroom with a damn cafeteria worker. On the fucking school grounds while classes were in session and your wife was in the building. You just keep scraping the bottom of the barrel," Silas barked angrily.

"I already apologized for that," Jax replied.

"Fuck your apologies Jaxon! Before I let you disgrace my family's name, I'll have your ass fired and disown you. Your brothers never gave us any problems and neither did their wives," Silas noted.

Jax wasn't surprised by that because his brothers were just like their father. They treated their wives like one of their children. They probably did them the same way that their father did their mother. He should know because he was the same way when he first got married. Sienna was easy to train because she wanted to be with him so badly. He punished her the same as he'd seen his father do his own mother so many times before. Physical and verbal abuse was common in their home and that was all that Jaxon knew. Royce wasn't having it though and Jax never even tried. He got in her face and yelled at her one time and she made it clear that it better be his last. His sister, Ashley, had her husband wrapped around her finger too, and Silas wouldn't have it any other way. Especially since Broderick's father was a well-known judge who he often played golf with.

"Is there anything else?" Jaxon asked.

"Get your house in order Jaxon. I don't care how you do it, I just want it done. If your wife can't act like a lady in public, then you need to leave her ass at home," Silas ordered.

"Yes sir," Jax replied.

"And make that your last time getting your dick wet in my wife's school. That's your first and last warning. Now, I suggest you go home and have a talk with Royce about what's expected of her. She's a Davenport and she will behave like one at all times," Silas noted.

"Yes sir," Jax repeated.

"You're dismissed," Silas said as he waved him away like he was a peasant. He picked up his plate of food and started eating, letting him know that the conversation was over.

Jax got up and walked to the door, stealing one last glance at his mother, who was still kneeling in the corner of the room. Elena looked so pitiful as she faced the wall and cried silent tears. She had long ago bypassed the stage of embarrassment because her children had seen it all. Being in her early sixties, her body didn't take too kindly to the punishments as it had years before. Her knees ached daily, and she had become a pro at hiding bruises. She knew that her other daughters-in-law were probably just as good. That was why she admired Royce so much. She was stronger than the others and she would never allow Jaxon to treat her that way. Her other sons' wives reminded her too much of herself. They were weak and never spoke up for themselves. Just like Elena, they paid the ultimate price to live the good life. They too smiled in public and reserved their tears for behind closed doors.

Chapter 11

"**N**ow I see why they kept telling me that they needed more money," Brian said as he looked around Shanti's baby shower.

He was happy that everything had come to an end and all the gifts were opened. As usual, Brooklyn and his mother did too much, but Shanti was happy with the outcome. Brian stayed inside with her thanking their guests, while two of his brothers and hers saw to it that all the gifts got to her house. Shanti had a huge bag filled with greeting cards that she decided to open later.

"Everything was so nice. I didn't know that they were gonna do so much." Shanti smiled.

"I could have told you that. When my mama and Brook do something, it's always over the top," Brian replied.

"I have to call and thank them later," Shanti said, making a mental note.

"You can thank me later too," Brian said with a sexy smirk.

"You know I don't need a special occasion for that." Shanti smiled as they walked up to the table where Caleb, Royce, and her cousin were sitting.

Shanti had met Royce's cousin once, but she had been seeing a lot of Royce lately. Just about every time Caleb came to Brian's house, Royce was right there with him. She and Shanti talked all the time and they had really taken a liking to each other. Apparently, the same could be said for Royce and Caleb.

"What's up thugettes?" Brian joked with Royce and Uri.

It was still funny to him how Caleb and Royce hooked up and even funnier about how they met. Caleb seemed to really like her and that was proven by how much time he spent with her. Their mates had cheated on them with each other and it seemed as if they were doing the exact same thing.

"Thanks for coming y'all. And thanks for the gifts," Shanti said as she hugged both women.

"You're welcome boo. Only because I like you. Your man was about to catch these hands a few months ago though," Uri laughed as she and Royce got up to hug her.

"Don't do me like that. I though we squashed all that beef," Brian said as he held his hand out for her to shake.

"Yeah, we did. I'm just messing with you," Uri said as she shook his hand.

When they heard someone talking loudly right by the exit, they all looked up towards the door to see Jaden going off about something.

"Aww shit. Let me go see what's wrong with this nigga," Brian said as he walked off with Caleb following behind him.

When they got closer, they saw Jaylynn standing there with a boy, while Kia tried her best to calm Jaden down. She pushed him away from the door to make sure that no one heard what they were saying. The boy looked scared out of his mind, as Jaden went off on him and his daughter.

"Your sneaky ass disappeared for over an hour, so don't try to play with me, Jaylynn. You claimed you were going to your car and never came back. Then, I come outside and see you standing by the car talking to this lil nigga," Jaden fumed angrily.

"I did go to my car," Jaylynn said as she looked on in embarrassment.

Her father did entirely too much, and she couldn't believe that he was causing a scene while Hayden was standing right there. Sweets was at the baby shower too, so she didn't think it was a big deal when she called his nephew to come over. Everyone was so pre-occupied with watching Shanti open her gifts that they never paid her any attention. Jaden saw when she got up from the table, but she told him that she was getting something from her car. It was well over an hour later when he realized that she had never came back. He was furious when he stepped outside and saw her standing near her car talking to the same lil nigga that he ordered her to stay away from. He knew Hayden's father, Harold, very well because they were in the game together at one time. He and Harold were always cool, but he wasn't okay with his son trying to be with his daughter.

"You're doing too much Jaden. This is not the time or the place for this," Kia whispered to her husband as she pulled him away.

"Fuck that Kia. I don't like that lil nigga," Jaden fumed low enough for only her to hear.

"You don't even know him Jaden. You're doing her the same way that Mo did me. I had to lie and sneak around to be with you and you see how that turned out. I was a teenage mother because Mo was so strict on me," Kia reminded him.

"So, what are you saying Kia? You expect me to be okay with this lil nigga pushing up on my baby and shit?" Jaden asked.

"Look at her, Jaden. She's not a baby anymore. She's not the same little girl who used to follow you around and cry when you left home. Be thankful that she's not giving us any real trouble at her age. She's a young lady and you better start treating her like one," Kia argued.

"I don't give a damn what you say; I'm not feeling her having a boyfriend right now," Jaden maintained.

"She's sixteen Jaden. How old does she have to be to start dating?" Kia questioned.

"Twenty-one," he answered seriously.

"What! You can't be serious," Kia replied.

"I'm dead ass. Fuck them lil niggas," Jaden spat.

"I'm not doing this with you right now. We really need to have a serious talk about this later," Kia said as she started to walk off back to where everyone else stood.

"Talk all you want, but I ain't listening to shit," Jaden mumbled as he followed behind her.

"What is my nephew doing out here?" Sweets asked when he and Co-Co walked outside.

"He's about to get his lil ass whipped out here trying to sweet talk my baby," Jaden threatened.

"Don't get distracted by the lace front and heels boo. I'm still a man underneath all this makeup," Sweets replied.

"And that's exactly why I won't feel bad if I have to knock you the fuck out," Jaden noted.

"Don't be threatening my friend, Jaden. He must be saying something that she wants to hear. She's smiling like she's auditioning for a toothpaste commercial. Y'all better put her hot ass on some birth control pills," Co-Co replied while looking over at Jaylynn.

"What!" Jaden yelled angrily.

"Co-Co, shut the hell up. Stop making shit worse," Kia fussed.

"I'm just saying. It's better to be safe than sorry." Co-Co shrugged.

"Fuck that lil nigga," Caleb said, waving him off.

"What are y'all getting mad with him for? Jaylynn is a pretty girl. If it wasn't Hayden, it would be somebody else," Sweets noted.

"The next nigga can get it too," Brian chimed in, as Jaden nodded in agreement.

"Y'all kill me with that shit. Y'all walk around here fucking everything that move but want to put a chokehold on a nigga that your niece is talking to. Jaden gon' get all that shit back that he put Mo through when Kia was younger. He used to have her sneaking around to be with him, but he gets amnesia whenever somebody bring it up. We never like it when the shoe is on the other foot, but you reap what you sow," Co-Co fussed.

"Amen," Sweets agreed.

"Fuck what you got to say Co-Co. You better get queen sugar and get the fuck on. I'm not in the mood for your bullshit. I already feel like snapping on a muthafucker," Jaden replied angrily.

"No, this nigga didn't," Sweets gasped dramatically.

"Jay, finish talking to your friend and we'll see you at home," Kia said, making Jaden frown while their daughter smiled.

"Okay," Jaylynn replied.

She appreciated her mother's understanding attitude because she often had to come to her rescue. Jaden was stubborn, and Kia often had to play referee with the two of them. Still, even though he made her mad sometimes, Jaylynn would forever be a daddy's girl.

"Let's go Jaden," Kia ordered her husband.

Their son was with Mo and she was ready to get him and go home. Jaden was standing there staring at his daughter until Kia grabbed his arm and pulled him away.

"What happened?" Shanti asked when she walked outside with Royce and Uri.

"Nothing happened. Are you ready?" Brain asked her.

"Yeah, but you can bring me home," Shanti replied.

"Why?" Brian asked with a frown.

"What do you mean why? I have to unpack all that stuff and put it in place. Knowing my brothers, I'm sure they just threw everything in there and left," Shanti replied.

"We can take care of that later Shanti. How much do you really think you can accomplish at eight months pregnant?" Brian asked.

"I'm not an invalid, Brian. Pregnancy is not a handicap. I can get around just fine," Shanti argued.

"Let's go. You can worry about that later. You need to open your envelopes and see what's in them first," he replied as he grabbed her hand.

"Are you ready?" Uri asked while looking at her cousin.

"Yeah, I'm ready. I guess we'll talk later," Royce said while looking at Caleb.

"I'm not ready for you to leave yet," he whispered so that only she could hear.

"I have to. Uri is my ride. My car is parked at her house," Royce replied.

"I can bring you to get it later. Do you have to be home at a certain time?" he asked.

"Really Caleb?" Royce asked, looking at him like he was stupid.

"I was just asking," he chuckled.

"Let me walk Uri to her car and I'll be right back," she said as she walked off behind her cousin.

"Let me find out that your soft ass is falling in love," Brian joked.

"I'm trying to get like you. Only difference is I won't deny it when it happens," Caleb said, making his brother frown and walk away.

He stood outside of his car and waited until Royce was done talking to her cousin. He really didn't have anywhere specific to take her, but he wasn't ready to let her go just yet. He and Royce usually parked near the levee and sat in his car and talked. Occasionally, they would walk around and watch the boats as they coasted up and down the river. They used that alone time to talk and get to know each other better. He and Royce were like night and day, but their opposites attracted them to each other. Caleb loved that she had a career and didn't solely depend on her husband to take care of her. Sienna was always looking for a handout and that was what had started to turn Caleb off the most. He couldn't believe that she and Royce had been married to the same man. They were nothing alike and that was a plus in Caleb's eyes.

***

"You need to start her a bank account with all this money Shanti. It's never too early," Brian said as he sat there watching her open all the envelopes that she got from the baby shower.

Shanti had already opened more than fifty cards with cash and gift cards inside and she had even more to get through. A few people mailed theirs in and some of their customers dropped some off to the shop. Shanti was loved and that was proven by the number of gifts she had for the baby. She didn't even know some of the people who they were from, but she appreciated their generosity. Brian's mother had invited some of her friends from work and she was sure that some of the gifts came from them.

"Yeah, that's what I'm gonna do," Shanti replied as she read over another card.

"Who is Marvin?" Brian asked when he picked up one of the cards and read yet another man's name. He'd lost count of all the men who had stuffed cash in a card for Shanti and her unborn.

"He's a friend of my brother," Shanti replied, just like she'd done the other times that he asked.

"Hold up! Kerry sent a gift too? You invited that nigga to the baby shower?" Brian asked angrily, referring to her ex-boyfriend.

"No, he must have dropped it off. I didn't see him there," Shanti replied.

"How did he even know where it was?" Brian continued to question.

"The shit was advertised all over social media Brian. Everybody and their mama knew when and where it was going to be. You need to calm the fuck down with all that yelling!" Shanti snapped.

"You can throw that shit away. My baby don't need nothing from no other nigga. That's what I'm here for," Brian fumed.

"Oh, so she's yours again this week?" Shanti replied sarcastically as she read the card from Kerry and smiled.

"The fuck is you smiling for?" Brian fumed as he snatched the card from her and read it.

Shanti grabbed the three hundred-dollar bills that were in the card before they could hit the floor. She quickly stuffed them into her purse where the rest of the money was before Brian did something stupid. She didn't care what he did with the card, but he wasn't about to play with the money.

"You need to grow up," Shanti said when Brian ripped the card up and threw the pieces on the floor.

"Fuck that nigga," he spat as he grabbed some more cards for her to open.

Shanti shook her head and laughed, as Brian continued to fuss under his breath. They fell into a comfortable silence again while reading over the cards. Shanti was almost done when she pulled out an envelope that was so thick, it had to be taped.

"What the hell is in this thing? I hope it's money," she laughed as she used the scissors to pry it open.

Brian was just as curious as she was. When the envelope was finally opened, he began to pull the contents out, right along with her. His face twisted in anger when he got a look at the papers and pictures inside.

"This bitch," Brian hissed angrily.

"But you wanna complain about one of my male friends sending me a gift," Shanti said as she tossed everything at him and stood to her feet.

Brian was heated as he looked over the ultrasound pictures and paperwork showing positive pregnancy results from over a year ago. Mya was a dumb bitch and Brian was getting sick of her. She just couldn't get over the fact that Shanti was having a baby and she aborted hers. Brian didn't put a gun to her head. He told her that he wasn't ready for kids and he suggested abortion. Mya was claiming that he made her do it, but she sounded stupid every time she said it.

"Where you going?" he asked when Shanti grabbed her purse from the table and walked away.

"To my house and away from your bullshit," Shanti snapped angrily.

"What! I didn't even do nothing," Brian maintained as he jumped up and blocked her path.

He was sorry that he took her home to get her car after the baby shower. He was content with her depending on him to drive her around.

"Yeah, so you say. I can't see this bitch doing all this if you weren't still entertaining her," Shanti replied.

"Don't even go there with me, Shanti. We both do our thing and we always have. It ain't like we're in a monogamous relationship or nothing," Brian countered.

"You're absolutely right. So, you shouldn't care if I go home or not. Move out of my way," Shanti ordered.

"Me wanting you here ain't about you, it's about my baby," Brian fussed.

"Nigga, please. I'm eight months pregnant with a baby that you barely claim. Miss me with the bullshit," Shanti said as she tried to go around him.

"You can't fault me for the dumb shit that Mya does. I can't control her actions."

"I never said that Brian, but you allow her to do the shit because you never put her in her place. You stop fucking with her for a little while and then be right back in her face. You made that hoe too comfortable, but you know I'm not the one. I can't wait until I have my baby. I got something for her nasty ass," Shanti fumed angrily.

"You don't even need to do all that. I'll tell her about it," Brian swore.

"Yeah right," Shanti hissed skeptically.

"I promise. I'll make sure I tell her about herself whenever I see her again. Just sit down and relax. Stop getting worked up over nothing," Brian advised.

He wasn't accustomed to begging, but Shanti always got him close to that point. He tried to play hard in the presence of others, but he was a different person when they were alone. Shanti was the only woman that he'd ever had feelings for, but he didn't know how to handle them. Love was a foreign emotion, but he couldn't deny what he felt for her. His boys were always clowning him, telling him that he was attracted to hoes and he didn't want that to be true with Shanti. He had to get over caring about what people said and learn to do what made him happy.

"I'm really getting sick of this Brian," Shanti argued.

"I know you are, but let me handle it. Our day was perfect up until now. Let's watch a movie and relax," Brian suggested once he had Shanti calm and relaxing on his plush leather sofa.

"I need to take a shower first," she said as she got up and walked off towards his bedroom.

"Am I invited?" Brian asked flirtatiously.

"Nope. Go take a bath with Shaky. Bitch water might be black as fuck, with her dirty ass," Shanti said, making him laugh.

"Man, fuck Shaky," Brian snapped as he started to strip out of his clothes.

"I'm not playing with you, Brian. I don't feel like being bothered with you right now," Shanti replied.

"Please," he pleaded as he kissed Shanti's ear.

Being pregnant always had her horny as hell. Brian could hardly look at her without her wanting to jump on him. Shanti didn't want to give in too easily, but she didn't have time to play hard to get. When Brian started to pull her dress over her head, she didn't even bother trying to stop him. She held on to his shoulders when he bent down to remove her underwear, right before following him into the master bathroom.

Chapter 12

"**D**amn nephew, you don't know how much I needed this shit," Shaq said as he watched the dancer drop down in front of him and work her way back up.

His eyes were fixated on her, as he threw a few dollars her way and watched as she stooped down to pick them up. He was happy as hell when Brian asked him if he wanted to join him and his boys, Ronnie and Trent, at the strip club. Shaq had been working nonstop for two weeks straight and he welcomed the idea. Since being released from jail two years prior, he was trying his best to stay out of trouble and do things right. Thanks to Jaden, he had a nice one-bedroom apartment and a decent vehicle to get around in.

"That nigga Caleb was supposed to come with me, but he flaked at the last minute," Brian replied.

"He must be with ole girl," Shaq said, referring to Royce.

"He is. Nigga pussy whipped and ain't even get the pussy yet," Brian joked.

"I don't blame him. It's not every day that you run across a good one. As soon as I find me somebody to settle down with, I won't be doing this shit too much either. You better enjoy it too nigga. Fatherhood ain't no joke," Shaq noted.

"Yeah man. I know I'll be stuck inside for a while once Shanti have the baby. I've been stacking my chips, so I can take some time off from the shop too," Brian said as he sipped his drink and watched the dancers do their thing.

Jaden had introduced him to the club a while back when he was messing with one of the dancers, and Brian had been a regular ever since. He met Mya during one of those visits and he took her to a hotel the same night. Brian slipped up a few times and had unprotected sex with her, which resulted in the unexpected pregnancy. He swore that he wasn't the father, but he really wasn't sure. Mya wasn't main chick material, but she was trying hard to be his one and only. Brian had to take some of the blame for that though. He always lied and told her what she wanted to hear, and she believed whatever he said.

"Yeah, it's almost that time," Shaq replied, pulling him away from his thoughts.

Shanti was now three weeks away from her due date, but she was still working every day, against Brian's wishes. Brian and his brothers situated everything in her house and all they were doing now was waiting for the baby's arrival. Shanti was adamant about going back to her house once the baby was born and nothing that Brian said was changing her mind. She let him take a few items to his house, but the bulk of the baby's things remained at hers.

"Nigga, you better make sure that baby is yours while you're making plans to be a family man and shit," Ronnie spoke up, making Brian look at him and frown.

It was no secret that Ronnie didn't care for Shanti too much. Mya's sister, Katrice, was his girlfriend of three years and he wanted Brian to be with the other woman. He was always throwing shade Shanti's way and Brian had to always shut his ass down

"The fuck you care for anyway? Worry about that big, bad built stripper hoe that you're in love with and less about Ashanti," Brian said, referring to Mya's sister who was a dancer at another club.

Ronnie was always complaining about her not making money stripping and Brian knew why. No nigga in their right mind would pay her to get naked, especially when most niggas didn't even want to see the shit for free. Katrice was about five feet tall and weighed at least two hundred fifty pounds or more.

"Every stripper ain't a hoe. And I know you ain't calling my girl big. Shanti ain't too small her damn self," Ronnie defended.

"But she fine as fuck, thick and all. Katrice big nasty ass don't need to be nowhere near a thong. Who the fuck is paying Big Bastard to strip for them anyway?" Brian said, making Trent laugh.

"All that because I'm asking if Shanti's baby is yours or not?" Ronnie questioned angrily.

"Mind your muthafucking business before I break your jaw. Bitch ass always worrying about the next nigga," Brian snapped angrily.

That was something else that he had to take the blame for. He had to stop saying shit when he was mad. People tended to throw shit back in your face and Ronnie was known to do that. Brian sometimes vented to his boys about Shanti, so he couldn't even get mad.

"That nigga act just like a hoe," Trent spoke up with a scowl.

Trent and Brian had gone to high school together and they met Ronnie a few years later through another mutual friend. Ronnie and Brian clicked immediately, but Trent never really liked him. Ronnie was a hater who seemed to take pleasure in other people's downfall. Trent tolerated him on the strength of Brian, but he wouldn't hesitate to knock him out if it ever got to that point.

"Don't get mad at me. That nigga was the one who said the baby wasn't his." Ronnie shrugged uncaringly.

"You need to make your circle just a little bit smaller," Shaq said so that only his nephew could hear him.

"Yeah, I'm starting to see that for myself," Brian said, right as Mya walked out of the back room.

He wasn't surprised when they locked eyes and she made her way over to them.

"Really Nikki?" Mya frowned as she looked at the other dancer who was over there entertaining them.

Everyone there knew of her and Brian's history. They also knew not to step to him when he came there because that was her job.

"Really what? They called for me to come over here. I'm sorry Shaky, but I got bills just like you," Nikki replied as she continued to dance.

"Okay, well, I'm here now. You can go work the other side of the room," Mya said dismissively.

"Nah, fuck that. You go work the other side of the room. You're good baby girl. Keep doing your thing," Brian said as he threw some money at Nikki's feet.

"Really Brian? That's how we're doing it now?" Mya questioned.

"Fuck you, Shaky. You lucky I don't knock your stupid ass out for that stunt you pulled," Brian hissed.

"What stunt?" she asked, feigning innocence.

"Play dumb if you want to," Brian replied.

"Fuck Shanti. I had to let that bitch know that she's not that special. She's not the first one to carry your baby," Mya smirked.

"Bitch, that baby probably wasn't even mine," Brian hissed, wiping the smile from her face.

"I hope you don't think Shanti's baby is yours. Just because I dance for a living doesn't make her better than me. That bitch got more bodies under her belt than I do," Mya spat.

Brian was just about to reply until he noticed Shanti's ex, Kerry, walk in with two other men. His jaw tightened in anger as the three men made their way over to their area.

"What's up Shaky? You trying to get some of this money or what?" Kerry asked as he flashed a knot of money in her face.

"Nope, I'm good right here. There you go Nikki. Go make that bill money that you were just talking about," Mya said, trying to get her to move away from Brian.

Nikki shook her head, but she got the hint and moved on to the other men who had just walked in.

"Get the fuck on Shaky. You can go over there right with her. Ain't nothing over here for you," Brian said, waving her off.

"Can we go somewhere and talk Brian? I'm sorry, but I was hurt and upset," Shaky whispered apologetically.

"We don't have shit to talk about," Brian hissed angrily.

"Oh, my bad, what's up fam? How's Shanti and our baby doing?" Kerry asked Brian with a smirk like he'd just noticed him sitting there.

"I see you got jokes, huh? We both know that you ain't even on the baby daddy list. That's one pussy that got my name written all over it," Brian laughed, making Kerry's blood boil.

"You sure about that?" Kerry asked, trying to plant the seed of doubt.

He knew without a doubt that Shanti's baby wasn't his, but Brian didn't. Kerry knew that he drove Brian crazy whenever he came around and he made it a point to do so every chance he got. Shanti was Kerry's first love and he was trying his best to get her back. He didn't care that she was pregnant with another man's baby. He would have gladly taken care of them both. Shaky was crazy in love with Brian and Kerry wanted them to be together. That was exactly why he didn't have a problem getting his sister, Kelsey, to drop Shaky's card off at Shanti's baby shower when she took his. Shaky was the one who told him when and where the shower was, but it was posted all over social media anyway. His sister and Shanti remained cool after their breakup. Shanti still did her nails and had been doing them for years.

"What's up Kerry?" Ronnie asked as he stood up and shook the other man's hand.

"Scary, punk ass nigga," Trent hissed.

No matter the time or place, Ronnie made it known that he and Kerry were cool. He didn't care that Brian didn't like him. That wasn't his beef. As for Trent, he had Brian's back no matter what. Kerry had never done anything to him, but he didn't like him on the strength of Brian alone.

"Tell her to call me if her and baby girl need anything else," Kerry said, not bothering to speak back to Ronnie.

"The fuck you still trying to talk to me for, bruh? You got all this pussy around you and you worried about the one that you can't have no more," Brian laughed.

"How do you know if I can't have it? Maybe I'm still getting it. I ain't coming around for nothing my nigga," Kerry chuckled.

"Do you, bruh. They got enough to go around." Brian shrugged, tired of the cat and mouse game.

Shit like that was why he was questioning if Shanti's baby was his or not. He wanted to be with her and make their relationship work, but she was too damn sneaky. She played the innocent role well and she was very convincing. His mind was saying fuck Shanti and all her games, but he needed his heart to cooperate and agree.

"What are y'all drinking?" Cookie asked when she came over to take their drink orders.

Her lust filled gaze was fixated on Kerry, but he just ignored her like always. He made the mistake of sleeping with Cookie one drunken night, but he made sure that it never happened again. She was annoying and not his type. Once she saw that Kerry wasn't giving her any attention, Cookie turned her attention towards Shaq. She winked at him, but he turned his head without a second thought. His entire family hated Cookie, so he wasn't even about to entertain her. Besides, she wasn't the type of female that he saw himself settling down with. He was done with the streets and the women in them.

"I'll be right back. Let's go," Brian said to Mya, right before downing the rest of his drink.

After smiling and winking at Cookie, Mya happily followed him out of the club and down the alley to the back of the building. Brian didn't have to tell her what he wanted because she already knew. He could never resist her for long and Kerry's rant helped to speed up the process. Once they were out back, Mya grabbed the buckle of Brian's belt and unhooked it before doing the same with his jeans. As soon as she freed his erection from his boxers, Mya dropped to her knees and started sucking him up. Brian used one hand to hold the back of her head while his other hand rested on the brick wall behind him.

"Shit," Brian hissed through short labored breaths.

His moans of pleasure were all the motivation that Mya needed to go harder. She took him further into her mouth, sucking him slow and hard, savoring her favorite flavor. Her womanhood moistened as his erection slid in and out of her warm mouth. His pleasure was all that concerned her and nothing else mattered.

"Get up," Brian ordered as he pulled her up by her hair.

He grabbed a condom from his pocket, tore it open, and slid it over his erection. Mya turned around and faced the wall, right before he gripped her waist and plunged deep inside of her.

"Ughh! Ughh!" she panted as he thrust in and out of her, making their skin slap on impact.

Brian was never a gentle lover and that was fine by her. Hard and rough was how she liked it and he never disappointed. Shanti was going to die when she saw what her so-called baby daddy and man was up to and Mya couldn't wait for it to happen.

***

After being out with his uncle and friends for a few hours, Brian had finally made it back home. He was happy that Trent drove him because he went a little over his normal drinking limit. He enjoyed his night, but banging Mya outside the club was a mistake that he was already starting to regret. She had already called him three times and he hadn't even been gone that long. Sending her mixed signals was what had her stalking him in the first place and he hadn't learned his lesson yet. But hearing what Kerry had said about Shanti had him in his feelings and he reacted off emotions.

"What are you doing up this late?" Brian asked Shanti as soon as he walked into the house.

She was coming out of his bedroom, but something about her appearance stood out to him. Shanti was in pajamas when he first left, but she was dressed in sweats and one of his oversized t-shirts now. When she tried to walk around him without answering, Brian grabbed her arm and made her stop and face him.

"Get your dirty ass hands off me!" Shanti screamed, taking him by surprise.

"The fuck is wrong with you, girl?" Brian asked in confusion.

They were fine when he left a few hours ago. She was acting like a crazy person now and he didn't know why.

"I'm going back home. Don't call me, text me, or even speak when you see me. Once the paternity test is done, we can work out financial and visitation arrangements. I've wasted enough time on you and I'm done. I don't have the energy to keep going through this same shit," Shanti rambled.

"What are you even talking about Ashanti?" Brian asked as he stood in front of her and grabbed her arm again.

"Just let me go Brian. I'm tired and I'm ready to go to sleep," Shanti replied.

"Go get in the bed then," Brian argued.

"I am, at my own house," Shanti said as she headed for the door.

"You ain't going no damn where. You got three weeks until you have the baby and you don't need to be at home alone," Brian reasoned.

"I'll be fine. My brothers don't live too far away from me," Shanti noted.

"Don't do this Shanti. Can we just sit down and talk?" Brian begged.

"We don't have shit to talk about," she replied.

Brian shook his head at the irony of the conversation. It was almost identical to the one that he'd had with Mya not too long before. The only difference was that the tables were turned in a different direction and he was now doing the begging.

"I didn't even do shit. I don't know what the hell is wrong with you," he maintained.

"You can tell me what you want, but this video ain't lying," Shanti said as she turned her phone towards him.

Brian dropped his head in defeat as he watched the video of Mya on her knees sucking him up behind the building of the strip club. He didn't even know how much of the act was recorded because he stopped watching. There was no need for him to wonder how she got it. That nigga Kerry was a straight up hoe, but Brian couldn't wait to cross paths with him again.

"The shit wasn't even that deep man," Brian said honestly.

"It's cool Brian. We're not in a committed relationship, remember? Your words, not mine," Shanti reminded him.

"Don't try to act like you don't be on no bullshit Shanti. You're supposed to be pregnant with my baby, but still letting that nigga Kerry hit it," Brian accused.

"Wow. This conversation is over and I'm gone," Shanti said as she walked around him and headed for the door once again.

"Nah, it ain't over. The nigga already told me what was up. Just keep it real," he barked angrily.

"How can a nigga who lies as much as you do tell me anything about keeping it real? I'm so happy that I see you for who you really are. I'm good on you and all this dumb shit. I really wish you weren't my daughter's father. Then I wouldn't have to deal with you at all," Shanti said as the tears that she'd been holding in started to fall.

She hated to show weakness around him, but she couldn't help it. As hard as she tried to fight it, she couldn't deny her love for him. It hurt her to know that he didn't feel the same way. All the bullshit that Mya did, and he still went back and kept fucking with her. She was tired of the back and forth and she was over it all.

"I'm sorry, but I swear it wasn't that serious for me. I was pissed, and I acted off emotions," Brian admitted as he wrapped his arms around her waist.

[118]

"It's cool Brian. I take the blame for everything that's happened between us. My biggest mistake was thinking that this was more than what it was," Shanti confessed.

"Don't even say no shit like that. That wasn't a mistake. Man, Shanti, I fucking love you. I just don't know if I can trust you. I'm not trying to get my heart broken," Brian admitted as he wiped away her tears.

"That makes two of us. And that's exactly why we can't be together," she said as she stepped out of his embrace and headed for the door.

"It's late Ashanti. Just go to sleep and wait until later to leave," Brian requested.

"I'll be fine. I don't even want to be around you right now."

"Shanti please, just get some rest and wait until later," Brian pleaded.

"No Brian. I'm going home. I'll be back to get my stuff later."

"Man-" Brian said before she cut him off.

"And for the record, I haven't slept with Kerry since we broke up three years ago," Shanti noted before she walked out the door and slammed it behind her.

She and Kerry had dated for a while, even though her brothers were against it. Kerry was heavy in the streets and they didn't want that for their one and only little sister. Shanti didn't care what they had to say. She loved him and she refused to leave him alone. Against their wishes, she moved out of the house with her brothers and got an apartment with Kerry. Three months after moving in with him, someone kicked in their door when they weren't home and ransacked the place looking for drugs. Her brothers were there the same day to move her out and she was done with Kerry after that. They were still friends and probably always would be, but a relationship never happened again. Kerry always expressed his wishes to have her back, but Shanti wasn't interested. She was too busy loving on Brian's no-good ass, even though he didn't deserve it.

"Damn man," Brian sighed in defeat as he walked out of the house and got into his car.

He was tired and tipsy, but he would be okay. Shanti had just backed out of the driveway, so he did the same and drove in the same direction. There was no way that he was letting Shanti go home alone that time of morning, so he followed her and made sure that she got inside safely. He wanted to go inside with her, but he knew that she wouldn't let him. Stupid decisions were all that Brian seemed to be making lately and it was time for him to get it right. He had to do better if he wanted them to be a family and he promised himself that he was going to try.

Chapter 13

"Stop acting like it's the end of the world Royce. Shit ain't as bad as you're making it out to be. It's not the first time that you missed your cycle. You might just be stressed again. Your boring ass is trying to juggle a husband and a man on the side and you're overwhelmed," Uri fussed as she drove.

"I can't believe this shit. I can't have a baby with a man who I don't even love or want to be with anymore. I can't be tied to Jax like that for the rest of my life," Royce whined.

"He's your husband, Royce. If you felt like that, you should have divorced his ass a long time ago," Uri replied.

"I'm not having it. I'll get an abortion before I reproduce with his ass," Royce swore.

"Bitch, please. You couldn't even flush your goldfish down the toilet when they died. Am I supposed to believe that you would kill a whole baby?" Uri laughed.

"This is not funny Uri. I was all set to tell him that I want him to move out and file for divorce. It's bad enough that I have to wait six months for that to be finalized. Having a baby means a lifetime commitment. I just can't do that," Royce said.

"You're really serious about divorcing him, huh?" Uri questioned.

"I told you that I've been doing my research," Royce replied.

"Yeah, but I never knew that you made a definite decision. You know I'm behind you all the way, but you have to keep a few things in mind Royce," Uri explained as they arrived at their destination.

"Like what?" Royce questioned.

"Jax is not gonna go away that easily. He's not gonna want his parents to know that y'all are separated, so he's gonna put up a fight. Not to mention, y'all work together and his mother is your boss. I just want you to be prepared, in case things get ugly. Thankfully, the house is yours, but I don't think you should stay there by yourself. I don't trust his ass."

"Fuck that house. I don't want to live there anyway. I don't want anything that reminds me of Jaxon Davenport. And that's exactly why I can't have his baby," Royce noted.

"We don't even know if your pregnant yet, bitch. Let's just go in here before you're late for your appointment," Uri said as she got out of the car in front of Royce's doctor's office.

Uri led the way, as Royce slowly followed behind her. She felt like a child on their way to be reprimanded by their parents and she dreaded the outcome. Once Uri saw how far behind she was, she pulled Royce's arm and made her walk ahead.

"Stop rushing me, bitch," Royce snapped.

"Girl, that nigga Caleb is really turning you out. Ain't no more sweet, innocent Royce. Nigga got you cussing and everything," Uri laughed, as Royce signed in to be seen.

"Don't blame it on Caleb. I should have been doing me a long time ago," Royce replied.

"I hate to see how you act when he finally breaks you off with the dick."

"I don't even want to think about that right now. I just want to see what's up, so I can know how to proceed. I'll gladly be a single mother. Pregnant or not, I want a divorce," Royce swore.

"I'll get divorced for the dick. Be a single mother for the dick," Uri sang, making her cousin laugh.

"I hate you. Why do you always make a joke out of everything?" Royce laughed.

"Because you need to lighten up bitch. It's not that serious," Uri replied.

She had taken the day off from work to accompany her cousin to her doctor's appointment. Royce was supposed to work a half day, but she ended up calling off because her nerves were so bad. It was crazy to Uri because her cousin was more worried about Caleb than anything else. Royce was terrified that she would have to tell her side nigga that she was pregnant by her own husband. That was a hot ass mess if she had to say so herself.

"Royce Davenport," the nurse called after they'd been sitting there for about twenty minutes.

"It's showtime," Royce mumbled while standing to her feet.

Uri stayed in the lobby and flipped through some magazines while Royce went to the back.

"I see that you think you might be pregnant. Did you take a test at home?" the nurse asked as she handed Royce a gown to put on.

"No, I didn't, but I missed my cycle," Royce replied.

"Okay. Take this cup and fill it up to the line as much as you can. I'll also need to get some blood from you," the nurse told her while handing her a cup to urinate in.

Royce took the cup from her to go into the bathroom to do as she was told. Once she filled the cup up, she wrapped it up with a few paper towels and washed her hands. The nurse took the sample from her and sat it on her cart. After taking a tube of blood, she assured Royce that the doctor would be with her soon. Royce sent a text to Uri, letting her know that she was almost done. She was sadly mistaken because it was over an hour before the doctor walked in with some papers in her hands.

"I have your results," her doctor said, as Royce crossed her fingers and prayed for the best.

***

"What is this bitch doing?" Uri mumbled to herself.

Royce claimed that she was almost done, but that was two hours ago. Uri tried texting and calling her, but she never answered. Even Uri's husband called to make sure they were okay, but she didn't have anything to report. She didn't even know what was going on. When the double doors flew open a few minutes later, Royce came rushing out and Uri knew that something was wrong. Royce's red-rimmed eyes and tear-stained face were all the proof she needed to know that the news wasn't what she wanted to hear.

"Let's go," Royce demanded as she rushed out the doors and in the direction of Uri's car.

Uri ran to catch up with her and she was out of breath when she did. Her heart broke when Royce got to her car and broke down crying.

"It's okay cousin. You know I'll do whatever I can to help you. Having a baby is a blessing, no matter how they are conceived. You don't have to stay with Jax just because you're pregnant and don't even think that way," Uri said as she pulled her into a hug.

"I'm not pregnant," Royce sobbed.

"What's wrong then? You should be happy," Uri replied in confusion.

"That dirty dick bastard gave me an STD," Royce fumed.

"What! How could they tell so soon? I thought you had to wait at least a day or two before they could tell you something like that," Uri stated.

"Technology is changing Uri. I don't know how she found out so soon, but that bastard gave me chlamydia. She gave me some nasty liquid shit to drink and I have to come back in a week to make sure it's cleared up. I took a stress test and my levels were through the roof. She said that was probably why I missed my cycle. I'm stressed out and unhappy and I can't take this shit no more. I just want that disease infested muthafucker out of my house today!" Royce yelled.

"Say no more. Let's go pack his shit up and have it waiting on his ass," Uri said, ready for whatever.

"I'm getting my locks changed and resetting the password on my alarm too," Royce said as they got into the car.

As Uri drove to her house, Royce made the necessary calls to the alarm company and a locksmith. Jax usually went straight to the gym after work so that would buy them a little time. As soon as they pulled up to her house, Royce and Uri got right to work. They grabbed the oversized black garbage bags and stuffed all of Jaxon's belongings inside. Royce was like a woman on a mission. She packed hygiene items, dirty clothes, and anything else that she could think of. She was tired from running up and down the stairs, but her adrenaline kept her going.

"I need a break boss. I'm tired as hell," Uri said as she flopped down on the sofa.

"Me too, but that should be everything," Royce said while handing her a bottle of water.

Half the floor in her living room was covered with Jaxon's belongings and she was happy about that.

"What are you gonna do about work? Putting Jax out of the house is one thing, but you still have to see him at work," Uri reminded her.

"I know, but it's too late in the semester for me to do anything now. I can put in for a transfer, but his father is the one who has to approve it. That woman-hating bastard is over all that kind of stuff."

"He's gonna know that something is wrong when you do that," Uri noted.

"I don't even care anymore. That's Jaxon's problem. I'm putting in my transfer as soon as I get settled and get on my laptop. I don't want to work under Elena or my mama anymore," Royce noted.

"I don't blame you, cousin. And you know that you don't have to sleep here tonight if you don't want to. My spare bedroom is yours for however long you need it. Ashton said the same thing," Uri said, referring to her husband.

"Thank you, cousin, but I'll be fine. If the boredom gets to be too much, I'll be over there," Royce replied.

"Maybe Caleb can come keep you company. I'm sure he'll be happy to," Uri suggested.

"Hell no, Uri. I'm too ashamed to even look at him right now," Royce admitted.

"Why? You don't have anything to be ashamed of Royce. It's not like you slept with a bunch of different niggas. Jax is your husband and he's the one at fault here. And, honestly, if you plan to pursue a relationship with Caleb, you need to let him know what's up," Uri remarked.

"No way in hell am I telling him that. It's not like we're having sex," Royce noted.

"No, but your partners were. Sienna is the common denominator here. She was screwing Jax and Caleb at the same time. What if she gave it to them both? If you and Caleb have sex, you'll be infected all over again," Uri pointed out.

"Oh, my God. Things just seem to keep getting worse," Royce said as she buried her head in her hands.

"Just be honest with him, Royce. Don't start off whatever y'all plan to build with secrets and lies," Uri warned.

"I won't. If we do decide to be together, I want things to be the total opposite of what I have with Jax."

"It will be. Caleb and I started out on the wrong foot, but I like him," Uri said.

"Me too, with his sexy ass," Royce blushed.

"Okay, I got my second wind now. What else do you need to do?" Uri asked.

"I think that's it, minus whatever he has in the basement," Royce replied.

"Let's go down there and see. Don't give his pathetic ass any reason to come back over here," Uri said as she stood up.

Royce got up too and led the way to the basement. She rarely went in Jax's man cave and she didn't have a reason to. He kept the area neat and clean and that was all that she cared about.

"At least his sad ass keeps it clean down here," Royce hissed.

"Bitch, it is nice down here. You should have kept this area for yourself," Uri complimented.

"Girl, you know how tore up this basement was when my daddy first got me this house. I didn't want no parts of it. That's why I didn't care when Jax decided to fix it up for himself," Royce replied as they looked around.

Aside from a stack of mail, a laptop, and tv, there wasn't much of anything in there to get rid of besides the furniture. Royce thumbed through the huge stack of mail, trying to see what else her husband was up to. She came up empty handed when all she saw were a bunch of fitness magazines and protein powder coupons. Jax was a health nut, so that was no surprise.

"What the...," Uri exclaimed, letting her words trail off.

"What?" Royce asked as she walked over to her.

Uri had picked up Jax's laptop that he'd obviously forgotten to log out of. Royce's hand went up to her mouth as she looked at a video of her husband having sex with his ex-wife. A few more videos showed him in compromising positions with various women at his gym. Royce now knew why he insisted on going to the gym every day after work. He was doing way more than just exercising. Uri opened another video and a movie starring Jax and Angelique started to play. Royce would recognize the black and white tiled walls in the background from anywhere. They were in one of the bathrooms at the school. She watched in disgust as her husband pounded into another woman, right before she dropped to her knees and took him into her mouth. What Royce wasn't prepared for was Elena bursting through the door and catching them in the act.

"Now I know why she doesn't work there anymore," Royce said once the video shut off.

She knew that Angelique didn't work in the cafeteria anymore, but she didn't know that she had been fired. Elena made it very clear in the video that Angelique's actions had guaranteed her dismissal.

"That's messed up. Why did she have to lose her job and he got to keep his? I don't like her ass from what I've heard about her, but they did her dirty. That whole family is foul," Uri replied.

"Who the fuck am I married to?" Royce mumbled, as Uri opened another tab on the computer that Jax never bothered to close.

"This nigga is a fucking freak. Look at this shit. Hotel rooms, porn sites, playboy movie rentals," Uri said, reading off all the transactions on Jax's bank statement.

"That's not who we bank with," Royce said as she looked at the online statement.

"This nigga is really foul. I don't give a damn what you say Royce, but you are not staying here tonight. Pack you a bag and be prepared to leave when I leave. This muthafucka is sick in the head," Uri snapped.

"What if he has me on camera too?" Royce asked in panic.

"I'm about to go through all these videos on here and see," Uri replied as she went to each one and pressed play.

There were over fifty different videos saved but, thankfully, Royce wasn't in any of them. Maybe it was because she was his wife, but she was just grateful that she had been spared. She didn't know what she would have done if her husband had recorded some of their most intimate moments.

"I need to talk to my daddy about getting rid of this house. I'll get an apartment until I can find another one if I have to," Royce said.

"And keep this computer somewhere too, just in case you need it. You can make that nigga jump through hoops with the shit that's on here," Uri said as she handed Royce the laptop.

They locked up the basement and went back upstairs. After packing a few bags and placing them in the truck of her car, Royce and her cousin sat in the living room and talked, waiting for Jaxon to get there.

Chapter 14

66 What the fuck do you want me to do Angelique?" Jax yelled into the phone angrily as he drove home.

"Did you even try to talk to your mother Jax? After all, I wasn't the only guilty party," Angelique replied.

"Talk to her and tell her what? I caught just as much heat behind that shit as you did," Jax argued.

"Yeah but, unlike me, you got to keep your job," Angelique pointed out.

"Oh well, shit happens," Jax replied uncaringly.

"Maybe I need to see what kind of shit will happen if I go to the school board office and tell them what really happened," Angelique raged.

"Are you threatening me, Angelique?" Jax questioned.

He wasn't worried about that because all complaints had to go through his father and hers wouldn't get anywhere.

"It's more like a promise," Angelique taunted.

"See, I was about to have a heart and throw a few dollars your way to help you out, but fuck you. Your threats don't scare me. My family is the school board bitch!" Jax snapped before hanging up in her face.

Every woman in his life was starting to give him a headache and he was tired of it. He thought sure that he and Royce were getting things back on track when she sexed him like a porn star, but he was sadly mistaken. Once the liquor and the hangover wore off, she was back to the way she was before. He tried not to think the worst, but he was starting to believe that his wife was having an affair. Royce was never home, and she stopped bothering to tell him where she was going. Not to mention the cologne that he swore he smelled on her when she came in late one night. When he confronted her about it, she laughed like it was a joke.

Then, there was Sienna, who was on some let's be a family shit that he wasn't trying to hear. Every time he went to the house to spend time with his kids, Sienna begged him to stay. She should have been happy with getting the dick, but she always wanted more. He bypassed going to the gym just to be with her and she still wasn't satisfied.

"The fuck is this bitch doing here?" Jax questioned out loud when he pulled up and saw Uri's car in their driveway.

She was a disrespectful lil bitch. She always made it a point to park in their driveway, knowing that his and Royce's cars were the only two that belonged there. Royce's other car was in the garage and she rarely drove it anymore. It was no secret that Uri hated him, and he felt the same about her. She was an undercover hoe and he hated when Royce hung out with her. If his wife was cheating, it was probably her cousin who put her up to it. Royce loved her like a sister, so that was a bond that he would never succeed in breaking.

"The hell? Royce! Open the door baby. My key ain't working!" Jax shouted as he banged on the front door.

He heard the locks being undone before he came face to face with Royce. She had a scowl on her face and so did Uri, who was standing right beside her.

"Why are you just standing here baby? Let me in," Jax said as he pushed the door and made his way inside.

He didn't get very far before Royce grabbed his arm and stopped him.

"This is far enough," she said as she stood there with her arms crossed over her chest.

It was at that exact moment that Jax noticed all the black trash bags that were on the floor. His heart did a nosedive in his chest as the reality of the situation hit him like a ton of bricks. Royce was leaving him. There was no way that he was letting that happen. He didn't care if he had to cry, beg, and plead. He needed his wife more than she knew. His actions didn't always show it, but it was true. His parents would die if his wife left and put a spot on their blemish-free appearance.

"Royce baby, please don't do this. I know that things haven't been too good with us, but we can make this work. Just, please don't leave me," Jax begged.

"I'm not leaving Jaxon," Royce said, making him visibly relax, "you are."

"What?" Jax asked in confusion.

"You heard me. This is my house that I had before I married you, so you have no claims to it. Here are all your belongings. Take it and get the fuck out," Royce snapped, as Uri stood there with a smirk on her face.

"Baby, please don't do this to us. We can go to marriage counselling or something. I'll do whatever you want me to do," Jax pleaded.

"The first thing I want you to do is go get that chlamydia infected dick treated so you don't give the shit to nobody else. And maybe you need to find out which one of your nasty ass hoes gave it to you so that bitch can get cured too. Make no mistake about it, this marriage is over and it should have been over a long time ago. If you don't want me to embarrass you by sending the papers to your parents' house or the school, I suggest you comply and sign when I ask you to," Royce rambled.

"That's some bullshit! I've never had an STD before in my life and you want me to believe that I have one now. I'm not stupid Royce. I see the way you've been moving lately. You're cheating on me and you're trying to blame what the other nigga did on me. If I do have anything, you're the one who gave it to me," Jax fumed.

"You sound like a damn fool, but you're right about one thing. There is somebody else in my life but, unlike you, I never fucked him."

"Yet," Uri interjected.

"Yeah, not yet," Royce agreed with a giggle.

She felt much better than she had earlier that day, thanks to Uri. She loved her cousin more than she would ever know for how she was always there for her.

"Bitch!" Jax yelled as he wrapped his hands around Royce's neck.

She clawed at his face to make him stop and she succeeded for a while. When Jax lifted his hand to hit her, Uri was ready for him.

"Do it nigga. I dare you. Hit her, so I can fill your punk ass with more lead than a number two pencil," Uri threatened as she aimed her small gun at Jaxon's head.

He got his mind right real quick and backed up until he was outside on the porch.

"Baby, please, I'm sorry for losing my temper just now, but we need to talk, alone," Jax said as he looked at Uri.

"You need to talk to a doctor. Go get that leaky dick checked," Uri laughed.

"Fuck you, bitch. It was probably you who put her up to cheating with your hoe ass," Jax snapped.

"It takes one to know one," Uri replied as she grabbed one of the bags and threw it outside.

"Don't touch my shit," he fumed as he caught the bag in midair.

"We're trying to help you out," Royce replied as she too threw a bag out the door at him.

Soon after, Jax was ducking black garbage bags, as both women threw his belongings out on the front porch. Royce had turned into an entirely different person over the last few months and he didn't know who she was anymore.

"This shit ain't over Royce. You think you can just kick me out after all the money that I've spent on upgrades to this place? This is just as much of my home as it is yours," Jax noted.

"Tell it to the judge," Royce countered.

"Do you really think you would win Royce? I'm a Davenport baby. My name alone will guarantee me a victory. I'm the best man that you'll ever have and even your mother knows that. We both have an image to uphold. Don't play hard in front of Uri because you know that this is not what you want."

"Don't flatter yourself boo. The Davenport name ain't shit. Let's not forget that I'm the same bitch who you told all your family's secrets to. I'm sure a lot of people would be interested in knowing why Elena's knees are so bad," Royce replied.

"Who's going to believe you? My family is good at making stories disappear," Jax smirked.

"Maybe so, but your computer has enough shit on it to bring your entire family down to its knees. Stories can disappear, but evidence can't. Don't fight me on this Jax. It won't be pretty if you do. You're sick and you need more help than what I thought," Royce said, wiping the smile from his face.

"Where is my laptop? You had no business touching my personal belongings."

"You'll get it back once you cooperate with this divorce. I need a little insurance to keep you in check," Royce noted.

"Please don't embarrass my family like that Royce. I fucked up, but they don't have anything to do with this," Jax pleaded.

"Don't try to humble yourself now nigga. What happened to the big bad Jaxon Davenport who was talking all that hot shit just now?" Uri questioned.

"Will you please just mind your business for once?" Jax snapped.

"She is my business nigga," Uri replied.

"Don't even argue with him, cousin. I've said all that I needed to say and you need to leave," Royce said while looking at Jax.

"I really need my laptop Royce. I have a lot of important documents on there," Jax begged.

"Yeah, I know all about how important they are. I saw all your hotel rentals on the bank statement that I knew nothing about. Like I said before, you'll get your computer once you sign the papers. When you see me at work, act like you don't know me. Don't try to call me and don't show up here. I would hate for your computer to end up in the wrong hands if you do. Don't forget that my cousin and father work for the newspaper. We can make some shit happen too," Royce threatened.

"Nasty bastard," Uri chimed in, right before Royce slammed the door in his face.

"Fuck!" Jax yelled in anger as he started grabbing his belongings and throwing them in his truck. Everything was going wrong and he didn't know what to do to fix it. His parents were already pissed, and Royce kicking him out would only make things worse. There was no way in hell that he was going to their house. He didn't want to go by any of his siblings or friends either. He didn't know anyone who was single and he couldn't see himself staying with someone else and their family. Sienna was the only person who came to mind and he hated that she was his only option. He owed her an ass whipping anyway. If what Royce said was true, then she was probably the bitch who infected him. There was no telling what kind of niggas she was fucking while working at that club.

[133]

***

"It's bed time guys. Put your toys away and brush your teeth," Sienna said to her son, Jayce, and daughter, Jewel.

"Are we going to Auntie Yada's house tonight?" Jayce asked.

"No, I'm off tonight," she replied.

Either Yada or her sixteen-year-old daughter would keep Sienna's kids if she had to work, but that wasn't the case that night. She had the next two days off and she needed them to rest.

"Is daddy coming back?" Jewel asked her.

"No baby. Just brush your teeth and go to bed. You have school in the morning," Sienna said, feeling down.

Her kids were so happy when they got home from school and saw their father there. He spent about twenty minutes with them before he ran off to go home to his bitch. The kids begged him to stay for dinner, but he declined. He only came over to fuck her and leave, just like always. And just like always, Sienna let him do it. If it weren't for his parents, he probably wouldn't have cared about their living arrangements. He knew that Sienna loved him too much to put him on child support, so he did the bare minimum and paid the few bills that she had. Between lights, water, and cable, that wasn't even five hundred dollars that he was giving up.

A sudden banging on her door shook Sienna from her thoughts as she eased down the hall to peep out the window. She couldn't see who it was, but she smiled when she saw Jaxon's car. She was upset when he left, so maybe he had come back to make things right. Sienna found out just how wrong she was when she opened the door and was met by Jax's open palm across her face. He slapped her so hard that she fell to the floor and started scooting away from him.

"Bitch, you gave me a fucking disease? Huh? Your nasty ass been out there fucking them niggas raw and gave me something," Jax fumed.

"What? No, I didn't give you anything. I wasn't having sex with nobody else," Sienna swore.

And that was the truth. Aside from Caleb, who she hadn't had sex with in months, Jaxon was her only partner.

"Don't fucking lie to me," Jax fumed as he snatched her up by her hair and slapped her twice more.

"I swear, I'm telling the truth. I had my annual about a month ago and I was fine. Besides that, we've been using condoms for the past few months," Sienna cried as she tasted the blood inside her mouth.

"Mommy!" Jewel yelled when she walked into the room and saw what was happening.

"Go to your room Jewel," Jax demanded.

"Please, don't hurt my mommy," Jewel cried, breaking Sienna's heart.

Jax was a heartless bastard. He saw his daughter standing there crying, but he refused to let Sienna's hair go.

"Take her to her room, Jayce, and you go to yours," Jax told his son when he walked into the room.

Jayce grabbed his little sister's hand and hurried out of the room like he was told to.

"Bitch, you better have some proof to back up this clean bill of health that you claim to have," Jax fumed as he dragged her down the hall to her bedroom.

Sienna had never thought she would feel anything outside of love for Jax but, in that moment, she hated him. It had been years since he put his hands on her, but old habits were hard to break. Jaxon was definitely his father's son.

"Get up!" Jax yelled angrily, finally deciding to release the grip that he had on her hair.

Sienna moved away from him before hurrying to her feet. She ran to her closet and grabbed her folder with all her important papers inside. She flipped through some papers until she came across what she was looking for.

"Here, I told you that I'm clean," Sienna sniffled.

Jax snatched the papers from her hand and read over everything. Sienna was telling the truth, but he was still pissed. The fact remained that he apparently had an STD and his wife had left him behind it. The first thing he needed to do was get tested and treated and then find out which one of them nasty hoes gave it to him. Aside from Angelique and Sienna, Jax had slept with two of the ladies that he frequented the gym with. They had flirted back and forth for months before he finally got them to give it up only one week apart. It only happened once both times, but that was all it took.

[135]

"I'm sorry Sienna, but you need to understand how I feel," Jax apologized.

"Fuck your apology Jaxon. You come here accusing me of something that I didn't even do. I need to get myself checked again, just to be on the safe side."

"You just said yourself that we always use condoms," Jax reminded her.

"Yeah, but you obviously weren't using them with other people," Sienna snapped.

"I haven't been with anybody else other than my wife," he lied.

"How do you know that her sneaky ass didn't give it to you? That bitch ain't as perfect as you think she is," Sienna said as she wet a rag and cleaned up her face.

"We just had an argument about it and I left her," Jax lied again.

"You left Royce?" Sienna asked in shock as she turned to face him.

"Yeah, I did and now I don't have anywhere else to go. I should have never moved in with her knowing that the house was hers before we got married."

All the hate that Sienna had felt a moment ago vanished as she processed the news that she'd just received. Jax and Royce not being together was like a dream come true. In her mind, Royce was the only thing standing in the way of them becoming a family again.

"You always have somewhere to go as long as I have a roof over my head. Besides, this is your family's house," Sienna replied.

"Yeah, but I can't let anyone know that I'm staying here Sienna. You already know how my parents are. You need to keep this to yourself," Jax instructed.

"Okay, I will," Sienna promised.

Satisfied with her answer, Jax went to his car and started unloading his belongings, while Sienna put everything away. Sienna was a fool for real. He'd just beat her ass, but she was so excited that he was moving in with her. Jax didn't want to rain on her parade, but his move was only temporary. He was sure that he could finesse his way back into Royce's life; he just had to get her alone. She had courage as long as Uri was there but, the minute she was by herself, she would fold like a towel. Royce had never gone as far as putting him out of the house. That act alone let him know just how bad the situation was.

Even if she didn't take him back, he needed to get his laptop back. He was kicking himself for being so careless and never locking the device or putting a password on it. Royce never stepped foot in the basement and he got too comfortable. Left in the wrong hands, his laptop could get him in a world of trouble. Recording someone in a sexual act without their permission was against the law, but that would be the least of his worries. As much as he wanted to call Royce and beg for her forgiveness, he didn't want to make her mad enough to do something stupid with his computer. He had to put a call in to her mother as soon as he could. If anyone could help him, it would be Sondra. He just had to switch the story up a little to make it sound believable. He also had to find out who the mystery man was that she claimed to be seeing. Jax had cheated too many times to count, but he was having a hard time accepting that Royce was doing the same.

Two days after settling in at Sienna's house, Jax went to his doctor to get tested. Just like Royce had said, he was infected with chlamydia and had infected her too. Sadly, he couldn't even point out who had given it to him. Sienna got checked just to be sure, but she was cleared. Jax could scratch one name off his list of suspects, but he still had a few more to go. His marriage was officially over. If he never knew it before, he definitely knew it now.

Chapter 15

"Did she answer?" Caleb asked Brooklyn as he paced back and forth in front of the building with the phone up to his ear.

"Yeah, but she keeps saying the same thing. She said she'll call you as soon as we hang up," Brooklyn replied.

"Her ass ain't call me yet and it's been five days since we last talked," Caleb replied.

"Damn. I hope she's okay. That's not like Royce," Brooklyn noted.

"Her ass is alright," Caleb snapped.

"How do you know that?" Brooklyn questioned.

"Because I'm looking right at her car in the parking lot of her job. Shit can't be that bad if she's still at work."

"I know damn well your stupid ass ain't at that school," Brooklyn fussed.

She got her answer when Caleb called her on FaceTime and showed her exactly where he was.

"Think it's a game if you want to," he replied.

"You do know that her husband works there too," Brook reminded him.

"Fuck that nigga!" Caleb snapped angrily.

"You and Brian are really nuts. First, he's sleeping in his car outside of Shanti's apartment like he's homeless and you're stalking this girl on her job," Brooklyn laughed.

She thought that Shanti was playing when she said that Brian was outside of her house asleep in his car, until she sent her a picture. Shanti said that he begged her to let him in, but she never did. She ignored him at the shop, and he was losing his mind. There was no need for him to deny it any longer; he was head over heels in love with Shanti and his actions proved it.

"I'm not a stalker, but I need to know what's up. We were good for months and she just switched up on a nigga for no reason. If it's over, then she needs to be a woman and say that shit to my face," Caleb argued.

"I never knew that anything had started," Brooklyn said.

"How many times in the past few months have you seen me without Royce?" Caleb quizzed.

"I don't know Caleb. Not that many," she answered.

"Exactly!" he yelled. "We didn't have to say the words to make it official. Our actions showed it."

"But, she's still married Caleb. You seem to keep forgetting that."

"And you seem to keep forgetting that I don't give a fuck. And stop trying to give me relationship advice Brooklyn. You don't have no room to talk."

"Whatever Caleb," she said, since she didn't have a rebuttal.

She really didn't have room to talk because her relationship with her husband was dysfunctional as hell in the beginning. He was engaged when they met and married when she got pregnant with their second child. It was old news to her, but her brothers never let her forget it.

"For the past few months, I've been more than a husband to her than he has anyway," Caleb bellowed.

"Just be calm when you talk to her, Caleb. Royce is not like the rest of them ghetto birds that you're accustomed to. Don't go at that girl with all that rowdy shit."

"She better say some shit that I want to hear or I'm about to go bat shit crazy on her ass out here," Caleb swore.

"Let me find out that you're falling in love with my friend," Brooklyn teased.

"Bye Brooklyn. I'm not in the mood for your games man," Caleb replied before hanging up on her.

He continued to pace the sidewalk, deep in thought. He really wanted to smoke something, but he was asking for jail time if he had drugs anywhere around a school zone. He had enough with Mrs. Lockwood already. He didn't need to give her any other reason to mess with him.

"The fuck is this girl at?" Caleb questioned out loud. The dismissal bell had rung at least twenty minutes ago and most of the kids had filed out of the building to their busses or rides that awaited them. Royce's car was still out there, so Caleb knew that she hadn't left.

"To what do I owe the honor of this visit? I'm hoping this has nothing to do with Sienna," a male voice said from behind, as Caleb continued to pace.

When he turned around and saw Jaxon standing there with a smug expression on his face, Caleb was tempted to knock his punk ass out.

"Fuck you, dude. And fuck Sienna too," Caleb replied while waving him off.

"Don't worry, I am," Jax smirked, letting him know what was up.

"As if I give a fuck. I should knock your punk ass out for divorcing her in the first place," Caleb threatened.

"Your threats don't scare me, but I am curious. Why does me divorcing Sienna have anything to do with you?" Jax questioned.

"If you would have stayed with the bitch, I would have never met her trifling ass," Caleb replied.

"I didn't need to stay married to her to still enjoy all the benefits. I just think of it as having two wives instead of one," Jax chuckled, happy to be taunting the other man.

Admittedly, he was jealous of Caleb for a while when Sienna first got with him. She had put Jax on the back burner and wouldn't even talk to him if it wasn't about their kids. He was used to Sienna being at his beck and call, so that didn't sit right with him. Since he had her back under his thumb, he had no reason to be envious.

"Dude, I'm really not in the mood to entertain your bullshit right now. If you know what's best for you, you would get the fuck on and stop talking to me," Caleb warned angrily.

"Gladly," Jax said smugly as he strolled to his car and sped away.

He didn't think Caleb had any kids, so he didn't know why he was at the school. Truthfully, he really didn't care. He had bigger things to worry about concerning his marriage.

"Stupid clown ass nigga," Caleb mumbled, right as he spotted Royce walking out of the building.

She paused for a second, surprised to see him standing there. She'd purposely waited until she saw Jaxon leave before she made her exit. Jax had been begging her for another chance, but she was done. He was trying to avoid his parents finding out about their separation, but it was almost inevitable.

"What are you doing here?" Royce quizzed when she walked up to Caleb.

"Don't ask me no stupid ass question like that. What's up with you, Royce?" Caleb questioned angrily.

"Nothing," Royce said as she tried to walk away from him.

"The fuck? Are you really trying to walk away while I'm talking to you?" Caleb asked as he pulled her back by her arm.

"Just let me go Caleb. I have a lot going on right now. I'll call and talk to you later," Royce said as she tried to keep her composure.

"Fuck that Royce! I'm right here. You can talk to me now," Caleb fumed.

"I... I..." Royce stuttered before she slumped her shoulders and burst out crying.

"Shit, baby, I'm sorry," Caleb apologized as he pulled her into him for a hug.

Brook had just told him not to go at her on no rowdy shit, but he didn't listen. He felt bad as he held her up while her entire body shook as she cried. Once she had calmed down a little, Caleb walked her to his car and sat her down in the back seat. Her legs were outside of the car, so he squatted down so that they were at eye level.

"You didn't do anything wrong Caleb. I just have a lot going on right now," Royce said, repeating her earlier statement.

"Like what Royce? For the past few months, we've been talking about everything. You could have called me," Caleb replied.

"I filed for divorce yesterday," Royce confessed.

"Why? What happened?" Caleb asked.

"We were already having problems but shit just got worse. It's too damn embarrassing to even talk about it," Royce sniffled.

"Since when are you embarrassed to tell me anything?" Caleb asked.

"I don't even know where to start," Royce sighed.

"Let's go take a ride," Caleb said as he helped her up.

"What about my car?" she asked while getting comfortable in the passenger's seat.

"I'll bring you back for it later," Caleb replied when he got into the car.

"I'm sorry for ignoring you," Royce said as she grabbed Caleb's hand.

"It's cool, but I need to know what's up and don't leave nothing out," he demanded.

"Okay," Royce replied as she ran everything down to him, starting with the night that she had drunk sex with her husband. As embarrassing as it was, she even had to tell him about her pregnancy scare and doctor's visit. Caleb looked like he was pissed, and she just hoped she wasn't the cause of his anger. Technically, she hadn't done anything wrong.

"So, that nigga not only fucked around on you, but he came home with an STD too?" Caleb asked, just to be clear.

"Apparently so. I should have done what Uri said and called you the day that I found out. You need to get tested too," Royce replied.

"Why? We never had sex before," Caleb reminded her.

"I know that Caleb, but what if he got it from Sienna?"

"I'm good either way. I haven't fucked with Sienna like that in months. I always used a condom whenever I did."

"I still think you should do it. Just to be on the safe side," Royce cautioned.

"Okay, I'll do it." Caleb shrugged like it was no big deal.

"I have another appointment tomorrow, just to make sure I'm good. This is so damn embarrassing," Royce said as she stared out of the window.

"You don't have anything to be embarrassed about Royce. It ain't like you were fucking a bunch of different dudes and caught something. That nigga is your husband and he's foul as fuck for that shit," Caleb fumed.

"That's why I always made sure that we used protection. This was a lesson learned for me too," she noted.

"That's fucked up that you can't even have unprotected sex with the person that you're married to," Caleb said, shaking his head.

[143]

"I agree. Do you always use protection with that police lady too?" Royce asked, right as they pulled up to one of her favorite restaurants.

"She's my probation officer, but don't even mention that thirsty bitch." Caleb frowned.

During one of his and Royce's many talks, he was upfront with her about his situation with Mrs. Lockwood. She thought it was hilarious that he had to trade sex for his freedom, but Caleb didn't get the joke.

"I'm just asking." Royce shrugged.

"I've never have unprotected sex with anyone," Caleb replied.

"Good." She smiled.

"I hope you ain't still living under the same roof with that clown ass nigga," Caleb said while turning to face her.

"Hell no!" Royce shrieked. "Uri and I packed his shit up the same day I went to the clinic. I don't want no parts of that house no more. I've been staying with Uri."

"Damn man. I gotta stop procrastinating and get me a place to stay. Don't worry about nothing baby. I'll buy us a house."

"I can't buy another house right now Caleb. I haven't even talked to my father about selling the one that I still have. I'm dreading this entire situation. My mama is gonna die."

"I said I'll buy us a house. You don't need to do anything but pick it out and move in," he replied as he pecked her lips.

"You make everything sound so easy."

"It is easy. Your house is in your name, right?" Caleb asked.

"Yes," Royce answered.

"Well, you have nothing to worry about. My brother and his father-in-law can help you with that," Caleb said, referring to Jaden and Rob.

"But, my father got the house for me. He might not care if I sell it, but my mama is a different story altogether."

"It doesn't matter who purchased it. The name on the deed is the only one that counts. I can have your back all day long and I will, but nobody will have your back like you. You only get one life Royce. Live it the way you want to live it. Stop always worrying about what people think or what they have to say. No wonder you're always stressed out and shit. I've never even met your mama and you got me not liking her ass already," Caleb spat.

"Good, because I can promise you that she won't like you either," Royce laughed.

"Excuse my language, but I really don't give a fuck. As long as you like me, I'm good," Caleb replied.

"Yeah, I think I like you a little too much. Hell, maybe it's more than like," Royce admitted.

"And the feeling is mutual," Caleb said as he kissed her again.

Royce felt better than she'd felt in a while when she and Caleb exited the car to go eat. They talked for hours and she hated when it was time for him to leave. He wanted to make things between them official, and she happily agreed. It didn't matter that she still had a husband. It never mattered to Jaxon that he had a wife either.

The following day, Royce was so excited to be given a clean bill of health from her doctor. All her other tests came back fine and that was music to her ears. Caleb had gone to see his doctor and his results came back fine as well. That was one situation that Royce could put behind her, and now it was time for her focus on other more important matters.

Chapter 16

"Hey daddy," Royce said when she entered her parents' home.

She was so happy when she called her father and was told that her mother wasn't there. She needed to talk to him in private and she didn't need the added dramatics. Sondra had been blowing her phone up, but she was not in the mood to talk.

"Hey baby," Patrick said as he got up from the sofa and hugged her.

"Where's your wife?" Royce asked, as if that wasn't her mother.

"Out with Elena somewhere. Probably spending up all my money," he chuckled.

"That sounds about right," Royce said while rolling her eyes.

"Is everything okay baby? You sounded weird on the phone," Patrick stated.

"Uh, no daddy, everything is not alright. That's what I wanted to talk to you about. I filed for divorce and I want to sell the house," Royce blurted out.

"Whoa! Wait a minute. Let me digest one thing before you hit me with another," Patrick said while raising his hand in the air.

"I'm sorry daddy and I don't want you to think that I'm ungrateful. I really appreciate you buying my house for me, but I just can't stay there anymore. I want a new start and I don't want anything that reminds me of Jaxon," Royce said as her eyes filled with tears.

"It's okay, baby. I don't think you're ungrateful at all. I got that house for you to do what you want with it. If selling it is what you want to do, I have no problem with that," Patrick assured her.

"I'll give you every dime it sells for, so you don't have to worry about that," Royce assured him.

"The money is yours to keep Royce. I didn't let you borrow the house. I bought it for you. That's not what concerns me though. What happened to make you file for divorce?" Patrick asked as he grabbed her hand.

Royce saw the look of concern all over his face and that's what she loved about him. Her father was on her side no matter what happened, and her feelings always came first. She opened her mouth to speak, but the front door flew open before she had a chance to. Sondra was fuming when she walked through the door. She was excited when Elena called her and asked her out to lunch. That wasn't unusual, since they always had lunch and shopping dates with or without Royce. It wasn't until she got there and saw that Silas was with her, did she realize that something must have been wrong. It wasn't enough that Royce got drunk in front of her in-laws, she just kept doing stupid shit and making Sondra look like a fool.

"I've been calling you for over an hour Royce. Why didn't you answer me?" Sondra asked angrily.

"Hello to you too, mother. Yes, I'm fine and you?" Royce replied sarcastically.

"Don't get flip with me, girl. You just don't get tired of embarrassing me, do you? What the hell is this?" Sondra yelled as she threw some papers in her daughter's lap.

"It's my transfer papers. I want to be transferred to another school," Royce replied calmly.

"Are you crazy Royce? Why would you want to work somewhere else, when your mother-in-law is the principal of the school you're at now? How is that going to look to everyone else? You are a Davenport!" Sondra shouted.

"Not for long. I filed for divorce," Royce said, making her mother wide-eyed and speechless.

Sondra had to take a seat because she felt like she was going to pass out from the shock alone. She'd just talked to Jaxon on the phone and he didn't mention anything about that.

"Please tell me you didn't," Sondra managed to choke out.

"Calm down honey. Royce is a smart girl. She's not gonna file for divorce and sell her house for nothing," Patrick tried to reason.

"Wait a damn minute! This is going too far now. You're trying to sell your house too? Are you trying to give me a heart attack Royce? What is going on?" Sondra rambled.

"I'm not happy and I haven't been happy for a while. I'm tired of trying to please everybody else while I'm miserable," Royce replied.

"Does this have anything to do with this other man that you're seeing? Jaxon told me that you confessed everything to him," Sondra said.

Jax sounded so hurt when he called her to talk about Royce. She had turned into a completely different person and Sondra was seeing that for herself. She was shocked when he told her of Royce's admission of cheating, but that certainly explained her less than normal behavior lately. Just like her, Jax was trying to save face with his parents. He didn't want the situation to get ugly and embarrass the Davenport name.

"What? You can't be serious right now. Just like always, you take his story and run with it without even asking your own daughter what happened!" Royce bellowed in anger.

"Calm down baby. It's okay," Patrick said as he rubbed his daughter's back.

"I told you not to put that house in her name, but you didn't listen. Now look at what's happening. She's ruining her life, all behind some low life who probably has bunch of kids and nothing going for himself," Sondra fumed.

"It's her damn house Sondra. Why wouldn't I put it in her name?" Patrick questioned, surprising his wife when he raised his voice.

"Look, let's just all calm down and talk like the educated adults that we are. Now, Jax is hurt, but he loves you, Royce. He's willing to forget the past and make your marriage work. He even mentioned something about marriage counseling," Sondra said with a smile.

"Fuck Jaxon and his marriage counseling! I'm done and nothing that he says or does will make me change my mind," Royce noted.

"That's enough! You are not selling your house and you're damn sure not divorcing your husband. You better come to your senses Royce and you better do it quickly," Sondra warned.

"It took me long enough, but I finally did come to my senses. I'm grown, and I'll be damned if I let you continue running my life. The days of you pulling the strings are over. I'm not your puppet," Royce snapped.

"What happened baby? I know that you and Jaxon have had minor problems in the past, but nothing to warrant a divorce," Pat said as he grabbed his daughter's hand and looked at her.

"Our problems have never been minor. I just swept most of them under the rug and overlooked the rest. Jax can't be faithful and that was our biggest problem. He's a liar and a cheater and that will never change."

"You're only going by what other people tell you," Sondra butted in.

"Let her talk Sondra," Patrick said, holding up his hand to prevent his wife from saying anything else.

"He gave me a disease," Royce whispered as she dropped her head in shame.

"He what!" her father shouted as he jumped up from his seat.

"Wh... what kind of disease?" Sondra stuttered, fearing the answer that her daughter was about to give.

"I had to get treated for chlamydia," Royce confessed.

"That dirty muthafucka! He doesn't deserve you, baby. I'm in your corner all the way Royce. Whatever you want to do, you have my full support," Patrick promised.

"Thank you, daddy." Royce smiled through her tears while giving him a hug.

"Are you serious right now Patrick? You're in agreement with her ruining her life?" Sondra asked.

"Exactly how is she ruining her life Sondra? You think I like seeing my daughter unhappy and crying all the time. I let you have your way about everything else, but not this time. Do you know how I feel right now as a father? I walked my baby down the aisle and gave her away to that bastard. He shook my hand and promised to love and cherish her. And how does he do it? By giving her a fucking STD," Patrick snapped angrily.

[150]

"Oh, please Patrick. You act like it was AIDS or something. And how do we know that Jaxon gave it to her. She's the one who admitted to having an affair," Sondra countered, making Royce look at her like she was insane.

"Fuck you!" Royce yelled as she stood to her feet.

"Excuse me," Sondra said, as she too stood up and looked at her only child like she had lost her mind.

"You heard me. Fuck you and the entire Davenport family. Auntie Lydia was right. Jax makes you happier than he's ever made me. I'm your only child and you never even tried to be there for me. From the moment I met and married Jaxon, it became all about you and what you stood to gain. After today, you don't ever have to worry about me again. It wasn't like you ever worried about me anyway. I'll call you later daddy," Royce said as she kissed him and made her way outside to her car.

She didn't shed one tear as she started her car and drove away. She was done crying over every little thing. She finally felt like she had the backbone that Uri always told her that she needed. Speaking of her cousin, Royce dialed her number and listened as the phone rang through her speakers.

"Hey cousin," Uri said when she answered the phone for Royce.

"I just cussed your auntie out," Royce revealed.

"Bitch! Hold on. Don't say nothing else. I need to step out on the porch right quick. I don't want to disturb my kids," Uri said as she fumbled with the phone.

"Nosey ass," Royce laughed.

"What the hell happened?" Uri asked once she was on her porch, free to talk as loud as she wanted to.

"I feel bad for how I talked to her, but I'm fed up," Royce replied as she ran the entire story down to her cousin.

"I know the hell Auntie Sondra didn't say no shit like that," Uri fumed.

"She sure did. Trying to say like I was the one who gave his dirty ass something. Girl, I just lost it after that," Royce said.

"I don't blame you. And I see my uncle was not with the bullshit either," Uri laughed.

It was funny when Royce told her how upset her uncle was about everything. Patrick was the sweetest man that anyone would ever have the pleasure of meeting. Uri couldn't remember a time that he wasn't there for her and Royce and she loved him for it. When she and Royce got married, nothing was too good for them in Patrick's eyes. He paid for everything and even sent them on their dream honeymoon. Uri never worried about who was going to walk her down the aisle because her uncle was her only choice. She had other uncles, but none of them were like Patrick. His love was genuine, and Uri loved that about him. Her mother's brothers always had something negative to say, but that was never the case with him. He even spoiled her kids and they were crazy about him too.

"Girl, I've never seen my daddy that mad before in my life. I'm sure they're probably in there arguing right now," Royce laughed.

"Are you sleeping here tonight?" Uri asked.

"Nope, I'm going by Caleb again," Royce replied.

"Y'all are too damn old for that shit. How his overgrown ass be sneaking you in his mama's house like that? And the funny part is your crazy ass be going," Uri laughed.

"I know. I feel like a teenager all over again. The house is so damn big; I doubt if she'll ever find out," Royce laughed.

She was scared to death when Caleb asked her to stay the night at his parents' house with him. He assured her that they would never know, and he was right. The room that Caleb occupied was downstairs and his parents rarely left the comforts of their bedroom. She had been there three nights in a row and had never run into any problems. Brooklyn's mama was always sweet whenever Royce saw her, but she didn't want to be on her bad side. Brooklyn always told her that Mrs. Pam had no filter and she believed her. Most times, Royce would be gone before anyone ever woke up. Mrs. Pam and her husband both went to work at nine and Royce had to be at the school no later than eight.

"I can't believe y'all made it official and you're still married. This bitch got a boyfriend and a husband on the side," Uri laughed.

"I don't even care. Jax has been having side bitches since before we got married. Forget what anybody has to say," Royce replied.

"I know that's right cousin. Did you talk to his brother about helping you sell the house?" Uri asked.

"Yeah, he said he got me. Him and his father-in-law did a walk through yesterday. They said I shouldn't have a problem selling, especially with a renovated basement," Royce replied.

"What are you gonna do until then? You can't keep sneaking in and out of that lady's house like that," Uri noted.

"I know. I'll probably be back by you in a few days until I figure out a permanent solution. But, I need your help with something else too."

"Okay. What's up?" Uri asked.

"Caleb's birthday is in two weeks and I want to buy him something special. I really appreciate everything that he's been doing for me and I want to show him."

"Uh oh Caleb, he's about to get some of that fire ass head," Uri laughed.

"Bitch, shut up. And how do you know that it's fire? Have I ever sucked your dick?" Royce asked.

"Shut up dummy. You know Tariq was losing his mind over that head game. Nigga was stalking me to get to you," Uri laughed, referring to Royce's ex-boyfriend.

"That nigga was just crazy," Royce noted.

"No bitch, you drove that man crazy. All he cared about was you giving somebody else head. Nigga was talking about cutting out your tongue and shit. That's why Jax dog ass put a ring on it."

"Shut up Uri. Are you gonna help me or not? You know I suck at stuff like that," Royce admitted.

"You know I got you, cousin. Send me a text once you sneak in for the night, so I won't worry," Uri snickered at her own joke.

"Alright, with your goofy ass," Royce said before she hung up with her cousin and dialed Caleb's number.

Chapter 17

"Shanti got that nigga about to cry out here," Caleb teased as he watched Brian dial Shanti's number for the fourth time in a row.

She answered for him the first time and said what she had to say. She was done talking after that and she didn't bother picking up again.

"That shit not even funny bruh. She gon' make a nigga beat her stupid ass up with all these games she keeps playing," Brian fumed.

"Boy, daddy will stomp your stupid ass if you even think about it. Grown ass man and all, you know he don't give a fuck," Caleb noted.

"Her stupid ass is two days overdue and want go to a drag show with Co-Co and Sweets stupid asses. She know she should be at home relaxing and shit," Brian fussed.

"Calm down bruh. She's in good hands," Caleb replied as he passed his brother the blunt that had been in rotation.

"I don't want that shit man," Brian said while angrily waving him off.

"Don't get mad with me because your baby mama would rather be around drag queens than at home with your ass," Caleb laughed.

"Keep talking and watch I tell mama that you be sneaking Royce up in her house every night. Ole childish ass nigga."

"Why you always gotta hit below the belt? Sensitive ass lil boy," Caleb taunted.

"Why don't you just get another apartment, dumb ass?" Brian asked.

"I'm seriously thinking about it man. I really want to be done with renting. I'm trying to buy something. And what the fuck are we still sitting in front of Shanti's house for when you know she ain't home? You got me fucked up if you think I'm sleeping out here in the car with your stalking ass. Brook already told me about that shit," Caleb noted.

"Man, it wasn't even like that. I came over here to make sure her ass was straight, since she kept complaining about her back hurting and shit. Her stubborn ass wouldn't even open the door for me, but I didn't feel right just leaving her like that. What if she would have gone into labor or something?" Brian questioned.

"You full of shit nigga. Just admit that you love the broad and you want to be with her. Ain't nobody trying to judge you for how you feel. Shit, I'm falling in love with a muthafucker who ain't even divorced yet. And if that ain't bad enough, I ain't even get nowhere near the pussy yet," Caleb said, shaking his head.

"Damn," Brian said as he doubled over with laughter.

"You can't help how you feel about somebody though." Caleb shrugged, right as his phone rung and Royce's picture popped up.

"The fuck is you smiling all hard for? Looking all stupid and shit," Brian teased.

"What's up baby?" Caleb said as he answered the phone and tuned his brother out.

Brian was fine with that because he didn't feel like talking anyway. He was stressed, and Shanti wasn't making it any better. Usually when she said that she was done with him, a week was all it took for her to calm down and let him back in. It had been a few weeks since their last argument and she still wasn't fucking with him. He had also found out that it was Cookie, and not Kerry, who had sent her the video of him and Mya behind the strip club that time. He had a feeling that Mya's snake ass was in on it too and that's exactly why he wasn't dealing with her shady ass no more.

His uncle Shaq went there without him one time and one of the other dancers had told him about it. She was heated because Cookie's messy ass used her phone to record and send the video. That was why Shanti didn't recognize the number. Brian was pissed, and Cookie seemed to think it was funny when he confronted her. He was ready to pay somebody to whip her ugly ass and not think twice about it. Bryce told him to leave it alone, but he was having a hard time listening. He couldn't wait until her lease was up at the shop, so she could get the fuck on. When Brian's phone rang displaying Shanti's number, he visibly exhaled, praying that she was on her way home.

"Where you at Ashanti?" Brian asked by way of greeting.

"Meet me at the hospital," Shanti said with an attitude.

"Why? What's wrong?" Brian panicked, as Caleb looked over at him.

"What do you think is wrong dummy? My water broke," Shanti replied.

"You see, this is the shit that I was talking about. You ain't had no damn business going out knowing that you could go into labor at any time. You don't listen man. Just like I told your ass to stop working and you did it anyway," Brian fussed as he pulled off and sped towards the hospital.

"Bye Brian," Shanti said before hanging up.

"What's up bruh?" Caleb asked as he buckled his seat belt. Brian was driving like a mad man and he was shook.

"Shanti's water broke," Brian replied.

"Oh shit. Come meet me at the hospital Royce. I don't have my car and this nigga probably ain't leaving no time soon. Which hospital are we going to?" Caleb asked.

He repeated the information that Brian had given him to Royce and she assured him that she was on her way.

***

About three the following morning, Shanti gave birth to a healthy seven pounds, six-ounce baby girl. Her labor wasn't as bad as she heard it would be, but she was happy that it was over. Brian, Mrs. Pam, and her aunt Karen were there to witness the birth and they were just as excited as she was. Her aunt was a retired social worker and she had already volunteered to babysit. Mrs. Pam swore that the baby was a replica of Brooklyn when she was born, and Brian was ready to sign the birth certificate. Shanti was done playing games with him though. As soon as she got set up in her room, she put in a call to DNA solutions to have them send a representative out as soon as they opened. Both Shanti and Brian were swabbed, along with the baby. She didn't want him to have anything to throw up in her face whenever he got mad.

"Aww, I can't wait to spoil her," Brooklyn said as she looked down at the baby in Brian's arms. They all stayed at the hospital for hours until she was born and they took turns going into the room to see her.

"You and me both," Brian beamed proudly.

"Y'all make a nigga want another one," Dominic said as he looked over at his wife.

"We're done with having kids boo. You got the original, the encore, and the remix," Brooklyn replied, speaking of their three kids.

"What did y'all decide to name her?" Dominic asked.

"Brielle Rene Andrews," Brian answered while looking at Shanti.

He felt a connection with his daughter already, so she had to be his. Now he knew what people meant when they spoke about feeling a special bond between them and their kids. He was experiencing it firsthand.

"That's pretty." Brooklyn smiled.

"Come on baby. We need to get going and let somebody else come in for a little while," Dominic said while grabbing her hand.

"Okay, I'll be back later. And make sure you call me as soon as you get settled in at home Shanti. I'll come over and cook for y'all," Brooklyn said before they left.

"I will and thanks for everything Brooklyn," Shanti replied before they left.

As soon as the door closed, Brian turned to Shanti and said what had been on his mind for the past few days.

"We have to come to some kind of agreement Shanti. I know that we live in two separate houses, but I don't want to miss out on important moments in my daughter's life because of that," Brian stated.

"I understand that Brian, but you know that I would never keep you away. We have to get along, if for no other reason than our child," Shanti replied.

"That's not what I mean Shanti. I want to be there at night to give her a bath and put her to bed. Simple shit like that is what matters most. I don't want to be the kind of father who is only there financially. Why can't we try to work on us while raising our daughter under the same roof?" Brian questioned.

"That's not happening. I tried with you, Brian, more than once. I can't keep letting you bring me through all these emotional changes. And I damn sure don't want you to want me just because we have a child together," Shanti replied.

"I want you because I love you. Don't think for a minute that this is easy for me, Ashanti. At least you've been in relationships before. This is all new to me. You're the first woman that ever made me even want to try. It's not just about us having a baby together," Brian replied as honestly as he knew how.

"Look, I know I can't stay away from you because of Brielle and I won't try. I want us to be the best co-parents that we can be, but that's about all that I can offer you. We can share space at my house and yours for the sake of our daughter, but nothing more."

"So, that's it Shanti? I sat here and poured my heart out to you, only for you to tell me some bullshit about co-parenting," Brian fumed.

"I'm not gonna let you keep breaking my heart Brian. Only a fool walks towards fire and doesn't expect to get burned," Shanti replied.

"I'm done with all that Shanti, I swear. I want us to be a family. Just you, me, and our baby. I know I didn't act like it before, but I really do love you," Brian confessed.

"Love is an action word Brian. Stop telling me and show me," Shanti said, right as someone knocked on the door and opened it.

"Hey boo. How are you feeling?" Royce asked as she and Caleb walked in.

"Hey girl. I'm fine. Just happy that it's over with," Shanti replied.

"Congrats nigga. Looks like everybody got a damn baby but me," Caleb joked as he gave his brother dap.

"You better stop letting Royce play with you and take that shit," Brian joked.

"Shut up Brian. I'm sorry that baby looks like your ugly self. At least she's cute with it," Royce replied.

"You think she looks like me?" Brian asked as he smiled down at his sleeping daughter.

[159]

"More like Brooklyn if anything," Caleb replied.

"You wanna hold her?" Brian asked his brother.

"Nah man. I gotta go shower and change clothes. I smell just like weed. We been sitting up in the lobby all night." Caleb yawned.

"Yeah, I forgot about that. You can take my car if you want to," Brian offered, since Caleb rode there with him.

"I'm good. My baby is bringing me home," Caleb said while making Royce blush.

"Are y'all a couple now or what?" Shanti asked.

"Yes, but I have so much to tell you, girl," Royce replied.

"At least some damn body is a couple," Brian mumbled loud enough for her to hear.

"I know you're probably tired, but make sure you bring your ass back up here later. Don't keep me in suspense," Shanti replied while looking at Royce.

Just like her, Royce didn't have many female friends. Her cousin Uri and Brooklyn were the only people that she really talked to and she had added Shanti to that short list. For a while, Keller had been Shanti's only friend, so she was happy to have other women to spend time with.

"Okay. Do y'all need me to bring any food or anything back?" Royce asked them.

"Yes, please. I can't stand this nasty ass food that they serve here." Shanti frowned.

"Okay, I'll call before I come to see what y'all want," Royce replied.

She and Caleb said their goodbyes and walked out of the room, right as Keller and Tigga were about to enter. Their hands were filled with balloons and gifts, so they spoke and kept going. Royce waited until they got on the elevator to say what was on her mind.

"You need to stop smoking Caleb," she said while looking over at him.

"Where did that come from?" he asked while frowning in confusion.

"Since we've made things official, I don't feel comfortable with you having to sleep with your probation officer just to stay out of jail. If you stop smoking and can pass the drug test, then you won't have to," Royce reasoned with him.

"Damn man," Caleb sighed while running his hand through his waves.

"You know what, fuck it. Just know that I'm done being anybody's fool. If it's good for you, then it'll be good for me too. You can keep fucking her, but don't get mad when I start doing the same," Royce said angrily.

"Girl, you got me all the way fucked up. I ain't even hit the pussy yet and you think you about to give it to the next nigga. And stop talking all that gangsta shit cause you ain't even on it like that. If you want me to stop smoking, then I'll stop," Caleb replied.

"Now see, was that so hard?" Royce asked as she stood on her toes and kissed him.

"Yeah, that shit is hard, but I respect your mind enough to do it. But check it. You can't be making these kinds of demands and ain't letting a nigga hit it. You gotta give me some kind of reward for this shit," Caleb fussed as they got off the elevators and walked out of the building.

"Good things come to those who patiently wait." Royce smiled as she threw him her keys for him to drive.

Chapter 18

"Come on Royce. Stop acting like you a virgin and let a nigga hit it," Caleb begged as he tugged at her pajama bottoms.

"Hell no, Caleb. I'm not fucking you in your mama's house. It's bad enough that I'm sneaking in here with your ass," Royce whispered, even though his parents' room was upstairs.

"Man, this is some bullshit. My birthday is tomorrow and I got blue balls," Caleb fussed.

"You'll be fine. Don't you have to go see your probation officer today," Royce said sarcastically.

"Don't even start with that dumb shit. I might be going my black ass straight to jail too," Caleb replied.

Two weeks had passed since he'd stopped smoking like Royce had asked him to. She had him drinking green tea and all kinds of herbal bullshit to cleanse his system. Caleb wasn't a chronic smoker, and Royce swore that his system should have been nice and clean. He had to fake sick the week before to miss his weekly appointment with Mrs. Lockwood, but she wasn't gonna buy that stomach virus story two weeks in a row. He promised Royce that he wouldn't sleep with the other woman anymore and he was going to honor that promise. He was prepared to take a urine test and he prayed that it worked out in his favor.

"You are not going to jail Caleb. Uri's husband does this all the time and he never has any problems. And he smokes way more than you do," Royce noted.

"You better be right about this Royce. I don't want to be spending my birthday behind bars," Caleb replied.

"You'll be good, I promise," Royce said as she got out of bed and tiptoed to the closet.

"Scary ass," Caleb laughed as he watched her quietly move around the room to get ready for work.

"I just got some new underwear and I can't find them anywhere," Royce mumbled as she searched through her belongings for the three pairs of lace thongs that she'd just purchased a few days before.

"What you telling me for? It's not like I've ever seen them on or off your body," Caleb fussed as he laid around.

He wasn't in a hurry to do anything, but he always walked her out to her car. When he saw that Royce was almost done, he got up and threw on a shirt, preparing to see her off to work. As usual, Caleb peeped out into the hallway before he grabbed Royce's hand and ushered her towards the front door. He had to disable the alarm before he opened the door. They were almost there when they were startled by the living room light being turned on. Royce squealed, as Caleb's heart took a dive in his chest.

"Good morning," Pam said, making them both jump in shock.

"Damn ma. You scared the hell out of me," Caleb replied while holding his chest.

"Yeah, I bet I did," Pam replied.

"Good morning Mrs. Pam," Royce spoke nervously.

"Y'all come on in the kitchen. I made breakfast," Pam said as she turned to walk away.

Caleb didn't want to, but he walked towards the kitchen with Royce following right behind him. He and Royce sat down, as Pam sat a plate of food in front of them both. Royce was happy that she was earlier than she needed to be because she was about to tear into her food. She was nervous, but that didn't stop her appetite.

"I guess I don't have to tell y'all that this is unacceptable because I'm sure y'all already know. I think you're a sweet, beautiful girl Royce, but I also know that you're married. Caleb is a grown man and I can't stop him from dealing with you, but I can't allow it to happen under my roof," Pam said as she looked back and forth between the two them.

"I understand how you feel ma, but she already filed for divorce," Caleb spoke up.

"Filing for divorce and being divorced are not the same Caleb. You know how I feel about these situations. I didn't agree with it when your sister did it and I don't agree with it now," Pam replied.

"I'm sorry Mrs. Pam. I just have a lot going on right now and I didn't feel comfortable staying in the house by myself," Royce admitted.

"I have no problem with you being here if you have nowhere else to go, but you can't shack up with Caleb under my roof. Excuse my language, but ain't nobody fucking in here but me and my husband," Pam said, letting the ratchet side of her surface.

"Trust me, ma, it ain't even like that," Caleb said while looking over at Royce.

"Shut up Caleb. But no, Mrs. Pam, it's not like that. Caleb and I have never been intimate with each other. And I definitely wouldn't have done it in your house," Royce assured her.

"Well, that's good to know. Do you not have anywhere else to go Royce?" Pam asked her.

Caleb was shaking his head telling her to say no, but Royce didn't want to lie. She wasn't homeless and, if things got bad, she still had her own home that she could go to.

"Yeah, I can stay with my cousin," Royce admitted.

"Man!" Caleb yelled as he threw his hands up in the air.

"Shut the hell up Caleb. You know better than to do some shit like this anyway. But, you better hurry up and get you a damn house. Your ass is too old to still be living up under my roof. And got the nerve to be sneaking in company like you pay bills," Pam fussed while Royce laughed.

"How did you even know that she was here? She's been here for over two weeks now," Caleb admitted, as Royce looked at him in shock. She couldn't believe that he was telling his mother how long she had been sleeping over there.

"Don't look so shocked Royce. If y'all are gonna do dirt, y'all need to be more careful," Mrs. Pam said as she threw the Macy's bag containing the lace thongs that Royce had been looking for on the table.

"Oh God," Royce gasped as she dropped her head in shame.

"Yeah, you must have dropped these one night when you snuck in. I know damn well I don't wear them strings up my ass," Pam replied as she stood up and left them in the kitchen.

"Damn man. Even my mama got to see the thongs before me," Caleb said, shaking his head.

"Shut up Caleb. I'm so embarrassed right now. I'll never be able to look your mother in the face again," Royce said as she pushed her empty plate away.

"Stop all the dramatics. This ain't shit to my mama compared to what we've done in the past. She ain't on it like that my baby," Caleb assured here.

"Come walk me out, so I don't be late," Royce said as she got up and walked to the door.

"Why did you tell her that you have somewhere to stay? You could have been over here with me," Caleb said as he disarmed the alarm and walked her to her car.

"I didn't want to lie Caleb. I do have somewhere to stay," Royce replied.

"Man, we gotta get an apartment or something. I'm too old for this shit."

"I thought you wanted to buy a house," Royce reminded him.

"I do, but that takes time Royce. This sleeping in different houses shit is for the birds. We're not kids," Caleb said.

"I know, but we'll figure something out."

"Call me when you get a break. We need to discuss what we're gonna do for my birthday tomorrow," Caleb said as he kissed her.

"Okay. I'll see you later. Call me and let me know how you make out at your probation appointment," Royce replied before she got into her car and pulled off.

She couldn't wait to tell Uri about what had just happened. Her cousin told her that she was going to get busted and her prediction had come true. Royce was laughing to herself, so she knew that Uri was going to fall out.

***

Caleb sat in his car, dreading that he had to go inside the building. He had filled up on green tea before he left home and his bladder was nice and full. He prayed that Royce was right about his urine being clean. He would be spending his born day in jail if it wasn't.

"Fuck it," Caleb sighed as he got out of the car and walked into the building.

He signed in and took a seat, waiting until it was his time to be seen. He smiled when he got an encouraging text message from Royce, but that smile faded the minute the receptionist called his name and led him to the back.

"You can go in Mr. Andrews," she said as she walked away.

Caleb wanted to walk off with her, but he took a deep breath and entered Mrs. Lockwood's office. She was standing behind her desk talking on her phone, but she walked over to the door and put the *do not disturb* sign on the outside before locking it. When she wrapped up her call, she kicked off her heels and started to lift her dress over her head.

"I need a cup," Caleb said, halting her movements.

"Why?" Mrs. Lockwood asked with a frown.

"The fuck you mean why? I'm here to take a drug test, right?" he questioned.

"Really Caleb? Are you sure that this is how you wanna do it?" Mrs. Lockwood asked.

"Man, just give me a cup," Caleb snapped irritably.

"Okay, I'll play your little game. Here you go," Mrs. Lockwood smirked while handing him a cup.

Caleb went into the bathroom inside her office, praying the entire time that things worked out in his favor. He knew without a doubt that she wouldn't send him to jail. Worst case scenario was, he would have to break his promise to Royce and dick her down to avoid it.

"Here," he said when he walked out of the bathroom and shoved the sample cup into her hand.

There were a series of tests that had to be done, in addition to testing for drugs. Caleb stood there and watched as she did them all. It was crazy to him that they tested the temperature on the urine, but Jaden told him why. Apparently, your urine had to be a certain temperature to administer the test or they wouldn't accept it. Jaden used to use Kia's urine all the time and Caleb needed to know how he did it. He didn't think that he could give up smoking altogether, especially since his birthday was the following day. The turn up always included smoking and drinking until he passed out. He just had to come up with a plan to keep Royce happy and stay out of jail at the same time.

[167]

"What brought about this sudden change?" Mrs. Lockwood quizzed as she completed her tasks.

"Just give me my results so I can go," Caleb replied in disgust.

"You're very sure of yourself, huh? I hope these results work out in your favor. I might decide to lock you up and fulfill my sexual needs elsewhere," Mrs. Lockwood teased.

"All that behind some dick. Just get the shit from your husband like other married women do," Caleb huffed.

"Don't flatter yourself honey. I can get dick from anywhere," Mrs. Lockwood snarled.

That was true. She could get sex from any one of her parolees and she did. None of them were packing like Caleb was though. She didn't care that he was never really into it. She knew what to do to get off and she always did. She was looking forward to a release, but he put a damper on her plans. As much as she hoped for the results to be in her favor, it just wasn't in the cards for her that day.

"Can I go now? Judging by the look on your face, I know I'm clean," Caleb beamed.

"What's her name? It must be a woman involved for you to go to this extreme," Mrs. Lockwood said with jealously dripping from her tone.

"Mind your business my baby. I'm out. I'll see you next week." Caleb smiled as he headed for the door.

"No need for the weekly visits anymore. I'll see you next month," Mrs. Lockwood said to his departing back.

Caleb damn near ran to his car with a smile almost as bright as the sun. Royce had come through for him and she was right. Two weeks was all it took for him to cleanse his system and pass his drug test. Since he was seeing Mrs. Lockwood once a month, he would be able to smoke and be clean before he had to see her and be tested again. School was almost out, and he couldn't wait to call Royce to tell her the good news. He was ready to rent a room and celebrate his birthday the right way.

Chapter 19

Royce was drained. Aside from administering her weekly Friday spelling test, she had to break up two fights right outside of her classroom. One of her students took sick with an asthma attack and another one threw up his entire lunch after recess. She had the day from hell and she was ready for it to be over. When the bell sounded, it was like music to her ears, as she ushered her kids out of the classroom and into the hallway to go home. She had a busy weekend ahead of her and she still needed to hit up the mall to get Caleb a gift. Uri had given her some great ideas and she already knew what she was going to get. She was still happy that her cousin was going with her though.

When her phone rang, she frowned when she saw that her mother was calling her yet again. Between Elena and Sondra, Royce didn't know who was bothering her the most. She had been doing great avoiding both women, but she knew that it wouldn't last for long. The only reason why it lasted as long as it did was because they had both been in conferences for weeks, discussing important school business. Royce ignored her call just like always and kept busy by straightening up her classroom. She would usually be walking out right with her students, but she was bound to run into Jax if she did. He had been keeping his distance like Royce told him to, but he was still begging her for his laptop. He'd signed the divorce papers with no problem, but Royce was making him sweat. When her phone rang again, Royce was ready to go off until she saw who it was calling.

"Hey boo." Royce smiled when she answered the phone for Caleb.

"What's up baby? You left work yet?" Caleb asked.

"No, but I'll be leaving in a minute. How did it go?" Royce asked, referring to his appointment.

"I'm not calling you from jail, so you should already know," Caleb replied.

"I told you that it would work. And you didn't have to prostitute yourself to stay out of jail," Royce laughed.

"I see you got jokes today, but I'm happy as hell that everything worked out," Caleb said.

"Me too." Royce smiled.

"Park your car by Uri and I'm coming to get you. I want to go somewhere tonight. I'm trying to spend my entire birthday weekend with you," Caleb said.

"I can't Caleb. I already made plans with Uri for tonight," Royce replied.

"What? You better cancel that shit!" Caleb barked.

"I can't do that Caleb. I already promised her," Royce added.

"Are you being serious right now Royce? You would rather hang with your cousin than spend some alone time with your nigga?" Caleb asked angrily.

"I'm sorry baby, but I'll make it up to you," Royce promised.

"Whatever man. Just call me whenever you make time," Caleb replied, right before he hung up.

Royce laughed because he didn't even give her a chance to reply. He was pissed, but she was sure that he would get over it. Once her classroom was straight, Royce grabbed her purse and prepared to leave. She barely got out of the classroom good enough before she ran right into Elena.

"You're a hard woman to catch up with Mrs. Davenport," Elena said, putting emphasis on her last name.

"Hi Elena. I've been busy," Royce replied.

"Too busy for your mother-in-law?" Elena asked as she gave Royce air kisses to both cheeks.

"What is it that you need Elena?" Royce asked, trying her best to remain professional and polite.

The video of her walking in on Angelique and Jax replayed in her head, and Royce got disgusted all over again. She didn't expect Elena to tell on her son, but she wasn't gonna pretend like it was all good either. The sweet, docile Royce was gone, and she had no problem letting everyone know that. Elena was just as foul as her son and husband were, if not more.

"Sondra and I have been talking and we've decided to have a long overdue family meeting. It's been called to my attention that you and my son have been having some marital issues. I didn't think it was that serious until my husband informed me about your transfer request," Elena pointed out.

"Yeah, and speaking of my transfer, when am I gonna be moved?" Royce asked.

"I really don't think that's the answer Royce. You and Jaxon need to see a counselor. Maybe take a vacation to rekindle the spark in your marriage," Elena suggested.

"That flame flickered out a long time ago. I'm not sure if you're aware Elena, but I've already filed for divorce," Royce said, making her briefly stop her stride.

"What?" Elena questioned as she looked at her through narrowed eyes.

"Yes, and Jaxon has already signed the papers," Royce revealed.

"Why would he do that when he doesn't want a divorce?" Elena asked.

"He didn't have a choice. You think I would stay with his ass after all that he's put me through? He didn't even have enough respect to keep the shit away from me. Fucking in the school's bathroom when I was right downstairs in my classroom."

"Who told you that? How do you know that it's even true?" Elena questioned.

"I know for a fact that it's true and so do you. After all, you walked in and caught them in the act," Royce said, making all the color drain from Elena's face.

"I was just trying to do the right thing Royce. Angelique was the problem, so I got rid of her. I didn't want you and Jaxon to separate behind a stupid mistake," Elena tried to reason.

"The only mistake made here was me marrying your son. There is no hope for us and there never will be. We don't even live under the same roof anymore," Royce informed her.

"Where is he living then?" Elena asked.

"You'll have to ask him that." Royce shrugged as they made it outside in front of the building.

She wanted to scream when she saw that Jax was still standing out front. He usually left right after school was out and headed straight for the gym. He looked as if he'd seen a ghost when he saw Royce and his mother walking out of the building together.

"I need to see you in my office Jaxon. Now!" Elena commanded as she turned on her heels and walked away.

Jax and Royce made eye contact, and she smirked at the stupid looking expression on his face. There was no doubt in his mind that Royce had told his mother everything and he was sure that's why she wanted to see him. Royce walked away with her head held high and went to her car. She paused when she got closer and saw a woman standing there crying. It took her a minute to recognize who it was, but that explained why Jax was lingering around after hours. Royce wanted to get into her car and pull off, but her conscience just wouldn't let her. She had to be a fool to sympathize with a woman who was sleeping with her husband, but she had a heart if nothing else.

"Are you okay?" she asked while handing Angelique a pack of Kleenex.

"I'm fine, thanks," Angelique replied, shocking Royce with how nice she was being.

Angelique seemed to always have an attitude with her, so it was a welcomed change.

"Let me guess; Jaxon, right?" Royce said, making her snap her head up in shock.

"No. Why would your husband have anything to do with what's wrong with me?" Angelique asked.

There was no way in hell that she could tell Royce that she was there to confront her husband because he gave her a disease. That was just too embarrassing, especially when she was still denying messing with him at all.

"You can kill the act sweetie. Everybody in the school knew that you and Jax were fucking, including me. You're one of the reasons why I'm divorcing his ass," Royce answered.

"Divorce?" Angelique questioned in shock.

"Yes, and it's been a long time coming," Royce acknowledged.

"You're way too good to be married to his dog ass anyway," Angelique said, deciding to stop fronting.

[172]

She was wrong for her hostile attitude towards Royce. After all, she was messing with her husband. She had no right to dislike Royce because she had developed feelings for Jaxon.

"You ain't telling me nothing that I don't already know," Royce countered.

"I owe you an apology too, Royce. You didn't deserve my attitude and I'm sorry," Angelique said humbly.

"It's all good Angelique. I already knew what the problem was. It's sad that fucking him caused you your job though. It wasn't even worth it."

"His bitch of a mother made that decision. Never mind her son, who was just as guilty as I was," Angelique spewed angrily.

"And you let it go down like that?" Royce asked with raised brows.

"It's not like I can get my job back. What was I supposed to do?" Angelique asked.

"You might not get your job back here, but you can be placed at another school. She could have just transferred you instead of having you fired, with her evil ass."

"Well, it's too late for all that now," Angelique shrugged.

"It's never too late boo. Put your number in my phone," Royce said as she handed Angelique her iPhone.

"Why would you want to help me when I just admitted to sleeping with your husband?" Angelique questioned skeptically.

"Girl bye. Jax sleeps with everybody. This ain't about you though. They need to know that just because their last name is Davenport, it doesn't make them untouchable."

"It seems like they are," Angelique replied.

"Honestly, she did have grounds to fire you, but her son should have been fired too. Don't let them get away with that shit. I'm sure you need your job just as much as he needs his," Royce said.

Angelique nodded in agreement as she grabbed Royce's phone and saved her number to her contacts before giving it back. Royce called her phone so that she would have her number as well.

"I'll be in touch," Royce said right before she turned and walked away.

She had more important things to worry about, but she was going to be in touch with Angelique sooner than she thought.

***

"What was I supposed to do mother? I can't make her stay married to me," Jax said as he sat in his mother's office. Thankfully, Sondra was already gone for the day.

"Did you even try to fight for your marriage Jaxon?" Elena asked angrily.

"Of course, I did, but she's not trying to hear me. Sondra has even tried to reason with her, but she's being stubborn," Jax replied.

"You signed the damn papers Jaxon. I guess we would have found out once the divorce was final," Elena said as she paced back and forth.

"That doesn't mean anything. We can stop it at any time, as soon as Royce comes to her senses," Jax noted.

"And why did you tell her about me catching you in the bathroom with Angelique? That was just stupid," Elena said, making him snap his head up in her direction.

He would have never done something so stupid and his mother should have known that too. He could never tell her how Royce found out though. That would mean that he had to admit to the videos that were on his computer. That wasn't happening.

"I didn't say anything. Maybe Angelique told her," Jax lied.

"What did you do Jaxon? What made her go to this extreme?" Elena questioned.

"I didn't do anything. She's the one who's cheating on me!" Jax yelled.

"And you expect me to believe that shit. You're a liar and a cheater and you always have been. Something happened to make her file for divorce, but I don't expect you to be honest about it. And exactly where are you living at now?" Elena questioned.

"I'm looking for an apartment," Jax answered.

"That's not what I asked you." Elena frowned.

"I've been staying with Sienna and my kids," Jax said while dropping his head.

[174]

"Oh God. It's even worse than I thought. First a divorce and now this. Your father is going to be livid," Elena said as she resumed her pace.

"I don't know why. People get divorced every day," Jaxon replied.

"That's not the point Jaxon. We have a lot of important events coming up that the entire family, including Royce, needs to attend. Your father is more than likely going to be named Zulu king for next year and there are a lot of functions involved with that as well. We need everything in our family to appear as perfect as possible," Elena noted.

"Appear is right because there's nothing perfect about it," Jax flippantly replied.

"Excuse me?" Elena questioned as she turned to face him.

"Nothing. Just forget it," Jax said, waving her off.

"No Jaxon. Say what's on your mind. You obviously have a lot to say," Elena pressed.

"Why didn't you leave?" Jax asked, taking his mother by surprise.

"What?" Elena mumbled.

"For years, I blamed my father to the point of hating him, but you're just as much to blame as he is. All the years of mental and physical abuse that we endured while you just sat back and watched. We needed you, ma. We needed you to be strong for us, but you couldn't even find the strength to help yourself," Jax replied.

"You don't know what you're talking about so just shut up. How do you think you were able to get a good education and great paying job? Your father might be a little old fashioned in his thinking, but he's always been a great provider for us. We've always had the best of everything and we never went without."

"But, at what cost ma? I might have been young, but I remember everything. I remember the times that he didn't come home, and you cried yourself to sleep. He was pissed about me having sex in the school, but he had half the teachers on the payroll when he used to be the principal. You talk about me disrespecting Royce, but you worked at the school when he did it too. At least Royce could stand up to me without the fear of retribution. I remember the times that you questioned him about things and were knocked unconscious because of it. We were kids and had to help our

[175]

mother nurse the black eyes and busted lips that our father gave her. There is nothing normal about a woman in her sixties being made to kneel in the corner like a child. What's so perfect about us?" Jax questioned.

"I don't expect you to understand Jaxon. Your father comes from a very powerful family. Things aren't always as easy as it seems. We lived a great life and I made sure of that. You need to worry more about getting your wife back and less about the past. I can only imagine what you did to make her leave you."

"I gave Royce chlamydia. You know, the same STD that my father gave to you a few years ago. That's why she left me. As much as it pains me to lose my wife, I don't blame her for loving herself more than she loved me. Not too many women can say that, including you," Jax said.

"Get out!" Elena yelled as tears poured from her eyes.

She knew without a doubt that her family was far from perfect, but she didn't appreciate her son holding a mirror in front of her face. They were flawed, as were many other families. They just did a great job of hiding it from the outside world. The only reason that Jaxon knew of her medical mishap was because he walked down on her and his father arguing about it. Silas was a man and he did what most men did; he cheated. Still, Elena would never dream of leaving him for any reason. He was the reason behind her success as a principal and she would never forget that.

"You're so quick to call me a liar and a cheater, but I am my father's son," Jax said as he walked out of her office and slammed the door behind him.

He knew without a doubt that he was about to feel his father's wrath and, for the first time ever, he really didn't give a fuck.

Chapter 20

"Happy Birthday nigga," Brian said when he walked into the kitchen of his mother's home.

He gave Caleb a one-armed hug before joining him at the kitchen table. He and Shanti were bringing the baby over to see his parents, but he didn't expect to see his brother there. Caleb usually turned up hard for his birthday and he just knew that he and Royce were going to be gone somewhere.

"Thanks man. I hear you got a reason to celebrate too," Caleb said, speaking of the paternity results that Brian had gotten back a few days after Brielle's birth.

"Yeah man. You just don't know how happy I was to see that shit. Honestly, I felt the connection the minute I held her," Brian replied.

"That's what's up. But, what's the deal with you and Shanti?" Caleb asked.

"Ain't shit up with us. I've been by her house since her and Bri came home, but she ain't fucking with a nigga like that. I'm trying, but she ain't trying to hear it," Brian admitted.

"She gon' come around eventually. Shit just takes time," Brian said.

"Yeah, I know, but she got to leave my mistakes in the past. We can't move forward if she keeps bringing up old shit."

"The shit ain't that old though, bruh. You fucked up a few weeks before she had the baby. Y'all work together and be up under the same roof. It's almost impossible for y'all not to work it out," Caleb said as he checked his phone again.

He hadn't heard from Royce since she told him that she had made plans with Uri the day before. She sent him a happy birthday message, but it wasn't the same as calling. Caleb was in his feelings and he couldn't wait to tell her about herself.

"I hope you're right about that. But, what's up with you? I'm surprised your ass is home. The turn up usually be real for your birthday," Brian laughed.

"Yeah, I know, but Royce is on some bullshit. I'm really wondering if I made a mistake by fucking with her so soon," Caleb replied.

"Damn bruh. What happened like that?" Brian questioned.

"She just been on some other shit since she left here yesterday. I wanted to rent a room and lay up all weekend, but she told me some bullshit about going somewhere with her cousin." Brian frowned.

"What kind of shit is she on? How you turn your nigga down for your cousin?" Brian questioned.

"That's what the fuck I'm trying to figure out. Maybe I should have let her figure out her divorce and all that other shit before we jumped into a relationship."

"You think she still fucking with her husband?" Brian asked.

"Nah, I think she's done with that clown. I really don't know what's up with her, but I'm good on this relationship shit. I don't do the games. I'm too old for that dumb shit," Caleb replied.

"I like Royce ole lame ass though. I hope y'all can figure it out and make it work," Brian said.

"Man, forget all that. Let me go hold my lil niece. The way shit looking for me, my nieces and nephews might be the only kids I ever have." Caleb shrugged as he got up and walked into the living room where Shanti and his parents sat.

Holding Brielle turned out to be boring as hell because all she did was sleep. Brian and Shanti chilled over there for hours and Caleb hadn't heard from Royce once. Caleb was done playing games with her though. He was just about to hit up one of his old flings to go chill when Brian suggested going out for drinks. Pam wasn't ready for the baby to go, so Shanti agreed to stay there until they returned. It was even better when Brian hit Jaden up and he agreed to roll with them. Business was slow at the shop and he really wasn't doing anything.

"The fuck is you looking all sad and shit for? It's your birthday nigga. It's time to pour up," Jaden said to Caleb as soon as he got into the car.

"I hate to see a grown ass man cry, especially on his birthday. I had to do something to cheer this nigga up. Royce hurt my bro's feelings," Brian joked, trying to lighten the mood.

"I'm straight nigga. She showed me what it is and I'm good on her." Caleb shrugged like it was no big deal.

"That's fucked up though, bruh. How you do a nigga dirty on his born day?" Jaden questioned.

Brian was about to reply until his phone rang, displaying Shanti's number.

"What's up?" Brian asked when he pressed the talk feature on his steering wheel.

"Am I on the speaker?" Shanti asked, making Brian look at his brothers.

"Nah. What's up?" Brian questioned, hoping that Shanti wasn't about to say something to embarrass him. He was always getting fussed at and he didn't need his brothers clowning him.

"Is Caleb around you?" Shanti asked.

Jaden was shaking his head telling Brian to say no, but there was no need for the coaching.

"No Ashanti. He's in the bar. I stepped outside to answer your call. What's up?" Brian asked again, more impatiently than before.

"I need you to come get me and bring me to my car," Shanti replied.

"For what? What kind of shit are you on Shanti?" Brian asked with a frown.

"Don't say shit Brian, but something is up with Royce. She's at a hotel and she asked me to bring her some money. She said she didn't want to call Uri or Caleb because they would be mad with her," Shanti replied, making Caleb's blood boil.

"What hotel?" Brian asked.

"I'm not telling you shit. You're only gonna repeat whatever I say to Caleb. Can you just come get me please?" Shanti begged.

"That don't make sense Ashanti. I'm already out here. It's crazy for me to come get you and bring you home

[179]

to get your car. I can go bring her a few dollars," Brian offered.

"No Brian. She doesn't want Caleb to know. Didn't I just say that?" Shanti asked.

"The fuck is she doing at a hotel anyway? She probably in there with her husband. Ole sneaky ass," Brian fumed.

"As if you have room to talk," Shanti snapped.

"Look, just give me the info. I'll make up some shit to tell my brothers."

"Promise me that you won't say anything Brian. You're always begging me to trust you, so this is your chance to show and prove," Shanti said.

"Yeah," Brian replied in disgust.

"Yeah what?" Shanti asked, wanting him to say it.

"I promise I won't say shit," Brian said, knowing that he was lying.

"Okay, I'll tell her that you're coming," Shanti said as she told him what hotel Royce was staying in and gave him the room number.

Caleb didn't even have to tell Brian to take him over there because he made a U-turn in the middle of the street and headed in that direction.

"I swear I wish I had my gun on me," Caleb fumed, as Brian sped to their destination.

"You know I got you covered bruh," Jaden replied as he handed him the gun that he'd just removed from his waistband.

"Nigga bout to be an accessory to murder out here," Brian said, shaking his head.

"Ain't nobody worth me doing football numbers in jail. I might beat the nigga down, but he'll live. He can have her ass though. It ain't even that real with me," Caleb replied.

"Man, I thought Royce was one of the real ones too. I was just telling Kia how I thought she was good for you. Looks are deceiving like a muthafucka," Jaden fussed.

"Fuck it. At least I can say that I tried." Caleb shrugged.

"Got me working hard trying to sell her house and she trying to play my damn brother. I'm pulling out of that shit," Jaden fumed, as Brian pulled up to the hotel.

Caleb looked around and got pissed when he spotted Royce's car among the others in the parking lot.

"Aye Jaden. Ain't that the lil nigga who Jaylynn be talking to?" Brian asked when he saw Hayden walking up to the front door.

"Yeah, that's his ass. See what I'm saying bruh? That's exactly why I didn't want Jay fucking with his ass. I told Kia I wasn't trying to hear that dating bullshit. Now, she's hanging out with her friends and this nigga is laid up in a room with somebody else's daughter," Jaden fussed as they got out of the car.

Hayden looked right in their direction and seemed to move faster than he was before.

"At least the nigga ain't play her cheap. These bitches are nice on the inside. Me and Shanti used to get rooms over here all the time," Brian said.

"Shut the fuck up nigga," Caleb snapped angrily as he led the pack into the hotel's lobby.

Jaden looked around to see if he could spot Hayden, but he was nowhere to be found. He couldn't wait to tell Kia what he had seen. She was so adamant about letting Jaylynn date him and he had just proved Jaden's point about him being too advanced for her.

"This way bruh. The elevators are over here," Brian instructed.

He knew that Shanti would be pissed, but he would just deal with that later. There was no way in hell he was going to knowingly let somebody play his brother for a fool. He could tell that Caleb was really feeling Royce, but all of that was about to come to an end. Sadly, it was happening on his birthday of all days.

"Handle your business nigga. You know we got your back," Jaden said when they arrived at the room.

"No doubt," Brian agreed as he stood right next to his brothers.

Caleb nodded and proceeded to knock on the door with the butt of the gun. He was enraged and there was no telling what he would do to the nigga who Royce was in there with.

"Who is it?" Royce asked from the other side of the door.

"Open this bitch up and see," Caleb snapped.

"Caleb?" Royce questioned.

"Don't make me kick this bitch down. Open the muthafucking door!" Caleb barked angrily.

[181]

"The fuck is taking her so long? She might be trying to hide the nigga," Brian instigated.

"Don't worry, we gon' check this bitch from top to bottom," Jaden noted.

When Caleb banged on the door again, they heard movement on the other side. A few seconds later, Royce swung the door open. All three men rushed inside and stopped as soon as they did.

"Happy birthday baby." Royce smiled, as Caleb stood there in awe.

The entire suite was decorated in red and black, including the comforter set that Royce had purchased. Balloons floated all over the ceiling and a heart made of rose petals adorned the bed. Two champagne glasses rested next to a bottle of limited edition Dom Perignon. Massage oils and chocolate covered strawberries rested on a tray and more chocolate treats sat on a nearby table. Small heart-shaped candles illuminated the room, while soft music played in the background.

"I told you, bitch. I should have recorded their asses," Uri said as she laughed at the expression on their faces.

"What kind of games are y'all playing?" Jaden questioned.

"Shanti know your ass like a book. You did exactly what she said you would do," Uri laughed while looking at Brian.

"Man, y'all play too much. Got my dude ready to put his murder game down. Wait til I see Shanti ass," Brian fussed.

"I'm happy this shit is over with. This was the hardest thing that I ever had to pull off. I'm going home. Call me tomorrow cousin," Uri said as she grabbed her purse and left.

"Have fun boy. We out," Jaden laughed as he and Brian walked out with Uri.

"Girl, I was about to act a fool on your ass up in here. Had me ready to break up with you and everything," Caleb said as he pulled Royce close and wrapped his arms around her.

"I'm sorry for ignoring you, baby, but now you see why I had to. I just wanted to give you a nice gift and take you out to dinner, but Uri wasn't having it. She went overboard as usual," Royce replied.

"I'm happy as hell that she did," Caleb said as he let her go and looked around. His face lit up when he saw three rolled blunts sitting on the tray. He looked over at Royce in shock, but she couldn't take the credit.

"Uri did that. You know I don't know how. She does it for her husband all the time," Royce replied.

"That's what's up," Caleb said, nodding his head in approval.

"So, about your birthday gift," Royce cooed seductively.

"I thought this was my birthday gift," Caleb replied as he turned around to face her.

He never noticed the floor-length black silk robe that adorned her frame. When she untied the belt, his mouth fell open as the robe fell from her body and hit the floor. Caleb smiled in appreciation at the royal blue thong and bra set that Royce had underneath. She was more toned than she appeared to be when she was dressed, and he loved her defined curves.

"I told you to be patient. Now, it's time for your reward." Royce smiled as she pulled him to her by his shirt for a kiss.

Caleb was a little surprised at her forwardness, but he let her do her thing. He tried to lift his shirt over his head, but Royce slapped his hand. She wanted to do it all, so he stood still while she took her time and undressed him from head to toe. The good girl had been replaced with a sexy vixen and Caleb loved seeing that side of her. When Royce pushed him back on the sofa and kneeled, Caleb smirked, wondering what she was doing. Royce was so prim and proper' he couldn't imagine her really knowing how to give head. It was the thought that counted, so he wasn't going to make her feel bad if it was garbage. When she grabbed his dick and started stroking it, Caleb decided to mess with her.

"What you trying to do with that?" he asked with a smile.

Royce loved to show and prove, so she didn't even bother answering him. She wasn't skilled at everything in the bedroom, but she was a pro when it came to oral. Some things just came naturally and, for her, that was one of them. Caleb thought it was a game until she took him into her mouth and made him disappear down her throat.

"Fuck!" he yelped in both pleasure and shock.

He watched in amazement as Royce worked him in and out of her mouth like a certified professional. Saliva dripped all over his shaft, as she massaged up and down while using her mouth like a suction cup. His hands massaged her scalp as he thrusted his hips upwards. A look of bliss covered his face as he groaned in satisfaction. He was surprised when he looked down at her and found her staring right back at him. She seemed nothing like the shy Royce that she was when they first met. She was in her element and there was nothing amateur about her oral skills.

"Shit Royce. Ease up a minute," Caleb begged as her warm mouth continued to engulf him.

He was losing it and he hadn't even hit it yet. The sensation from Royce sucking and massaging him at the same time was just too much to bear.

"Oh shit. Raise up Royce," Caleb begged when he felt his release building up.

Royce ignored him as she sucked harder than she was before. Caleb grabbed on to the sofa cushions for support as he felt himself hitting the back of Royce's throat. He had to admit that he sounded like a bitch with all that screaming, but he didn't give a damn. Royce had him feeling like his soul had departed from his body as he came, and she kept sucking like it was nothing. Caleb wanted to push her away, but he was too weak to move after that. Royce didn't seem to care that he unloaded in her mouth. She just kept sucking him up until he was hard again.

"Are you enjoying your birthday so far?" she asked as she stood up and stripped out of her lingerie.

"The best one yet," Caleb admitted as he watched her walked away to grab a condom.

"I aim to please." Royce smiled while walking back over to him.

He was wowed once again when Royce put the condom in her mouth and used her tongue to roll it onto his erection. When she straddled him, Caleb grabbed her hips and slowly entered her. They both moaned at the invasion, but he quickly took control after that.

"Oh shit! Ahh!" Royce screamed, as Caleb rapidly bounced her up and down his length.

He leaned down and took one of her nipples into his mouth and softly bit down on it. Royce was soaking wet and it felt like her juices were pouring from her body. Good was too weak of a word to describe how she was feeling. As Caleb pounded into her, all the troubles in her life seemed to fade into the background She didn't care about her failed marriage or anything else. All she wanted was for him to keep doing what he was doing. When he stopped, Royce's eyes popped open to see why. He lifted her up, allowing their connection to be temporarily broken. Caleb picked her up as if she weighed nothing and walked her over to the bed.

"Caleb!" Royce squealed, as he threw her on the bed.

Her body landed on the rose petals, making them scatter everywhere. She didn't have a chance to get comfortable before Caleb grabbed her legs and pulled her to the edge of the bed. Royce prepared for his reentry, but he had other plans. Her back arched and her legs spread wider when she felt the first flick of Caleb's tongue at her opening.

"We need our own damn house for real now," Caleb said in between licks.

"Okay baby," Royce replied, willing to agree to anything at that point.

It was Caleb's birthday, but he made it his business to please her just as much as she pleased him. He and Royce didn't get much sleep that night, but neither one of them were complaining. She only had the room for one night, but Caleb wanted it extended for the entire week. He swore that he was going to the front desk to make it happen as soon as he rested up for a while.

***

"What the hell are you calling me for? Don't you have a fine ass man and a hotel room to enjoy?" Uri asked when she answered the phone for Royce the next morning.

"I'm not in the room. I left to go get us some breakfast. I'm on my way back there now," Royce replied.

"How was it?" Uri questioned.

"Bitch, it was everything. That nigga is paying for us to stay there the entire week." Royce smiled.

"I know you lying," Uri laughed.

"Nope and he wants us to go apartment hunting too," Royce replied.

"Jax can hang it up for real now. Caleb is that nigga!" Uri yelled, right as Royce pulled up to the hotel. She was about to reply, but something else got her attention.

"Girl, I must be seeing things," Royce replied.

"Why? What happened?" Uri questioned.

"I thought I saw Jaden and Kia's daughter getting in a car just now. It looked like her, but I'm not sure. She was moving too fast," Royce said.

"Nah, that can't be her. That nigga Jaden is nuts. I can see that and I haven't even known him long," Uri noted.

"Yeah, you're right about that." Royce shrugged as she grabbed their food and got out of the car. It wasn't her business and she didn't want to cause any confusion.

She laughed when she walked into the lobby and saw Caleb standing there talking to the receptionist. She ended her call with Uri and walked over to him.

"I was just about to call and see where you went," he said, as she grabbed the bags from Royce's hands and gave her a kiss.

"I had to feed you." Royce smiled.

"You fed me a lot last night and this morning," Caleb said with a wink.

"Freak," Royce laughed.

"I just paid for another week," Caleb informed her.

"I can't believe that you were serious about that," Royce laughed.

"You damn right I was serious. I'm too grown for all that dumb shit. You need to get on finding us an apartment," Caleb replied.

"I just have so much on my plate right now Caleb," Royce sighed as they headed back up to the room.

"I know you do baby. I'm not trying to stress you out or nothing. Just handle your business and I'll work on everything else," Caleb offered.

"I just don't think it's a good idea for me to have anything in my name right now while I'm still married," Royce said, right as her phone rang.

"Take your call and we'll talk when you're done," Caleb said before he walked into the room.

"I thought I said that I'll be in touch with you," Royce said when she answered the phone for Angelique.

"I know and I'm sorry. I just ran across some text messages and stuff on my phone that I thought might be useful to you with this thing with Jax," Angelique replied.

"None of it is gonna be useful to me but, hopefully, it will help you to get your job back. I'll tell you what to do and the rest is up to you," Royce replied.

"Okay, I'm ready. I'll do whatever I have to do to keep a roof over my head," Angelique said eagerly.

Royce was sorry that she'd agreed to help but, the sooner she got Angelique off the phone, the better. She wanted to spend time with Caleb with no interruptions, so she gave Angelique all the information that she needed. Silas might have been a big deal at the school board office, but there were a few people even higher than he was. He kept a lot of things from his colleagues and handled it himself. Angelique just had to get the info into the right hands and Royce had everything she needed to do so.

Chapter 21

"I'm outside baby," Caleb said when Royce answered the phone.

He was there to take her to lunch, and she was starving. She was back at Uri's house, but Caleb had rented them another room the night before. She was still sleepy from being up all night and she didn't have time to eat breakfast.

"Okay, give me a minute to get these kids to the playground and I'll be there," Royce replied before they disconnected.

Two weeks had passed since his birthday and he couldn't seem to get enough of Royce. She had a good heart and kind spirit; traits that were hard to come by. Caleb could just see himself spoiling her, but he wanted her all to himself first. The fact that she was still married to Jax was stopping her from moving how she wanted to. After spending a week in the hotel, Caleb made good on his promise to get another apartment. He found a nice one and had just come back from paying his deposit. Royce didn't want her name on the lease because she didn't want anything to come back on her during the divorce.

Jaden had made an offer for the house that Caleb wanted, and he was almost sure that he was going to get it. Even if he did, there was a lot of work that needed to be done before he could move in. The house was a double that Caleb planned to convert into one big single-family home. There were two bedrooms on each side, which would give him four bedrooms and two baths with lots of living space. Caleb wasn't trying to overwhelm her, so he didn't even tell Royce anything about it. He was really feeling her, but he would understand if she wasn't ready to move in with him so soon after being divorced. He wasn't even pressuring her to move into his apartment. If she just wanted to spend a few nights sometimes, he would be cool with that too.

"Am I missing something? Do you have kids, or do I need to get the police involved? I hope Sienna didn't have a pedophile around my kids," Jax said when he walked up and saw Caleb standing there.

"Just because I don't want these kids to witness you getting your ass beat, I'll let that comment fly," Caleb said as he turned around to face him.

He was so deep in thought that he didn't even see the other man walking up on him. Jax was in a foul mood after just having a meeting with his father and some other top school board officials, but he couldn't pass up on an opportunity to mess with his one-time rival.

"I'm just double checking. A grown man having relations with kids is against the law," Jax chuckled, right as he spotted Royce walking out of the building.

She looked good in her pin striped skirt and matching button-down ruffled shirt. The strappy heels that she wore made her legs look even more toned than they were. Jax wanted to pull her into a hug, but she probably would have swung on him if he did. He missed having their daily lunch dates and he was regretting not doing right by her when he should have. It was like he no longer existed to Royce. She ignored him whenever she saw him, and she dared him to speak to her. Rumors were circulating around the school about their split and that drove both their mothers crazy. Royce was still holding his computer hostage, so she had him by the balls.

"Nah dude. My girl is all woman." Caleb smiled, as Royce walked over to them.

"Hey baby. Let's go, I'm starving," Royce said as she kissed his lips.

"The fuck," Jax mumbled as he watched them walk away holding hands like the perfect couple.

He didn't even know that Royce and Caleb knew each other, but he was curious as to how they did. After seeing them drive off together, Jax grabbed his phone from his pocket and called Sienna.

"Yeah," Sienna answered the phone sounding disgusted.

Having Jax back under the same roof with her and their kids was not what she thought it would be. Sienna thought that she was getting her family back, but Jax wasn't interested in that. She was nothing more than a housekeeper, cook, punching bag, and sex object to him. He didn't even sleep in the same bed with her. That's if he decided to sleep there at all. She was over it and ready for him to go. She didn't care about being back with him anymore, since nothing about him had changed. Sienna was taking steps to better herself, which was why she was trying to enroll in school again. She had been looking for a better job and she'd had a few interviews lined up. Things in her life were looking up, except for her situation with Jaxon. She wanted him out of her house and she didn't care that it belonged to his parents.

"You ever told your ex-boyfriend anything about my wife?" Jax asked, getting right to the point.

"What ex-boyfriend?" Sienna questioned with a frown.

"That nigga Caleb," Jax replied.

"No. Why would I tell Caleb anything about Royce?" she asked in confusion.

"I don't know, but I'm trying to see how the hell my wife and your ex nigga are together now. That shit don't even sound right to me," Jax fumed as he paced the sidewalk.

"Royce ole stuck up ass ain't even Caleb's type," Sienna snapped irritably.

"She must be his type. I just watched her walk up to the nigga and kiss him on the lips. Then, she got in the car with him and left."

"You sure sound like you're mad, even though you and Royce are no longer together," Sienna noted.

"I'm not mad, I'm pissed. I already got enough on my plate as it is. I can't have people seeing my wife on the arm of another man. Nobody even knows that we're getting a divorce. People are already talking and shit is about to get worse," Jax fumed.

"How long did you think you would be able to keep up that charade Jax? Y'all work together and don't even speak. People were bound to have questions sooner or later," Sienna replied.

"Yeah, but her parading another man around the school is not a good look. I don't know why they didn't just transfer her when she asked them to."

[191]

"Because your father is an asshole who loves to throw his position around," Sienna replied.

"I hope he's not holding out on hope of us getting back together. She's done and she made that clear when she put me out. I've never seen her more serious about anything in my life," Jax said.

"I thought you said you left her," Sienna said, catching him in an obvious lie.

"Bye Sienna!" Jax yelled before hanging up in her face.

He had enough to deal with and he wasn't trying to let her add to the stress that he was already feeling. He'd already had a hearing at the school board office that morning that didn't work out in his favor. Angelique had more heart than he gave her credit for. She was done threatening him and she made good on her promises. Jax was shocked when his father told him about the complaint that she had filed against him and his mother. She was threatening to sue the school board for wrongful termination and they immediately held a hearing. After all the smoke cleared, Angelique was rehired to work at another school and Jax was written up for the part that he played in everything. His father was livid, and he made sure to tell him so. As usual, Jax, the black sheep of the family, had managed to embarrass him once again. Elena was verbally reprimanded too and Jax hated to see what was going to happen to her once she got home.

***

"Hello," Royce said when she answered the phone for Angelique.

She was ready to be done with her and the entire situation with Jax. Royce hated to be annoyed, but that was her own fault. She should have never even entertained Angelique in the first place. She had an affair with a married man and she was paying for it. Royce just didn't like the fact that Jax didn't have the same consequences as she did.

"I got my job back!" Angelique yelled excitedly.

"Really? That's great," Royce said, happy that she wouldn't have to call her anymore.

"Yeah, well, not at the same school, but at least I'm working again," Angelique replied.

"I'm happy for you, Angelique, but I have to go. I'm having lunch with my boyfriend and it's rude for me to be on the phone," Royce noted.

"Oh, sorry Royce. I just called to tell you the good news and to thank you for your help," Angelique said.

"No problem Angelique. I'm happy that everything worked out for you," Royce said before she disconnected.

"You're better than me, baby. I wouldn't have helped her ass with nothing. Bitch keeps calling you like she wasn't fucking your husband." Caleb frowned.

"I keep telling you that it wasn't about her. Jax does shit because he always gets away with it. He needed to be reprimanded, right along with her. And stop throwing stones Caleb. You're sleeping with somebody else's wife too. I'm not divorced yet you know," Royce reminded him.

"That's different though, Royce. You and ole boy were still together when they were messing around," Caleb said.

"That's no excuse Caleb. The fact remains that I'm still married, and we started messing around before Jax and I split up. There's no justifying that and I'm not trying to. It is what it is. I'm happy and that's all that matters."

"You better be happy." Caleb smiled.

"So, what's going on with the apartment?" Royce asked, since he never mentioned it.

"I signed a six-month lease and paid the first three months of the rent," Caleb replied as he ate.

"When were you gonna tell me?" Royce asked.

"I'm telling you now," he replied.

"You know what I mean Caleb," Royce countered.

"I know you got a lot going on right now and I'm not trying to overwhelm you. I'm not trying to move too fast for you. I won't be mad if you decide not to move in. My door is always open, so you can come and go as you please," Caleb offered.

"Did I tell you that I didn't want to move in with you, Caleb?" Royce questioned.

"No but..." he started.

"No buts Caleb. I've had enough of people thinking and talking for me. I can speak for myself. Now, I'm not going back home and I'm tired of being the outsider at Uri's house. There's no way in hell that I'm going by my parents.

[193]

I'd die before I did that. I'm moving in with you and I'll pay the other three months of the rent," Royce rambled.

"You don't have to do that baby. I got the bills covered," Caleb replied.

"I know you do Caleb, but I want to pull my own weight. I don't want you doing everything for me. I want us to do for each other," Royce said, making him smile.

"That's what the fuck I'm talking about. Grown woman shit." Caleb nodded.

He had no intentions of letting her pay for anything, but he appreciated the fact that she offered. He wasn't rich, but he made enough to make sure that he and Royce lived comfortably.

"What about furniture and stuff?" Royce asked, right as her phone started to ring.

Her mood instantly changed when she looked at who the caller was.

"Who is that?" Caleb quizzed.

"My mother," Royce said, rolling her eyes.

"You can't run from her forever Royce," Caleb said.

"I'm not running from her now. I see her every day at school and I ignore her there too. She owes me an apology and I have no words for her until I get it. I'm tired of giving her a pass."

"I can't say nothing about that. It was fucked up what she said to you. You'll always be her daughter, even when ole boy is no longer her son-in-law," Caleb noted.

"My point exactly," Royce said as her phone rang again.

This time, her reaction was the exact opposite. She had a huge smile on her face, making Caleb wonder who the hell was calling her now.

"The hell you smiling so hard for? Who is that?" Caleb asked.

Instead of replying, Royce answered her phone to let him know.

"Hey daddy," she beamed when she connected the call.

The frown that she once wore had returned and Caleb was as confused as ever. When Royce put the call on speaker and lowered the volume so that only the two of them could hear, he soon found out why.

"I guess the only way I get to talk to you is if I call from your father's phone," Sondra snapped angrily.

Royce was happy that they were done eating because her appetite would have vanished if they hadn't. Caleb threw some money on the table and signaled to Royce that he was ready to leave. He didn't want her conversation to get heated and draw attention to their table.

"What is it that you need?" Royce asked, void of any emotion.

"What is going on with you lately Royce? Your attitude has completely changed and I don't like it," Sondra fussed.

"Well, it's a good thing that I don't give a damn about what you like, huh?" Royce asked sarcastically.

"I am still your mother Royce Davenport and you better respect me as such!" Sondra yelled.

"Last time before I hang up. What do you want?" Royce asked through clenched teeth.

"I'm sure you don't know this, but Silas has been chosen as next year's Zulu king," Sondra informed her.

"I know damn well you didn't call to tell me that foolishness," Royce said as she looked at the phone like Sondra could see her.

"I'm not done. Your father has been appointed to sit on the chairman's board and they're having a ceremony to make the announcements," Sondra revealed.

"When and where?" Royce asked sternly.

"I'll text you the date and time. It's a black-tie affair, so make sure you dress to impress. Oh, and Jax told me all about your little boyfriend picking you up from the school not too long ago. Make sure you leave him home because he's not invited," Sondra spat before she hung up the phone.

"Man, your mama better calm down. How she in her feelings about a nigga and we ain't never met?" Caleb questioned.

"As if I give a damn about how she feels anymore." Royce frowned.

"I know I don't," Caleb countered.

"What do you have to do this weekend?" Royce asked.

"Nothing that I know of. Why? What's up?" he questioned.

"We need to go shopping for you a tux," Royce replied.

"A tux for what?" Caleb asked.

"You heard what my mama just said. It's a black-tie affair," Royce answered.

"Yeah and I also heard her say that I wasn't invited. I'll fuck around and go to jail messing with your mama, girl. I'll meet your people eventually, but I think I better sit this one out."

"Are you my man or not Caleb?" Royce questioned as she stood there with her hands on her hips.

"Girl, the way I been knee-deep in that pussy for two weeks straight, you shouldn't even fix your mouth to ask me no shit like that," Caleb replied with a smirk.

"Okay then. I want my man on my arm when I walk in the room. Is that going to be a problem?" Royce asked.

"Nah, it ain't a problem. Just don't get mad when you and your pops be picking your mama up when I knock her evil ass out," Caleb replied, making her laugh.

Chapter 22

"Girl, fuck Brian! Stop acting like he's the only nigga that you can get. If he wants that bitch, let him have her," Katrice snapped as she looked over at her sister.

"That nigga ain't been home since she had that baby," Ronnie instigated as he played on his game.

"I can tell when the bitch is not around because he always answers the phone. If she's not his girl like he claims, he should be able to answer all the time," Mya fumed.

She never mentioned that he never answered from her number. She always had to use another phone, but Brian didn't really have anything to say to her.

"She might not be his girl right now, but he's trying hard as hell," Ronnie noted.

"How do you know that?" Mya asked with a frown.

"He's one of his best friends. If anybody knows what's up, he does," Katrice responded in her man's defense.

"Shit, I'm surprised that the baby was really his," Ronnie spoke up.

"Me too, since you said her ex-boyfriend was claiming to be the daddy," Katrice replied.

Ronnie got under Mya's skin sometimes with his feminine ass ways. He swore that he was helping with the info that he provided but, most times, he only made shit worse. He rubbed it in for an entire week when the paternity test results came back. He kept showing Mya pictures of the baby that Brian posted on Instagram, as well as the ones that Shanti posted of the father and daughter together. Katrice had to make him sit down and shut up, and Mya was grateful for small favors. He swore that he wanted her and Brian to be together but, sometimes, she wasn't so sure.

"That nigga Kerry said that he fell back. He said Shanti be acting funny since Brian be there, so he don't really call her no more. She was kind of salty about him telling Brian that he was still fucking her too," Ronnie said, interrupting her thoughts.

"I would never want a friend like you. Nigga talk everybody's business," Mya said with a frown.

"Brian is my boy, but we're family. I'm just looking out for you. I don't want to see you get messed over by nobody, friend or not," Ronnie spoke up.

He and Brian had met Shaky and Katrice at the same time. Katrice worked at a different club, but she was there to watch her sister's performance that night. He and Brian both left the club with them, but their relationships took a different direction. Katrice had Ronnie gone from day one, but Brian wasn't feeling Shaky as much. He was looking for sex and she was looking for a commitment.

"They got mad niggas that be trying to get at you. I don't know why you're so stuck on Brian. That nigga ain't all that," Katrice said.

"And Ronnie is?" Mya asked sarcastically.

"Bitch, don't come for him just because you're mad with that other nigga," Katrice snapped.

Mya only ignored her because she was used to her coming to Ronnie's defense. He was a dummy who Katrice treated like her child. She was a few years older than Ronnie and he was like her puppet. She was always getting mad when other people talked crazy to him, but she dogged him out the most. Mya lost count of how many times he got beat up trying to come to Katrice's rescue. He was a boy trying to do grown man things.

"I got you, sis. Let me call that nigga for you," Ronnie offered as he paused his game and grabbed his phone.

"Don't tell him that you're calling for me. Just let me hear what he's saying," Mya said as she got closer to him to listen in.

She watched with baited breath as Ronnie dialed Brian's number and put him on speaker phone. She smiled when Brian answered the phone because she missed hearing his voice all the time.

"What's good nigga?" Brian asked when he answered.

"Ain't nothing, just calling to see what's good with you," Ronnie replied.

"I'm relaxing man. Just got baby girl to sleep and me and Shanti about to watch a movie," Brian said.

"You still ain't bring your ass home yet?" Ronnie questioned.

"Nah, we might go spend a few weeks there soon though," Brian replied.

"Who is we?" Ronnie asked.

"Me, Shanti, and Bri," Brian answered.

"Y'all really doing the family thing I see," Ronnie said, fishing for answers.

"What's up bruh? What you called for?" Brian asked.

"I'm trying to see when you're going back to work. You know I don't really like nobody else to cut my hair," Ronnie said, coming up with a believable excuse.

"I'll be back next week. My baby got her six-week checkup that Monday and me and Shanti are going back to work that Tuesday. Come fuck with me," Brian replied.

"Alright bruh, I'll be there," Ronnie said before they disconnected.

"There you have it sis. That nigga is a family man now. I know that it hurts to hear him talk about his baby, knowing that you got rid of yours. When you meet the right man, you can start a family with him. Let Brian's ass go and move on. He made his choice and it wasn't you," Katrice said, breaking her baby sister's heart.

Mya wasn't trying to hear anything that Katrice was saying. In her eyes, she didn't have room to talk and her advice was garbage. Before she got with Ronnie, she had been the side chick to a married man for years. He made a fool of her and she did whatever he told her to. She stalked him for months when he broke it off, until he got a restraining order on her. She used to go to him and his wife's jobs and she even lurked around their children's school. Katrice was a big girl, but she had lost weight and her mind over somebody's else's husband. It took her a while to get back right and, now, she wanted to act like a relationship expert. Mya didn't want to hear nothing else that she had to say, so she got up and went to her bedroom. As soon as she laid down, she picked up her phone and called Cookie.

"Hey boo," Cookie said when she answered the phone.

"I need to make a hair appointment," Mya replied.

"Okay. When?" Cookie asked.

"I want to come Tuesday," Mya replied, giving her the day that Brian was scheduled to return to work.

"Okay boo. You know I work at the club Monday night, so you can come around noon. That'll give me a little time to rest up," Cookie replied.

"That's cool. I'll see you then," Mya said before she hung up.

Cookie wasn't the only person that she would be seeing. Since Brian didn't want to answer his phone, he would be seeing her face to face on his first day back.

***

"No Jaylynn. I'm not doing this with your sneaky ass today. You are not coming to my house to meet up with Hayden!" Co-Co yelled into his phone.

He stepped outside to take her call, since she had been blowing his phone up all morning. She had been begging to talk to him about something, but he wasn't trying to hear her. His gut told him that she was trying to get him to take her to get some birth control, but that wasn't happening. It wasn't his job and he wasn't about to overstep his boundaries. Sweets said that Hayden had been throwing hints at him about the same thing and he flat out said no.

"I'm not trying to be sneaky and I'm not meeting up with Hayden. I just want to talk to you about something. It's important," Jaylynn begged.

"If it's that important, you need to talk to your mama and daddy. What is it with everybody in this family calling me with their problems?" Co-Co questioned.

"You already know how they are. My daddy won't even let me have a boyfriend, so I can't talk to him about how I'm feeling. If I tell my mama, she's just gonna run back and tell him whatever I say. I just need some advice. Can I just come over later Co-Co? Please?" Jaylynn cried.

"You can stop the waterworks bitch because I'm not buying it. Whatever mess you've gotten yourself into is not my problem," Co-Co fussed.

"You and Sweets are being so mean to us," Jaylynn fussed.

"That's because you and Hayden are not our responsibility. Now, I gotta go, but I suggest you discuss whatever is going on with your parents and Hayden needs to do the same," Co-Co said before hanging up.

"Six weeks later and you're still on the same shit," Brian joked as he and Shanti walked up.

"Welcome back mommy and daddy." Co-Co smiled as he ushered them inside the shop.

Everyone greeted them with warm welcomes as they both went to their work stations and prepared to get their day started.

"I know it felt funny leaving Bri for the first time," Candace said as she braided her client's hair.

"I was fine. Your cousin looked like he was about to cry," Shanti laughed.

"Aww. You were having separation anxiety Brian?" Candace asked.

"No man, but my baby didn't want me to leave her. She can't talk, but I saw the way she was looking," Brian said, making his cousin laugh.

"Stop lying boy. She was sleep when we dropped her off," Shanti said, right as her first appointment walked in.

"Forget all that small talk. Are y'all together now or what? I mean, y'all got Bri and y'all damn near live together. And I didn't miss that y'all came in the same car. Stop trying to be all secretive and shit," Co-Co blurted out.

"Mind your business nigga," Brian replied.

"I'll take that as a no. Shanti must have shot his ass down again," Co-Co snickered.

"We're taking our time," Shanti replied, making Brian smile.

That was music to his ears because it was a start. Shanti didn't flat out say no, letting him know that she was still open to the idea of them being together. When Brian's customer walked in, he got right to work cutting his hair. The day was going by smoothly and he knew that it was because Cookie wasn't there. He and Shanti were getting along fine and had even made plans to go to lunch together.

He knew that it was too good to be true when Cookie walked through the door a few hours later accompanied by Mya. Of all the days for her to come into the shop, she just had to come in on his and Shanti's first day back. Brian was far from dumb and he knew that her presence had Ronnie's name written all over it. It was no coincidence that he told Ronnie when he would return and Mya came in the same day. Brian couldn't wait to call and tell his pussy ass off. That nigga was a hoe and his actions just kept proving that.

"Welcome back y'all," Cookie smirked as she walked over to her work station.

Both Brian and Shanti had customers, so they ignored her greeting. Mya had a scowl on her face as she looked at Shanti, but she was too busy to notice. Co-Co paid attention to everything and he always spoke up when he did.

"Some of these hoes need to build a bridge and get over their feelings," Co-Co said as he played on his phone, waiting for his appointment to arrive.

"I'm selling edge control y'all. I learned how to make it myself and it's the truth. Let me know if y'all want to buy some," Cookie said as she held up a small label-free jar for them to see.

"I'll pass. A bitch without edges selling edge control is like a man with no teeth selling dental plans. The struggle ain't that real," Co-Co cracked, as Cookie laughed.

"The fuck is you laughing for when he's cracking on you?" Mya whispered, making sure that he didn't hear her.

She knew all about Co-Co's slick mouth and she wasn't in the mood to argue with him. She probably wouldn't have won anyway, so it wasn't worth it.

"That's my friend girl. He just be messing with me," Cookie naïvely replied.

Mya just let it go because her girl was a damn fool. Co-Co was not playing with her and a blind man could see that. If Cookie was okay with being made a fool of, there was nothing that she could do about it.

"Hey everybody," Uri said when she walked into the shop.

She had an appointment with Co-Co and it was her first time going to him. She'd seen his work before and she liked what she saw. She left work for a few hours to let him do her sew-in like he'd done Royce's a few weeks before.

"Hey boo. What's going on with you today?" Shanti asked with a smile.

"Girl, just trying to let Co-Co get this hair right. I didn't know that y'all were back at work," Uri replied as she sat in Co-Co's chair.

"Yeah, we just got back today," Shanti replied.

"Did you get on him for telling Caleb about Royce being at the hotel?" Uri asked Shanti.

"I fussed at his ass as soon as he came to pick me and Bri up from his mama's house," Shanti replied.

"Y'all play too much," Brian laughed while shaking his head.

"Who's keeping the baby?" Uri questioned.

"She's with my auntie," Shanti replied.

"Girl, that six weeks passed so fast. Who's spoiling her?" Uri asked while Co-Co started braiding her hair.

"Me," Brian admitted with a smile.

"I should have known," Uri laughed, right as Mya got up from Cookie's chair and walked over to Brian's.

"Can you line me up right quick?" she asked as she stood way too close for his liking.

She usually wore wigs at the club, but Mya's hair was short with a tapered back.

"Nah, I have another appointment coming," Brian lied with no emotion in his voice.

Tuesdays were usually slow, and he wasn't waiting for anyone else. He would take a walk-in if they came in, but that was about it.

"It'll only take you a minute. I wanted to ask you that when I called the other day," Mya said, letting Shanti know that she was still in the picture.

"It's a good thing that your auntie is watching her, Shanti. You know people don't like to watch no spoiled babies. Mine were rotten too and my mama kept them both while my husband and I worked," Uri said, changing the subject.

"I can't wait until Bri gets big like your girls." Shanti smiled, right as she finished with her customer.

She collected her payment and stood up to stretch. She was starving, but she no longer wanted to go to lunch with Brian. She tried to act unaffected by Mya's comment, but she was pissed. Brian was begging her for another chance, but he still seemed to be playing games.

[203]

"My baby would have been two years old by now. Right Brian? Two or almost two," Mya spoke up, making the tension thick once again.

"Didn't you come here to get your hair done? Maybe you need to focus on that and less on other people's conversations," Co-Co snapped irritably.

"Come on and let me shampoo you, Shaky," Cookie said, trying to diffuse the situation.

Problems with Co-Co was not what her girl wanted, and she needed her to know that.

"You ready to go to lunch?" Brian asked Shanti, as Mya frowned in anger.

She wanted to scream and act a fool, but that wouldn't have gotten her far. If they were anywhere else, she would have been trying to swing on Brian and his bitch at the same time.

"Yeah, I'm ready," Shanti said while grabbing her purse.

She didn't want to let Mya know that her words affected her, so she let Brian grab her hand and lead her out of the shop. She felt Mya's eyes on them the entire time and she was happy that she kept it classy. As soon as they got out of everyone's view, she snatched her hand away and walked ahead of him.

"What's wrong with you?" Brian asked.

"I'm done playing games with you and your bitch. I'm not pregnant no more. I'll deal with that hoe and anybody who comes behind her," Shanti snapped.

"The fuck is you getting mad with me for though?" Brian questioned.

"Because you be entertaining her stupid ass. And you wonder why I'm not in a hurry to be with you again. You still talking to the bitch and everything."

"Man, I don't talk to that damn girl. I answered the phone for her twice and that was only because I didn't recognize the number. As soon as I heard her voice, I hung up and never looked back. For the first time in my life, I'm not talking to or dealing with no other females. I told you that I'm done with the games. I want my family and I'm trying to show you just how serious I am. I know that it won't happen overnight, but I need you to trust me."

"I'm trying Brian. I really am. That bitch just disturbs my peace and I hate that shit. We've been getting along fine, and I don't want that to change. I have to stop letting stupid shit like that get to me though," Shanti admitted.

"I understand that Shanti, but you're giving her exactly what she wants. I told you that it's all about you and Bri from now on and I mean that shit," Brian swore as he grabbed her hand and kissed it.

"I believe you." Shanti smiled.

He was taking the advice that Shanti gave him when she was in the hospital. He was trying to show her that he loved her, as opposed to just telling her. The past six weeks let Brian know just what he had been missing from his life. A family of his own was what he had longed for and he didn't want to give that up. Mya and no other woman was worth him losing what he was trying so hard to build with Shanti.

Chapter 23

"I think an up-do will look better with the dress you're wearing," Uri said as she watched Co-Co applying Royce's makeup.

"I told her stubborn ass to let me pin her hair up," Co-Co fussed.

Brooklyn, along with Royce and Uri, were at Co-Co's house helping Royce get together. Royce had a beautiful black, form-fitting, off the shoulder dress that looked great on her. Co-Co had tightened and curled her sew-in and he was almost done with her makeup. She was thankful that Co-Co let her use his house to get ready. Royce and Caleb had just moved into their apartment and everything was all over the place. They were in the middle of unpacking and it was a mess. They had purchased all new furniture, since Royce didn't want to take any of hers. She decided to sell her house as is, furniture and all. Two people had put in offers, but it still hadn't sold.

"Is it too late to pin it up?" Royce asked.

"I'll do it after you get dressed," Co-Co replied.

"How is Shanti making out? I swear, I wanted to pop that Shaky bitch in the mouth when I was there," Uri said as she and Brooklyn sipped from their long island iced teas.

"What did that bitch do now?" Brooklyn questioned.

Uri ran the story down to her about what happened when Co-Co did her hair. Mya was a piece of work and that was Uri's first time ever seeing her. She stayed there for hours even after her hair was done, just frowning at Brian and Shanti. They ignored her, but she seemed to be used to the treatment.

"That be Cookie keeping up all that mess," Brooklyn noted.

"I'm trying to see how that bitch got hired as a topless bartender. Them saggy ass titties look like she's been nursing a litter of puppies. Looking at her takes my gay away," Co-Co said, making them weak with laughter.

"I'm so happy that Brian is done with her ass. Him and Caleb picked the two dumbest bitches in the world." Brooklyn frowned.

"That bitch Sienna is a few books short of a series," Co-Co replied.

"She must be crazy to go from being the wife to the side bitch," Uri commented.

"It's hard being a wife when you're cut from the cloth of a side chick. She's only doing what she's been taught," Royce replied with a shrug.

"These niggas just need to stop buying mutts and get themselves a pure bred," Co-Co said, right as he finished with Royce makeup.

"Now ain't that the truth," Uri laughed.

Royce went into the spare bedroom and put on her dress and shoes. Uri helped her with her accessories, as Co-Co styled and pinned her hair to one side.

"Now that's a bad bitch," Co-Co sang as he danced and snapped his fingers.

"Are you nervous cousin?" Uri asked.

"Nervous about what?" Royce countered.

"Bitch, you're about to bring your new man around your parents and your in-laws for the first time. And I'm sure that Jax will be there too. I hate that Zulu shit, but this is one time that I should have made an exception," Uri replied.

"I don't give a damn about none of them. I'm only going to support my daddy. Everybody else can kiss my ass," Royce snapped.

"This bitch been going off lately. She was so quiet and calm when we first met," Brooklyn laughed.

"Between Caleb and the alcohol, I don't know who turned her out the most," Uri replied.

"We need to have a ladies' night. Kia has been trying to do one for a while now," Brooklyn spoke up.

"Don't let that bitch Keller do it again. She went got in the bed with her husband and left us by ourselves," Co-Co replied.

"Y'all are family now, so y'all have to come. I promise that y'all will have so much fun. Co-Co and Sweets will make sure of that," Brooklyn said.

"Yes honey. Me and my bestie are always the life of the party," Co-Co replied.

"Just tell us when and where," Uri replied.

Royce took a few pictures while she waited for Caleb to pick her up. He was having trouble with his bowtie, so he had to swing by his father's house for some help. When he got there, he and Royce took a few pictures together and they were on their way soon after.

"Once my daddy is done with what he's doing, we're leaving," Royce informed Caleb as he drove.

"You know that's cool with me. This bowtie is choking a nigga already," Caleb complained.

"I know this ain't your first time wearing one," Royce replied.

"Nah, but I haven't worn one since Jaden and Kia's wedding. That was some years ago," Caleb replied.

"Do you think you'll ever get married?" Royce asked him.

"Why? Are you asking?" Caleb smirked.

"Stop playing Caleb. I'm serious," Royce pouted.

"Yeah, I want all that one day. Marriage, a house, and kids," Caleb replied.

"You got the house, even though you tried to keep it from me," Royce said, rolling her eyes.

Caleb had purchased the double home that he wanted, and he was making plans to get it renovated.

"I wasn't keeping anything from you. I just didn't want to overwhelm you with so much. You were already stressed out," Caleb replied, right as they pulled up to the Zulu Club.

"I'm so not in the mood for this fake bullshit tonight." Royce frowned.

"It's all good baby. Let's just get this over with without me having to knock nobody the fuck out," Caleb replied as he found a place to park.

***

"Congrats to the king and queen," Sondra said as she held up her glass of lemon water like she was making a toast.

"Thanks, my darling. Congrats to you as well, Patrick. Sitting on the board is a great accomplishment," Elena replied.

"Thank you," Patrick replied as he smiled politely.

"Where the hell is our daughter? People are asking and I'm running out of excuses. I promised Silas and Elena that she would be here," Sondra whispered to her husband.

"She'll be here honey. She promised that she would," Patrick assured her.

"All of Silas and Elena's kids are here with their spouses except for Jaxon. How embarrassing is that?" Sondra mumbled.

"They are not together anymore Sondra. I don't expect her to come in here and be cordial with his ass and I don't blame her," Patrick fumed.

"Oh, and you're one to talk. Like you don't have any skeletons in your closet. Let's not forget about your past transgressions. I'm reminded of it every day," Sondra snapped.

"Do you really want to discuss this right now Sondra. Do you, because I don't mind?" Patrick replied angrily.

He was tired of having his past mistakes thrown in his face whenever things didn't go Sondra's way. He made mistakes just like any other human being.

"No, I don't," Sondra replied as she looked around.

She was happy that everyone else seemed to be engaged in conversations of their own and no one paid attention to their minor disagreement. Elena's sons seemed to be the life of the party, but their wives never opened their mouths. Once they were introduced and spoke, they were mute the entire night. Elena's daughter, Ashley, and her husband were very social, but they were used to the black-tie scene. They were a part of the in crowd, so they knew how to socialize.

"Is everybody ready for the big announcements? We have about thirty more minutes before we get started," one of the club's presidents walked over and said.

"We're ready." Silas smiled as he shook his hand.

"And where is your lovely wife tonight?" he asked while looking over at Jaxon.

Jax looked like he was at a loss for words and Sondra wanted to disappear. Elena looked embarrassed and Silas looked downright upset.

"There she is. Running a little late, but she's here," Jax smiled when he saw Royce walking through the front door.

His smile gradually faded when he saw her strolling over to their table holding hands with Caleb. His parents looked like they were ready to snap, and he understood their frustration.

"Oh, okay. I guess I'll talk to you guys a little later," the other man said, looking just as uncomfortable as they all felt. He hurried away like he wanted no parts of what was about to take place.

"Oh, my God. I specifically told her not to bring him here," Sondra mumbled to herself.

She had never met her daughter's boyfriend, but it didn't take a genius to know who the other man was. Royce looked beautiful, but that was overshadowed by the situation that she'd created.

"Good evening everybody. Hi daddy," Royce said as her father stood up to hug her.

"Hey baby. Hello young man," Patrick said while shaking Caleb's hand.

"Daddy, this is my boyfriend, Caleb." Royce smiled.

"It's nice to meet you sir," Caleb politely replied.

"Caleb, this is my mother Sondra," Royce introduced, void of any emotion.

"Yes, and this is her husband, Jaxon, and her in-laws," Sondra rudely commented as she introduced Jax and every member of his family.

Caleb was about to have a snappy comeback, but something else got his attention. He didn't want to accompany Royce to the gathering at first, but he was happy that he did when he saw who was seated next to Jax.

"What's good Mrs. Lockwood?" Caleb asked with a huge smile covering his face.

"Hello," Mrs. Lockwood replied, barely above a whisper.

"How do you know Ashley?" Royce questioned.

"She's my probation officer," Caleb smirked.

"Are you serious?" Royce asked angrily.

She knew all about Caleb being forced to sleep with his probation officer, but she never dreamed that Jax's sister was the one. Ashley had been on the board of the probation and parole department for years, courtesy of her father-in-law. She and Broderick didn't have any kids, but they seemed to be happy and in love. She would have never thought that she was cheating on him, especially with her probationers. The entire Davenport family was more fucked up than she thought they were and they just kept proving her right.

"Oh, my God! You're on probation?" Sondra asked, snapping Royce away from her daydream.

"I was, but not anymore. Ain't that right Mrs. Lockwood? Or is it Ashely?" Caleb smirked.

"She's Mrs. Lockwood to you. Don't disrespect my wife," Broderick spoke up.

"She disrespected herself," Royce spoke up.

"What the hell is that supposed to mean?" Broderick questioned.

"Are you seriously standing here defending another man in the presence of your husband, Royce?" Sondra questioned.

"I'm not defending another man. I'm defending my man," Royce replied, as Caleb snaked his arm around her waist.

"Okay, let's all calm down here. Royce, you and Caleb have a seat and let's act like adults," Patrick said as he motioned towards two chairs that were right next to Sondra.

Royce took the seat closest to her mother and let Caleb have the other. She would have preferred to sit next to her father, but she wasn't going to make a big deal out of it. She noticed the angered look on Silas' face, but she didn't give a damn. She had never met a man who loved pussy but hated the women who he got it from, including his own wife.

"How could you do this to me, Royce? I'm so humiliated. I told you not to bring him here," Sondra whispered.

"As if I care about what you say. If it weren't for my father being recognized, I wouldn't be here at all," Royce replied.

"How can you go from a great man like Jaxon Davenport to this common criminal?" Sondra questioned.

"You don't know a damn thing about him so keep your comments to yourself," Royce fumed.

"He just admitted to being on probation. I'm sure he's also the reason for your lack of respect these days. I don't like him already," Sondra noted.

"I don't give a damn if you like him or not and I know for a fact that he doesn't either. That common criminal, as you call him, has a great career that pays him way more than Jaxon's ever did. And if you don't want me to embarrass you further, I suggest you stop talking to me. I'm not feeling up to using my inside voice anymore. I would hate to have this discussion loud enough for everyone to hear," Royce threatened, making Sondra pipe down.

A few minutes later, the ceremony got under way and Royce was happy for that. Dinner was served as the program went on and that was another plus. The sooner they got it over with, the sooner they could leave all the drama behind. Royce was happy to see her father and Caleb talking throughout the night. Patrick got along with anyone and had always been that way since Royce could remember.

"I need to run to the bathroom. I'll be right back," Caleb whispered to Royce before he got up and walked away.

Royce was too busy engaged in a conversation with her father to see when Jax walked over and took the seat that Caleb had just vacated.

"Did you have to bring him here of all places Royce? I get it, I pissed you off, but why would you do this to my family?" Jax asked lowly.

"Fuck you and your family. You must be crazy if you think I'm gonna hide my man and my relationship to spare anybody's feelings," Royce replied.

"This shit is crazy man. How the hell did you manage to hook up with Sienna's ex?" Jax wondered out loud.

"Imagine my surprise when I found out that my friend Brooklyn's brother was the same man who I confronted about Sienna cheating with you. Ironic, ain't it?" Royce chuckled.

It was indeed ironic, but Jax didn't find anything funny. He remembered hating Caleb for a long time because Sienna wanted nothing to do with him when they were together. He got over those feelings once he had Sienna under his spell again. Now, that hate had intensified since Caleb now had the heart of the one woman who he'd ever truly loved. Jax didn't bother replying. He got up from the table and headed towards the bathroom. As soon as he walked in, he was greeted by Caleb's smirking face standing at the sink washing his hands.

"Leftovers are never as good as the original meal you know. Maybe you should try getting your own plate sometimes," Jax said as he stood next to him.

"Now, that's where you're wrong at my man. Sometimes, I purposely save my plate for later. Everybody knows that the food is always better the next day," Caleb replied.

"She's only using you to get back at me for cheating on her. It'll never last. You're not even Royce's type. She hates thugs and that's obviously what you are," Jax countered.

"She might hate thugs, but she loves that thug dick. But, then again, so does your sister," Caleb laughed.

"You don't know shit about my sister, aside from her being your probation officer," Jax snapped.

"I know that she's doing more with her probationers than just testing their piss. I also know that she can't suck dick worth a damn, but my baby is a pro," Caleb teased.

"That's bullshit. My sister wouldn't go anywhere near you," Jax said, waving him off.

"I guess I just imagined that heart-shaped tattoo with her initials that she got tatted on her ass cheek then, huh?" Caleb said, making him jerk his head around to face him.

Jax knew that tattoo well because his parents had a fit when they found out about it. Ashley got it during her freshman year in college. They went on their annual summer vacation and her swimsuit gave her away. The fact that Caleb knew about it meant that he had indeed seen Ashley outside of her normal work attire. Ashley always spoke so negatively about the people who she supervised on parole, so that bit of information came as a surprise. Cheating just seemed to be in their DNA, thanks to Silas.

"I know that it's a hard pill to swallow. I've been with your ex-wife, your sister, and now your current wife. I know you probably hate a nigga right about now. Shit, if I were you, I would hate me too. But, I thank you, bruh, I really do," Caleb said, interrupting Jax's thoughts.

"Thank me for what?" Jax questioned.

"For not appreciating what you had in front of you. You know how many niggas wish they had a woman like Royce? And to think, your fuck up literally sent her right to my front door. I didn't even have to go looking for her."

"You can have her," Jax replied, sounding just as bitter as he was.

"You can't give me nothing that already belongs to me, my dude. That's what's wrong with you niggas now. Y'all need to start appreciating what you have before they become what you had. Be easy fam," Caleb said as he patted his back and walked away.

Chapter 24

"I just can't believe that he was fucking Ashley of all people. I really wanna fight that bitch right now," Royce slurred as she sipped from her fifth drink of the night.

Two weeks had passed since they went to the Zulu function and she found out that her sister-in-law was Caleb's probation officer. Royce must have asked him a million questions when they left that night and he answered them all. She hated that Caleb had blessed Ashley with the dick to keep his freedom, but he was done with her and his probation. He swore that he wasn't going back to see her, and Royce didn't want him too. She had no problem putting Ashley on blast if it ever became a problem.

"That's your last drink for the night bitch. You've clearly had enough," Uri fussed.

"Leave her alone honey. This is the Royce that I love to see," Co-Co countered.

"Those cups are too damn big to be drinking out of and her shit was filled to the rim," Kia replied.

"I'm calling Caleb to pick her up. Ain't no way in hell I'm driving her ass home," Uri said.

"Leave her alone. She's feeling herself," Sweets laughed, as Royce continued to rant about Ashley.

"Bitch ain't never had a fight in her life and talking about beating somebody up," Uri chuckled.

"I bet I drop that hoe the next time I see her. And Sienna can get it too!" Royce yelled.

"I'm so weak," Brook said as she fell out laughing.

"Get them hoes Royce. Don't take no shit off nobody," Co-Co instigated as he refilled her cup.

"Stop giving her liquor. She's fucked up enough," Brooklyn fussed.

"Come on Royce. Let's show these hoes how to twerk. With all that wagon you're dragging, I'm sure you can make it clap," Co-Co said as he pulled her up from the sofa.

"That bitch don't know how to dance," Uri laughed.

"Wait, let me finish my drink," Royce said as she turned the cup up to her lips and drained it.

Co-Co put on one of Big Freedia's twerk songs as he and Sweets starting dancing.

"Show me how to do my booty like that Co-Co," Royce requested as she tried to imitate his movements.

"Arch your back and put your hands on your knees," Co-Co instructed.

Once he had her in the right position, he showed her how to move her butt cheeks to the beat. Royce caught on quickly and, before long, Shanti had jumped up to join her. Mrs. Pam had Bri for the weekend and Shanti was happy that she was off the following day.

"Fuck it up Royce!" Co-Co yelled, bucking her up.

"Brian is about to get him some tonight," Shanti said as she danced on beat with the music.

"Bitch please. Brian been getting it," Co-Co said, calling her out.

Shanti only smiled because it was true. The same day that she was cleared by her doctor, she gave it up. She and Brian were both working through their trust issues and taking things slow. She and Bri had been at his house for the past weekend and they were doing a great job of co-parenting. Shanti was even assisting him with putting the finishing touches on decorating his house. Brian was a true bachelor, but she needed him to do better.

After hours of dancing, drinking, and pigging out, everybody was worn out. It was only a little after eight, but they started early. Jaden cut hair for a wedding earlier that morning and he was out having drinks with Brian, Shaq, and Caleb. Bryce and his family were on a cruise, so he and Taylor weren't in attendance. Tigga was home with his kids, so he wasn't with the men either. Tessa was missing too, but she had been down with the flu for a few days.

"Good evening everybody," Jaylynn spoke as she rushed into the house with her little brother and went straight to her room. She was at one of her friends' houses, but Kia asked her to stop by Mo to grab Juice before she came home.

"Well damn speed racer!" Co-Co yelled after her.

"Hey Co-Co." Juice smiled at his big cousin.

"Get your bad ass away from me. You know I don't trust you," Co-Co replied.

"Go tell your sister to run you some bath water Juice. I know you're probably dirty as hell coming from by Mo's house," Kia instructed her son.

"Is Jay okay? She usually likes to chill with us for a little while," Keller said.

"I need to have a talk with her. She hasn't been herself for the past few months," Kia noted.

"What do you mean?" Keller asked, concerned about her only niece.

"I can't explain it. We used to sit around and talk all the time, but she's been acting strange lately. We used to go shopping together, but she doesn't even want to do that anymore. She's even been dressing weird," Kia replied.

"Jay has always been a daddy's girl, Kia. Don't go getting all in your feelings now," Keller said.

"She barely talks to Jaden either. It's like she's been depressed or something. She stays in her room all the time. We live in the same house, but I feel like I hardly see her," Kia replied.

"Yeah, you might want to have a serious talk with her. That depression shit ain't no joke. Kids be taking their own lives behind that shit," Sweets replied.

"Y'all ever suck a nigga dick so good that he started crying? I think I made Caleb cry last night," Royce said out of the blue.

"The fuck is this bitch talking about?" Candace asked aloud.

"Let me call her man to come and get her," Uri said as she called Caleb.

"I sucked his dick in the movie theater too," Royce blurted.

"Bitch, this is not confession and we are not priests. Keep that shit to yourself," Co-Co fussed.

"Bitch, I'm about to pee on myself," Uri said as she held her stomach and laughed.

"Is Caleb on his way to get her?" Brooklyn asked.

"Yeah, he said he's coming. Where's your bathroom Kia?" Uri asked.

[219]

"Juice is probably taking his bath in the hallway bathroom. Let me show you to the other one," Kia said as she got up.

"Royce got me about to piss on myself," Uri giggled as she followed behind her.

Kia checked on her son to make sure he was straight, before showing Uri to one of her three bathrooms. She never let anyone use the one in her bedroom, so she walked her to the other side of the house close to Jaylynn's room.

"Here you go boo," Kia said as she swung the door open.

"Ma! I'm in here!" Jaylynn yelled as she tried to cover her naked body.

"Oh, my God, Jay! No baby! No!" Kia screamed as she burst out in tears.

She wasn't ready, and nothing could have prepared her for the small, perfectly round belly that Jaylynn tried hard to cover. She felt weak and she was so thankful that Uri was standing there to hold her up. Uri just stood there in stunned silence, as Kia fell apart. She remembered Royce saying that she thought she saw Jaylynn at a hotel, but she didn't believe that it was really her. Now, seeing her standing there trying to shield her baby bump, Uri wasn't so sure anymore.

"What happened girl?" Co-Co asked as he and the rest of the crew rushed to Kia's side. Royce was the only one who wasn't with them because she was too tipsy to move.

"Oh Lord! You're pregnant Jay?" Keller asked in shock.

"Jesus, have mercy," Sweets said as he covered his mouth with his hands.

There was no doubt in his mind that his nephew was the father. His sister and brother-in-law were going to die. Jaylynn stood there naked and embarrassed as everyone looked at her like she was some kind of science experiment. She had been going crazy trying to keep her secret hidden and she had done well for months. It helped that she wasn't really showing, and all her weight seemed to be in her ass and hips. Her breasts had gotten huge, but wearing baggy clothes and jackets helped with that. Kia always questioned her about wearing jackets when it was so warm, but she always had an excuse. Her classes were cold she would say and that would be the end of the discussion. She tried talking to Co-Co about her dilemma, but he wanted no parts of it. Hayden was just as scared as she was, and they went months trying to figure out what they were going to do.

"Jaden is about to murder everybody in New Orleans and the surrounding areas," Co-Co said as he stood there in shock.

Now he knew why Jaylynn had been trying to talk to him for the past few months. He couldn't help her then and he damn sure couldn't help her now. He knew that she was lying when she claimed to not be having sex. All the signs were there, but he would have never expected a pregnancy.

"Put some clothes on and come into the living room Jay. Come on Kia. Calm down boo," Brooklyn said as she hugged her distraught sister-in-law and led her back to the front of the house.

Shanti comforted Keller because she was just as torn up as Kia was. Jay was like her baby too. She was her only niece and had been the only grandchild for years.

"My baby," Kia sobbed as her entire body shook.

Just like her, Jaylynn was going to be a teenage mother. Kia didn't want that for her daughter and she was sure that Mo didn't want that for her either. Jay was going to be seventeen the following month, the same age that Kia was when she had her. A generation of curses that she wanted her daughter to break. Things didn't always work out like they wanted, and Kia was seeing that firsthand. Everyone seemed to have forgotten about Juice, so Candace made sure he took his bath and put on his pajamas.

"What's wrong with my mama?" Juice frowned when he walked into the living room and saw Kia crying.

"Your mama is okay baby," Brooklyn assured him, right as Jaylynn walked into the room.

Her face was wet with tears as she slowly made her way to the sofa and sat down. She hated to see her mother crying, especially since she was the cause of it. Even still, that wasn't what had her shook up the most. As much as she loved Kia, Jay loved her father twice as much. Disappointing him was worse than finding out that she was pregnant in the first place. She tried hard to prevent it, but it happened anyway.

"I'm sorry ma," Jaylynn sniffled as she hugged one of the sofa pillows. She was too ashamed to look at anyone, so she kept her head down.

[221]

"Why didn't you come to me, Jay? I could have made sure that you were well protected," Kia said.

"I was scared. I knew that you would have told my daddy and he was going to be mad with me," Jay replied.

"How do you think he's going to feel now? You're pregnant and I have to be the one to break the news to him. How far along are you?" Kia asked.

"I don't know," Jay replied as she fiddled with the strings on the pillow.

"That bitch is lying. You know when you last saw your period, so don't even come with that stupid sounding shit," Co-Co interjected.

"Have you even seen a doctor yet?" Keller asked.

"Yeah, once," Jay admitted.

"Once!" Co-Co yelled. "You look like you're a few months along and you only saw the doctor once?"

"I went when I missed my period, just to take a pregnancy test," Jaylynn replied.

"Does my nephew know about this?" Sweets asked.

"Yeah, he came with me," Jaylynn admitted.

"Lord Jesus, protect my nephew from Jaden's crazy ass," Sweets said as he looked up to the sky.

"Ain't no need to get mad at Hayden. He didn't do it all by himself. Jay was a willing participant," Co-Co noted.

"The first thing we need to do is get her to a doctor to make sure that the baby is healthy. Do you feel any movements in your belly Jay?" Brooklyn asked.

"Yeah, it moves all the time," Jaylynn replied.

"I just want to know how far along you are. You have no idea how many months you are?" Kia asked as she cradled Juice in her arms.

"No," Jaylynn whispered, dreading them finding out the truth.

"Stop lying!" Co-Co yelled angrily. He could spot bullshit a mile away and Jaylynn was spitting plenty of it right now.

"How many periods did you miss before you went to the doctor?" Brooklyn asked.

"Two," Jay answered.

"Okay, so you should have been around eight weeks or two months by then," Brooklyn calculated.

"Right, so all we need to do is see how long ago that was and do the math. How long ago did you see the doctor Jay?" Candace asked.

Jaylynn dropped her head again but didn't answer. She knew exactly how far along she was, but that was going to be another shocker once she revealed it.

"You better open your damn mouth and say something little girl. How long ago did you see the damn doctor?" Co-Co asked loudly.

"Five months ago," Jaylynn whispered.

"Five months!" Kia and Keller both shouted at the same time.

"This baby is damn near ready for high school," Co-Co said as he dramatically fanned his face.

"You're seven months pregnant Jaylynn?" Brooklyn questioned.

"Yes," Jay replied, making Kia break down and cry again.

"My sister is going to lose her mind," Sweets mumbled to himself.

Hayden was the youngest of her four boys and he was on his way to college on a full basketball scholarship. He was staying locally, but having a baby was going to change things for him. His father, Harold, was a no-nonsense kind of man and he didn't play with his boys when it came to being responsible. Hayden was going to do right by his child and Harold was going to make sure of it.

"Who turned off the music?" Royce sat up and asked.

"This bitch," Uri mumbled.

Royce had dozed off, but it was too quiet in there for her. The party was live before she went sleep and she wanted to make it live again. Everybody ignored her, as she grabbed Co-Co's phone and started up the bounce music again. When no one got up to dance, she lowered the music to see what was going on.

"Come on Co-Co, let's twerk," Royce said as she got up and started dancing on him.

"Bitch, go sit your drunk ass down somewhere. Ain't nobody in the twerking mood," Co-Co said as he pushed her away.

Royce was in a world of her own, as Kia heard keys fumbling outside her front door.

"Jaden's here," Brooklyn said out loud.

"I'm scared mama," Jaylynn cried as she grabbed on to her mother's arm.

[223]

"It's okay baby. I'll talk to him," Kia said as she tried to pull herself together.

As soon as the door opened, Jaden walked in, followed by Shaq, Caleb, and Brian. As soon as Royce saw her man, her face lit up as she ran over to him.

"Look, baby. Co-Co taught me how to twerk!" Royce yelled as she bent over and made her butt cheeks bounce.

"The fuck is she on?" Brian laughed as he watched Royce dance all over his brother.

"Y'all ain't right for this shit man. Y'all know she can't handle her liquor. The fuck y'all let her drink so much for," Caleb fussed.

"Ain't nobody here to babysit Royce's ass. Take her drunk ass home and put her to bed," Co-Co replied.

"I told them about the movie theater too," Royce giggled.

"Alright baby, just relax. We're about to go home," Caleb replied as he picked her up and threw her over his shoulder.

Jaden immediately noticed Kia's puffy eyes and tear-stained face. Jaylynn looked like she'd been crying too, and he needed to know what was up.

"What happened?" Jaden asked as he looked back and forth between the two of them.

"Um, I think it's time for us to go," Brooklyn said as she stood to her feet.

"Yeah, it's getting late," Uri said as she grabbed her purse.

"The fuck is going on? Why is everybody trying to rush out of here all of a sudden?" Jaden questioned.

"We'll talk a little later," Kia said as she wiped a few stray tears.

"Talk about what Kia? What's wrong?" Jaden asked loudly.

"Jay is having a baby, daddy," Juice blurted out.

"Aww shit," Shaq groaned as he saw the look on his nephew's face.

"Whip his lil bad ass. He need one of them old-fashioned, stay in a child's place ass whippings," Co-Co fussed.

Jaden didn't utter a word. He turned right back around and headed straight for the door.

"Baby, wait! Where are you going?" Kia yelled after him.

[224]

"I'm so sorry daddy," Jay cried as her father walked out of the house and slammed the door behind him.

"Jaden!" Kia yelled as she jumped up to go after him.

"Calm down niece, I got him. Let me talk to him. He'll be alright," Shaq promised as he stopped her from going outside.

Jaylynn was inconsolable, as Kia nodded her head and let Shaq go after her husband. She knew that Jaden was going to take the news harder than she did. She would have preferred to sit down and talk to him, but Juice just had to open his mouth. Kia looked at her son and was tempted to do just what Co-Co said and whip his ass. She was emotionally drained, and she didn't have the energy to deal with him or anything else.

"I need somebody to get Juice away from me before I kill him. I'm not in the mood to look in his bad ass face tonight," Kia sighed.

"I wanna go with Co-Co," Juice requested.

"The devil is a liar. I'm not trying to go to jail messing with you, lil boy," Co-Co replied.

"I'm gonna be good. I won't put no salt in your food or nothing," Juice promised.

"Hell no! Stop talking to me, lil boy. You're giving me flashbacks and I really wanna fight you right now," Co-Co replied.

"Co-Co, stop fussing with that baby," Candace laughed.

"That future inmate ain't no damn baby. What part is everybody missing?" Co-Co yelled.

Kia was happy when Brooklyn packed Juice a bag and took him home with her. She took a nice hot shower and snuggled up with her daughter and talked to her about how she was feeling. She tried to assure Jaylynn that her father would come around, but Kia wasn't so sure about that herself.

Chapter 25

Jaden and Shaq ended up at the same bar that they had just left from. Jaden's heart damn near beat out of his chest once Juice revealed what was going on. Pregnant. His baby was having a baby and he just couldn't seem to wrap his mind around that fact. Jaylynn was his first love, besides Kia, and he was having a hard time letting her grow up.

"My fucking baby, man. I can't believe this shit," Jaden said as he shook his head and sipped from his cup. He felt like crying, but the tears just wouldn't come.

"Jay is young, but she's not a baby anymore bruh. I told you to ease up off her with that not having a boyfriend shit," Shaq fussed.

"What are you trying to say? You making it seem like her being pregnant is my fault," Jaden said while pointing to himself.

"The only two at fault here is Jay and the lil nigga that knocked her up. It's fucked up, but it's not the end of the world." Shaq shrugged.

"I didn't want this for her though, bruh. My baby was supposed to graduate from high school next year and go off to college. She ain't supposed to be some stupid ass lil nigga's baby mama," Jaden fumed.

"What do you mean was? What's stopping her from still doing all that bruh? Kia was a teenage mother and she still handled her business. You think Mo wanted her baby to have a baby at seventeen years old? You're not exempt from life happening to you too," Shaq pointed out, making Jaden think.

He had to be honest with himself, if no one else. Mo tried her best to keep Kia away from him when she was younger, but he wasn't having it. They came up with all kinds of ways to sneak around and be together. They were successful for a while until Kia popped up pregnant. He imagined that Mo probably felt the same way that he was feeling now.

"If I wasn't cool with that lil nigga's daddy, I would put a bullet in his head," Jaden fumed.

"And what would that solve? Your daughter would be a single mother and your grandbaby would be without a father," Shaq noted.

"A fucking grandpa though, bruh. That title don't even fit a nigga like me," Jaden argued.

"You better make it fit. It's happening weather you like it or not." Shaq shrugged.

"The fuck was Jaylynn thinking though, bruh? It's bad enough that she was fucking. Why wouldn't she use protection?" Jaden questioned.

"Why didn't you and Kia?" Shaq countered.

"I wish you stop comparing shit. This ain't about me and Kia," Jaden snapped.

"I'm just trying to get you to see how fast the shoe can be placed on the other foot. You put Mo through the exact same thing, but you're sitting here pissed because it's now happening to you. The universe gives you back exactly what you put out."

"Here you go with this earth and universe shit," Jaden said, waving him off.

"It's true though, bruh. All those years in jail taught me a lot. I would have been on the same wild, crazy shit I was on before if it didn't. I know it hurts nephew, but you gotta suck it up and be the man that your family needs you to be. Your wife and daughter are all fucked up and you just walked out and left them to deal with the shit alone. Our kids don't always do what we want them to do, but we have to love them despite their faults. Shit, how do you think I feel having a daughter who got more balls than my son? I'm still waiting for that nigga to come out of the closet. The shit gone kill me, but I love him regardless," Shaq said, trying to lighten the mood.

He was happy to see Jaden laughing and that was his goal.

"You think cuz is gay?" Jaden asked.

[228]

"Yep, but he swears he's not. The nigga been soft, but I thought he would have grown out of it by now. He got a bunch of women, but that don't mean shit." Shaq shrugged.

"Damn man. I guess I need to bring my ass home and face the music. I really want to knock Jaylynn's ass out, but that's still my baby. She got me fucked up if she thinks I'm babysitting though," Jaden replied.

"You say that shit now, but that baby gon' steal your heart. I used to say the same shit before Quell gave me my first grandson," Shaq laughed.

"I still can't believe that her and Pluck had a damn baby," Jaden laughed as he stood up and threw some money on the table.

"Honestly, I'm happy that they did. That was exactly what they needed to calm down and do right," Shaq replied.

Jaden couldn't depute that because it was true. Pluck and Quell had an apartment and they both worked decent jobs. They weren't on that rowdy shit anymore and they were good parents. After dropping his uncle off at home, Jaden headed home himself. He felt bad for walking out like he did, but his emotions were all over the place. He had been gone for hours and he was sure that his family were in bed by now.

When he walked into the house, everything was still and quiet. Jaden was about to head down the hall to his bedroom, but he saw a small sliver of light coming from the kitchen. He knew that it was coming from the fridge, so he went that way to see who was still up. When he locked eyes with Jaylynn, she dropped her head and looked down at the floor. She was nervous, and Jaden saw the fear in her eyes. Her hand was shaking and the bottle of apple juice that she was drinking looked like it was about to fall. Jaden felt bad as he grabbed the bottle from her and sat it on the counter. Jay had tears falling from her eyes as he pulled her into a hug.

"I love you, baby. We're gonna get through this, I promise," Jaden said as he rocked her back and forth.

"I love you too, daddy," Jaylynn sniffled, melting into her father's embrace.

He cringed when he felt the small baby bump pressed into his body. Shit was real. His baby was having a baby.

[229]

Sweets comforted his crying sister, as her husband Harold paced their hardwood floor. Harold poured Jaden a glass of Hennessey, but he was drinking straight from the bottle. A few days after learning of their daughter's pregnancy, Jaden and Kia had to break the news to Hayden's family as well. Jaden was shocked once again when he learned that he only had two months to prepare for the new addition to his family. Everyone was in shock, but not more than he was. They didn't have time to do a baby shower, so they would have to purchase everything that the baby needed themselves. They had a spare bedroom, so Kia wanted to make that out of the baby's room.

"How fucking stupid can you be bruh? You're about to start college on a full scholarship and you go make a fucking baby?" Harold yelled as he looked at his youngest son.

All four of his boys were there, along with Jaylynn and her parents. He and Jaden had known each other for years, but they would have never thought they would be connected by a grandchild someday. Harold used to be a dope boy, but he didn't want his boys to follow in his footsteps. He took his dirty money and cleaned it up by opening three car washes in different parts of the city. Hayden worked at one of them on the weekends to keep money in his pockets and he would need all the money he could get now.

"I'm just worried about the baby. Jaylynn hasn't been seeing a doctor and that's not good," Hayden's mother, Mona, spoke up through her sniffles.

"I made her an appointment to see a doctor tomorrow," Kia replied.

"Okay, I want to come, if that's alright with you," Mona said.

"Yeah, it's fine," Kia smiled.

"And you better be ready because your ass is going too," Harold said as he pointed to his baby boy.

"Yes sir," Hayden mumbled obediently.

"And you can forget about all them Jordan's and that other dumb shit that you be spending your money on lil nigga. Every dime you make better go towards making sure your baby is straight. We'll do our part as the grandparents, but that's your muthafucking baby. You gon' handle your business or you gon' have me to deal with," Harold warned.

"Yes sir," Hayden repeated.

"Let us know whatever y'all need us to do Kia. We'll buy whatever the baby needs," Mona assured her.

"Yeah man, I'm pissed the fuck off, but I want my grandbaby to have everything that he or she needs," Harold agreed.

"This shit is just crazy. I feel like I've been robbed of the nine months that it takes to prepare for some shit like this. Nigga gon' be a grandpa in two fucking months," Jaden complained as he downed his drink.

"Fucking babies having babies. I'm not stopping my life for this shit though bruh. I'll help out when I want to, but I'm not making their responsibility mine," Harold swore.

"I already told her not to even ask me to babysit. That shit ain't happening," Jaden replied.

Kia and Mona talked amongst themselves and made notes of everything that they would need to purchase. They wanted to know the sex of the baby and that would make things easier. After wrapping up their meeting with Hayden's parents, Jaden took his family out to dinner before going home.

The following day, Jaden and Kia accompanied Jaylynn to the hospital. Harold, Mona, and Hayden were already there when they walked into the building. Once Jaylynn checked in, they all sat down and waited for her name to be called. Kia was still employed by the hospital, even though she now worked from home. She was happy that she was cool with a few of the doctors because she had to call in a favor to have Jaylynn seen.

"You feel okay baby?" Mona asked as she grabbed Jaylynn's hand.

"Yes ma'am," Jaylynn replied with a smile.

"When do we find out the sex of the baby?" Harold questioned.

"Hopefully today," Kia replied, right as they called Jaylynn's name.

"I'm staying out here baby. Y'all can go ahead," Jaden told Kia.

Harold nodded in agreement, since he felt the same way. When he saw that his son didn't move, he turned to him with a frown.

"The fuck you still sitting here for nigga? You don't get to choose. Get your ass up and go see about your baby," Harold fussed, as Hayden jumped up and followed the women to the back.

Jaylynn was given a gown to change into while Kia and the doctor who she was friends with made small talk. Kia told her that they wanted to know the sex of the baby and she assured her that she would be able to tell.

"Any pain or anything Jaylynn?" Dr. Harris asked, as she began her examination.

"No," Jaylynn replied.

"Your stomach is tiny, but that doesn't mean anything. You might just be carrying in other places," she replied as she pressed some buttons on a machine.

"What's all that weird noise?" Hayden asked with a frown.

"Are you the father?" Dr. Harris asked politely.

"Yes ma'am." Hayden smiled.

"Well, that weird noise, my dear, is your baby's heartbeat. It's very strong, so that's a good sign," Dr. Harris replied.

After giving Jaylynn a thorough examination, everyone was pleased to know that her and the baby were fine and healthy. Although it was late in the pregnancy, Dr. Harris prescribed her some vitamins to take twice a day. Once that was done, she did an ultrasound to check the baby's growth and tell everyone the sex. The grandfathers to-be were deep in conversation when they all walked back into the waiting room, but Harold could tell that his wife had been crying.

"What's wrong Mona? Everything all good with the baby?" Harold asked.

He was ready to kill his son the day before, but he had embraced the idea of being a grandfather since then. It wasn't like he had much of a choice anyway.

"No, everything is fine," Kia spoke up.

"What's with the tears baby?" Harold asked, as Mona buried her face in his chest.

"It's a girl Harold," Mona sniffled as she wiped her eyes.

"Aww shit," Harold chuckled as he rubbed his wife's back.

Mona had wanted a daughter ever since she got pregnant the very first time twenty-three years ago. Three pregnancies later and her wish still wasn't granted. After boy number four, she was over it and had her tubes tied. Things didn't work out with her having a girl of her own, but a granddaughter was just as good. Harold already knew that Mona was about to go crazy shopping. He didn't mind, just as long as his wife was happy.

"A girl huh? What's her name gonna be?" Jaden asked.

"Hayley," Jaylynn replied.

"I like that. And I'm happy that it ain't nothing ghetto. Damn babies can barely spell their own names," Harold fussed.

"Whose last name will she have?" Hayden asked.

"Yours, dumb ass, so you can be ready to sign her birth certificate. Shit is different for you now, my nigga. It ain't about you no more. Me and your mama always put you and your brothers first, and I expect the same thing from you with your daughter. Real men make moves, not excuses," Harold told his son as they walked out of the doctor's office.

"You wanna go get something to eat Jay?" Hayden asked as he looked over at Jaylynn.

He drove his own car because his parents had to go somewhere else afterwards.

"Is it okay?" Jaylynn asked as she looked over at Jaden.

"Go ahead. Ain't no need to trip now. The damage is already done" Jaden shrugged.

He still didn't like the lil nigga, but Hayden was his granddaughter's father. It wasn't like he could do anything worse than what he'd already done. Once the kids were gone, everyone else went their separate ways. Jaden was still in shock that in just seven more weeks, he would be a grandfather. He kept saying that Jaylynn was on her own, but Kia felt the opposite. She was going to help her daughter out as much as she could, and she hoped that her husband came around soon. Jaden was worried about Jaylynn finishing school and going to college. So many young girls had babies and forget all about their plans for continued education. He didn't want that for his daughter. Jay was smart, and he wanted her to use it.

Kia was happy because Jay would be having the baby during the summer, so she wouldn't have to miss any days from school. Jaylynn was making seventeen in three weeks, and she would be a senior when she went back to school. Unlike Jaden, Kia wasn't worried about their daughter doing the right thing. She was in the same predicament as her when she was her age and she still finished high school and college. She understood Jaden's apprehension, but she had faith that everything would work out just how they wanted it to.

Chapter 26

"This shit is crazy. How the fuck is my lil niece having a baby before me?" Caleb fussed, as Jaden lined up his hair.

It was a Sunday, but he and Brian had gone to Jaden's house for a little while. Kia, Jaylynn, and Shanti had gone shopping while Brian kept the baby. It was Jaylynn's birthday and she wanted something cute to wear. Royce was at one of her cousin's baby shower with Uri, so Caleb had a little free time.

"Don't even remind me, bruh. I feel like crying every time I pass by that room and see all that baby shit," Jaden replied.

They were now down to four weeks before their new addition arrived, and Jaden felt lightheaded every time the subject came up.

"How the fuck did she manage to hide the shit for seven whole months?" Brian wondered as he cradled his now three-month-old baby girl.

"I don't even know bruh. Her stomach ain't that big, but I can see it now since she ain't wearing all them big ass clothes. I'm still trying to wrap my mind around the shit," Jaden said as he brushed the access hair from Caleb's shoulders.

"Hold her for a minute bro. Let me get touched up right quick. I don't feel like doing the shit myself," Brian said as he handed Brielle off to Caleb.

"What's up pretty girl? You're getting thick as hell," Caleb said as he made his niece laugh.

"This nigga bout to be a grandpa. What she gon' call you, bruh?" Brian asked Jaden.

"She gon' call me Jaden, just like everybody else. Fuck you thought," Jaden replied.

"Nigga, you can't have your grandbaby calling you Jaden," Caleb laughed.

"She damn sure won't be calling me no grandpa," Jaden snapped.

"Leave that nigga alone before he clicks out," Brian laughed.

"Nigga, you laughing and shit, but you got your own drama going on. You ain't tell me that your P.O. is Royce's sister-in-law. You fucking the whole family," Jaden said while looking at Caleb.

"I didn't know that until I went to that Zulu shit with Royce. I was shocked my damn self," Caleb replied.

"You still go see her?" Brian questioned.

"Hell no, and I don't plan on it. I took myself off probation," Caleb replied.

"Fuck with that lady if you want to. Stupid ass gon' end up right back in jail. She has to be the one to release you from probation. You can't release yourself," Jaden said.

"Fuck her. Let her do what she do," Caleb replied, right as Brian's phone started ringing.

"This nigga," Brian said as he ignored the call.

"That must be Ronnie's ole punk ass. I don't even know why you still fuck with his shady ass." Caleb frowned.

"I ain't been fucking with that nigga. I don't even want to cut his hair no more. I know it was him who told Shaky when I was going back to work. That shit wasn't no coincidence," Brian replied.

"What's up with Trent?" Jaden asked.

"That's who that was calling. Nigga trying to get me to go to Miami with him and his brother," Brian replied.

"For what?" Jaden asked.

"You know his brother is a DJ. That nigga be having gigs all over the place," Brian said.

"Why you ain't going?" Jaden asked.

"Shanti," Caleb answered before Brian had a chance to.

"I just can't up and leave her with my baby to go to Miami," Brian noted.

"You full of shit nigga," Caleb laughed.

"Nigga probably scared that Shanti gon' cheat on him. You safe though, bruh. I heard that nigga Kerry got a girl now," Jaden replied.

"Fuck Kerry! That nigga wasn't a threat even when he was single." Brian frowned.

"Yeah okay," Jaden smirked knowingly.

He finished up with Brian's hair and cleaned up his mess. Brian stayed inside with his daughter, while Caleb and Jaden went out back and fired up. When Shanti came back, she and Brian left, and Caleb wasn't too far behind. Jaden was taking his family out to dinner to celebrate Jaylynn's birthday. As much as he didn't want to do it, he gave Jaylynn the okay for Hayden to come along as well. As hard as it was, Jaden knew that he had to embrace the situation that he was in, no matter how much he hated it.

***

"I don't know which one of us is getting off first, but we'll be here to get her soon after," Shanti promised her auntie.

"Take your time honey. This is my only company during the week," she replied with a smile.

"Bye Bri Bri. I love you," Shanti said as she kissed her daughter's chubby cheek.

She and Brian usually drove to work in the same car, but she had to hit up a few stores. She needed a few supplies and she didn't want to hold him up. For the first time in a while, she and Brian seemed to be on the same page. It was like they were together without actually saying so. They had been at his house more than hers, but she wasn't complaining. Brian loved to share his space with her and Shanti never felt like a burden. He seemed to have matured since their daughter was born, and Shanti fell even deeper in love with him. Shaky and Kerry had been staying their distance and that helped things to run smoother. She didn't know how long their peace was going to last, but she was enjoying it.

After stopping at three different supply stores, Shanti had everything that she needed. Brian told her that he was getting them some lunch, so she didn't have that to worry about. When she pulled up to the shop and didn't see his car, she knew that he was probably gone to get their food since it was almost noon. Shanti got out and grabbed her bags, preparing to head into the shop.

"What's up Shanti?" someone yelled in the distance.

Shanti cringed when she turned around and saw Kerry parking in the middle of the street. He turned his emergency lights on so that the other cars could go around him. Shanti felt like she had talked him up, but he was not a welcomed sight.

"Hey Kerry," Shanti replied dryly.

"Damn. Why it gotta be like that?" Kerry asked, looking offended.

"Like what? I said hey," Shanti replied.

"You don't have to sound all dry and shit. I know you and your baby daddy are together now, but we're still cool. We were always friends, even when we weren't lovers," Kerry said.

"We are friends, but I try to avoid drama as much as I can," Shanti noted.

"So, speaking to me causes drama? I know that nigga ain't that insecure," Kerry smirked.

"He's not insecure at all, but your ass is petty," Shanti said, calling him out.

"Petty is for bitches," Kerry replied defensively.

"If the shoe fits." Shanti shrugged.

"What are you even talking about Ashanti?" Kerry asked.

"I'm talking about you telling Brian that we were still fucking, even though we haven't gone there in years."

"I was just fucking with his ole sensitive ass," Kerry said, waving her off.

"Fucking with him but disrespecting me at the same time. I've always been cordial with you, even when I was in relationships with other people. For some reason though, Brian has always intimidated you. Maybe it's because you knew how I feel about him, but he's the only man since we broke up that you've always had a problem with," Shanti replied.

"Don't no nigga intimate me, baby girl," Kerry snarled.

"Okay Kerry. I'm not trying to argue with you. I just didn't appreciate you lying on me, but it's all good," Shanti replied, right as Brian walked up.

"What's up?" Brian asked as he looked at Shanti.

"Nothing. I just got here," she replied while ignoring Kerry's presence.

"You be easy Ashanti," Kerry said, getting the hint that their conversation was over.

Brian's face showed exactly how he was feeling as he walked away carrying the food that he'd just purchased them for lunch. They walked into the shop together, but he went straight to the break room. Shanti dropped her bags off at her work station and followed right behind him.

"The fuck was that nigga doing around here?" Brian snapped as soon as she walked into the room.

"Excuse you? You better talk to me like you got some fucking sense," Shanti clapped back.

"What's good Ashanti? You still fucking with that nigga or what?" Brian asked.

"You can't be serious right now. We've been joined at the hip for the past three months, so when would I have the time?" Shanti countered.

"I'm not understanding how you always smiling in this nigga's face though," Brian fumed.

"How was I smiling in his face and I just pulled up? He spotted me as soon as I got out of my car and walked up to me. I know you saw him parked in the middle of the streets with his emergency lights on."

"Y'all shouldn't have shit to talk about though. That's what's confusing to me."

"What part are you not understanding? I just told you what it was. I haven't seen or talked to Kerry since I was pregnant. I could have gone without seeing him today, but he approached me," Shanti noted.

"Whatever you say Ashanti. Here's your food," Brian said angrily.

"Fuck you and that food!" Shanti countered, just as upset.

"Oh yeah, and I'm going to Miami in a few days," Brian said, deciding to take Trent up on his offer.

"You can go to hell for all I care," Shanti snapped as she stormed off and left him standing there.

Brian didn't care that she was upset. He was just as pissed off as she was. He had to talk himself out of going up to Kerry and knocking him the fuck out. He wasn't trying to bring no more drama to the shop, so he decided to chill. Shanti was always claiming to be so innocent, but she stayed smiling up in the same nigga's face. Granted, Brian did see Kerry's car parked in the middle of the street with his lights flashing, but that didn't mean shit to him. The entire scene looked suspicious to him and he wasn't feeling it.

"What's up fam?" Trent said when he answered the phone for Brian.

"When do we leave nigga?" Brian asked him.

"What nigga? Shanti letting you go now?" Trent asked.

"I'm a grown ass man. I don't need nobody's permission to do shit," Brian replied.

"Alright then, nigga. I'll text you all the info in a minute," Trent said before they disconnected.

Brian was having second thoughts the moment they hung up, but he'd already put his foot in his mouth. He had never been away from his baby since she'd been born and that was going to bother him the most. Still, he was doing what he always did when he got upset. He was acting off his emotions, instead of taking the time to talk things out. He and Shanti had been good since Brielle was born but, as always, nothing good ever lasted too long with them.

Chapter 27

Shanti looked down at her phone and rolled her eyes to the ceiling. Brian was calling her on Facetime again and she ignored it like she'd been doing since he'd left three days ago. He had her fucked up to think that she was going to give him updates on Brielle when he just up and left like he did. Shanti wasn't used to doing everything on her own because Brian was always there. She had to get up earlier in the morning to get herself ready and then focus on her baby. For the past three days, she had gotten a taste of how it felt to be a single mother with no help. Shanti was so overwhelmed that she didn't even go in to work, and Saturday was usually one of her busiest days. When the phone rang again a few minutes later, Shanti was ready to ignore the call again. When she saw that it was Mrs. Pam calling, she quickly answered for the woman who she had grown to love like a mother.

"Hey Mrs. Pam." Shanti smiled when she answered the phone.

"Hey baby. Are you and Bri okay?" Pam asked.

"Yeah, we're fine. Why?" Shanti questioned.

"Brian is driving me crazy thinking that something is wrong. He said he's been trying to Facetime with you and Bri, but he's not getting an answer," she replied.

"Fuc... I mean forget Brian. If he was that concerned about us, he wouldn't have up and left like he did. I'm not ever answering the phone for him," Shanti replied.

"Okay baby. I'm not trying to get in y'all business or nothing. I just wanted to make sure that everything was alright."

"I don't care if you know what happened or not. Let me tell you what's going on," Shanti said as she ran everything down to her.

"So, this wasn't a trip that he'd been planned?" Pam asked.

"No. He told me that Trent asked him and he told him no. He only agreed to go because he got mad at me. I packed up me and Brielle's stuff and came right back home. I can't even eat or take a bath until she goes to sleep because I'm in here trying to do everything by myself," Shanti said as she started to cry.

It had been a while since she shed tears over something that Brian had done and she wasn't about to start again. She had become emotional just that fast and she hated to feel weak.

"I'm on my way over," Pam replied.

She didn't even give Shanti a chance to reply before she hung up the phone. It was Saturday and Shanti hated to bother her. Mrs. Pam was only off on the weekends and she usually spent that time with her husband. Her grandkids would be by her sometimes too, but Shanti didn't want to be a burden. It took about twenty minutes before Shanti heard her doorbell ringing. As soon as she opened the door, Mrs. Pam engulfed her in a motherly hug.

"Where's my sweet baby?" Pam asked as she looked around for Bri.

"She just went to sleep. Thank God," Shanti replied.

"Okay, well, have a seat and let's talk," Pam said as she took a seat on her sofa.

"Okay," Shanti said as she sat next to her.

"First off, I just want to say that I'm pissed," Pam said angrily.

"Why? What happened now?" Shanti asked.

"This entire situation has me in my feelings. I don't give a damn what happened between you and Brian. I don't appreciate Brielle being thrown in the mix. He had me under the impression that this trip had been planned for a while and you were okay with it."

"He's a damn lie if he told you that," Shanti replied.

"He didn't come right out and say it, but it was implied. Brian is selfish, and he's been that way since he was younger. I'm telling you right now Ashanti, don't take that shit and make him think it's okay. I know my sons and sometimes you have to show them that you ain't the one to play with. Taylor had to do it to Bryce and Kia did it to Jaden. If you start accepting it now, don't expect it to get no better later. Show his ass better than you can tell him. And you heard that bit of info from his own mama," Pam said.

"That's the thing though, I can't just up and leave my baby for days like he did," Shanti replied.

"Why not? He did it. That doesn't make you a bad mother, just like it doesn't make him a bad father. That's what's wrong with these niggas now. They dish it and expect women to take it. Kia had Jaden's ass crying like a baby, but I bet he got his mind right."

"I can't picture Jaden shedding tears," Shanti laughed.

"Honey, tears, snot and everything else. His ass used to be up under me like a newborn baby," Pam chuckled.

"Thanks Mrs. Pam. I feel much better," Shanti sighed, feeling like she had released some of her frustration.

"That's good to hear. Now, go get dressed and pack Bri a bag. It's too nice outside for you to be sitting in here all depressed and shit," Pam said.

"You don't have to tell me twice," Shanti replied as she jumped up to go get Bri together.

As soon as she saw Mrs. Pam and her baby off, Shanti took a shower and put on some clothes. She didn't have anywhere to go, but she would have walked around the mall by herself if she had to. Thankfully, she didn't have to be alone. When Brooklyn called and asked if she wanted to go out to eat with her, Royce, and Uri, she jumped at the chance. Royce was stressing about whatever was going on in her life and she needed to get away. Shanti could relate because she felt the exact same way.

***

"I thought you were supposed to be coming back one day next week," Caleb said when he picked Brian up from the airport.

"I was man, but Shanti is on some bullshit. I couldn't even enjoy myself because she wasn't answering the phone. I didn't even know if her and my baby were straight or not," Brian replied.

[243]

He cut his trip short, turning a week-long vacation into only three days. By day four, he was booking his flight home and calling Caleb to get him from the airport.

"If you felt like that, you should have never left. You said you weren't going, but you up and left anyway."

"I wasn't going until she pissed me off," Brian replied.

"You need to grow the fuck up bruh," Caleb said, shaking his head.

"Nigga, talk to me when your live-in girlfriend don't have a husband. Fuck outta here trying to give me advice. Like you got room to talk," Brian snapped.

"Lil emotional ass always trying to pop off," Caleb smirked.

"Just bring me home bruh," Brian said, trying to end their conversation.

"I don't know why. Shanti and Bri ain't there no more," Caleb informed him.

"The fuck they at then?" Brian questioned.

"I guess she went back home." Caleb shrugged.

"How do you know?" Brian asked.

"She was with Royce yesterday and she said that her and Uri dropped her off at home," Caleb answered.

"Bring me over there," Brian demanded.

He was already aggravated. Knowing that Shanti and his daughter were back at her house didn't make him feel any better. Brian was on edge the entire ride until Caleb pulled up to Shanti's apartment. He exhaled loudly, relieved that her car was parked out front.

"You want me to wait for you, nigga? She might not let your stupid ass in," Caleb said.

"I'm good. Keep my stuff in your trunk and I'll get it later," Brian replied as he got out and walked up to her door. He pressed on the doorbell and kept his finger there until he heard Shanti's voice.

"Who the hell is it? Ringing my damn doorbell like you're crazy," Shanti snapped.

"It's me, girl," Brian replied.

Shanti took her time, but she opened the door to let him in a short while later.

"What's up?" Brian asked as he strolled in like everything was all good.

"Fuck you, nigga," Shanti mumbled under her breath as she walked away.

Brian obviously didn't hear her because he would have replied if he did. Bri was in her swing looking around and he quickly snatched her up.

"Daddy missed you, baby. I know you missed me too," Brian said as he planted kisses all over her chubby face.

Shanti wanted to grab her baby and tell him to go back to wherever he'd just come from. Since she had something else in mind, she decided to let him make it. Bri was a bald mouth traitor, smiling and laughing in his face like he hadn't done anything wrong. She was probably happy to see him, but Shanti wasn't.

"Why did you come back home?" Brian had the nerve to ask.

"You can't be serious," Shanti replied.

"I'm dead ass serious," Brian countered.

"Why would I be dumb enough to stay at your house when you weren't even there?" Shanti questioned.

"What does that mean? You're always there when I'm not."

"Yeah, for a few hours, not a few days. It ain't like you give a fuck about what's going on with us anyway," Shanti fumed.

"Don't even start that dumb shit. I called and Facetimed you the entire time I was gone. You never answered for me once. I had to get updates about you and my baby from my mama."

"You got me fucked up. I wish I would have answered for you when you just up and left like you didn't have responsibilities at home," Shanti snapped.

"I just needed to get away for a while Ashanti. I had to clear my head before I snapped and did something stupid."

"All the way in Miami though, Brian!" Shanti yelled.

"The opportunity presented itself, so I took it." He shrugged like it was no big deal.

"It must be nice to be a father. Y'all still get to jump up and do whatever it is that y'all want to do, while us mothers have to stay behind and take care of the kids," Shanti said as she laughed sarcastically.

"Don't even go there with me, man. I take care of Bri just as much as you do," Brian said, waving her off.

[245]

"That's bullshit! If I were to up and leave you alone with her for three days, you wouldn't even know what to do."

"I would handle my business, just like always," Brian replied cockily.

"Okay, well, here's your chance. You know where everything is when you need it. Good luck," Shanti said as she grabbed her purse and keys and headed for the door.

"Wait, what? The fuck is you going Ashanti?" Brian asked as he jumped up and hurried out the door behind her.

"Bye Bri. Mommy loves you," Shanti said as he got into her car and started it up.

"I'm not fucking around with you, Ashanti. Quit playing and come here girl. Ashanti!" Brian yelled, as she backed out of her parking spot and drove out of the complex.

She had a bag packed in the trunk, along with her work supplies. She had appointments lined up, but she'd already made arrangements to go to her customers, instead of having them come to her. Mrs. Pam was right. If she didn't put her foot down with Brian, he would be running circles around her and she wasn't having it. He needed to know that whatever he did, she was capable of doing it too. Her brother and his girlfriend were cool with her staying with them for a few days and they had an extra bedroom. Shanti hated to still be playing games at that point in her life, but Brian needed to know how she felt. She was finally ready to settle down and be a family, but he obviously wasn't.

Chapter 28

"What's wrong now Brian?" Pam asked when she answered the phone for her son.

"Can I feed her again ma? She just had a four-ounce bottle and she's still sucking on her fingers," Brian replied.

"Yes Brian. She'll let you know when she's had enough. Stop counting ounces and feed her until she's full," Pam replied.

"That's a dumb muthafucker," Brian heard his father say, letting him know that he was on speakerphone.

Brian had been driving his mother crazy since Shanti left three days ago. He worried about every little thing and he was getting on her last nerve. She had to rush over there the day before because Bri slept longer than usual. Brian swore that something was wrong, but the damn baby was tired. He smiled in her face all day and she probably couldn't get any rest.

"Man, I don't know all that kind of stuff. I usually just do whatever Shanti tells me to do," Brian admitted as he stuck the warm bottle of formula into Brielle's mouth.

"She should be good for a nap after she eats. Let her sleep Brian. You have all the time in the world to play with her once she wakes up. And you don't have to hold her while she sleeps either. That's what her crib is for," Pam said.

"Okay. Shanti needs to bring her stubborn ass back home. What kind of mother leaves their three-month-old baby for three damn days?" Brian asked.

"The same kind of father that does it. Double standards my love," Pam replied.

"Don't take her side ma. You know she was foul for leaving us like that," Brian fussed.

"And you weren't? You got life fucked up if you can't see what you did wrong."

"I'm not saying that I was right, but it's not the same. She's a mother," Brian reasoned.

"And you're a father. What's your point?" Pam countered.

"Nothing ma. You don't get what I'm saying. Don't even worry about it," Brian replied.

"I know exactly what you're saying, but you sound stupid saying it. It never feels good when the dirt you throw starts to fly in your own eyes."

"I'm trying ma," Brian sighed as he put Brielle on his shoulder to burp her.

"Nigga, you don't get no points for trying. You're a grown ass man with responsibilities. Trying ain't gon' keep no food in your daughter's mouth. I never tried, I made shit happen. Y'all keep making all these fucked up mistakes and expect my wife to fix the shit. You better man the fuck up and act like you got some sense boy," Bryce Sr. fussed.

"Calm down baby," Pam said while rubbing her husband's back.

Her sons knew how their father was, but she hated when he got upset. Bryce was a man in every sense of the word and he expected the same from his sons. He didn't do excuses and they knew not to bring him any. He was barely twenty years old when he started a family and he's provided for them ever since then.

"Did you hear what I just said Brian?" his father asked.

"Yeah, I hear you, bruh. I'm getting my shit together," Brian replied.

"You better," his father warned.

"What is Bri doing now?" Pam asked while changing the subject.

"She just burped and now she's falling asleep," Brian replied.

"Okay baby. Call me if you need me," Pam said.

"Don't call here no more boy. I'm sick of this shit!" his father yelled, making him laugh.

"Alright y'all," Brian said before they disconnected.

He chuckled when he heard Bri lightly snoring in his ear. Brian had her blanket laid out in the bed, so he slowly stood up and headed to Shanti's bedroom. He didn't go back home like she did when he left. He still had clothes at her house, so he decided to stay there. Once he laid Bri down, Brian made sure that she had more bottles made before he stretched out in the bed next to her. He was bored out of his mind and he missed Shanti something serious. He was already missing her after being gone for three days and she added three more days to that. Their time apart put a lot of things in perspective for him and he was seeing things in a different light. He didn't only love Shanti; he was in love with her. He had women throwing themselves at him in Miami, but he didn't even entertain them. Shanti and his daughter stayed on his mind the entire time and that's when he knew that it was real.

Brian was deep in thought when he heard the front door open and close a short time later. Shanti threw her keys on the counter like she always did and walked into her bedroom. Brian wanted to be mad and go off on her, but he had to be honest with himself. He started the bullshit by leaving first and she had every right to follow his lead. Bri was on her back sleeping, as Shanti planted light kisses on her face. She missed her baby and she was happy to be back home.

"What about me? I can't get no kisses?" Brian asked.

"You can kiss my ass, but that's about all that I can offer you," Shanti replied as she walked away.

Brian got up and placed a few pillows around Bri before following her into the living room. Shanti sat on the sofa and flipped through the channels on the tv while Brian stood their staring at her.

"I guess I deserved that," Brian spoke up.

"I guess you did." Shanti shrugged.

"I know it's way too late for this shit, but I'm sorry. I fucked up and I'm man enough to admit that. I always let my insecurities cause me to do stupid shit and be regretting it later. I was wrong to just up and leave you and Bri like I did," Brian admitted, shocking Shanti with his apology.

She thought they were going to argue the minute she walked through the door and continue until the sun came up. That's how it was in the past, but she was happy that things had changed.

"Thank you for apologizing Brian. I know that was hard for you to do," Shanti replied.

"Nah, it wasn't. I fucked up, so it is what it is. I just gotta stop letting stupid shit get to me," Brian admitted.

[249]

"We were doing too good for that Brian. I just feel like all the progress we made was for nothing. We're right back to square one."

"We don't have to be though Shanti," Brian replied.

"I don't see how you can say that. You claim to want to be with me, but you obviously don't trust me. For every step forward, we've taken two steps back. I can't be in a relationship like that and I won't be," Shanti swore.

"I do trust you, Ashanti. I told you that it's my own insecurities that makes me act the way I do. I did so much dirt in my life and I'm scared as fuck that the shit is gonna come back to me. You and Bri are the best things that ever happened to me. I don't want us to co-exist. I want us to be a family," Brian replied.

"How do I know that you won't just up and leave us again if something goes wrong?" Shanti asked.

"Honestly, you don't, but I hope you believe me when I say that it will never happen again. My word is all that I have until I can prove myself. I love you, baby, and, if you let me, I promise to make you the happiest woman in the world or die trying," Brian said, giving her goosebumps.

"I love you too, Brian, but I just need a little more time," Shanti replied.

"Take all the time you need. I'm not going anywhere," Brian said as he turned and walked back into the bedroom.

✱✱✱

"What's up nigga? You trying to hit up the strip club tonight or what? That's the least you can do since you left me hanging in Miami," Trent said over the phone to Brian.

Two weeks had passed since he and Shanti had their talk and things were looking up. They were back to how they were before, but they still weren't official yet. Brian wanted to ask her about it again, but he decided against it. When the time was right, he would know it.

"Nah man. I'm on daddy duty tonight. Shanti is going somewhere with my sister and Royce," Brian replied.

"You still at Shanti's house?" Trent asked.

"Yeah man. We're supposed to be going back to my house tomorrow," Brian replied.

"Tell Shanti to give up that damn apartment and move in with you. Y'all can be saving money with just one place," Trent noted.

"I said the same thing, but her ass is stubborn. She's still on this co-parenting bullshit that I'm tired of hearing."

"Her ass better stop all that playing. Ain't no damn co-parenting. She's wifey."

"You already know," Brian agreed.

"You and Shanti being together is a good look though," Trent said.

"I think so too, but you need to tell her that," Brian laughed.

"Damn man. The strip club gon' be lit tonight too. They got two parties up in that bitch," Trent replied.

"Fuck that club. I wouldn't go, even if I didn't have my baby. I'm not trying to see that bitch Shaky. She already been coming to the shop three times a week with her stalking ass."

"The fuck is she coming to the shop three times a week for? Bitch don't even have that much hair," Trent said.

"Cookie ole messy ass be having her up in there. I can't wait until her lease is up. I don't know what Bryce was thinking giving her ass an eighteen-month contract," Brian fussed.

"Yeah, that was bad business, but he didn't know. Bitch finessed her way right through the front door," Trent laughed.

"That fuck boy Ronnie be on that bullshit too. Lame ass nigga." Brian frowned.

"I told you, bruh. I can read a muthafucka like a book. I never did like that nigga from day one. I knew he wasn't right," Trent replied.

"The nigga was alright until he got with Katrice big nasty looking ass."

"He was never alright with me," Trent said, right as Shanti walked out of the bedroom with Bri in her arms.

She had just given Bri a bath and handed her to Brian to feed. She needed to get dressed and she didn't want to be late.

"I gotta go bruh. My boss is here and my shift is about to start," Brian joked before he hung up the phone.

"Lil nasty thing pissed in her water. I had to let it out and run some more," Shanti laughed.

"Come on Pissy Missy," Brian said as he stuck the bottle in her mouth.

"Did you make some more bottles, or do I need to?" Shanti asked.

"I already did it. What time are you coming back?" Brian asked.

"I don't know." Shanti shrugged as she walked away.

A teacher that Royce and Brooklyn knew was having a birthday party in a club and they invited Shanti. She didn't really get out much, so she took them up on their offer. Brian didn't really want her to go, but he had to keep that to himself. He fed Bri and laid her on his chest as she slept.

Almost an hour later, Shanti walked out of the room and made him sit up to look at her. Shanti was always thick, but having Brielle made some of her best parts even better. She would be considered fat to some, but she was just right for Brian. Her cute baby face was one of her best assets, in his opinion.

"What?" Shanti questioned when she noticed him staring at her.

"Why you gotta wear that?" Brian asked with a frown.

Shanti had on a cream colored off the shoulder bandage dress. The gold strappy heels gave her short frame some height and put her thick legs on full display. Her hair was curly and pinned up on one side and her makeup was light and natural. The jealous hearted nigga that lived inside of Brian wanted to throw the Coke that he was drinking on her so that she would change. The part of him that was trying to do right took over and instantly calmed him down.

"What's wrong with what I have on?" Shanti asked as she looked down at her outfit.

"You look good baby, but damn," Brian sighed.

"Don't worry, I'll behave. I'm almost spoken for," Shanti smirked.

"Almost," Brian repeated.

"Yes, almost. We haven't made anything official," Shanti replied.

"Whose fault is that?" Brian asked.

"Let's not do this right now Brian. I'm already running late," Shanti said.

[252]

She gave him a peck on the lips and kissed Brielle's cheek. Once she grabbed her purse, she rushed out of the house to go meet her girls. Brian was in his feelings the minute the door closed behind her. He flopped back on the sofa to watch a movie, but he couldn't get Shanti off his mind. She probably hadn't even made it to her destination and he was already ready for her to come back home. Bri must have felt the same way because she woke up not even an hour after her mother left.

"You want your mama home too, huh? Don't worry about it. Your daddy is about to make it happen," Brian said as he dialed his mother's number.

"Hey baby," Pam said, answering the phone.

"What's considered a high temperature for a baby?" Brian asked.

"What's wrong with my baby?" Pam asked in concern.

"Calm down and just answer the question ma," Brian replied.

"Anything over one hundred is high. What's her temperature?" Pam asked.

"What can an infant take for a high fever?" Brian questioned, without replying to what she'd asked.

"Infant Tylenol or Motrin. Where is Ashanti? Are you alone with Bri?" Pam asked.

"Yeah. Shanti is with Brooklyn and Royce," he replied.

"I'm on my way," Pam said.

"Ma, no, I'm good. I got this," Brian assured her.

"Boy, if something happens to my grandbaby, I'm fucking you up," Bryce Sr. threatened in the background.

"Why you always gotta have people on speakerphone?" Brian asked.

"I don't even know why you called me, Brian. You know how worried I get. Jaylynn is about to have this baby, Juice is beating up all the kids in school, and now Bri is sick. Y'all are gonna drive me crazy," Pam fussed.

"Have a drink and relax ma. I can handle my own baby."

"Just promise that you'll call if you need me, Brian," Pam said.

"Yeah ma, I promise. You worry too much," Brian laughed.

"Okay baby," Pam sighed before she hung up.

[253]

"Come one Bri. Your daddy is about to put the p in petty. Don't tell nobody about this either," Brian said, making her laugh.

He sat Bri in her swing and ran to the bathroom in Shanti's bedroom. He walked back into the kitchen with the infant Motrin and the baby thermometer. After reading the instructions on the medicine, he took the dosage out that was appropriate for Brielle's age. He dropped the medicine in the sink and ran some water to rinse it away. He then took the lighter out of his pocket and put fire to the metal tip of the thermometer as he watched the digital numbers go up. Once he was satisfied with his handy work, Brian pulled out his phone and snapped a picture. He typed up a message along with the picture and sent it to Ashanti. He grabbed Bri out of her swing to change her diaper and waited for his phone to ring.

Chapter 29

"Baby, Shanti is cutting it up on that dance floor," Uri said as she watched Shanti doing her thing with some random man who asked her to dance.

Shanti had been pulling niggas all night, but she never did more than dance with them. As soon as they asked for her number, she shot them down and kept it moving.

"She doesn't really get out too much no more since she had Bri. I'm happy that she's enjoying herself," Brooklyn replied.

"I know the feeling. It took me a while to start enjoying myself after I had my kids. My husband be damn near throwing me out of the house now," Uri laughed.

"I guess I'll be able to relate one day." Royce shrugged as she sipped on her juice.

"No crown apple and Sprite today Royce?" Brooklyn laughed.

"Caleb got that bitch scared to drink," Uri replied.

"Bitch, I'm grown. Caleb can't stop me from doing nothing. I feel like I need something stronger than that anyway," Royce said.

"Why? What's wrong?" Brooklyn asked.

"I just feel stressed out and overwhelmed," Royce replied.

"Oh Lord. Here she goes with the stress again," Uri sighed.

"I'm serious Uri. I got a lot going on and it's starting to get to me. I've been arguing with my mama every day and I'm about ready to lay hands on her disgusting ass. Not to mention, Jax has been blowing my phone up begging for his laptop. I'm trying to help Caleb with the renovations to the house, as well as sell my own," Royce rambled.

"You worry too much, and you always have. I don't know why you're even entertaining your mama with that dumb shit with Jax. Y'all are gonna be divorced in a little over a month, whether she likes it or not," Uri replied.

"Why are you still holding on to Jaxon's computer? He signed the divorce papers already," Brook noted.

"Girl, he can have that cheap ass laptop. I forgot I even had the damn thing." Royce frowned.

"What happened to the people who were interested in buying your house? I thought the deal was almost done," Uri said.

"The bank wouldn't finance their broke asses, so the deal fell through. I'm praying that this other couple can get financed. They seem to really want the house and they have a down payment. I don't want to be paying property taxes and stuff on a house that I'm no longer living in. Caleb and I will have to do all that at the new house once we move in," Royce said.

"I didn't know that Caleb asked you to move in with him," Uri noted.

"He didn't ask me, but I'm going. What's understood don't need to be explained," Royce said, making her cousin and friend laugh.

"What happened to the shy, timid Royce?" Brooklyn asked.

"That bitch is dead and gone," Royce said, right as Shanti came back over to their booth.

"Sit down and drink some water girl. You look like you're about to pass out," Brook said while handing Shanti some bottled water.

"Girl, that old man wore my ass out," Shanti said as she fanned her face with a napkin.

"I saw him giving you a run for your money," Uri laughed.

"My damn feet are killing me in these heels on," Shanti complained.

"I guess so if you've been dancing in them for over an hour," Brook replied.

Shanti downed half of her water as she looked around the semi crowded club. The lady who the gathering was for was the life of her own party and she hadn't sat down yet. There were a lot of older people in attendance, but they had more energy than people half their age. Shanti's last dance partner said that he was sixty-five, but he was a livewire. She had been ready to tap out, but she couldn't let him outdo her.

"Where is my purse?" Shanti asked as she looked around the area that they were seated in.

"Here," Brooklyn said as she handed it to her.

Shanti fumbled around inside until she located her phone. She had texted Brian earlier to make sure that her baby was okay, but she wanted to check again. She had an unread message from him that she immediately opened. It was sent almost an hour ago, but that didn't matter.

"Oh God! I have to go!" Shanti shrieked as she jumped up from her seat.

"What's wrong?" Brooklyn asked as she stood up and walked over to her.

The look on Shanti's face had her heart thumping rapidly in her chest. When Shanti handed her the phone to read the message, she understood why. Brian had sent her a picture of a thermometer with a temperature that was well over the norm for an infant. He also sent a picture of the medicine that he'd given to Bri, telling her that he had it under control and not to worry. Shanti wasn't trying to hear that shit and Brooklyn didn't blame her. No mother wanted to be away from their baby when they were sick, and she understood why Shanti was rushing out of there. Brook walked her out and one of the security guards made sure that she got to her car safely. Shanti was happy that the roads were clear because she ran red lights and all trying to get home to her baby. As soon as she pulled up, she rushed inside and straight to her bedroom. Brian was stretched out across the bed, while Bri laid on her back right next to him.

"Don't make no noise. I just got her back to sleep," Brian whispered.

"We need to bring her to the hospital Brian. That's a high fever for an infant," Shanti said as she touched her baby's forehead.

Bri didn't feel warm, so maybe the medicine that he gave her helped. Brian felt like shit when he saw the look of concern covering Shanti's face. He probably went overboard just to get her home, but his plan worked.

"She's fine Ashanti. I gave her some medicine and she feels better," Brian replied.

[257]

"How do you know that Brian? It ain't like she can talk and tell you that she's okay," Shanti fussed.

"Calm down baby. She's good," Brian tried to assure her.

"Give me her thermometer," Shanti demanded.

Brian got up and gave her Brielle's thermometer and watched as she stuck it under the baby's arm. Shanti waited until the device beeped before she looked at it to make sure it was normal.

"I told you that she was okay. Her temperature is back to normal," Brian said while rubbing her back.

"I feel like shit. I'm never going out again," Shanti replied as she stared down at her baby.

"Stop being so damn dramatic girl. You left for three whole days and she was fine," Brian reminded her.

"Yeah, but your mama had my back. She kept me updated and made sure that she was straight," Shanti replied.

"She was trying to come over here tonight," Brian laughed as he sat her down on the bench at the foot of the bed.

He kneeled and removed Shanti's heels before pulling her up again. Shanti stood still while he unzipped her dress and pulled it off. Her jewelry was next to go, leaving her in a half-bra and thongs. When Brian lifted her up, Shanti wrapped her arms around his neck and went with the flow. After carrying her to the other bedroom, he laid her down on the bed before taking off the rest of her clothes. Shanti's eyes never left his as he removed his pajama bottoms and the boxers that he had on. She opened her legs wider when Brian climbed on top of her, giving him enough room to get comfortable. When Brian's soft lips connected with hers, Shanti closed her eyes and enjoyed the feeling. She was ready for whatever, but Brian had other plans.

"Let's talk," he said, making Shanti's eyes pop open in shock.

"Talk? Nigga, we're laying here butt ass naked and you want to talk," Shanti replied.

"Yep," Brian smirked as he rubbed his hand up and down her side, making her shutter.

"Let's talk about how many positions you're about to fuck me in," Shanti said as she grinded on him.

"Nah, I don't want to talk about no sex. I want to talk about us. You get all the benefits of being my girl, but you're still refusing to make a commitment. Me and my dick are tired of being used," Bran joked.

"Stop playing so much Brian. You got me all hot and bothered and now you're acting stupid," Shanti fussed.

Her breath got caught in her throat when Brian started raining kisses all over her face and neck. Shanti grabbed on to his erection and tried to put it in herself.

"Stop girl," Brian said as he stuck his tongue in her ear.

"Oh, my God," Shanti moaned as she tried to grind on him again.

"What's good Ashanti? You trying to make us official or not?" Brian asked as he continued to tease her.

"Okay," Shanti hissed as he slipped a finger inside of her and moved it around.

"What does okay mean?" Brian asked as he slipped another finger inside of her and watched her lose control.

"It's official. We're official," Shanti panted.

"Don't play with me, Ashanti. Don't say that shit just because you want the dick," Brian said as he stopped moving and looked down at her.

"I'm not. It was only a matter of time before we made it official anyway. I'm tired of all the dumb shit. We're already together, whether we admit it or not," Shanti replied.

"You know I love you, right?" Brian asked as he looked her in her eyes.

"I love you too, baby," Shanti said as she smiled at him.

"That's all I needed to hear. I've been holding back on you, but now you can get that official dick," Brian said as he picked her up and make her straddle his face.

Shanti's entire body shook when she felt the first flick of his tongue at her opening. Maybe it was because they made it official, but the sex that night was even better than before. For the first time in a while, Shanti felt complete. She had the family that she always wanted and, to her, nothing was better than that.

Shanti woke up the next morning to the loud ringing of Brian's phone, but he was no longer in the bed with her. After showering the night before, she and Brian had gone back into the room and got in bed with Bri. When Shanti looked in her bassinet, Bri was gone too. Brian's phone was still going off, so she grabbed it and went to the front of the house to give it to him.

"What's wrong?" Brian asked when Shanti walked into the living room.

He was giving his baby girl a bottle while he watched a college basketball game. Bri had woke up crying earlier, so he took her out of the room to let Shanti get some rest.

"Your phone has been ringing off the hook," Shanti replied.

"Who is it?" Brian asked, never taking his eyes off the game.

"I don't know. I didn't look," Shanti replied.

"Answer it," Brian said as he continued to feed their daughter.

He didn't have anything to hide and he needed Shanti to know that she could trust him. She tried not to let her face show it, but Shanti was too hyped. She remembered her and Brian arguing once before when she answered his phone, but he had matured since then.

"Hey Jaden," Shanti said when she looked at the screen and answered the phone for his brother.

She listened to what Jaden had to say before she hung up the phone.

"What's going on?" Brian asked.

"Jaylynn is in labor. Jaden said that they're at the hospital now," Shanti replied.

"Okay. Hold her while I get dressed. I'll dress her while you get yourself together once I'm done," Brian said while handing her their baby.

His first great niece was coming, and he wanted to be there for his brother. He was sure that Jaden was a nervous wreck, but having his brothers around would keep him calm.

Chapter 30

"She looks like a pale rat," Co-Co said as he looked down at Jaylynn's baby in Sweets' arms.

Jaylynn had been in labor for only three hours before she gave birth to six-pound, three-ounce Hayley Kemora Williams. Kia, Hayden, and Mona were by her side as her bundle of joy entered the world. Once Jaylynn was moved into her room, her grandparents and some other family members came there to see her and the baby. Everyone was saying how cute the baby was, but Co-Co was not about to lie. He was sure that her looks would change over time, but he just had to wait until that time came. Until then, his opinion remained the same.

"Don't talk about my great niece. She is beautiful." Sweets smiled as he looked down at Hayley.

"No comment," Co-Co replied as he rolled his eyes up to the sky.

"Get fucked up in here if you want to Co-Co," Jaden threatened angrily.

Hayden's mother, Mona, looked like she wanted to say something, but she had the right one. Co-Co didn't care that she was his best friend's sister; she could get it too. She had a mug on her face like she didn't like what he was saying about her granddaughter, but he didn't give a damn.

"Shut up boy. She's barely a day old. Her looks haven't even hit her yet," Pam fussed.

"I hope they hurry up," Co-Co mumbled.

"Now, let somebody say something about his niece and nephew. He'll be ready to fight," Sweets spoke up.

"Bitch, my niece and nephew were beautiful when they were born, and nothing has changed. Fuck you mean," Co-Co snapped.

Everybody knew that he was an entirely different person when it came down to David and Candace's kids. Spoiled was too vague of a word to describe how rotten he had them. Nothing was too good for them and they knew it. His sister gave birth to them, but they were his babies.

"Not today and I mean that shit. I'll clear this room out if we're going to have a problem," Pam fussed while looking at her nephew.

"I'll be good auntie, but you know I don't play about them two," Co-Co said as he looked at his best friend. He couldn't wait to get Sweets alone to tell him about himself.

"How are you feeling Jaylynn?" Mona asked as she looked over at her.

Hayden was quiet as he sat in the chair next to her bed and watched his baby being passed around. He didn't want to give her up, but everybody was asking to hold her. He didn't care what Co-Co said; his baby was beautiful to him. He was scared out of his mind, but he wanted to be a good father. He was set to move into his dorm room the following day to start basketball camp, and that scared him too. College was already a scary thing, but being a young father was even scarier. There was no room for errors where Hayley was concerned. His father wasn't having it and he let that be known.

"I feel okay. Just happy that all the pain is over," Jaylynn replied, shaking Hayden from his thoughts.

"I wish his ass could have felt some of it too," Harold said, referring to his son.

"I want to know when the doctor is coming back up in here. We need to discuss some birth control," Jaden replied.

"Daddy," Jaylynn said in embarrassment.

"Don't daddy me, with your sneaky ass. You snuck this one in on me, but I bet that shit won't happen again. My eyes are wide open now," Jaden noted.

"I'm with you on that," Harold agreed while giving him dap.

Jaylynn only shook her head and smiled, but she understood their concerns. She knew better, but she was young and careless. Kia had talked to her about sex enough for her to know what to do. She and Hayden started out using protection, but he convinced her that the pull-out method worked just as good. They both found out the hard way that that was a lie.

"Are y'all putting her in a daycare when you go back to school?" Sweets asked.

"Over my dead body. I'm home every day. She'll be with me," Mona spoke up.

"She's just trying to spoil her," Harold said, laughing at his wife.

"No, but I don't want her to be with just anybody," Mona replied.

Jaylynn turned over and closed her eyes as her parents and Hayden's made decisions for their baby. She already knew that was how it was going to be, but there was nothing that she could do about it. Hayden looked like he had a lot on his mind as well, but he just sat there and listened just like she did.

✳✳✳

Two weeks later and Jaylynn was bringing her baby girl to have her first checkup. She was happy that she'd given birth during the summer because she had to adjust to waking up all during the night with a baby. Hayden had moved into his dorm room the day after Hayley's birth, but he came to their house every day to see the baby. Things seemed to be different between the two of them, but Jaylynn didn't know why. Hayden called her on Facetime all the time when he wasn't there, but he only wanted to talk about Hayley. Before the baby was born, he and Jaylynn talked about everything. Now, it seemed like they were no longer a couple and were just parents to their daughter. He claimed that he was so busy with camp, but his social media pages showed a different story. Hayden had been living it up, going to parties and hanging with some of his new teammates.

"Y'all want me to come to the back with y'all?" Mona asked her son and Jaylynn.

Kia had a conference call for work, so Mona went to the clinic with them. Jay didn't want anyone but Hayden to go, but Mona didn't miss a beat with her granddaughter.

"No, it's okay," Jaylynn replied while Hayden played on his phone.

He hadn't said too much since they picked her and the baby up, but Jaylynn wanted some answers. Mona signed Hayley in and they all took a seat and waited for her name to be called. Once the nurse called them to the back, Hayden picked up the car seat and followed Jaylynn to the back room.

"Are you okay?" Jaylynn asked him once they were in the room alone.

"Yeah," Hayden replied as he helped her to undress their baby girl.

"Did I do something because you've been acting kind of distant lately," Jaylynn noted.

"How am I acting distant? I call and come to see my baby every day," Hayden noted.

"Yeah, but you act like I don't exist."

"I'm just focusing on school, basketball, and my daughter right now," Hayden said, making her heart drop.

"What are you trying to say Hayden?" Jaylynn questioned.

"I just said it. I don't have time for no girl and all that right now. I got too much going on for all that," he replied, refusing to even look her in the eye.

"Yeah, but you sure find time to party with your new teammates and stuff though, huh?" Jaylynn questioned.

"I'm in college Jay. That's all they do is party." Hayden shrugged.

"Why didn't you just tell me that you didn't want a girlfriend anymore?" she asked.

"Because I didn't feel like that until recently. I just want to focus on school and my baby right now. I don't have time for nothing else," he replied.

"Cool," Jaylynn nodded, trying to sound unaffected. She wanted to break down and cry, but she wouldn't give him the satisfaction.

Jaylynn held it together as the doctor examined Hayley. She got her first set of shots and they were on their way soon after. The ride back to her house was quiet and Jay was happy when they finally pulled up. Hayden helped her get the baby out of the car and promised to call her on Facetime once he got settled into his room. Jaylynn laid her baby down in her bassinet before climbing into her bed to watch some tv.

[264]

"How did it go?" Kia asked when she walked into the room. She peeked at Hayley before taking a seat at the foot of Jaylynn's bed.

"She's doing good. She got her first set of shots," Jaylynn replied.

"I'm happy I wasn't there. I don't want to see her cry," Kia pouted.

"She didn't cry very long," Jaylynn noted as she looked down at her nails.

"What's wrong Jay? You sound sad," Kia pointed out.

"Sad about what? What happened?" Jaden asked as he walked into the room and looked down at his sleeping granddaughter.

"Nothing. I'm fine," Jaylynn lied.

"No, you're not Jay. I can tell when something is wrong with you," Kia pressed.

"Hayden and I broke up," Jay admitted.

"Good," Jaden mumbled loud enough for them to hear.

"Don't say that baby. What happened Jay?" Kia asked sympathetically.

"He just said that he wanted to focus on school and Hayley and he doesn't have time for a girlfriend," Jaylynn shrugged.

"Wait, hold up. That nigga broke up with you?" Jaden questioned angrily.

"Really Jaden? Would it have made a difference if she had broken up with him instead?" Kia asked.

"You damn right it would have! I never liked that high yellow pretty muthafucker anyway!" Jaden fumed.

"But that's not a bad thing though, Jay. Focusing on school and his daughter shows maturity," Kia reasoned.

"I know damn well you ain't buying that bullshit ass excuse girl," Jaden said while looking at his wife sideways.

"He's lying. He's always at parties and stuff every time I look on his Snapchat or Instagram," Jaylynn pointed out.

"Exactly. That nigga is in college and he's trying to be a hoe, but fuck him," Jaden snapped.

"Aww, I'm so sorry baby. I hate that this happened to you," Kia said as her daughter's eyes filled with tears. She pulled Jay in for a hug, as Jaden looked on angrily.

"I dare you. You better not shed one muthafucking tear over that nigga and I mean that shit. Ain't no nigga worth your tears," Jaden fussed.

"Don't do that Jaden. She's hurt. Hell, I shed enough tears over your ass to fill a river. Now you're mad because somebody else has your daughter wanting to do the same thing," Kia replied.

"I don't want to hear that shit right now Kia. This is my baby that this lil nigga is trying to fuck over. You already know what's up with me. I'll go knock on that door and put a bullet in everybody up in that bitch," Jaden fumed.

"Daddy! Oh, my God! I'm fine and it's not that serious," Jaylynn laughed.

"I don't find nothing funny about this shit Jay. Nigga got you pregnant, then decided that he didn't want the responsibility no more. Lil pussy," Jaden ranted.

"That's not true daddy. Him breaking up with me has nothing to do with Hayley. He calls and comes to see her every day. My feelings are hurt, but I'll get over it. I'm only seventeen. Just like I met Hayden, I can meet somebody else." Jay shrugged.

"Yeah, but you better not bring no more damn babies up in here," Jaden warned.

"I won't daddy," Jaylynn laughed.

"Lil light bright bitch got my baby girl looking just like his ass," Jaden said as he looked over at Hayley.

"Are you really okay baby?" Kia asked as she held her daughter's hand.

"She better be okay. You ain't no punk Jay. Fuck that nigga. I need to make Pluck come out of retirement to beat his ass," Jaden said, making them laugh.

Just like always, Jaden made his daughter feel better about her situation. He had her and Kia laughing for hours until Hayley woke up for a bottle. When Hayden called Jaylynn later that night, she did exactly what he had been doing lately. She kept the conversation strictly about Hayley and nothing more. She was young, but she was nobody's fool, baby daddy included.

Chapter 31

66 No! Stop!" Sienna screamed, as Jax's closed fist came down and connected with her face once again.

The look on his face made Jax look like the devil himself as he continued to throw her around the room and hit her. Jax was already angry and Sienna had just pushed him over the edge. After months of begging and pleading, Royce had finally given him his laptop. He and Royce both taught summer school, so she handed it over to him one morning before work. Jax had learned his lesson from before and put a passcode on his device. He had his computer hidden in his bottom drawer under his folded clothes. Jax had left for work that morning, but he forgot his gym bag. He was pissed when he walked into the house and found Sienna in his hiding place, trying to take his computer out. There was nothing that she could do with it, but he was heated that she even tried.

"Stay in your fucking place. Don't touch my shit and this is my last time saying it," Jax fumed angrily.

Things in Jaxon's life had spiraled out of control and he often took his frustrations out on Sienna. His parents were still on his ass about the situation with Angelique, not to mention the way that Royce had embarrassed them at the club. He was the black sheep of all their children and they never let him forget it. They would probably die if they knew that their one and only daughter wasn't as perfect as they thought she was. Ashley had as many skeletons in her closet as he did, if not more.

"I want you out of here," Sienna cried as she backed up into a corner.

"Bitch, this is my family's home. You'll leave before I do," Jax replied. He grabbed his laptop and gym bag, right before he walked out of the room.

As soon as the front door slammed, Sienna ran to look out of the window to make sure that he was really gone. When she saw his car speeding out of the driveway, she ran back to her bedroom and grabbed her phone.

"I'm on my way!" Yada yelled as soon as she answered the phone for her best friend.

"I'm fine Keyada. He just left," Sienna replied as she walked into the bathroom.

"You need to call the police Sienna. Stop letting him put his hands on you and get away with it," Yada said to her girl.

Sienna's kids were at her house because she had to work the night before. When Yada called to tell her that she was bringing them home, she heard Jax yelling at her in background before the phone went dead. She left Sienna's kids with her daughter while she rushed to her best friend's rescue once again.

"You know I can't do that," Sienna said after a long pause.

"Why not? You keep trying to spare that nigga when he doesn't give a fuck about you. I'm tired of doing this same shit with you every other day. I don't know why you let him back in your life. You need to put his ass on child support and be done with it. You're struggling with his kids and he got money to help you," Yada fussed.

"He does help me," Sienna defended.

"No bitch, his mama and daddy help you and only when they feel like it. You had to hit rock bottom for them to even give you a place to stay. Stop being so fucking stupid!" Yada yelled angrily.

"I'm just so scared Yada. What if I put him in jail and his parents put me out? I just don't know what to do," Sienna sniffled.

"Where is he at now?" Yada asked.

"He just left to go to work."

"I thought school was out," Yada said.

"He's teaching summer school," Sienna replied.

"Okay and that's exactly where we're sending the police," Yada said.

"What! No Yada. I can't do that," Sienna panicked.

"Why the fuck not?" Yada asked.

[268]

"His parents already hate me. It'll be even worse if I have their son arrested at school," Sienna replied.

"Open the door. I'm outside," Yada said before hanging up the phone.

Sienna wet a towel and tried to clean some of the blood from her face before she went to the door. She knew that her friend was really going to go off once she saw all the damage that Jax had done.

"It's not as bad as it looks," Sienna said as soon as she let her in.

"Are you out of our damn mind? You can barely open your fucking eye!" Yada yelled.

Sienna's left eye was almost swollen shut. Her bottom lip was almost twice it's normal size and her nose was dripping blood like a leaky faucet. She looked horrible and she was still trying to defend her sad ass ex-husband.

"I'm okay Yada, really, I am," Sienna said, trying to convince her best friend as well as herself.

That was a lie and she knew it. She was broken, mentally and spiritually. She wasn't a bad person, but she continuously made bad decisions. She wanted love, but she always found it in the wrong places. Yada always told her that she had to be okay with being alone before she could truly be happy with someone else. She didn't want to hear it at first, but Sienna was starting to see that for herself. She no longer wanted a man to make her feel complete. She had two beautiful kids for that. She had to get her life together for them, if not herself.

"I'm done Sienna. I can't keep doing this with you. I'll bring the kids home later, but my daughter and I won't be helping you with them anymore. You're draining me, and I've had enough," Yada said as she turned to leave.

"Please don't do this to me, Yada. You're the only friend that I have," Sienna cried as she dropped down to her knees.

"I'm trying to help you, Sienna, but you don't seem to want it. You're a beautiful person inside and out, but I can't make you believe that. I've been your friend for over ten years and I've always been here for you. I just don't know how much more I can take. You've been physically and mentally abused for as long as I can remember and I'm tired of watching it. As your best friend, I hurt whenever you hurt, and I can't take the pain anymore."

Sienna had a heart of gold, but she gave it to the wrong people. Yada hated that she was so passive because she forgave the unforgivable. There was no way in hell she should have let Jaxon back into her life, but she was desperate for the family that she never had.

"I'm ready for a change, but I don't know where to start," Sienna sniffled.

"Start by making Jaxon accountable for his actions. Look at your face Sienna. You or no other woman deserves that kind of treatment," Yada said as she pulled her best friend up from the floor and hugged her.

"I agree. I deserve better. Jax has taken enough from me. I can't lose my best friend too. Where's my phone?" Sienna questioned.

"Why? Who are you trying to call?" Yada asked.

"I'm calling the police," Sienna exhaled.

"That's what the hell I'm talking about. Here, you can use mine," Yada said with a smile.

***

"Did you decide what you wanted to eat?" Caleb asked as he looked over at Royce.

"I'll probably just get a smoothie until later. Maybe we can go out to eat when I get off," she replied with a yawn.

"Sleepy?" Caleb asked her.

"I wonder why," Royce smirked as he drove her back to work.

"I'm sorry baby. You know my sex drive is through the roof," Caleb laughed.

Royce was on her lunch break and Caleb went to get her. He wanted to check on the progress of the house and he wanted Royce to go with him. They were pleased with what had been done so far and it was almost finished. Royce had basically invited herself to move in with him, but Caleb was fine with that. It saved him the trouble of having to ask her. He didn't want her to do anything, but Royce insisted on helping him financially. Caleb was shocked when she handed him a cashier's check for ten thousand dollars. If he never knew it before, Caleb knew then that she was the one. They had about three or four more months left before they would be able to move in. Caleb's plans were to give Royce her money back to go towards decorating their new space.

Her divorce would be finalized in less than a month and things were looking up for them.

"What the hell is going on around here?" Royce asked when they pulled up to the school.

There were three police cars out front and a small crowd had gathered around them. Caleb was happy that he and Royce were together because he would have been worried if he had pulled up and saw that.

"Damn man. I hope nothing ain't happen to none of the kids," Caleb said.

"Me too," Royce replied as they both got out of the car.

Royce spotted her mother in the crowd and walked over to her. She saw that Caleb had stopped walking, so she grabbed his hand and pulled him along. Patrick had invited them out to dinner a few times and Sondra made it a point to let Caleb know how much she disliked him. She ignored his presence, and Royce ignored her in return. Most times, she and Caleb talked to Patrick as if Sondra wasn't even there. It was crazy that she insisted on coming to dinner knowing that she hated the person who they were dining with.

"What happened?" Royce asked when they walked up to Sondra.

"I don't know. I just came back from lunch and saw the police cars out here," Sondra replied.

She and Royce hardly talked without arguing. Thanks to Caleb always being around, she couldn't even talk to her daughter about Jax anymore. She knew that he and Royce were almost divorced, but that didn't mean anything to her. Things were going from bad to worse and she felt the strain in her relationship with Elena. They barely talked anymore, and they worked in the same office. Elena used to invite her out to lunch all the time, but she hadn't done that since Royce showed up at the club with her new man. Securing the principal's job once Elena got promoted seemed like wishful thinking now, but she was still hopeful.

"How you doing Mrs. Calloway?" Caleb spoke politely.

"Go to hell," Sondra replied with a smile like she had said nothing wrong.

"After you, ma'am," Caleb replied with a smirk.

[271]

"And this is the kind of trash that you want to be with Royce? He doesn't even respect your mother," Sondra hissed.

"Maybe my mother needs to give respect if she wants to get it," Royce replied, right as one of the police officers exited the building.

"Oh Lord!" Sondra gasped when she saw another officer following behind him with Jaxon in handcuffs.

"The fuck did this nigga do?" Caleb wondered out loud.

Everyone was shocked to see one of the most popular teachers and son of the principal being placed in the back of a squad car. Sondra spotted Elena rushing out behind him with her purse dangling from her arm. She had her shades on, probably trying to hide her embarrassment.

"What's going on Elena? Is there anything that I can do?" Sondra rushed over to her and asked.

"I need you to take over in my absence. If anyone asks about what happened here, you have no comment. I don't think I'll be in tomorrow, but I'll keep you posted," Elena replied.

Her husband was going to blow a gasket once he found out. Elena was pleased to see that no cameras were around. All she had to do now was get her son out of jail to buy herself some time. She had to tread lightly with Silas or there would be hell to pay.

"Okay. I'll take care of everything Elena. Don't worry," Sondra replied.

"Good riddance," Royce said, right as the patrol car pulled off with Jax inside.

"That is still your husband you know," Sondra pointed out.

"Three weeks and four days from now he won't be," Royce chuckled.

She shook her head in pity, as Sondra walked away like the flunky that she was. Royce saw Caleb off before going back to her classroom to do what she was being paid to do. The Davenport empire was crumbling before their very eyes and they had no one else to blame but themselves.

Chapter 32

It was like déjá vu for Jax when he pulled up to Sienna's house the following day. Sienna and Yada had packed up all his shit and had it waiting for him. Unlike Royce, who kept his belongings indoors, Sienna had everything out on the front porch. She had taken out a restraining order on him and she didn't want him nowhere around her. He was never the best father anyway, so she didn't even care if he stayed away from their kids. Jax was still having a hard time believing that she'd gone as far as getting the police involved. He was sure that her girl had a lot to do with it, which was why he never liked her anyway. Thankfully, it was early in the day when he was arrested, and he was able to get bailed out the same day. Elena was livid, but that was nothing compared to how he knew Silas would feel. Jax was in a bind, but there was no way in hell that he was living with his parents. He was going to store some of his belongings there, but he refused to live under the same roof as his father. Silas already treated him like a child and things would only get worse if he lived with him. Elena still hadn't told him about the arrest and, thankfully, no one else had either. When Jax pulled up to the house, he sat in his car for a while before he went inside.

"Hey... I mean hi mother," Jax spoke when he walked into the house.

As usual, Elena was in the kitchen preparing whatever meal her husband had requested. She wanted to take the day off from work, but she didn't want to make him suspicious. She knew that people were whispering, and she wasn't in the mood for the stares that she was sure to receive. Sondra did a great job of keeping people away and she appreciated her for that. Elena had been avoiding her since the Zulu function, at Silas' request. He felt that Royce and her entire family were bringing shame to the Davenport name. The last straw for him was when Royce showed up at the event with another man. Silas didn't tolerate disrespect and that was a slap in his face.

"Hello Jaxon," Elena replied after a long pause.

"Where is he? Did you tell him yet?" Jax inquired.

"No, I didn't, but I have to do it today Jaxon. I should have said something as soon as it happened. God forbid if someone else had gotten to him before me," Elena worried.

"So what ma? You're not a child and neither am I. We're not perfect, no matter how hard you try to pretend that we are. I'm human and I make mistakes," Jax rambled.

"Yeah, but you make them too often Jaxon. My God. What were you thinking about son? Her face was horrendous," Elena replied.

She had seen Sienna when she came down to the courthouse to sign the restraining order. She looked terrible with her swollen eyes and busted lip. She tried talking to her, but her friend stepped in and shut her up.

"Maybe I should have hit her below the neck so that she could cover it up like you do," Jax fumed.

"Don't you dare disrespect me in my home," Elena whispered harshly.

Silas was down the hall in his favorite room and she didn't want him to hear. She was already nervous about having to talk to him and Jaxon wasn't making it any better. He was an ungrateful bastard and always has been.

"I'll be upstairs whenever the lion is ready to roar," Jax said, speaking of his father.

"What is wrong with you, Jaxon? This is your mess, not ours. And just like always, we'll be spending our hard-earned money to make this go away. I knew that moving in with Sienna was a bad idea, but you never listen."

"I apologized a million times, but I don't know what else you want from me. I'm tired of trying to live on this pedestal that you've built for me. We're damaged goods and we always will be. As much as you hate to admit it, you have your husband to thank for that," Jax replied as he walked away.

Elena dropped her head, but she didn't bother with a reply. Jax wasn't her only child who blamed his father for his mannerisms. Her other two sons felt the same way.

According to them, they treated their wives identical to the way that they saw their father treat her. It was learned behavior. Jaxon wasn't the only cheater in the family. He was just the only one who always got caught.

"Who were you in here talking to?" Silas asked when he walked into the kitchen.

"Oh, hi honey. That was Jaxon. He's upstairs. Go have a seat and relax. Your dinner is ready. I was just about to bring it to you." Elena smiled.

Silas ignored her instructions and walked closer to where she stood. Elena felt his presence, but she was too afraid to turn around and face him. She didn't know why he was still standing there, but she found out soon enough. The snap of the leather jolted her before a sharp pain to her back had Elena doubling over in pain. When she looked up and saw Silas swinging the belt in her direction again, Elena held her hands up and begged for mercy. Her pleas fell on deaf ears as Silas' belt connected with every part of her body.

Jax heard his mother's cries from upstairs, but he didn't bother going to see what was wrong. It made no sense, when he knew that she was going to tell him to mind his own business. She was fine or at least that's what she would tell him. Over sixty years old and still being treated like a child. Her weakness disgusted him. Jax turned the volume up on the radio and tuned her out, just like he did when he was younger.

"Get up!" Silas commanded angrily.

Elena's entire body was sore, and her skin was on fire. She knew better than to disobey her husband, so she slowly stood to her feet. When Silas shoved his cellphone in her face, Elena scanned over the email that he had pulled up for her to read.

"I was going to tell you," Elena mumbled, angering her husband all over again.

"Bullshit!" Silas roared as he delivered a vicious slap to her face that dropped her to her knees.

"Silas, please," Elena said, begging for compassion.

"I had to find out from my colleagues that my own son was arrested at my wife's school. Do you know how that makes me look? Weak, Elena. That's how it makes me look. Like I can't run my own damn household!" Silas barked.

"I'm sorry," Elena apologized.

"Do I look weak to you, Elena?" Silas asked.

[275]

"No, you don't," she whimpered.

"Tell me everything," Silas demanded.

From her place on the floor, Elena told him everything that she knew. She didn't have many details other than the obvious. Jaxon had beat Sienna and she called the police on him.

"I tried talking to her, but her friend didn't let me get a word in," Elena replied.

"Get her on the phone. Now!" Silas bellowed as he handed his wife his phone.

Elena hurriedly dialed Sienna's number and passed the phone to her husband. She listened as her husband spoke with her ex daughter-in-law over the phone. She didn't know what Sienna was saying, but it was obviously something that Silas didn't want to hear. After a few minutes of going back and forth, he finally got her to agree to meet with them. Sienna didn't trust anyone in the Davenport family, so she picked the meeting place.

"Another fucking mess that I have to fix," Silas fumed.

"Sienna will listen to me, Silas. She always has. Just tell me what you want me to do," Elena begged.

"The only thing I want you to do right now is go to the corner. The sight of you disgusts me." Silas frowned.

Elena went to stand, but a firm hand on her shoulder pushed her back down to the floor.

"Who told you to stand?" Silas asked menacingly.

"But, you told me to go to the corner," Elena said in confusion.

"Crawl!" Silas ordered in a hate-filled voice.

Elena's shoulder slumped as she got on all fours and crawled to the corner like her husband told her to. When Silas called for Jax to come down a few minutes later, he shook his head at the sight of the pathetic woman who called herself his mother.

***

"Hold still Sienna. I know you don't want to leave out of here with a black ring around your eye," Yada said as she applied makeup to her friend's face.

"Sorry girl. I'm just so nervous. Why did I even agree to meet with them?" Sienna questioned out loud.

"Because you have questions and you need answers. Either Jaxon agrees to pay you a set amount each month for your kids or you bring his ass to court for child support. You always want to make sure that you and your kids will have a stable place to stay."

"I can't say all that Yada. You know I've never been the aggressive type. I'll fuck around and agree to everything that they say. You should come with me," Sienna replied.

"Hell no, Sienna. I can't stand nobody in that family. I'll be in jail before the ice melts in my drink," Yada said, making her laugh.

"Please Yada. I'll feel better knowing that you're with me," Sienna begged, right as her phone started ringing.

Yada was happy for the interruption because she needed a minute to think. She continued to apply makeup to Sienna's face as she talked on the phone. The smile on her friend's face was a welcomed sight and Yada smiled with her. When Sienna hung up, she jumped up from the chair and started screaming excitedly.

"What happened? Who was that?" Yada asked.

"That was my children's school. Remember when I put in the application to be a classroom assistant last year?" Sienna asked.

"Yeah," Yada nodded.

"They just called and said I got the job!" Sienna yelled.

"I'm so happy for you, Sienna. Things are really starting to look up." Yada smiled.

"I did two interviews a while ago, but I never heard back from them."

"I guess they were saving the best for last," Yada smiled.

"Getting Jax out of my life for good was the best thing that I could have ever done. Everything has been looking up for me since then."

"That black cloud was bringing bad karma your way. This is only the beginning of your happiness. I can't wait until you get all the blessings that you deserve," Yada said, making Sienna blush and smile.

She continued the task of putting on Sienna's makeup before she got dressed. Sienna looked great and there was no evidence of any bruises anywhere on her face. Yada wanted to decline, but she decided to accompany her friend to the restaurant. When they pulled up and saw Jaxon's car, she was happy that she did.

"I knew it. I knew that he was going to be here. Lying bastard claimed that it was only gonna be him and his wife," Sienna said, referring to Silas.

"Don't worry about it friend. I got my stun gun, mace, and my brass knuckles. And if that ain't enough, I'm coming back out to my trunk. I got multiple choices for their asses," Yada said, making her laugh.

"Come on and let's get this over with," Sienna said as she exited the car.

She and Yada walked up to the entrance of Texas Roadhouse right as someone was coming out. Sienna locked eyes with Caleb before her gaze drifted over to Royce.

"Hi," Royce spoke politely.

"Hi Royce. Hi Caleb," Sienna spoke back.

"What's up?" Caleb replied.

She was shocked that Royce said anything to her, but she didn't expect Caleb to speak back. They didn't end on the best terms, but there were obviously no hard feelings. Sienna didn't want to stare, but her ex looked better than she remembered. He had a firm grip on Royce's hand as he held the door open for them with the other. Sienna hated to admit it, but they made a cute couple. She was sure that it killed Jax to see their exes together, but that was good for his ass.

"Girl, this is some crazy shit if I might say so myself. Your ex-husband's soon to be ex-wife is with your-ex-boyfriend now. That sounds like a tongue twister," Yada laughed.

"Yeah, but that's my ratchet ass life." Sienna shrugged as they walked inside.

They informed the hostess that they were meeting someone before they ventured further into the restaurant. Sienna spotted Jax looking angry as always. His mother looked worn out and his father looed downright scary. Silas was never a friendly man and it seemed as if nothing had changed.

"Sienna, thanks for meeting us," Elena greeted with a phony smile.

"No problem. This is my best friend Keyada," Sienna said while introducing her girl.

Jax twisted his face up into a frown and Yada did the same. Both women sat down at Elena's urging and waited for the meeting to start.

"First," Silas started, "I want to apologize for what my son did to you."

"It's not you who should be apologizing," Yada snapped angrily.

Sienna nudged her friend, silently begging her to be behave.

"Like I was saying," Silas continued while staring Yada down, "things got too far out of hand and we need to come to an agreement of some kind."

"The only thing I want is financial support for my kids and a stable place for us to stay," Sienna replied.

"We can arrange that," Silas assured her.

"I'm listening," Sienna noted.

Silas looked at Elena, giving her the okay to speak.

"First, I just want to let you know that we love our grandkids more than anything. When we make decisions, we must do so with them in mind. With that being said, Silas and I have agreed to sign the house that you're living in over to you," Elena said with a smile.

"Okay," Sienna said, void of any emotion.

"Is that a yes or no?" Silas questioned.

"It's a yes, of course, but Jax is still not off the hook. I'm very appreciative of a place to stay, but I still need financial assistance," Sienna replied.

Yada nodded her head, happy that her friend was finally learning to speak up for herself.

"Of course." Elena smiled. "We're also willing to give you four hundred dollars every month to help with the children's expenses. That's two hundred per child," Elena pointed out.

"I'm not taking anything less than five hundred per child," Sienna replied confidently.

"Man, I told you. She's fucking ungrateful," Jax snapped angrily.

He was already upset about seeing Royce with Caleb a few minutes ago. The last thing he wanted to do was kiss Sienna's ass to make her act right.

"Shut up Jaxon. This is your mess, and don't you forget it," his father sternly replied.

"I'm ungrateful?" Sienna asked while pointing to herself. "I've done everything by myself for years, even

[279]

when we were married. You paid a few bills, but you were living there too. You buy a few outfits and some shoes and think you've done something. How dare you try to offer me four hundred dollars per month. I spend more than that just to feed them."

"Five hundred per child is doable," Silas agreed, stopping an argument before it got started.

"What's the catch?" Sienna asked while looking over at them.

"Excuse me?" Elena asked.

"I appreciate everything, but I know that you're not giving me a house and money just because I have your grandkids. I've been having them for years and you've never offered more than a few gifts every now and then. So, again, what's the catch?" Sienna repeated.

"These charges that you have against Jaxon, they need to disappear," Silas advised.

"I'll be happy to make them disappear as soon as I see everything that you've offered me in writing," Sienna said, making Yada proud once again. Her girl was wheeling and dealing, and she loved every minute of it.

"Already done," Silas said as his wife handed her a gold envelope with some paperwork inside.

"We'll just have to revise the monthly amount and send you a new copy. Once we do, you will need to read over everything, sign it, and have it back to us as soon as possible," Elena spoke up as she grabbed her purse and prepared to leave.

Jax seemed even angrier than he was when they first got there, but Sienna didn't give a damn. Even though she agreed to drop the charges, her restraining order was staying in place. He was not to be trusted. Once the Davenports were gone, Yada gave her friend a big hug.

"I'm so proud of you honey. A new job, a house, and one thousand extra dollars a month. I'm scared of you," Yada joked.

"Yes and, hopefully, I'll be going back to school at night too," Sienna replied.

"Look at God!" Yada shouted like she was in church.

"I owe you so much Yada. I don't know how I'll ever be able to repay you. But, I'll start right now by treating you to a meal. Get whatever you want, on me." Sienna smiled.

"You don't have tell me twice. Pass me the menu," Yada laughed.

Sienna had a genuine smile on her face for the first time in a while. For once in her life, the dark clouds had been lifted and the sun was shining on her once again.

Chapter 33

"What is going on with you, Caleb?" Pam said as soon as her son walked through the front door.

"I'm straight. What's supposed to be going on with me?" Caleb asked.

"This is the fourth letter that came here from your probation officer. Have you been going to see her like you're supposed to?" Pam questioned.

"I'm good ma. I got everything under control," Caleb assured her.

"That's not what I asked you boy. Have you been going to see her like you're supposed to?" Pam repeated.

"Nah, but I'm going," Caleb replied.

"Are y'all trying to give me a heart attack?" Pam asked, being dramatic just like always.

"Calm down ma. You be stressing for nothing," Caleb said while hugging her.

"Just stay out of trouble Caleb. That's all that I want from you," Pam begged.

"I'm good ma, I promise," Caleb said, hoping that he was right.

Mrs. Lockwood had been blowing his phone up, but he never answered for her. He deleted the voicemails without even listening to what she had to say. She obviously felt some type of way about him not coming to see her and that was clear by the number of letters sent and phone calls made. Caleb opened one of the letters that his mother gave him and almost passed out when he read it. Mrs. Lockwood was giving him one more chance to come see her before putting a warrant out for his arrest. It was Monday and she was requesting his presence that Friday. Caleb had been smoking like a chimney for the past few weeks and there was no way in hell that his urine would be clean by then. He needed to get at Jaden to see what he could do about that. He couldn't go to jail. He had too much going on to even think about it.

"What does it say?" Pam asked.

"I have to go see her Friday," Caleb replied.

"You better bring your ass to your appointment Caleb. Don't be stupid and get locked up. You have too many good things happening for you right now. Your house is almost ready to be moved into and you have a damn good job. Don't lose it all over nothing," Pam fussed.

"I got you, my girl," Caleb said while kissing her on the cheek.

"Big baby," Pam teased.

"I love you, ma," Caleb said while leaning into her.

"I love you too, honey." Pam smiled.

"You love me enough to do anything that I ask you to?" Caleb questioned.

"Depends on what it is. My love has limits baby. What do you want me to do?" Pam asked.

"Can you beat up Royce's mama for me?" Caleb asked seriously.

"Boy, go sit your overgrown ass down somewhere," Pam laughed.

"I'm serious though ma. That lady is the devil." Caleb frowned.

"Well, you know how to handle yourself without being disrespectful. You wouldn't want anybody to disrespect me, so give Royce's mother the same treatment."

"You ain't nothing like her though, ma. Her pops is cool, but her mama needs an exorcism. You don't have to beat her bad. Just punch her one good time and make her dizzy."

"Get out of my house Caleb," Pam laughed as she pushed him away from her.

Caleb stayed and talked with his mother for a while before he left. Once he found out that Jaden was home, he headed to his brother's house to get some advice. Caleb was new to the whole jail and probation thing, but Jaden was a pro. He knew all kinds of tricks to stay out of jail and Caleb needed to be taught a few. Caleb hadn't seen his great niece in a few days and he was looking forward to holding her again. When he pulled up and didn't see Jaylynn's car, he knew that spoiling Hayley for a little while would have to wait.

"Who is it?" Jaden yelled when Caleb rang the doorbell.

"Me nigga," Caleb replied.

"Come on," Jaden said when he unlocked the door.

Caleb was shocked when he walked in and saw his brother cradling Hayley in his arms.

"Where is Jaylynn?" Caleb asked.

"Outside with her friends somewhere," Jaden replied.

"Where's Kia?" Caleb questioned.

"Her and Juice went by Keller," he replied.

"Get the fuck outta here! This nigga is babysitting. All that shit you was talking while Jay was pregnant. I knew you were full of shit," Caleb laughed.

"Mind your business nigga. The fuck you want anyway. You're interrupting our bonding time," Jaden replied as he sat down and put Hayley on his chest.

Caleb didn't even ask to hold her because Jaden didn't look like he was gonna give her up.

"I knew you were gonna spoil her," Caleb said as he looked at his brother rubbing his granddaughter's back lovingly.

"I'm the only one that she likes," Jaden said as he smiled down at her.

"But aye, bruh, I need your help. I fucked up big time. Royce is gonna kill me," Caleb said, shaking his head.

"You cheated on Royce nigga!" Jaden yelled as his eyes widened in surprise.

"What? Nigga no. It ain't nothing like that," Caleb replied.

"The fuck you did then?" Jaden questioned.

"That bitch Mrs. Lockwood is trying to lock a nigga up. She said if I don't come see her Friday morning, she's putting a warrant out for my arrest."

"I told your stupid ass. You can't take yourself off probation dummy. The fuck is you supposed to be to make those kind of decisions," Jaden fussed.

"Man, I don't need a lecture right now. My urine is dirty as fuck. I been getting it in lately," Caleb confessed.

"You better get Royce to piss for you. Kia used to do it for me all the time," Jaden admitted.

"I remember you saying that, but how? That bitch be doing all kind of shit to a nigga pee. They test the temperature and everything else."

"You gotta keep it close to your body for the heat," Jaden replied.

"How though bruh?" Caleb asked.

"It's like this, Royce have to piss in a cup or something right before you go. You have to get a small zip lock bag and put some of it in there. Then, you tape it to the inside of your leg to keep it at the right temperature. You know, close to your nuts. It's always warm in that area," Jaden said.

"Man, hell no. I'm not doing that shit. What if it wastes?" Caleb asked.

"You gon' be on your R. Kelly shit then nigga," Jaden laughed.

"Quit playing man. This is some serious shit." Caleb frowned.

"I'm being serious with you right now though, bruh. You have to keep the urine close to your body to stay at the right temperature. Your body heat will keep it warm. I did the shit all the time and I never had any problems. No spills or nothing." Jaden shrugged.

"Damn man. It's not like have much of a choice. I know I'm about to hear her damn mouth when I tell her."

"Either she gives you some pee or come visit you in jail; her choice," Jaden said.

"You know how paranoid Royce be though. Every little thing stresses her out."

"I already know. That's why I'm happy that her house finally sold. She was driving a nigga crazy," Jaden laughed as he kissed the top of Hayley's head.

"This nigga is a fucking grandpa. I still can't believe this shit," Caleb chuckled.

"This my lil light bright baby. Looking like her pretty ass daddy." Jaden frowned.

"That nigga been handling his business? I would hate to fuck him up for playing with my lil niece," Caleb said.

"Yeah, the nigga be doing his part. He come through every day to see her and drop shit off. His mama is disgusting as fuck though. Her ass act like she don't know when to go home."

"They don't take the baby to their house?" Caleb asked.

"Not yet. She just made six weeks today, so she's about to start going over there," Jaden replied.

"Man, let me get my ass out of here. I might swing by the shop tomorrow for a cut," Caleb said as he got up and headed for the door.

"Just hit me up," Jaden replied as he got up and walked him to the door.

Caleb kissed the baby's hand before leaving his brother's house to head home. He knew that Royce was there because she sent him a text as soon as she got home. It took about fifteen minutes for Caleb to get to his apartment. He sat outside in his car deep in thought before he finally made his way inside. As soon as he closed the door behind him, Royce came running from the back with something in her hand. She jumped into Caleb's arms and wrapped her legs around his waist.

"Damn, you must be really happy to see a nigga," Caleb laughed.

"I'm always happy to see you, but that's not why I'm so excited. Baby, look. It's official. I'm no longer a Davenport." Royce smiled as she showed him her finalized divorce papers.

"That's what's up baby." Caleb smiled while kissing her cheek.

"Why don't you seem happy?" Royce asked as she jumped out of his hold.

"I am happy baby. I just have a lot on my mind right now," Caleb replied.

"Like what Caleb? What's wrong?" Royce asked.

Instead of replying, Caleb reached into his back pocket and pulled out the letter that Mrs. Lockwood sent to his mother's house. She didn't have his new address and she never would if he could help it.

"This bitch," Royce mumbled as she rolled her eyes.

"Man, ain't no way I can pass a drug test right now Royce," Caleb admitted.

"You've been smoking Caleb? When? I never see you smoke anything."

"Just know that I'm fucked if I go take a drug test Friday," Caleb replied.

"God, Caleb. I can't believe you right now. We're supposed to be celebrating and you hit me with this bullshit," Royce said as she flopped down on the sofa.

"I'm sorry baby, but there's a way around it," Caleb noted as he sat down next to her and grabbed her hand.

"How Caleb? What are you gonna do? Sneak some clean pee in there for her to test?" Royce yelled.

"Yeah, basically." He shrugged.

"Wait, what? Are you serious? That's so gross. Whose urine are you gonna use?" Royce asked.

"Yours." Caleb smirked.

"Mine!" Royce yelled.

"Yes, yours, unless you been blowing and ain't telling me about it," Caleb joked.

"Boy bye. My lungs are showroom new," Royce laughed.

"See, that's why I need you, baby. Jaden already told me what to do. I know you ain't trying to visit your man in jail."

"I'd die, but I'd rather see you behind bars than fucking Ashley's scandalous ass again. I still owe her an ass whipping," Royce said, making him laugh.

"Relax baby gangsta. Ain't gon' be none of that," Caleb assured her.

"Ugh, this shit is gonna stress me out. I just know it," Royce groaned.

"Girl, calm down. Everything stresses you out. You need to learn to relax," Caleb said while rubbing her back.

"What if this doesn't work Caleb? I don't want you to go to jail. You're gonna leave me all by myself," Royce said sadly.

"I love you, baby. I'm never gonna leave you if I don't have to," Caleb said, making her blush.

"Aww, I love you too boo." Royce smiled, happy to finally hear him say it.

"And stop worrying so much. Stress kills," Caleb told her.

"Okay, I'll try," Royce promised, as Caleb grabbed her divorce papers and read over them.

"It's about damn time. That was the longest six months of my life," he laughed.

"I know, but I don't even feel like celebrating anymore. I know you told me not to worry, but I can't help it," Royce replied.

"We'll be good baby, I promise. Now, come on in the room and let me give you some divorced dick," Caleb said while picking her up.

"Yes!" Royce cheered, as Caleb threw her over his shoulder and walked her to their bedroom.

Chapter 34

"**B**aby, please call me and let me know something. I have my phone right in my front pocket, so I'll be waiting," Royce said as she talked on the phone with Caleb.

"Okay, I will," he assured her.

"I'm serious Caleb. You know I'm nervous as hell right now," Royce replied.

"How do you think I feel Royce? I'm about to walk up in here with your piss strapped to my nuts," Caleb said, making her laugh.

"Eww, that sounds so gross," Royce giggled.

"Yeah, but that's my life right now. Go back in your class and I'll call you as soon as I know something."

"Okay. I love you," Royce said.

"I love you too baby," Caleb said before they disconnected.

Seeing Mrs. Lockwood again was not on his agenda, but he really didn't have a choice. He went about the entire situation the wrong way and that was his own fault. Jaden tried to tell him, but listening wasn't one of Caleb's strong points. Unlike other times, he wasn't trying to prolong his visit. In fact, he was thirty minutes early for his appointment. Once he signed in, he took a seat and waited. Caleb was too anxious to sit down for long, so he walked to the back of the building and went to the bathroom. He had to check and make sure that everything was intact before he went in for his appointment. Royce had secured the zip lock bag for him, but he still didn't want it to spill.

"I hate that bitch!" a man fumed when he walked into the bathroom.

He grabbed a wad of paper towels from the sink and ran some water on them. He didn't care that Caleb was standing right there. He dropped his pants and boxers and started wiping his dick.

"Damn," Caleb laughed as he turned his head.

"My bad bruh, but I hate these fucking people. I wish that bitch lose her job with her desperate ass," the man ranted.

"I feel you, man. I hate coming up in this bitch too. Nigga never know if he's going home or not," Caleb replied.

"I know I'm going home. All I gotta do is dick the bitch down and I'm good."

"You must have to see Mrs. Lockwood," Caleb replied.

"Yeah and I hate that hoe." The man frowned.

"That's who I'm here to see too, but I'm not fucking that bitch for my freedom. I'll go to jail first," Caleb swore.

"Man, I'm over this shit. That bitch wasn't even my probation officer when I first started coming here. I'm about to get my lawyers involved," the man said as he fixed himself up and walked away.

Caleb never even bothered going to one of the stalls. He headed out of the bathroom, just as the receptionist was calling his name.

"You can go right in Mr. Andrews," she told him as she walked away.

When Caleb walked into her office. Mrs. Lockwood was just walking out of her private bathroom. Nasty bitch probably had to freshen up before her next victim came to see her.

"So, I have to threaten you to get you to keep your appointments Caleb. You are still under active probation, just in case you forgot," Mrs. Lockwood said as soon as she saw him.

"Just give me a cup," Caleb said, not bothering to reply to what she'd just said.

"How long have you and Royce been together?" she asked as she looked him up and down.

Royce was a good girl, or so she thought. She would have never imagined that she'd be with a man like Caleb.

"Mind your muthafucking business and give me a cup," Caleb snapped angrily.

"You better watch your mouth. I'll have your ass locked up for failure to appear. You've missed several appointments with no explanation as to why," Mrs. Lockwood said as she handed him the cup.

Caleb snatched it from her hand and walked into the bathroom. He wasn't even nervous as he emptied the contents of the zip lock bag into the cup, filling it to the line. He threw the entire bag in the toilet and flushed it before washing his hands. The liquid still felt warm to the touch and Caleb was hoping for the best.

"Here," he replied when he walked out and handed Mrs. Lockwood the cup.

Caleb took a seat in the corner of the room as she did a series of test. Her face held no emotion and he didn't know if that was good or bad. It took almost ten minutes before she turned around and faced him with a stupid grin on her face.

"I should have your ass locked up," Mrs. Lockwood laughed, making him angry.

There was no way in hell that she could pay him to believe that Royce's urine was dirty. Maybe the temperature was off, but he knew that it was clean. Caleb was done playing her stupid ass game. If she wanted to lock him up, that was cool, but he wasn't going down that easily.

"Do it then," Caleb challenged as he stood to his feet. "I bet I'll be at your house as soon as I get out to have a talk with your husband."

"Is that a threat Caleb?" Mrs. Lockwood asked.

"Nah, that's a muthafucking promise. As a matter of fact, I might need to have a talk with him anyway. I need to know why that nigga ain't dicking you down like he's supposed to. Got your probationers suffering because he ain't doing his job. Shit, I might decide to play the victim and contact the newspaper. My father-in-law got me covered on that if I need help. I'm sure your mama and daddy would be happy to know what you've been up to," Caleb noted.

"Your threats don't scare me. Go right ahead. It'll be your word against mine." She smiled through her nervousness.

"Let's do it then. I'm sure your husband is gonna wonder how I know about that tattoo," Caleb replied.

He laughed when he saw the look of fear that crossed her face. She was bluffing, but he was ready and willing. He didn't have anything to lose, but she couldn't say the same.

"Just leave," Mrs. Lockwood said dismissively.

"Nah, I'm not going nowhere. I want to request a hearing with the board," Caleb replied.

"A hearing for what?" Mrs. Lockwood panicked.

"I'm trying to understand why I'm still on papers when I'm a first-time offender. Niggas who did serious crimes get off easier than I did. I feel like I was a victim of discrimination."

"Are you serious? How were you discriminated against?" she inquired.

"You had the authority to terminate my probation, but you refused because of the sexual relationship that we had. I need to talk to somebody about that."

"That's not discrimination dumb ass," Mrs. Lockwood snapped.

"Maybe it was rape. I said no, and you made me do it anyway," Caleb said, messing with her.

Caleb rambled on and on, as she went to her computer and typed at record speed. He didn't know if he was leaving the office in handcuffs or not and he really didn't care. He was ready to make good on his threats if she came at him on some bullshit.

"Here, you're free to go. Your probation has been terminated, effective immediately," Mrs. Lockwood said as she handed him a piece of paper.

Keeping him on papers wasn't even worth the risk. Caleb was a loose cannon and she believed that he would do exactly what he said. She couldn't take those kinds of chances. Royce knew too much about her family and she would probably be eager to assist him.

"That wasn't hard at all, was it?" Caleb asked as he got up and prepared to leave.

Caleb damn near ran to the door, trying to get away from her. He wanted to know what had made her threaten to arrest him, but he didn't care enough to ask.

"And by the way, you're pregnant!" Mrs. Lockwood yelled down the hall to his departing back.

Caleb stopped momentarily and turned to face her. He was looking for a hint of humor in her expression, but there was none. She knew all along that the urine he used wasn't his, but he wasn't expecting those results. He was happy as hell to be having a baby with Royce, but he wondered why she didn't tell him. He hoped she wasn't trying to get rid of it because they would have a serious problem if she was.

***

Royce was on cloud nine when she left from work. Caleb had told her the good news about being taken off probation and that was music to her ears. After stopping to get them something to eat, Royce raced home to spend some quality time with her man.

"Caleb! Where are you? I have food!" Royce yelled when she walked into the apartment.

She sat the bags of food on the counter and walked down the hall to their bedroom. She found Caleb stretched out across the bed in nothing but his boxers. It was always funny to her how he had a good paying job but was never at work. He got mad when he actually had to do something and that was even funnier.

"Baby, wake up. I have food. Come eat before it gets cold," Royce said as he climbed on top of him and kissed his neck.

"What time is it?" Caleb asked groggily.

"It's almost five," Royce replied.

"Where the food at?" Caleb asked as he looked around.

"It's in the kitchen," Royce replied as she tried to move off him.

Caleb held her in place and sat up with her still on his lap. Royce didn't know why he was staring at her, but she waited for him to speak.

"We don't keep secrets from each other, right?" Caleb asked while looking directly in her eyes.

He needed to make sure that she was being completely honest with him. Royce wasn't a liar and he trusted whatever she told him.

"No Caleb. We talk to each other about everything," Royce replied.

"Not telling is the same as lying Royce," Caleb noted.

"I know that Caleb. Where is this even coming from? What happened?" Royce asked.

"When's the last time you saw your period?" Caleb asked.

[295]

"What kind of question is that?" Royce yelled as she moved out of his lap.

"What are you getting defensive for? You got something to hide?" Caleb questioned.

"I don't have time for the riddles Caleb. Just say what you have to say," Royce demanded.

"Are you pregnant?" he blurted out.

"Wow," Royce laughed as she got up from the bed.

"The fuck does that mean Royce? Wow what?" Caleb asked.

"You sound stupid as hell Caleb. Don't you think I would know if I was pregnant? You would have been the first person I told."

"How do you know Royce? Do you even know when you had your last period?" Caleb questioned.

"That means nothing Caleb. I've missed before, and it was a false alarm every time," Royce said, waving him off.

"Yeah, well, Mrs. Lockwood tested the urine that I gave her and said something different."

"What are you even talking about?" Royce asked him.

She sat down on the bed and listened as Caleb told her everything that happened at his appointment. Royce was speechless because it sounded so unbelievable. She had missed her cycle the month before and she was late for the present month. Still, that meant nothing to her because it had happened before.

"I stopped and got another test," Caleb said as he got the bag that contained the pregnancy test and handed it to her.

"This is crazy," Royce said as she followed him into the bathroom.

"How do you think I felt? I thought you knew and were trying to kill my baby," Caleb replied.

"Boy! I can't even kill a fly. I would never kill a human being," Royce assured him.

"Good, now go pee on the stick," Caleb instructed.

"You should be tired of seeing my pee," Royce joked as she did what he said.

Once she was done, Caleb grabbed the test with a towel while she washed her hands. She stood right next to him, right as the two pink lines appeared.

"It's about damn time!" he yelled. "Where's my phone so I can take a picture?"

"You better not put that pissy stick on social media boy," Royce fussed.

"Oh shit, I'm trippin'," Caleb laughed.

"My daddy is gonna be so happy." Royce smiled.

Her father's birthday was the following week and that was the perfect present.

"Nobody is happier than me," Caleb said as he picked her up and hugged her.

"Me too," Royce replied.

She was shocked but happy at the same time. She remembered trying to have a baby with Jaxon when they first got married, but they never conceived. That was something else that she was thankful for, seeing as how they were divorced now. If she were being honest, Jax wasn't the best father to the kids he already had. She would probably be a single mother by now, just like Sienna. Although she hadn't known Caleb as long as she'd known Jax, she felt a deeper connection with him. She knew the real him and not who he pretended to be. There was no one else who Royce would have wanted to share her child or her life with.

Chapter 35

"**T**his is so cute Royce. He's gonna love it." Uri smiled as she read the mug that Royce had for her father.

"You know he drinks coffee like it's water, so I know he'll use it," Royce replied.

"It's gonna be his favorite one," Uri assured her.

It was Patrick's birthday and Sondra had a small dinner for him at her house. There were only a handful of people there and most of them had already left. Uri's husband was still there and so was Lydia. Patrick had opened his gifts and was out back playing with Uri's daughters while they put the leftover food away. Royce had one more gift to give him, but she didn't want everyone around when she did. The gift was special, and she didn't want her fake ass family ruining the surprise.

"Make sure you record everything on my phone, so I can show Caleb," Royce said.

"His scary ass should have come," Uri laughed, knowing that would never happen.

"You know he ain't coming around my mama if he doesn't have to," Royce replied.

"I wonder how she's gonna feel knowing that you're having a baby by the man she hates."

"Honestly, she doesn't even have to be a part of my baby's life. I'm good either way." Royce shrugged.

"That's not fair Royce. Auntie Sondra can be a bitch sometimes, but she's not that bad. This is her first grandchild and it will kill her if you keep her away," Uri noted.

"I won't try to keep her away, but I won't tolerate her bullshit either. She's gonna respect my decision to be with who I want to be with. I'm not going out of my way to accommodate her, just because she doesn't like my man. If she doesn't want Caleb around, then me and my baby won't come around either. If I start that with her now, it'll be like that forever. She's not getting her way with me ever again."

"You're right about that cousin. You have to draw the line somewhere," Uri agreed.

"What time are we leaving Uri? My fake ass family is gone and I'm ready to go too. I don't even know why I came," Lydia said when she walked into the house.

She had been drinking since she got there, and Uri knew that she was tipsy. Lydia turned on the stove and lit her cigarette, right as Sondra walked into the house.

"You know I don't allow smoking in my house Lydia," Sondra chastised.

"As if I give a damn," Lydia spat as she took a puff and blew out the smoke.

"Ma!" Uri yelled as she looked at her mother.

"It's okay Uri. I'm not in the mood for another one of her tantrums. Just let her be," Sondra said dismissively.

Uri never understood her auntie's passive attitude towards her mother. Sondra snapped on everybody else, but it was if she was afraid of Lydia. She never wanted to upset her, and she let her have her way like she was a child.

"Are you ready to do this Royce? I need to get her home before I lose my cool," Uri said while looking at her mother.

"You're the one who begged me to come to this bullshit. I don't go nowhere that I'm not welcomed," Lydia snapped.

"Uri," Sondra said while shaking her head. She was silently begging her to be quiet and not start an argument.

"Uri," Lydia mocked. "I hate that damn name. Shakira is what I wanted to name you, but that wasn't classy enough, was it Sondra?"

"Come on Uri. Don't forget to record," Royce said as she grabbed the box with the mug in it and walked out the back door.

Lydia and Sondra followed them outside and sat down. Patrick was pushing Uri's girls on the swing set that they had in the yard for them when Royce called him over. Uri's husband got up and finished pushing them, while Royce did what she needed to do.

[300]

"What's wrong baby?" Patrick asked when he walked over.

"Nothing is wrong. I have one more gift for you." Royce smiled.

"Another gift? You already gave me three," Patrick said as he took a seat.

"Yeah, but I saved the best for last." Royce smiled while handing him the box.

Patrick took his time and opened the box, carefully removing the tissue that surrounded the mug. He pulled out the mug that read *"Just when parents think their work is finished, someone calls them grand."*

At first, he had a look of confusion on his face, but realization set in soon after.

"You're pregnant?" Patrick jumped up and asked.

"Eight weeks." Royce smiled brightly.

"Congratulations baby. This is the best present that I could have received," Patrick beamed.

Royce was shocked to see her mother smiling too. The only emotion she expected her to show was anger. Sondra wiped a few tears from her eyes as she picked up the mug and read what it said. She felt horrible about the strained relationship that she'd caused between her and Royce. Her one and only daughter didn't even feel the need to include her in her good news. That hurt her more than anything.

"I'm gonna be a grandpa," Patrick said as he pulled Royce into a hug.

"Nigga please. You're already a grandpa," Lydia blurted out, making everybody turn to face her.

"Lydia, please," Sondra pleaded.

"What is she talking about daddy?" Royce asked with a perplexed look on her face.

"Nothing baby. It's nothing," Patrick replied uncomfortably.

"Nothing? Is that what you call it now?" Lydia asked.

"Ma, come on, let's go. You're obviously drunk and talking crazy. Girls, come say goodbye to everybody so we can leave!" Uri called out to her daughters.

"Yeah girls, come say goodbye to your grandpa!" Lydia yelled.

"Grand... grandpa?" Royce stuttered as her brows furrowed in confusion.

[301]

"Is this your idea of a joke?" Uri questioned. "Because I don't find it funny at all."

"Tell her Patrick. Tell your daughter or your nothing, as you called her, the truth," Lydia slurred.

"Daddy," Royce whispered as she looked at him with teary eyes.

"I'm sorry baby. This is not the way that this should have been discussed," Patrick apologized.

"Oh, my God! Are y'all fucking serious right now!" Uri screamed as tears poured from her eyes.

"Uri, baby listen," Patrick said as he went to grab her hand.

"Don't touch me! I can't believe that y'all would do this to me!" Uri screamed, as Royce's phone fell from her trembling hands.

Her husband rushed over to her side as her daughters looked on in confusion. Royce was crying her eyes out as her father tried to comfort her. Sondra looked at Lydia with fire in her eyes, but her sister was too drunk to care. Years of secrets had been revealed in a matter of seconds and things would probably never be the same. Ashton had to carry his wife out of the yard like a baby and that pained him to do.

"I need to get out of here," Royce said as she jerked away from her father and grabbed her phone from the ground.

She rushed inside to grab her purse and keys. She wanted to get home as soon as possible and crawl into her bed. Uri was just as upset, and they ended up leaving Lydia right in the yard with the other two liars. As soon as Royce made it home, she fell into Caleb's arms and cried until her eyes burned.

***

Two days later, Royce and Uri were sitting in the living room of Uri's home eating from a huge bucket of ice cream. Neither woman had talked to their parents since Patrick's birthday dinner and it was their first time talking to each other. Their emotions were all over the place and they needed time to process what they'd learned.

"This is so fucked up Royce. Like, I don't even know how to feel right now," Uri sighed.

"I'm just so angry with everybody. That wasn't fair to us. We grew up as cousins and were sisters all along. I mean, you've always been like my sister, but we deserved to know," Royce replied.

"Uncle Pat has always been there for me for as long as I can remember and now I know why. He wasn't being a good uncle; he was being a good father. How the hell am I gonna explain this shit to my kids?" Uri questioned as she wiped the stray tears from her eyes.

"I can't believe that my daddy slept with my auntie. That shit is just nasty. She was only seventeen years old when she had you. I can't talk about Jax, when our family is just as dysfunctional."

"Now it all makes sense. Auntie Sondra taking care of her and letting her have her way all the time. She was trying to keep my mama happy so that she wouldn't tell their secret," Uri pointed out.

"Auntie Lydia used to always drop little hints, but she always shut up when I asked her to explain. I guess she got tired of playing the game." Royce shrugged, right as Ashton was unlocking the door to come in.

Royce and Uri both were shocked to see Lydia walking into the house behind him.

"What is she doing here?" Uri asked with a frown. She wasn't ready to see her mother yet and Ashton knew that.

"Chill out Uri. She called me to pick her up and I thought it was a good idea. Y'all need to talk and get this shit over with. I'm taking the girls out for a little while," Ashton said as he walked away.

Lydia sat down on the smaller sofa right next to the one that Uri and Royce were on. She kept her head down while she nervously fidgeted with her hands. Ashton and the girls came back to the front of the house and said their goodbyes before leaving. The tension was thick in the room, but Uri broke the silence.

"You came here to talk so talk," Uri said to her mother.

Sighing deeply, Lydia said what was on her mind. "I first want to apologize for my actions. Although I wanted you girls to know the truth, I went about it the wrong way. I never meant to hurt anyone, especially you two."

"Yeah, well, you failed that mission," Uri spat angrily.

"Don't be mad at Patrick, Royce. He didn't do anything wrong," Lydia said while looking at her niece.

"Fucking his wife's seventeen-year-old sister and getting her pregnant wasn't wrong?" Royce questioned angrily.

"Yes, but it wasn't like that. I went at him, but he never took me seriously. Hell, he practically helped your mama raise me, so he didn't see me as the woman I thought I was. He turned down my advances every time until we both got drunk one night. Well, he was more drunk than I was. I always could handle my liquor better than the average person, but Pat is an occasional drinker. Seducing your father was never about me having feelings for him. I wanted to get back at Sondra for making my life miserable and he was the best way to do it. My plan was for her to walk down on us in her bed and everything went accordingly. What wasn't planned was me finding out that I was pregnant with Uri two months later. Sondra wanted me to have an abortion, but I refused. Then, she tried to make me sign over my rights, so that she could raise Uri as her own. I wasn't doing that either. I hated living under her roof and I didn't want her to turn my baby into one of her little perfect projects. When none of that worked, she moved me into my own apartment and told people that I was pregnant and didn't know who the father was. She was my only source of income, so I just went along with the lie. Pat didn't want to do it, but Sondra convinced us both that it was for the best. He's always been an important part of Uri's life and he made sure that she had everything that she's ever needed. He's always been a great father. You just knew him as your uncle instead," Lydia said, explaining the situation as best as she could.

"Wow," Uri said once her mother was done talking.

"So, you and my father were only together once?" Royce questioned.

"Once is all it takes." Lydia shrugged.

"It's just like my mama to sweep problems under the rug and act like they don't exist," Royce said, shaking her head.

"Sondra will never change. She was willing to take this secret to the grave, but I just couldn't do it. I see the love you have for Patrick and I don't want that to change," Lydia said, looking at her daughter.

"My love for him will never change, but I just need some time. My entire life changed in the blink of an eye and I need time to process it all. Royce and I will sit down and talk to him, but only when we're ready," Uri said, as Royce nodded in agreement.

"I understand, and I hope y'all can forgive me too. I'm sorry for how I behaved," Lydia said sincerely.

"We're family. That's what we do." Royce smiled.

"Bitch please. You still haven't forgiven your own mama," Uri laughed.

"Yes, I have. I just don't let her run my life like she used to. I'm not the same Royce that I was a few years ago."

"No, you're not," Uri agreed.

"I love the new you. You deserve to live your life however you want to live it. Sondra should have been stopped a long time ago," Lydia replied.

"Well, at least one good thing came out of this," Uri spoke up.

"What's that?" Royce questioned.

"I have a sister." Uri smiled while kissing Royce's cheek.

"Aww. Don't make me blush. You've always had a sister. It's just official now," Royce replied.

Uri and Royce enjoyed Lydia's company for a while until Ashton came back to take her home. The entire situation was still messed up, but they were happy that they knew the entire story. Uri and Royce decided to invite Patrick to dinner the following night to have a talk with him. He gave the same story that Lydia gave and he too apologized for the role that he played in everything. Uri thought it was best if they left things as they were. He would still be Uncle Pat to her and her daughters, and he didn't have a problem with that. They didn't want to confuse the girls and that was their main concern. He assured Uri that nothing would change, and she believed him. He had always been like a father to her and she wouldn't have it any other way.

Chapter 36

Sondra read over the email that she was about to send out one more time before she pressed the send key. She was a perfectionist and she had always been that way. Her mother demanded perfection and it was embedded in her. She used to think that being that way was a good thing, but she wasn't so sure anymore. Being a person who always cared about appearances had Sondra on edge all the time. She was constantly wondering what people were saying about her and it was draining. Not only that, but it was starting to cause problems in her home life. Royce barely said two words to her and it was like Patrick was her only parent. She called him every day and even invited him to her house sometimes. Patrick always went out to dinner with her and Caleb, but Sondra was no longer invited. She knew that it was because of her dislike for Caleb, so she wasn't expecting to get a call.

Truthfully, besides her love for Jaxon, she had no reason to dislike the other man. She never even gave Caleb a chance and she felt bad about that too. So many times, she wanted to pick up the phone and call her daughter, but she didn't know what to say. Sondra was never good at apologizing, since she had never felt the need to.

"Good afternoon," Elena said flatly when she walked into the office.

Sondra had her head down looking at her computer screen when the other woman walked into the office.

"Good afternoon Elena. How are you?" Sondra asked.

Elena had been at meetings all morning and that was Sondra's first time seeing her. In fact, she hadn't been seeing much of the other woman at all lately.

"I'm fine, thanks," Elena replied as she sat down at her desk.

"Is everything okay?" Sondra asked her.

Elena was usually full of conversation, but she had been distant lately.

"Yes, but we need to discuss a few things when you get a moment," Elena replied.

"I'm free right now," Sondra informed her.

"Okay, well, I just came from a meeting with my husband and some other school board colleagues. It's been made official and this is my last year as principal of the school. I'll be working alongside Silas in the school board office, overseeing the back end of everything," Elena said proudly.

"Oh, my God, Elena! That's great! Congratulations," Sondra said excitedly.

That was the news that she had been waiting a lifetime to hear. All the years of kissing up to Elena had finally paid off and she was getting what she had worked so hard to obtain. Although she was eligible to retire, becoming principal was a lifelong dream come true for Sondra. She deserved it and that much was certain.

"Thank you, but that's not all," Elena said, as Sondra held her breath in anticipation.

"Okay," she replied as she almost burst at the seams with excitement.

"Silas and I have decided to take things in a different direction. You are welcome to remain on staff here as assistant principal, but we've decided to go with a different choice for principal," Elena said, wiping the smile from Sondra's face.

"Excuse me?" Sondra asked, as if she didn't hear her the first time.

"Yeah, we think it's best if we get someone new with fresh new ideas. We spent the morning interviewing candidates and we've found the perfect choice. Jaxon is also being promoted to senior athletic director at the high school where he teaches track. His position is effective immediately, since they want him to start right away. Today will be his last day here," Elena noted.

"Wow. So, everyone in your family has been given a promotion, while I get handed your ass to kiss," Sondra said angrily.

"Let's remain professional Sondra. This is for the best. Things have been awkward between us since Jax and Royce aren't together anymore. Silas just feels that we need to cut all ties with each other and move on. We don't need the whispering and gossiping about Royce and Jaxon's divorce. That's why we had him moved to another school as well. And with Royce being pregnant, it'll only make things worse. People are already wondering if Jax is the father or not. And I don't want you to think of this decision in a negative way. You'll basically be running the show, since the new principal doesn't know the ropes yet," Elena replied.

"So, let me get this straight. You want me to do the work of a principal without the principal's pay. You and your husband basically screwed me out of a job that you all but promised to me because of your personal feelings about our kids not being together," Sondra snapped.

"This is not personal Sondra. This is business. Silas and I just have to do what we think is best," Elena reasoned.

"That's bullshit, and you know it. I'm done being your fool. I've done that long enough," Sondra fumed as she grabbed her keys and purse.

"What the hell is that supposed to mean?" Elena asked.

"It means that you and your husband can kiss my ass. Consider this my last day. I'm putting in for my retirement, effective immediately," Sondra snapped as she stormed out of the office.

She couldn't lie, she felt like a damn fool. Everything that she'd done over the years, including begging her husband to join the Zulu Club, was done to ensure that she was the next acting principal of the school. When Royce and Jax started dating and got married, she just knew that her position was solidified. She'd basically ruined her relationship with her daughter, all behind a dream that would never come true. It was embarrassing, but she had no one else to blame but herself.

Once she was in her car, Sondra let the tears that she'd been holding in fall freely. She'd always heard about karma, but she had never been unlucky enough to experience it firsthand. Now, she knew all too well how it felt to be on the receiving end of it. Royce had tried to warn her, but she didn't take heed. At one point, she couldn't see any wrong in the great Elena Davenport. Now, she realized just how much of a bitch that Royce always said Elena was. Sondra had to bite the bullet. As much as she hated to do it, she needed to call her daughter and beg for her forgiveness. She was wrong and, for the first time in her life, she had to admit it.

***

"You want to drop me off home and go meet her?" Caleb asked Royce over the phone.

"I guess so. I don't even feel like going, but I'm too nosey not to," Royce replied.

She was packing up her belongings to go home for the day and Caleb was coming to pick her up. Royce had sold the car that she had in the garage of her old house and her other car was at the dealership being serviced. She was shocked when her mother called and asked her to meet her for dinner, but she reluctantly agreed. She hadn't seen Sondra too much outside of work and she didn't really want to. Royce loved her mother the same as always, but she was hurt by her actions. Sondra did things without thinking about how it made other people feel. Royce was tired of being hurt by her, so she just stayed away.

"What's wrong baby? I can drop you off and come back for you if you don't feel like driving," Caleb offered.

"It doesn't matter Caleb. I'm sleepy, but I already gave my word," Royce said as she locked up her classroom.

"Okay, well, I'll be there in a minute," Caleb said before they disconnected.

Royce stopped at the classroom next to hers to talk to another teacher for a second. She was about to leave as well, so they walked out of the building together.

"Make sure you let me know about the baby shower Royce. I know it's still early, but I want my invite," the other woman said before she left and went to her car.

Royce smiled and waved to her as she pulled off, but her smile faded when she saw Jax standing there watching her. It was creepy how he just stood there staring at her like it was normal.

"And to think, I thought you were different from all the others," Jax said, shaking his head.

"As if I give a fuck about what you think. Take your dirty dick on somewhere," Royce said, waving him off.

"You were so pressed to be my one and only, but your new nigga ain't no better," Jax smirked.

"Get the fuck away from me, Jax. You can't tell me nothing about my man that I don't already know. He wasn't the only one who was fucking your sister for his freedom," Royce replied.

"Yet, you chose to have a baby by him. I never took you for one of these desperate hoes out here, but I guess I was wrong," Jax said as he turned to walk away.

As soon as he turned around, a vicious blow to the face made him stumble and fall to the ground.

"Watch your mouth lil bitch. Respect a queen when you see one," Caleb said as he frowned down on him.

"Hey baby." Royce smiled as he stepped over Jax and gave him a kiss.

They walked away holding hands, as Jax picked himself up off the ground. He was caught off guard and embarrassed, but he was no fool. Jax wasn't a street nigga so he would never go after Caleb, knowing that he wouldn't win.

"The fuck was that about?" Caleb asked as he opened the door for Royce to get into the car.

"His stupid ass was talking shit just like always," Royce replied as she strapped on her seatbelt.

Caleb walked around and got into the car and drove off to their destination. Royce was meeting her mother at a little café not too far from the school and it only took about ten minutes before they got there. She spotted Sondra's Silver Lexus backed into a parking spot right near the front door. Royce was starving, and she was happy that they were meeting at a place that served good food.

"I'm not leaving. I'll wait in the car until you're done. Knowing you, it won't take long anyway," Caleb said as he pulled up next to Sondra's car.

"Damn. Am I really that bad?" Royce asked as she laughed.

"Nah, but you and Lady Satan ain't been seeing eye to eye lately," Caleb replied.

"Did you just call my mama Lady Satan?" Royce asked as she fell out laughing.

[311]

"Yep," he said while laughing with her.

"You don't have to wait Caleb. I'll call you when I'm done. I don't know how long we're gonna be. I don't even know what she wants to talk about."

"I'm good. I'm going next door and grab me a few more games," Caleb said as he pointed to the Game Stop.

"Okay, I'll try to make this fast," Royce said as she kissed him and got out of the car.

As soon as she walked into the café, Sondra stood up and waved her over. Royce made her way to the table and took a seat, picking up her menu as soon as she did.

"How have you been Royce? Is everything good with the pregnancy?" Sondra asked.

"Yes, everything is fine," Royce said as she waved a waitress over and placed her order.

"That's good to hear," Sondra said, trying to stall.

Royce wasn't having it though. She needed to know why her mother wanted to meet up to talk so badly.

"What's going on ma? Why did you want to meet me?" Royce asked.

"Well, first thing is, I've decided that today is my last day as assistant principal at the school. I'm retiring," Sondra informed her.

"Congrats. I thought your whole life revolved around being principle once Elena left. What made you change your mind?" Royce asked.

"I didn't change my mind. Elena and Silas changed theirs," Sondra admitted.

"I can't even say that I'm surprised. I tried to tell you but, as usual, you never listen."

"Yeah, well, I found out the hard way just how right you were," Sondra replied as she replayed her and Elena's conversation back to her daughter.

"I won't even lie and say that I feel bad for you because I don't. You basically turned your back on your one and only child for people who don't even care about you. I was in a marriage that almost drained the life out of me and I couldn't even talk to my own mother about it," Royce said, feeling emotional.

"I know and that's why I asked you to come here Royce. I owe you an apology and I'm sorry," Sondra replied.

"Yeah, only because everything fell apart for you," Royce countered.

[312]

"Honestly, Royce, I've wanted to apologize to you for a while now. I'm not perfect, no matter how hard I pretend to be. I've made lots of mistakes, but I can't take them back. I know that it'll take a while for us to get to where we need to be, but I want to at least try. I want to be a part of my grandchild's life and yours too," Sondra said as she wiped her teary eyes.

"I would never keep you away from your grandchild, but a solid relationship between the two of us is going to take a while," Royce admitted, right as the waitress sat her food in front of her.

"I understand Royce. I did a lot of damage to our entire family and that can't be undone overnight. I'm sure Uri hates me just as much as her mother does."

"Uri isn't capable of hating anyone, but would you blame her if she did? You singlehandedly decided to alter everyone's lives like it was okay."

"I was ashamed and embarrassed Royce. My seventeen-year-old sister had a baby by my husband and I didn't even have one at the time. I only did what I was taught to do and tried to fix the situation. My mother always demanded perfection and she made sure that we did too. It wasn't until Lydia came along that things started to change. She was nothing like the rest of us. She was a free spirit who didn't live by anybody's rules. No matter how much I tried to tame her, she just didn't bend. I did what I thought was right, but I did more harm than good," Sondra admitted.

"Why didn't we have this talk a long time ago? I never understood why you did some of the things you did, and I resented you for years. I feel like I didn't get to know the real you because you always hid behind a perfect façade," Royce pointed out.

"Smile even when you feel like crying. A real woman hides a thousand tears behind the prettiest smile," Sondra said sadly, repeating what her mother always said to her.

It was at that exact moment that Royce realized just how unhappy her mother was. She was a pretender, but her eyes told the truth.

"You can't fake happiness ma. Either you're happy or you're not. There is no in between," Royce pointed out.

"It's sad that after all these years, I'm just now realizing that," Sondra admitted.

[313]

Royce spent over an hour just having a heart to heart talk with her mother. It probably would have been longer, but she didn't want to keep Caleb waiting too long.

"Don't forget to ask Uri about lunch this weekend. She and I have a lot to talk about too," Sondra said as she and Royce walked out of the building.

Caleb pulled up right on time and Royce was happy for that. He got out of the car to open the door for her and was shocked when Sondra waved at him. Caleb looked behind him to see who was there. It was hard for him to believe that Sondra was speaking to him.

"You are so wrong for that," Royce laughed when she got into the car.

"Shit, I was trying to see who she was waving at," Caleb said, laughing with her.

"Be nice Caleb," Royce giggled.

"To who?" he asked seriously

"My mama," Royce laughed.

"She's lucky that my mama is saved now. I was trying to get her to lay hands on her and not in a holy way," Caleb replied.

"You wanted Mrs. Pam to fight my mama?" Royce asked.

"Yeah, but she told me no," Caleb answered.

"Oh, my God. Wait until I tell this shit to Uri," Royce laughed as they drove away.

She felt better after having a talk with her mother, but she had to be realistic. The damage that had been done to their relationship couldn't be repaired in one day. And Royce still wasn't convinced that Sondra's sudden change of heart was sincere. She wondered if things hadn't gone left with the Davenports, would she would have felt the need to apologize at all. Royce tried to keep an open mind, so she wasn't going to dwell on anything negative. She wasn't the same Royce that she was before. If Sondra started up with her bullshit again, she had no problem cutting her off, just like she had done before.

Chapter 37

"The queen and the princess. Bitch please. Her fat ass and that funny looking baby," Mya said as she looked at the newest picture and caption that Brian had posted on Instagram.

He had been on some family shit lately and it was driving her crazy. Before, Brian would only post pictures of his customers after he cut their hair. For the past few weeks, his page had been cluttered with pictures of Shanti doing various things throughout the day. He even had pictures of the bitch when she was sleeping, like she was somebody special.

"I told you that they're together now. Ain't no more hiding and faking it. They be all out in the open hugging and kissing. You know I be ear hustling bitch. I heard that she's about to move in with him and everything. She's giving up her apartment," Cookie replied as she took inventory of the alcohol.

She and Mya were at work, but Mya hadn't started her shift yet. She was at the bar venting to Cookie about Brian, just like always. Mya still called him all the time, but he had finally answered for her a few days ago. He wasn't ugly or rude and that surprised her. He did, however, ask her to stop calling him because he was in a committed relationship with Shanti now. Mya went berserk when he said that, but he was unfazed by her outburst. He simply hung up the phone and added the number that she called from to the block list with all the others.

"That big bitch ain't nobody special. He's only doing that because she got his baby. I was pregnant by him first. If I wouldn't have terminated my pregnancy, that would be me instead of her," Mya fumed.

"Having a baby by a nigga these days don't mean shit. If he don't want you, having a baby won't change that. Honestly, I think he was feeling Shanti long before she got pregnant," Cookie pointed out.

"He was feeling me too and you know that. We were close before I got pregnant. Shit just went left after that," Mya replied.

"I don't know Shaky but fuck him. You are a pretty girl and you can get any man you want," Cookie complimented.

"Maybe so, but he's the only man that I want. Why doesn't he want me though?" Mya asked sadly.

"I don't know friend, but you have to let that go," Cookie advised.

"Why does everybody keep saying that? If it was that easy, I would have done it a long time ago. You think I want to be in love with a man who's in love with someone else. I have no problem letting go, but my heart won't comply," Mya said as she wiped her teary eyes.

"I know how you feel Shaky and you know that I've been there before. I loved a nigga so hard that I hit rock bottom and lost everything that I had. My stupid ass didn't even have a place to stay and was paying the note on a car that I couldn't even ride in. Love makes us do some stupid shit, but you have to force yourself to move on. My sister lost her life over a man because she couldn't let go. Don't let that be you too," Cookie warned.

Mya heard her, but she couldn't help how she felt. She had never been in love before and she couldn't handle Brian's rejection. She would usually fuck and duck, but she wanted more with Brian. When she found out that she was carrying his child, her love for him grew even stronger. She envisioned them being together and raising their child under the same roof. Sadly, Brian felt differently. He wasn't ready for kids, or so he said. Yet, he wasted no time doing the family thing with that bitch Shanti.

"I'm about to comment," Mya said as she went back to the picture.

"Bitch, did you hear anything that I just said? Leave that nigga alone and let that shit go," Cookie replied.

"I dare that bitch to play with me. She's tagged in the photo, so I know she'll see it," Mya said as she typed away.

"I give up. You got a one-track mind and Brian is the only thing on it," Cookie said, shaking her head.

Mya ignored her as she continued to do what she did best and tried to cause confusion in Brian's love life.

***

"Me and Dwight took a vacation and came back to all kinds of drama," Co-Co said as he got comfortable on Kia's sofa.

The whole crew was there filling him in on everything that he had been missing. Royce and Caleb had moved into their new house a little sooner than they anticipated, and Dwight was there mounting their televisions on the walls.

"Drama is right honey," Kia laughed.

"Where is my great niece?" Sweets asked.

"She's with your sister," Kia replied.

"How the fuck I leave and y'all are cousins, but when I come back y'all are sisters? What kind of shit is that?" Co-Co asked while looking at Royce and Uri.

"Ask my daddy uncle and my mama," Uri replied with a shrug.

"Not your daddy uncle," Kia said as she fell out laughing.

"Shit, that's what he is. Royce is my sister cousin," Uri replied, making them laugh.

"And I liked to died when I heard that Caleb's probation officer told him that he was pregnant. Y'all keep a bitch entertained around here," Co-Co laughed.

"That bitch period is unpredictable just like her. Every time she starts stressing, her shit go MIA," Uri laughed.

"Don't even remind me. I can't stand that bitch Ashley, with her nasty ass. I'm so happy that Caleb is not on probation no more. I'm sure she got somebody else fucking for freedom now," Royce said, rolling her eyes right as Jaylynn walked through the door.

"Hey everybody." Jay smiled and waved.

"Where are you coming from looking all cute?" Sweets asked.

"She had a date," Keller said with a smile.

"A date with who?" Co-Co asked.

[317]

"I just went to the movies with somebody that I met a few weeks ago." Jay shrugged.

"That bitch ain't waste no time I see," Co-Co said.

"Why should she? Them niggas don't waste no time either. She's young. Let her do her thing," Candace replied.

"Bitch better make sure she pops them pills," Co-Co ordered.

"Goodbye. I hear enough of that from my daddy," Jaylynn said as she walked away to the kitchen.

"Ain't no more pills bitch. Jaden wasn't feeling that shit. She's on the three-month shot now," Kia noted.

"Good," Keller replied.

"What else did I miss?" Co-Co asked everybody.

"Shanti and Shaky been having an internet war," Keller laughed.

"Fuck that bitch. Hoe called my baby ugly and everything. She better pray that I never see her nasty ass," Shanti fumed.

"Bitch, I know you ain't finger fighting on social media!" Co-Co yelled.

"That bitch came for me. She went under all the pictures that Brian had of me and Bri and commented. Who does that?" Shanti questioned.

"You gotta stop letting bothered people bother you. That bitch makes her money a dollar at a time. She's not even on your level," Sweets replied.

"I refuse to argue with a bitch who wears stale lacefronts. It's a waste of time," Co-Co replied.

"Everything doesn't need to be entertained Shanti. That's exactly what she wants you to do. I know it's hard to ignore when it involves your child, but you have to learn to fly with ruffled feathers baby girl," Sweets lectured.

"You're right. I'm done with it after today. Brian and I are good and that's all that matters to me," Shanti replied, right as the doorbell rang.

Kia got up and looked out of the window, shocked to see Hayden standing on her porch.

"Hayley is with your mama and daddy Hayden," Kia said when she opened the door.

"I know, I just put her to sleep before I left. Is Jaylynn home?" he asked.

"Yeah, come in. She's in the kitchen," Kia said as she stepped aside.

"Good evening," Hayden said when he saw everyone seated in the living room.

"Mmhmm," Co-Co mumbled under his breath.

"Don't do my nephew like that," Sweets chuckled, as Hayden walked into the kitchen.

"I'm going eavesdrop," Co-Co said as he got up from the sofa and tiptoed close to the kitchen.

He put his finger up to his lips, signaling everyone to be quiet as he listened to their conversation. No one tried to stop him because they wanted to know too. It wasn't like they were whispering, so they heard everything anyway.

"Hey," Hayden said as he watched Jaylynn eating the sandwich that she had just made.

"What are you doing here Hayden? You know your daughter is not home," Jaylynn replied.

"I called you a few times. Why didn't you answer?" he asked.

"Because your daughter is not here. Why are you calling me when you know she's with your mama and daddy?"

"You sure that's the only reason you didn't answer?" Hayden asked.

"What are you talking about?" Jaylynn asked.

"Did you go to the movies with Zander today?" Hayden questioned.

"How do you know Zander?" Jay questioned.

"He goes to my school. He's on the basketball team with me. How do you know him?" he questioned.

"I met him a few weeks ago at the mall," Jay replied.

She and Zander hadn't known each other very long, so she didn't know too much about him yet. She knew that he was in college, but they hadn't gotten that deep just yet. It was their first time going somewhere together because Jaylynn always turned him down when he asked. She was bored that day, so she decided to meet him at the movies when he begged her to. She enjoyed his company and promised that they could do it again.

"I can't believe this. He's been telling me that he met somebody that he was really feeling, but I didn't know that he was telling me about my own girlfriend," Hayden fumed as he paced the floor.

"You don't have a girlfriend," Jaylynn reminded him.

[319]

"What is that supposed to mean?" Hayden inquired with a frown.

"You broke up with me, remember?" Jay smirked.

"So, it's like that now. You're cutting me off for that nigga?" Hayden frowned.

"If I did cut you off, you handed me the scissors." Jaylynn shrugged.

"Can we go somewhere and talk Jay?" Hayden asked.

"Nope. I just got home and I'm tired. I'm going take a shower and watch Netflix and chill by myself," she replied.

"What about tomorrow? It's Sunday, so we can go somewhere early in the day. I know you don't really do anything on weekdays since school is back in. We can get Hayley and go out to eat," Hayden suggested.

"I don't know Hayden. I'll let you know. I'll talk to you later," Jaylynn said, dismissing him.

"Can I call you tonight?" he asked, almost begging.

"For what Hayden? I want to relax since I have some time to myself."

"Me and Hayley are gonna call you on Facetime in about an hour," he said, like he didn't care about what she'd just said.

She knew that he only threw their daughter in the mix to make sure that she answered for him. He kissed Jaylynn's cheek and turned to walk away. He didn't even see Co-Co standing there listening, but Jaylynn spotted him as soon as she walked out of the kitchen.

"You are so nosey," she laughed when she saw the shocked expression on his face.

"Bitch, you did that. My baby cousin is a fucking boss!" Co-Co yelled excitedly.

"You probably hurt my nephew's feelings," Sweets replied.

"And? She ain't doing no more to him than he did to her. That nigga played with the wrong one. He thought my cousin was gonna be sitting around here waiting on his lil high yellow ass, but she showed him. The fuck he thought," Co-Co countered.

"His ass thought since he was in college, he was gonna have his pick of the litter. They always think the grass is greener on the other side," Keller said.

"Everything ain't always what it appears to be honey. Even salt looks like sugar," Co-Co retorted with a snap.

"I know he was wrong for what he did Jay, but don't be too hard on him. Hayden is a good boy," Sweets defended.

"Fuck that shit! Make his ass suffer Jay. That nigga gave the ammunition. He can't get mad now that the gun is being fired!" Co-Co yelled.

"Y'all calm down. These are seventeen and eighteen-year-old kids that we're talking about here. Let them figure this shit out on their own," Kia suggested.

"We'll talk later Jay. Fuck what they got to say. That nigga gon' regret the day he broke up with you. Hayley ain't gon' be the only one up all night crying," Co-Co replied.

Jay smiled as she walked away to her bedroom. Co-Co sat back down and resumed the conversation that he was having before Jay got there. A few minutes later, Jaden came home with Juice following behind him.

"Hey Co-Co," Juice said while waving at his cousin.

"Hey, you future serial killer," Co-Co replied.

"Don't call my baby that," Kia laughed as she slapped his arm.

"Why do you only speak to Co-Co when you walk into the room? Don't you see your auntie and everybody else in here?" Keller fussed.

"Yeah, but that's my friend," Juice replied with a smile as he went and stood next to him.

"With friends like you, I damn sure don't need no enemies. Move away from me, lil boy. You know I don't trust you," Co-Co replied.

"Jay! Bring her to me!" Jaden yelled down the hall to his daughter.

"Hayley's not here baby. She's with Mona and Harold," Kia informed him.

"For how long?" he asked with a scowl.

"I really don't know." Kia shrugged.

"Muthafuckers get on my nerves man," he mumbled as he walked down the hall to their bedroom.

"If I didn't know that he was bat shit crazy, I would tell his ass about talking about my family," Sweets whispered.

"Let me get my ass out of here. Did you pack my babies' bags Candace? I haven't seen them in two weeks and I'm having withdrawals," Co-Co replied.

"They're packed and ready to go," Candace replied.

"Can I come too Co-Co?" Juice asked, looking all innocent.

"Aww, that's too cute," Sweets cooed.

"Bitch please. Don't let the puppy dog eyes fool you. This is the devil in Jordan's," Co-Co replied.

"I won't be bad, and I'll listen to you," Juice promised.

"Lord, I know I'm gonna regret this later but, yeah, you can come. But, let me tell your lil bad ass something. I'm not calling Jaden and Kia if you act up. I'm whipping your ass my damn self," Co-Co warned him.

"Whippings don't hurt me," Juice said as he ran down the hall to get Jaden to pack him a bag.

"What kind of special education shit is that?" Co-Co frowned.

He waited until Jaden had Juice packed up before he and the rest of the crew left Kia's house. He was happy as hell that Juice had gone to sleep as soon as they got into the car. He just prayed like hell that he stayed sleep all throughout the night.

Chapter 38

Elena and Silas read over the papers that were placed in front of them with mixed emotions. Elena was worried about the outcome, while Silas was thinking of ways to make it go away. Normalcy in the Davenport family was starting to sound like a foreign word. They were used to Jaxon fucking up every other day, but their daughter was as close to perfection as she could get. Aside from getting a tattoo when she was in college, Ashley was a parent's dream come true. She did everything right, including marriage. She could do no wrong in their eyes, or so they thought. It seemed as if Ashley had not only done something wrong, but she got caught too. According to the list of complaints filed against her, Ashley had been very busy.

"What did your father-in-law have to say about all of this? He's a judge for Christ's sake!" Elena yelled.

Ashley wiped the tears from her eyes and shook her head in defeat. "He says it might be best if I resigned from my position," Ashley replied.

"And do what!" Silas barked angrily as he slammed his closed fist down on the dining room table.

Ashley and Elena jumped in fear, as he opened and closed his fist menacingly.

"What did Broderick say?" Elena questioned.

"Things aren't good between us right now. He thinks I'm just as guilty as they're saying I am," Ashley admitted.

"Are you?" Silas questioned as his eyes bore into her.

"Of course not!" Elena shouted.

She immediately covered her mouth soon after, sorry that she had been so careless with her outburst. Silas gave her a look that let her know that she would be paying for that later. Maybe not that very day, but soon enough.

"You have over ten complaints from different people claiming that you forced them to have sex with you in exchange for bypassing their drug tests. One complaint is too many and you have multiples. Don't you dare try to sit here and claim to be innocent. I can see the guilt all over you. Are you that desperate that you would stoop so low as to sleep with convicts? I'm fucking disgusted just looking at you." Silas frowned in anger, making his one and only daughter cry harder.

Ashely was used to his verbal abuse, but she hadn't encountered it in years. Unlike Jax, she knew how to stay under the radar, or at least she used to. It was crazy how one fed-up person turned into several. One of her probationers contacted his lawyer and his lawyer reached out to some of the others. Caleb wasn't one of them, since he'd been let off probation shortly before. She thought sure her cover was going to be blown at the Zulu function, but she had been spared. Broderick had even questioned her about something that Royce had said, but she assured him that it was nothing.

Ashley loved her husband with her whole heart, but he just didn't do it for her sexually. Broderick was boring in and out of the bedroom and Ashley needed some excitement. She got a taste of a few bad boys in college, but she knew that she could never marry one. Broderick was perfect for her family's image and her father was pleased with her choice. Ashley tried to coach him in the bedroom, but he was a lost cause. It was cool because she had found a way to have the best of both worlds. Now, her greed had come back to haunt her in the worse way.

"Now what?" Elena questioned.

"I don't know ma. I'm under investigation," Ashely replied

"A fucking disaster! We hold two of the highest positions in the school board office right now. My brother is planning to run for a seat on the city council and another is planning to announce his run for mayor. We are set to be King and Queen of Zulu next year and I get hit with this bullshit. A media shitstorm at the worst possible time," Silas roared angrily, right as Jaxon walked into the house.

He didn't know what was going on, but he knew that it had to be bad. His sister was his parents pride and joy and she never got into any trouble. To hear his father raising his voice at her was shocking. Even more shocking was Ashley sitting there with a face full of tears. Jax hated to do it, but he had no choice but to move back in with his parents after his drama with Sienna. He slept out every chance he got, but he didn't get too many chances. Every woman in his life seemed to be looking for a commitment that he wasn't willing to give. He had just gotten out of his second marriage and he wasn't doing it a third time. He hated to stay the night with one of them because they never wanted him to leave. He wasn't ready to live with anyone else. He wanted to stick and move, but they didn't seem to understand that.

Jax found a way around that too. He started dealing with people who didn't even have a house to call their own. That way, he could take them to the hotel for a few hours and drop them off home right after. That was considered a perfect relationship in his opinion. A text came through, breaking him from his thoughts and confirming his plans for the night. Jax smiled, happy that things had worked out.

"Good evening," Jaxon said as rushed pass them and up to his room.

He didn't need to be in the middle of anymore bullshit and he wasn't trying to be. He was just happy that it was someone else other than him who was in trouble this time. Since he no longer worked at the school with his mother, he didn't see her as often as he did before. That was fine with him because he really didn't want to. And he felt the same way about Royce. She was having a baby with someone else and he didn't need that constant reminder every time he saw her. He still loved her and that would have hurt too much.

"Hand in your resignation before the media gets ahold of this. I'll have to see what our attorneys can do to make this go away. I don't even know if they can make it go away. It's obvious that your father-in-law wants no parts of it. Even he can see how fucked up this is," Silas said.

"But, resigning will only make me look guilty, won't it?" Ashley questioned like she wasn't.

"Get the fuck out of my house Ashley," Silas demanded in a calm but deadly tone.

"Honey-" Elena started before he cut her off after the first word.

"Shut up and don't open your mouth to speak again unless I tell you to," Silas ordered, making Elena clamp her mouth shut.

Ashley was scared to death. She grabbed her purse and made a mad dash for the front door. Upsetting their father was something that none of them wanted to do. Silas was a monster in an expensive suit and they knew that all too well. Ashley hated to go home to face her husband but arguing with him was better than dealing with her father.

***

"How did it go? Did anyone see you sneak in?" Jax asked as he drove home after work.

He was bypassing his trip to the gym because he was too tired to work out or do anything else. He had just gotten inside after two that morning and had to be up at six for work.

"No, I already had that part covered," his female companion replied.

"Sorry for keeping you out so late. I just couldn't get enough of you," Jax said, making her blush on the other end of the phone.

"Same here. I could barely keep my eyes open in my classes today." She yawned.

"Yeah, my students had a free day today too. I let them do whatever the hell they wanted to do, as long as they left me alone," Jax laughed.

"I wish I could say the same." She yawned again.

"When can I see you again? I know it takes time to get your story together, so I'm putting in my request early," Jax chuckled as he turned on his parents' streets.

His face twisted in confusion as he spotted two police cars and one unmarked car pulled up in front of their house. A little over a month had passed since Ashley had gotten into trouble and it seemed as if it wasn't over yet. It took a few days for him to get his mother to tell him what was going on, but he wasn't as surprised as they were. Caleb had already told him that his sister wasn't as perfect as they thought she was. Ashely's transgressions were catching up with her and her husband was threatening divorce. The

Lockwood family had more clout than they did, and it was an embarrassment to Broderick's family. Silas had been on a rampage and Elena was walking on eggshells around the house.

"You can see me whenever you want to," Jaxon's female friend spoke up, interrupting his thoughts.

He had quickly forgotten that she was on the phone because he was too busy trying to see what was going on. He didn't see Ashley's car, but he was sure that she would be there soon. She came over just about every day because she hated being home with her husband.

"Let me call you back later. I need to talk to my parents right quick," Jax said. He didn't even give her a chance to reply before he hung up the phone and parked his car.

"Do you have a warrant to search for anything in my home? What the hell is this about? I'm calling my attorney," Jax heard Silas bellow as he walked up the stairs.

His parents lived in an upscale subdivision and nothing ever happened in their area. He wasn't surprised to see their nosey ass neighbors standing around gossiping about the situation. That was nothing new to him though.

"My God, Jaxon!" Elena sobbed when her son walked through the door.

"What's wrong ma? Is everything okay with Ashley?" Jax asked.

Her face was soaked with tears as she ran over and wrapped her arms around his neck. Silas took long angry strides in his direction until he was standing right in front of him. His face was a mask of anger and hate as he looked down at his son.

"What the hell did you do?" he asked through clenched teeth.

"Me?" Jax questioned while pointing to himself.

"A fucking disappointment is all that you've ever been," Silas fumed.

Jax was confused, but he never got a chance to reply. Two uniformed officers and a detective came walking down the steps and right over to him. The detective had Jax's computer in a clear plastic bag, along with some other items that they'd obviously found in his room.

"What the hell are y'all doing with my stuff?" Jax asked angrily.

"Jaxon Davenport?" one of the officers asked.

"Yes, I'm Jaxon Davenport," he confirmed.

"You're under arrest for carnal knowledge of a juvenile," the police officer informed him.

"What! This is some bullshit! Y'all got the wrong man," Jaxon argued as he jerked away from the arresting officer.

"Stop resisting!" the officer yelled while slamming him to the tiled floor.

"Jaxon please. Don't move sweetheart. Don't resist," Elena begged through her tears.

"I didn't even do shit," Jax swore.

"Shut up Jaxon. Let the lawyers do all the talking. Don't open your mouth again," Silas ordered in his deep domineering voice.

Jax nodded his head as he was led out of the house in front of a crowd of onlookers. The gasps and whispers started as soon as the door opened, and he felt like a common criminal. Jax had managed to finesse himself out of many situations, but he didn't know if he was skilled enough to do it this time. He didn't think with the right head and he always ended up in trouble because of it. Working fulltime at a high school was too much temptation for a man like him and he couldn't resist it for long. Jax loved that younger girls were easier to deal with than women his own age. He didn't have to worry about them begging him to stay all night because they all lived at home with their parents. They weren't worried about a serious relationship because they knew that they weren't supposed to be dealing with him at all. His biggest issue was making sure that they stayed quiet, but someone had obviously talked. Whatever wasn't said would be revealed once they gained access to his laptop and cellphone anyway.

"God, our neighbors will never look at us the same again," Elena said as she closed and locked the front door. She stood on the porch and watched until the police cars were no longer in sight before going back inside.

"Our neighbors are the least of our problems right now. First Ashley and now this. You can bet your last dollar that heads are about to roll for this shit. I knew that putting him at a high school fulltime was a mistake. Now, we can add sex offender and pedophile to his long list of fuckups," Silas fumed.

"I never want to leave out of this house again," Elena sniffled, right as her husband's phone rang.

[328]

"Damn it," Silas bellowed when he saw who was calling.

"What's wrong honey? Who is it?" Elena asked.

"A call that I've been dreading since the police first knocked on the door. It's the school board chairman. I'm sure he's calling to tell me that Jaxon is out of a job. I dread to think about what his little mishaps will mean for us," Silas replied as he walked away to take the call.

Chapter 39

Jax looked around his newly obtained two-bedroom apartment and shook his head in disgust. His life had taken a drastic turn and he hated the direction that it had gone in. After being arrested a few months before, things had only gotten worse for him. After several videos were retrieved from his computer, Jax was hit with even more charges. His father tried his best to make the charges go away, but the authorities weren't having it. They took it seriously when minors were involved and Jax found that out the hard way. He thought his secret was safe, but he was sadly mistaken. Apparently, one of the students that he had been with was careless and left her phone lying around. Jax sent her an explicit text message and her mother got it instead of her. After questioning her daughter and finding out the truth, she immediately got the authorities involved.

Once Jax was arrested, two more students came forward and his father was livid. He wanted Jax out of his house and he wasted no time making it happen. It was no secret that his son had a problem but fulfilling his sexual needs with his students was the ultimate low. Jax knew that he was dead wrong, but most of his students had the bodies of grown women. He resisted for a while when he was just their part-time coach. He didn't have to see them every day, so it wasn't that hard. Once he became a full-time teacher, the temptation became too much. It started out as innocent flirting to see how they would respond. When they started to reciprocate, Jax was all in. He swore them to secrecy and things worked out for a while. But, just like always, karma paid him a visit and all hell broke loose.

"Hello," Jax said, answering the phone for his mother.

"Hey son. How are you?" Elena whispered.

"I'm good ma. Why are you whispering?" Jax asked her.

"You know how your father is Jaxon. He's still being stubborn about everything," Elena replied.

Silas had basically cut off all communication with his son. He forbad Elena from talking to him, but she snuck and did it anyway. He wanted to distance himself from Jax and all his drama, even though it was too late. Silas had been forced to resign from his position amid all the scandal and he hated his son for altering his life. He lost all his retirement benefits that he'd worked all his life to obtain. Elena resigned as well and was now trying to become principal at another elementary school. She wasn't so sure that she would get the position, but she tried anyway. They had enough money to live comfortably, but that wasn't the point. Being made to do anything didn't sit right with Silas and he hated when he wasn't in control. Besides, all the legal fees that he had to pay for Jax had put a huge dent in their savings.

"I don't want you to get into any trouble ma. Just call me whenever you're alone," Jax suggested.

"It's fine honey. Your father is taking a shower," Elena replied.

"How are you, ma? I know that things are kind of rough right now. I'm sure that you're feeling the impact of all that's been going on," Jax said, speaking in riddles.

He really wanted to say that he knew that the beatings had increased, but there was no need to state the obvious. Elena could barely breathe without Silas getting upset, so she stayed out of his way. He just needed some time for the smoke to clear and things would get a little better.

"I'm fine honey. I'm more worried about you and Ashley than anything," Elena replied.

"What's up with her? How did everything go?" Jax asked her.

"Not good. Thank God she's not facing any jail time, but she's still a nervous mess. I'm not sure what's going to happen with her and Broderick either. She said that he hasn't spoken to her since she admitted to everything," Elena replied.

"Damn," Jax sighed, feeling his sister's pain.

"How's your new job going?" Elena questioned.

"It doesn't pay as much as I'm used to, but it's a job." Jax shrugged as if she could see him.

It was a wrap for him ever teaching again, so he ended up applying for a job at the gym that he frequented. They needed a personal trainer and Jax was hired on the spot. He was a regular, so they knew that he was capable of getting the job done. Jax enjoyed being able to work out whenever he wanted to, and he loved that he had access to as many women as he wanted as well.

"Let me know if you need anything Jaxon. You're still my son, no matter what. I know that you have a lot of legal fees since your father stopped paying for everything."

"I'm good for now ma. I have a few dollars saved up. I just have to spend it wisely. I'll go out and get a second job before I bow down to your husband. It's only a matter of time before he's exposed for who he truly is," Jax replied.

"Don't wish bad luck on your father Jaxon," Elena scolded.

"I'll never do that, but karma has no expiration date. His luck will run out soon enough. I'm a living witness to that," Jax replied.

All the things that he'd been through in the past year had taught him a valuable lesson. Marriage wasn't for everybody and Jax added himself to that list. He liked to be with multiple women, so he decided that he wasn't going to commit to anyone else. He also promised himself that he was going to be a better father. His kids had been exposed to some of the same things that he had to witness while growing up. He didn't want them to grow up feeling about him how he felt about his father.

Just like his mother didn't deserve to be mistreated, Sienna didn't either. Jax had been in contact with her, but only for the sake of their children. Sienna still had a restraining order on him, so he had to get his brother's wife to get his kids when he wanted to spend time with them. He enjoyed bonding with them and they seemed to love spending time with him as well. Somebody had to break the Davenport curse and Jax wanted that someone to be him.

"I know that your father can be difficult at times, but he's always done the best that he could with his family," Elena defended.

"I hate that you actually believe that, but I can't change your mind. I just want you to be safe," Jax replied.

"I'm fine honey, but I have to go. I just heard the water shut off," Elena whispered in a hurry.

"I love you, ma. Make sure you keep in touch, so I won't worry," Jax replied.

"Okay, I love you too son," Elena said before she hung up.

Jax felt bad for his mother, but she was stuck in her ways. She saw the good in her husband, but she was the only one who did. Silas was an asshole and had been that way all his life. He thought he was hurting Jaxon by cutting him off, but he'd actually done him a favor. Silas had done something that Jaxon had been wanting to do for years and that was distance himself.

***

"When the hell did you become friends with Sienna?" Caleb asked Royce as they walked around the store.

"I'm not friends with her ass. Me and Uri saw her when we took the kids to Dave and Buster's earlier," Royce replied.

"How did y'all start talking?" Caleb questioned.

"I didn't even see her, but her kids spotted me. When she saw us sitting at the table, she spoke and started spilling all kinds of tea. She talks to one of Jax's brother's wives and she be telling her everything. She said that Jax had to register as a sex offender and his father put him out because of it. He didn't want his address associated with nothing like that. He's an asshole, so that doesn't surprise me." Royce frowned.

"Like father, like son," Caleb replied.

"She also said that Ashley's husband filed for divorce. She wanted to resign from her job, but they fired her before she had a chance to. She went from being the head of the probation department to being on probation her damn self. I told my mama that it was only a matter of time before the shit hit the fan with them, but she had to see it for herself," Royce rambled.

"Stop with all that messy gossiping and shit. You gon' fuck around and have my son come out acting just like Co-Co," Caleb fussed.

Royce was now in her sixth month of pregnancy and Caleb was excited to be having his first son. Uri and his family were planning a huge baby shower, and he and Royce were finishing up their registry.

"What's wrong with that?" Royce asked with a smirk.

"Don't play with me, Royce," Caleb said seriously as he looked at her and frowned.

"I'm just playing baby. Calm down," Royce laughed, right as his phone started ringing.

"What's up ma?" Caleb asked while answering the phone for Pam.

"Where is Royce? I called her phone and didn't get an answer," Pam said.

"She's right here. She left her phone in the car," Caleb replied.

"Oh okay. Well, Brook and I are looking at cakes online. I sent a few pictures to her phone. Tell her to let me know which one she likes best. And tell her to text me her mother's phone number," Pam instructed.

"What do you need her number for?" Caleb asked.

"Because I want to include her in the planning Caleb. We're getting input from Uri, but I'm sure her mother wants to be involved too. Royce is her only child," Pam noted.

"Don't do it ma, I'm telling you. That lady is the Anti-Christ," Caleb replied.

"Boy, stop being so stupid," Pam laughed.

"Keep thinking it's a game if you want to. You gon' end up laying hands on her just like I've been asking you to," Caleb replied.

"Just do what I said Caleb. I don't have a problem sitting her ass down if it comes to that. I'm really not the one for her to try that shit with," Pam said.

"That's what I'm talking about. I knew you were still bout that life," Caleb replied.

"Bye boy," Pam laughed before hanging up in his face.

"You better stop talking about my mama nigga," Royce fussed as soon as he got off the phone.

"How do you know who I was talking about?" Caleb asked.

"Because that's the only time you talk to your mama about fighting somebody," Royce laughed.

"Your mama started with me first. I be civil with her because of my love for you, but that won't stop me from letting my mama tag that ass," Caleb swore.

"I know she's a piece of work, but I'm just trying to keep the peace," Royce replied.

She and Sondra were working towards building a decent mother daughter relationship, but Royce was taking her time. Sondra tried too hard at times and that only made her daughter pull back from her. She was trying to rush progress on something that she had took years to ruin, and Royce wasn't having it. Sondra still seemed to dislike Caleb, but she tried her best to hide it. Caleb was very outspoken and that's what she hated about him the most. They had finally invited Sondra to their new home and she started up with her controlling bullshit a few minutes after walking through the door. She was making suggestions about their son's room and about names that Royce should consider. Caleb politely told her to mind her own business and she didn't like that very much. His son was going to be named after him and he didn't need her input.

"I'm not worrying about keeping the peace with her Royce. She ain't about to stress you out while you're carrying my son and no other time after that. She can either get with it or keep it pushing. It's as simple as that," Caleb noted.

"Why can't she just go with the flow like my daddy always does?" Royce wondered aloud.

"Because she wants to control everything. You and your daddy let her run shit for so long and now she don't know how to stay in her lane. You might want to talk to her and let her know that she got me fucked up," Caleb suggested.

"You know she volunteered herself to watch the baby since she's retired now," Royce said, dreading Caleb's response.

"I know you didn't agree to that bullshit!" Caleb snapped as he stopped to look at her.

"No, I didn't, but we don't have anyone else in mind. You already said that you didn't want him in nursery," Royce replied.

"He's not going to nursey. He's gonna be right at home with me," Caleb replied.

"That is not gonna work and you know it. What about the times that you have to actually do some work Caleb? Where is he gonna be then? You'll do anything to keep my mama out of the picture. You're being difficult for no reason," Royce argued.

"I'm not even doing this with you right now Royce," Caleb said, brushing her off.

"Whatever Caleb," Royce said as they continued to shop.

Once they were done, Caleb stopped to get them something to eat before they headed home. They hadn't said too much to each other since they were in the store and Caleb didn't like that. He and Royce never really argued about much and he didn't want to start. Royce had taken a shower and was in bed watching tv when Caleb laid down next to her. He pulled her close and rubbed her belly before he said what was on his mind.

"Look, I'm sorry if I came off too harsh, but I can't help the way that I feel. I really need you to understand my position though Royce. You think I want somebody watching my son who doesn't even like me. Ain't no telling what kind of shit she gon' be putting in his head. I hate what you said she did to you when you were growing up and you expect me to be okay with her keeping my son. That's not happening Royce. I don't need us to start arguing over dumb shit and I don't need you to be stressing over nothing either. Let me handle everything just like I told you from day one," Caleb said.

"Okay," Royce replied with a smile.

"Okay?" Caleb repeated. "I said all that and all you have to say is okay?"

"What else do you want me to say Caleb? I trust you to do exactly what you said you would do. I understand everything that you just said, and I agree."

"Well, what was the attitude about earlier then?" Caleb asked.

"I don't know. Hormones I guess." Royce shrugged.

"Three more months," Caleb said, shaking his head.

Not only was he ready to meet his son, but he was ready for Royce to get back to her old self. Her attitude was ridiculous, and Caleb had to remember that that wasn't her usual demeanor. There were many days when he was seconds away from calling her a crazy bitch, but then he would have to deal with the tears. He now understood why Brian was so stressed out when Shanti was pregnant. They were too emotional, and it was draining. Even through all that, Caleb was happy, and he wouldn't have it any other way. Royce hadn't even had his first son yet and he was already looking forward to baby number two.

Chapter 40

"This shit has gone too far Shaky. It was one thing for y'all to be arguing on social media, but y'all are playing a dangerous game now," Cookie said as she drove her friend home.

Shanti and Mya were still going at it via social media, but things took a drastic turn earlier that day. Cookie and Mya pulled up to the gas station to grab something to drink and ran into Shanti and one of her friends. Cookie had barely put the car in park before Mya was hopping out of it to confront the other woman. Thankfully, the woman who was with Shanti was not trying to let them fight. Cookie held Mya back while the other woman did the same to Shanti. Things seemed to be under control until Mya picked up a bottle and threw it in Shanti's direction. The bottle missed her by inches, but she was furious about it being thrown. When Shanti picked up a bottle from the ground, her aim was a lot better than Mya's was. The bottle hit Mya in the middle of her forehead and had blood streaming down her face soon after. Cookie thought that her friend needed stiches, so she rushed her to the urgent care center that wasn't too far from where they were. Thankfully, it was only a cut that was cleaned and bandaged up and no stitches were required.

"Fuck that Cookie. That bitch got me fucked up. I'm not hoping to run into her on the streets no more. I'm going to the shop for that hoe," Mya fumed.

"You better not go there with no bullshit Mya, I'm telling you. That's a family business and you're asking for a family beat down if you do," Cookie warned.

"Fuck them. I stay ready and you already know what's up with me," Mya replied as her leg bounced nervously.

"I told you to leave that dumb shit alone Mya. You shouldn't have commented on that man's pictures," Cookie said as she pulled up to Mya's house.

Katrice was standing outside ready and waiting to see what was up. Her sister had already called her, and she was pissed.

"I can say what the fuck I want. That bitch said just as much as I did!" Mya yelled as they both got out of the car.

"But, you started it Mya. You can't be talking reckless about people's kids and not expect them to react," Cookie replied.

"Okay, but did you not see what that bitch said to me? You're not considered a baby mama if you killed the baby. That hoe hit below the belt."

"And you didn't? Calling that girl's baby ugly and funny looking. That shit is just childish," Cookie countered.

She was over trying to tell Mya right from wrong. She didn't listen and still did whatever she wanted to do anyway. It was all fun and games when Cookie was reporting shit back to her just to get under Brian and Shanti's skin, but it was on a whole new level now. Cookie didn't even feel comfortable being at the shop anymore and she barely went there. She had sent Bryce a text that morning asking him to call her, but he hadn't called yet. Cookie didn't know what she had to do, but she wanted to be let out of her lease. She wasn't really making money anyway, so it was a waste. She did better with the tips that she got from the club.

"You dumb as fuck if you think she's your friend. She might be right in the shop talking about you with the rest of them hoes!" Katrice yelled from her spot on the porch.

"Bitch, I'm more of a friend to her than you are a sister. Who opened their door and gave her a place to stay when you let your married nigga put her out? That nigga didn't even live with you and was calling the shots. The fuck you mean!" Cookie yelled angrily.

"Water under the bridge hoe. No matter what happened in the past, I'm here now. She don't need no friends as long as she got me," Katrice replied.

"No bitch, she don't need no enemies as long as she got you. You better hope Ronnie don't want you out of here Shaky. You're gonna be homeless again," Cookie warned.

"Bye Cookie. I'll talk to you later," Mya said as she walked away.

Cookie really felt bad for her friend. With a big sister like Katrice, she was never going to do better. She encouraged the drama, instead of trying to prevent it. Cookie was guilty of that at one time too, but she knew when to stop and back away.

"Let me see your head," Katrice said when Mya walked up to her.

"I'm good," Mya replied as she lifted the bandage to show her the small cut that was underneath.

"So that bitch likes to fight dirty I see," Katrice fumed as they walked into the house.

"Yeah, but it's all good," Mya replied.

She didn't bother telling her sister that she threw the bottle at Shanti first. It wouldn't have mattered to Katrice anyway. She was always down for a good fight, no matter who started it.

"No, it ain't all good. I hope that bitch don't think that this is over. She gon' see me sooner than she thinks," Katrice said as she lit her cigarette to calm her nerves.

Mya smiled inwardly because that was exactly what she wanted to hear. Cookie was always trying to hold her back, but Katrice got out there and fought with her. Shanti just didn't know what she was up against, but she was going to find out soon enough.

***

"Bitch, we need some champagne up in here today. I'm going to the store and get us a few bottles too," Co-Co said excitedly.

Bryce had just left the shop, but not before giving Co-Co and everyone else some great news. Cookie had asked to be let out of her lease and Bryce happily obliged. He was tired of hearing the complaints but, most of all, he was tired of the drama. They made a clean break and he was happy that everything worked out. He was done trying to hire someone and he decided to leave that up to Co-Co. He worked at night, so he didn't have to see the new employee anyway. He knew that Co-Co was going to be like the police and screen the applicants accordingly.

"Hell yeah. It feels like a holiday up in this bitch," Brian agreed.

Having Cookie gone meant that Shaky would no longer be coming around either. That was the best news that Brian had heard in a while.

"Baby, the next bitch that comes through here is going through hair salon boot camp. We're doing background checks, dental exams, and everything else," Co-Co replied.

"Bryce need to stop doing them long ass leases. Who the fuck rents out space for eighteen months?" Brian questioned.

"That's over with too, cousin. We're doing month to month up in this bitch now. If we like you one month and can't stand you the next, your ass got to go," Co-Co replied as he prepared to leave.

"Where you going Co-Co?" Candace asked her brother.

"You must have thought I was playing. I'm going get some champagne bitch," Co-Co replied, right before he walked out the front door.

"Are you ready to eat Brian?" Shanti asked him.

"I will be in a minute," he replied as he cut his customer's hair.

"I'm going to China Doll and I already know what you want. Anybody else want something?" Shanti asked.

"Bring me some rice back Shanti. Come get some money from my top drawer," Candace said while braiding someone's hair.

"I got you, cousin," Shanti replied.

She walked to the break room to grab her purse before she left to go across the river. While walking to her car, she began the aggravating task of trying to place her order by phone, since that was almost impossible to do. China Doll was always packed, and their phones stayed busy. Shanti sighed in frustration as she dialed the phone for the fifth time and got the same results. She was about ready to give up and get something else to eat, but her mind was set on Chinese food.

After three more tries, Shanti finally got lucky and the phone started ringing. She was ready to place her order, but her attention was pulled in another direction when she saw someone rushing towards her. Shanti immediately dropped her purse and started swinging when Shaky got close to her.

"Bitch, you knew it wasn't over," Shaky said as her and Shanti went into a quick mix.

Shaky was holding her own, but Shanti was still getting the best of her. Three days had passed since their last altercation, but Shanti wasn't surprised to see her. Shaky lived for drama and she didn't know how to let shit go. She felt played about Shanti hitting her with the bottle, but she started the bullshit. Shanti swore that she was done entertaining her on social media, but she was tired of Shaky coming for her. Talking about her was one thing, but bringing her baby into it was going too far.

"Get off my lil sister, bitch!" Katrice yelled when Shanti slung Mya to the ground and tried to get on top of her.

"You want some too hoe!" Shanti yelled as she turned her attention to Katrice.

Shaky jumped up when the other two women started fighting and quickly jumped in, making it two against one.

Cars pulled to the side to watch them fight, but nobody made a move to break it up. Brian thought there had been a car accident outside, even though he didn't hear anything. When he and his customer walked outside, his face twisted up in a mask of anger. He saw Shanti fighting with Shaky and Katrice and he was seeing red.

"The fuck!" Brian yelled as he sprinted over to them.

He grabbed Katrice first and slung her to the ground. Shanti used that time to focus on Mya and really give her the business.

"Nigga, you got me fucked up. Don't put your fucking hands on me," Katrice fumed as she walked up on Brian.

"You better get your big nasty ass away from here and take this trashy bitch with you!" he yelled as he pulled Shanti away from Mya and pushed her close to her sister.

Brian was pissed when he saw the blood trickling from Shanti's lip. He used the bottom of his t-shirt to wipe it away as he inspected her face. His customer who walked outside with him tried to hold the other two women back, but Katrice was too wild. She broke away from his grasp and came charging at Shanti once again. Shanti was ready, and she swung, hitting Katrice in the mouth before Brian could stop her. He'd had enough of the drama and he was ready to put an end to it.

"Man, get the fuck on!" Brian barked angrily as he shoved Katrice hard enough for her to go crashing to the ground.

He wasn't in the habit of manhandling women, but they had him fucked up thinking that he was gonna stand there while they jumped his girl. Shanti was good one on one, but they obviously couldn't handle her that way.

"Y'all need to chill out," another man in the crowd said as he helped to hold Mya and Katrice back. Brian recognized him as the man who sometimes sold Cd's and DVD's in the area.

"Fuck you, Brian! You got me fucked up putting your hands on me!" Katrice yelled as she limped back to her car.

She fell on her ankle when Brian pushed her, and it was aching already. She was sure that it would get worse later and Ronnie was gonna be pissed when he found out what happened.

"You lucky he didn't knock your ugly ass out. Grown man looking ass bitch," Shanti replied.

"You gon' see me again hoe. Believe that," Shaky promised as she was carried off kicking and screaming.

Candace was late coming out of the shop and she caught the very end of the commotion.

"The hell happened out here?" she asked as she looked around.

"Two puppies escaped from the pound," Shanti replied, making her laugh.

"I'm so sick of this dumb shit man. Cookie's messy ass is gone, and this bitch is still coming around here with drama," Brian fussed as he picked up Shanti's purse from the ground.

"I lost my damn appetite messing with these hoes," Shanti said as he followed him back inside.

"So, it's a no on the rice?" Candace asked as she resumed braiding her customer's hair.

"My baby just got attacked by two pit bulls and you're worried about some rice," Brian said as he wiped Shanti's face with the paper towel that he'd just wet in the shampoo bowl.

"I'm hungry man. Let me call David," Candace said, referring to her husband.

"We're going get the food girl. Calm down," Brian replied.

He had a little time to spare, so he went with Shanti to go get the food. He didn't want a repeat of what happened before with Shaky, and he wasn't taking any chances. He was just happy that Jaden and Co-Co weren't there because things would have been much worse than they already were.

Chapter 41

"That shit gon' turn out bad bruh. Shaky is crazy just like that bitch Tori was. You can't underestimate them delusional hoes," Jaden said as he and Brian sat in his living room and talked.

Brian was filling him in on the events of the day before, but he wasn't surprised. He told Brian to leave Shaky alone a long time ago, but he didn't listen. He could spot crazy from a mile away and Shaky fit the description. He was happy that Cookie didn't work there anymore, but that didn't mean that Shaky would stay away. Then, there was Ronnie, who Jaden was sure was going to be a problem eventually as well. Katrice had him sprung, so that was to be expected. The nigga was lame as hell, so he was nothing to stress over.

"Where the fuck was you at anyway? You never miss work on Saturdays," Brian noted.

"In here drinking with Kia Friday night and was hungover. I was too fucked up to do anything. We ordered food and just chilled all day," Jaden replied.

"That's what the fuck I'm talking about. Fuck friends when you got your wife."

"The fuck you waiting on then nigga? You and Shanti live together and got a baby. Marriage is all that's left." Jaden shrugged.

"Nah bruh. I don't think I'm ready for all that right now," Brian said while scratching his head.

"Tell me what's the difference though, bruh. Y'all are already living like a married couple. The only thing missing is the paperwork and a ring. Life is short and you ain't getting no younger. And take it from me, ain't shit else out there. You've had enough hoes to last you a lifetime. You must be tired of the single life because you settled down with Shanti. Make that shit right. Don't just have Bri with your last name. Give her mama your last name too," Jaden suggested.

"I hear you, bruh, but I don't think I'm ready for all that right now," Brian replied, right as he heard Hayley crying from Jaylynn's room down the hall.

"Jay! What's wrong with her?" Jaden yelled.

"She's fine. I'm cleaning my room and she's in her swing," Jaylynn replied, as Hayley continued to scream.

"Pick her up man! Don't let her cry like that," Jaden bellowed.

"Crying won't kill her, daddy. She just got in there," Jaylynn pointed out.

"She got me fucked up," Jaden said as he got up and walked down the hall.

"She's fine daddy. She's already too spoiled, thanks to you," Jaylynn fussed when her father walked into the room.

Hayley knew that he was coming for her because she started kicking her thick legs and reaching her arms out for him. She was seven months old now and rotten to the core. Jaden swore that he wasn't ready to be a grandpa, but he could have fooled her. He had Hayley more spoiled than anybody else. She slept with him and Kia some nights and he watched her every Monday, since he was off from work. Hayden's parents had her spoiled too and Jaylynn couldn't win for losing. She was thankful for the help, but they turned Hayley into a crybaby.

"Don't make me sit this fucking swing out for the garbage man. You know she don't like this bullshit," Jaden fussed.

"How do you know when she's never in it? Nobody is ever gonna watch her crybaby self," Jaylynn argued.

"As if I give a fuck," Jaden replied as he walked away with Hayley in his arms.

"Nigga, you full of shit," Brian laughed when Jaden walked back in with the baby.

Jaden talked mad shit when Jaylynn was pregnant, but he got amnesia whenever somebody mentioned it.

"Mind your business nigga," he laughed, knowing what his brother was referring to.

"What's up with her punk ass daddy?" Brian asked.

"Lil pussy be over here every day kissing Jay's ass." Jaden frowned.

"She back with that nigga?" Brian asked.

"I don't know who she's with. She talks to some other lil niggas too. As long as she takes that shot every three months, I'm good. I'm not wasting my time being on her back like that no more. I did that before and still ended up with a grandbaby. Fuck it," Jaden replied.

"Let me get my ass up out of here and go home," Brian said as he stood up.

His phone rang to Shanti's ringtone as soon as he walked to the door.

"Just put a ring on it nigga," Jaden laughed as he walked him out.

"One day," Brian said as he walked to his car and pulled off.

Jaden made some good points, but he just wasn't ready. He and Shanti never really talked about marriage, so he didn't know how she felt about it. Brian wasn't opposed to marriage, but he wanted to make his first time his one and only. He knew without a doubt that Shanti was the one, he just hoped she felt the same way about him.

***

The following Tuesday at the shop started out quietly. Tuesdays were usually slow, and that day was no different. But, just like always, peace and quiet never lasted too long. Co-Co and Candace were trying to write up an ad for a new stylist while Shanti played on her phone. Brian and Jaden had just finished with a customer and were sitting in their barber chairs when Ronnie walked through the door. Brian stood up when he saw Shaky and Katrice walk in with him. That nigga was bold, and those silly bitches weren't any better. Jaden chuckled at their audacity. Ronnie walked through the door like he was a boss in the presence of two bad bitches. Shanti didn't have a customer, so she kicked off her heels and prepared for whatever. She went and stood next to her man and mean mugged right along with him.

"What's good Brian?" Ronnie asked as he pulled up his sagging pants.

Jaden watched him like a hawk and he paid attention to his body language. He stood up from his chair because he already knew that shit was about to go left.

"You tell me. You walked up in here like we got a problem," Brian replied.

"We most definitely have a problem since you think it's cool to put your hands on my girl," Ronnie replied, as Katrice smiled and nodded like he said something real.

"This goofy muthafucka," Jaden mumbled as he looked over at Ronnie.

He was nervous, and Jaden saw that when he first walked in. More than likely, Katrice put him up to defending her honor, but he wasn't even built like that. If he really wanted to do Brian dirty, he knew where he laid his head and where he hung out at. They had been good friends for years, so it wasn't hard. The fact that he decided to show up at Brian's job in broad daylight was a foolish move that only an amateur would make.

Brian chuckled at how lame Ronnie was. Trent always said it, but he was seeing it for himself right now.

"Man, you've been knowing me long enough to know that I don't do too much talking. Get the fuck on with that clown shit. McDonald's is up the street," Brian said, waving him off.

In true hoe form, Ronnie looked at Katrice before he made his next move. She gave a head nod and he reached for the gun that was tucked inside his waistband. Before he could even get it all the way out, Jaden hit him with a right hook that had him dazed and confused. The gun fell from his hands and Brian went into savage mode. He hit Ronnie with a quick two-piece that knocked him to the floor. Shanti grabbed Shaky's hair and slung her to the floor soon after. Katrice tried to pick the gun up, but Candace kicked it under Jaden's work station. She then pushed Katrice so hard that she fell and slid by the front door. The shop was pure chaos and Co-Co didn't know what to do first. Since Shanti was closer, he pulled her off Shaky and pushed her in the back towards the break room. Ronnie was still on the floor, but he wasn't fighting back. It was a waste for Brian to keep hitting him, so he let him make it.

"Get the fuck up out of here before you be needing a body bag nigga," Brian fumed angrily. His focus was on Ronnie and he never noticed Shaky coming at him with the knife.

"Ahh! Fuck! This bitch is stabbing me!" Brian yelled as his white Polo turned red with blood.

Shanti was screaming as Brian went down, clutching his chest. Shaky moved her blade with the speed of light as she tried to make Brian an afterthought. Jaden was too busy watching Ronnie to make sure he wasn't on no snake shit. It took him a minute to see that Brian was hurt.

"Bitch, get off my cousin!" Co-Co yelled as he swung his two hot flat irons like they were weapons.

They obviously did the trick because Shaky yelped in pain and dropped her knife. Candace sprang into action and grabbed her by her hair, pulling her away from Brian. Jaden was out for blood as he watched his brother on the floor bleeding profusely. His anger was reserved for Bryce too, since he forbad Jaden from bringing his gun to the shop. With all the drama that they had going on throughout the years, Bryce should have wanted them to stay strapped.

Jaden wanted somebody dead and he didn't care which one of the three it was or all of them if possible. He searched for the gun that Ronnie had dropped, ready to shed some more blood. By then, Ronnie and his two accomplices were out the door and rushing to the car that had been left running in the middle of the street. They'd obviously planned to handle business and make a quick getaway.

"Brian, baby, please hold on. Don't leave us. Me and Bri need you," Shanti cried as she cradled Brian in her arms.

"The ambulance is on the way," Candace assured her.

"You can't leave me!" Shanti screamed, making Jaden even more nervous than he was before.

He'd finally got his hands on the gun that he was looking for and ran out of the shop after his prey. Nobody was outside, but Jaden didn't care anyway. He started shooting at the car that Ronnie was driving, causing him to temporarily lose control. Jaden only fired three shots before the gun was empty and he was heated. Ronnie jumped the neutral ground and started driving on the opposite side of the street to keep from being shot. Car horns blared as motorists tried to get out of his way. He tried to turn a corner that was meant for incoming traffic and an eighteen-wheeler slammed into him.

"Oh shit!" Co-Co yelled when he walked outside and saw the car that Ronnie was driving flip several times before being hit by two other oncoming cars. Somebody flew out of the front window and landed in the middle of the street, right as the car came to a stop on its side.

Jaden had seen may things in his life, but nothing like he'd just witnessed. He was paralyzed with shock as he watched it all unfold. He heard sirens in the distance, but he knew that they were already too late. Shaky had been thrown from the car and her lifeless body laid motionless in the middle of the street. A few good Samaritans stopped their cars to offer aid, but the car was too mangled for them to even open the doors.

"Brian!" Shanti yelled, causing Co-Co and Jaden to rush back into the shop.

Brian was unconscious, and Shanti was losing it. Candace tried to get her away from him, but she was refusing to move.

"Fuck!" Jaden yelled as he picked his brother up, carrying him outside bridal style.

The ambulance was taking too long, and he couldn't wait any longer. He heard the wailing of the sirens, but they hadn't shown up yet.

"Over here!" Co-Co was screaming and waving when he saw the ambulance speeding up the street.

Police cars, fire trucks, and other first responders were on the scene, but an ambulance rushed over to where they were. Candace was the only one who was calm enough to explain what had happened because everybody else were panicking. Co-Co ran to lock up the shop as he and Candace prepared to follow the ambulance. He watched while they loaded Brian into the back, as Jaden and Shanti got in with him.

"Lord have mercy," Co-Co said as he held his chest. He no longer had to wonder if Shaky was dead or alive. His question was answered when he watched one of the police officers put up the black screens to shield her body from onlookers.

Chapter 42

Brian heard the voices around him, but he was too tired to open his eyes. His mind replayed the events of the night before and he couldn't believe that bitch Shaky had stabbed him. He couldn't wait to get out of there to deal with her and Ronnie's punk ass. The nerve of that nigga to show up to his job and pull a gun on him. *Who does shit like that,* Brian thought to himself. He didn't know who all was in the room, but he knew that Jaden and Shanti were amongst the visitors.

"It's fucked up, but they didn't want to live. Who does that kind of dumb shit? Whatever happened to moving in silence?" Jaden said.

Brian was fighting through his fatigue, trying to open his eyes. He needed to know exactly who Jaden was talking about.

"I feel bad, but it's better them than my man," Shanti replied.

"You good now sis? You had me scared for a minute," Jaden said.

"I'm good now. I'll take him with a few cuts rather than not have him at all," Shanti replied.

"I can't believe all three of them died though. That shit sounds so unbelievable," Co-Co spoke up.

"Who's dead?" Brian finally managed to ask.

"How do you feel baby?" Shanti asked as she leaned down to kiss him.

"Tired as hell. My mouth is dry is fuck," Brian mumbled.

"Let me pour you some water," Shanti said as she grabbed the pitcher and filled a cup with ice water.

"Where's my baby?" Brian asked once he drank some water.

"She's with my auntie," Shanti said as she rubbed his head.

"You feel any pain bruh?" Jaden asked.

"I don't feel shit. What are they saying is up with me?" Brian asked.

"You're full of pain meds, but you'll be fine. You got stabbed five times and lost some blood, but not enough to need a transfusion. That's what caused you to pass out yesterday," Shanti replied.

"Yesterday? I spent the night up in here?" Brian questioned.

"Yes. Everybody has been up here, but you've been sleeping," Shanti replied.

"That crazy bitch stabbed me five times. I can't wait to get well. I got something for her and Ronnie's punk ass," Brian fumed.

"Too late my nigga," Jaden replied.

"What you mean?" Brian asked.

Brian listened as Jaden and Co-Co ran the entire story down to him. He was shocked, but he didn't feel any remorse. After all, they came there to do him dirty and ended up losing their lives instead. If Cookie was still working at the shop, he was sure that it would have been four dead bodies instead of three.

"How you go to kill somebody and end up getting killed? That shit don't even sound right," Co-Co said, shaking his head.

"It happens all the time when amateurs try to do the job of a professional. I don't give a damn what Bryce says, I'm not getting caught slippin' without my gun ever again," Jaden replied, right as Pam and Bryce Sr. walked into the room.

"Hey, my baby. How do you feel?" Pam asked as she kissed Brian's cheek.

"I'm good. Why y'all not at work?" Brian asked as Shanti helped him sit up in the bed.

"Why would we be at work when our son is laid up in the hospital gutted like a fish?" his father asked.

"I had to finalize some things for Royce's baby shower and I had to make sure that you were okay," Pam said.

"That nigga Caleb bout to be a daddy," Jaden chuckled.

"The way y'all are having babies, we gon' need a damn school bus to take a family vacation," his father replied.

"That's exactly why I'm retiring. I want to enjoy my grandbabies while I can," Pam said.

"You know you ain't retiring. Both of y'all have been saying the same thing for years," Jaden said, waving her off.

"Well, it's really happening this time. We're officially retiring, and the paperwork has been done," their father spoke up.

"It's about damn time," Brian said, happy to hear the good news.

"It ain't like I'll be able to rest. Caleb has already asked me to keep his baby when he and Royce go back to work. I don't mind though. That's what grandmas are for." Pam smiled.

Throughout the day, Brian had visitors coming and going. Shanti's aunt came through with Bri and Brian was happy to see his baby. He was missing her, and he didn't want her to leave. Pam took her home, since Shanti's auntie had somewhere to go. Brian had about another day or two before he was released, and he couldn't wait to go home to her. He had stitches and they wanted to monitor him for infection. He felt fine minus a little occasional pain.

Once everyone was gone, Shanti helped Brian take a shower before she took hers. She had Keller pack them both a bag because she never left Brian's side. He wanted to be under her, so she climbed into bed with him and relaxed. She and Brian were face to face as she rubbed his back and he caressed her thigh.

"Are you in any pain?" Shanti asked him.

"No, I'm good. I wish my baby was here though," Brian replied.

"I know, but she's good. Your mama said that she's sleeping," Shanti replied.

"I love you, baby," Brian said as he kissed Shanti's lips.

He appreciated her being there more than anything. She could have gone home with their daughter, but she chose to stay with him instead. That meant more to him than she would ever know.

"I love you too." Shanti smiled.

"Marry me," Brian said while giving her direct eye contact.

Everything that Jaden had said to him a few days before came rushing back to his memory. Life was short, and Brian didn't want to live the rest of his without Ashanti by his side. Almost losing his life put a lot of things into perspective for him. He heard Shanti begging him not to leave her and he never would if he could help it.

"Are you high off pain meds Brian? Where did that even come from?" Shanti laughed.

"I'm serious Ashanti. We're already living like we're married. Let's make this shit official. Tomorrow ain't promised to none of us," Brian said as he looked at her.

"You're really serious, aren't you?" Shanti asked.

"Dead ass. Will you marry me, baby?" Brian asked.

"Hell yeah!" Shanti yelled. "Where's my ring?"

"I got you as soon as I get out of here. You can get whatever you want," he promised, making Shanti smile.

"When do you wanna do it?" Shanti asked.

"As soon as possible, unless you want to do something big."

"I don't care about that. It's not like I have anybody to invite anyway," Shanti said, waving him off.

"Cool, but this medicine is about to knock me out. We'll talk about it some more tomorrow," Brian said as he kissed her and closed his eyes.

✳✳✳

"Heeeeey Mrs. Andrews." Royce smiled when she hugged Shanti.

She and Caleb were walking around thanking the guests who attended their baby shower when she stopped to joke with Shanti and Brian. They were married the month before and she always referenced Shanti by her new last name. Brian was serious about making Shanti his wife and he wasted no time doing so. Besides a few scars, Brian was good after being stabbed five times. It was an open and closed case once the police investigated everything. The knife that Shaky had stabbed him with was still in the same spot where she'd dropped it. Ronnie was buried the week after he was killed, but Shaky and Katrice didn't have any family or life insurance. Cookie raised a little money to have them cremated and that was the best that she could do.

"Hey boo. Everything was so nice," Shanti complimented.

"Thanks girl." Royce smiled.

She was so thankful to everyone who attended. She had one more month before she gave birth and her son had everything that he needed and more. Even better was the fact that Mrs. Pam and her husband were officially retired now. Caleb was happy because he no longer had to worry about his son being in capable hands when they went back to work.

"Girl, my auntie is about to knock your mama out," Co-Co said when he walked over to Royce.

"It's about damn time," Caleb replied.

"What happened now?" Royce asked as she and Caleb walked away.

Sondra looked like she was upset about something, but Pam appeared to be fine. Royce walked over to where Uri and Lydia sat to see what they knew.

"Chile, I just love Caleb's mama." Lydia smiled as she sipped on her Coke.

Uri was so proud of her mother for trying to change and do better. Lydia hadn't stopped drinking altogether, but she didn't do it nearly as much as she used to. She found a part-time job as a waitress to keep busy and she loved the tips that she made. Sondra still paid all her bills and that would probably never change.

"What happened?" Royce questioned.

"Auntie Sondra is trying to run shit, just like always. She was trying to tell Caleb's mama that she was taking some of the stuff to her house since she would be watching the baby. Mrs. Pam politely sat her ass right on down and didn't even raise her voice while doing it," Uri giggled.

"That's good for her. She got the right one this time. Mrs. Pam don't play that shit," Royce laughed.

"I told my mama not to do it," Caleb said, shaking his head.

She knew that Mrs. Pam meant well, but Royce did not want her to involve her mother in the planning of her shower. Pam saw firsthand just why Caleb wanted her to knock the other woman on her ass. Sondra was bossy, and she expected everyone to do what she said. Her and Pam bumped heads a few times, but it was nothing that couldn't

[357]

be resolved. When it was all said and done, Pam didn't even include her in anything anymore. She got with Brooklyn and Uri and they made it happen on their own.

"Let me go say goodbye to my daddy," Royce said as she and Caleb walked over to the table where her parents sat. The shower was over, and she knew that they were probably about to go.

"Everything was beautiful baby girl," Patrick said as he hugged Royce and shook Caleb's hand.

"Thanks daddy, but I can't take any of the credit. Uri and Caleb's mother and sister put it all together," Royce replied, as her mother rolled her eyes discreetly.

"Did you enjoy yourself mother?" Royce asked, just to be polite.

"Yes, it was very nice," Sondra said with a forced smile.

"Do y'all have everything that he needs? I'll be happy to help if y'all need anything else," Patrick offered.

"No sir, we have more than enough, but thanks for the offer. My mama will take whatever was duplicated to her house. She's going to be watching the baby when Royce and I go back to work," Caleb smirked, as Sondra's head jerked around in Royce's direction.

"Okay, good," Patrick nodded in approval.

He could tell that his wife wanted to say something, but she remained tightlipped. It killed Sondra not to oversee everything, but she had to get with the program. Royce was no longer that docile, soft spoken young woman that she was before. She spoke her mind and she lived her life the way she saw fit. Sondra couldn't control her the way she used to and that drove her crazy. Royce loved who she wanted to love, and she didn't care what anyone said about it. Patrick was happy with whatever made Royce happy, but Sondra had a hard time adjusting. She was trying hard to rebuild her relationship with Royce, so she never said anything. She often vented to Patrick behind closed doors and he always told her to let it go. Sondra really believed that Caleb changed Royce into who she had become, but Patrick begged to differ. Life had a way of doing that all on its own. After being through so much with Jaxon, Royce deserved whatever happiness came her way.

Chapter 43

"Don't make me come get you, Royce. You ain't have no damn business leaving out of here when I was asleep," Caleb fussed.

"I'm coming right back baby. I wanted some cake and Uri offered to bring me to Whole Foods. I didn't want to wake you," Royce replied.

"I don't give a damn Royce. Your ass is nine months pregnant and overdue. You should know better," Caleb replied.

"Nigga, you better be my daddy," Royce snapped.

"Keep talking that hot shit and watch I come to that store and embarrass your ass," Caleb threatened.

"Okay, I'm coming right now," Royce swore before hanging up.

"Why you lied to that man?" Uri laughed as they pulled up to the store.

"He must be crazy if he thinks I'm coming home before getting my cake," Royce replied while getting out of the car.

Uri grabbed a basket and followed behind her. Royce was always claiming to go to the store for one thing, but she always came out with much more. Uri was tired of doing the balancing act while holding all her stuff, so she started using her head whenever she went with her.

"Don't take too long Royce. I don't need Caleb having us paged over the loud speaker like he did at Walmart the other day. That shit was just embarrassing," Uri reminded her.

"I just want my cake and some ice cream. We can go after that. Caleb just be doing too damn much," Royce said, shaking her head.

"I thought Jaden was the only crazy one, but Caleb and Brian ain't wrapped too tight either," Uri laughed.

"I could have told you that. Kia said that Bryce is the only calm one of the bunch," Royce replied as they walked up to the bakery.

She went there to get a berry cake, but her mouth watered when she saw the other desserts in the case. She didn't want to waste her money if she didn't like them, so she stuck to what she knew. Uri ordered her kids some cupcakes and they waited patiently while the clerk boxed up their sweets.

"What are you having?" a man asked as he walked up behind Royce and Uri.

"A baby that ain't yours," Uri replied when they turned around and saw Jax standing there.

He was wearing his gym uniform shirt and some sweats, but he wasn't embarrassed by being seen that way. A few months ago, he would have been, but he was over caring about the public's opinion. His life was much easier that way.

"A boy," Royce replied flatly.

She couldn't say that she was surprised to see Jax there because he was always in the Whole Foods stores. He was a health nut and he loved to eat those nasty protein snacks. He had buffed up a little since the last time Royce had seen him, but that was the only thing different about him. He was still the same old Jax and his lingering gaze confirmed that. His sneaky eyes roamed her body lustfully, like she wasn't carrying a nine-month pregnant belly in front of her.

"Congrats," Jax said as the clerk handed Royce and Uri their items.

"Thanks," Royce said as she attempted to walk away.

"Royce, wait, can I talk to you for a minute?" Jax asked as he stepped in front of her.

"About what?" Royce asked impatiently, as Uri stood there and waited.

She didn't need Caleb to make good on his promise and show up to the store. She would never be able to explain to him why she was standing there talking to her ex-husband.

"Alone," Jax replied while looking directly at Uri.

"Nigga please. She gon' tell me everything you say as soon as we get in the car anyway." Uri shrugged as she walked away.

She didn't go too far because she still didn't trust Jax. She gave him enough room to say what he had to say without being heard. He looked like he still wasn't satisfied with the distance, but he could kiss her ass.

"What's up Jaxon?" Royce asked.

"Look, I know that things didn't end too well with us, but I want you to know that it was nothing that you did wrong," Jax said.

"Oh, I already knew that honey. I was and still am a damn good woman. I never had any doubts about that," Royce replied.

"I agree, but I feel like I owed you an apology. You deserved so much more than what I gave you."

"Yes, I did and I'm happy that I found it," Royce said while rubbing her stomach.

"I regret a lot of things that I did in life and ruining our marriage is one of them. You deserve to be happy and it's good to see that you are," Jax replied.

"Thank you, Jaxon. I appreciate that," Royce said right as her phone started to ring.

Jax couldn't help but look at the screen and feel a twinge of jealousy. The maternity picture of Royce and Caleb was beautiful, and he could tell that they were in love. Although he would probably always love her, Jax meant what he said. No one else deserved happiness more than Royce and Sienna and he was happy for them both.

"Well, I won't hold you. I just wanted to get a few things off my chest. Good luck with the baby and congrats again," Jax said before he walked away.

He was meeting Elena for lunch, but she hadn't arrived yet. She had some free time on her hands since Silas was out golfing with some of his friends. Since being forced to resign from his job, the Zulu Club had also parted ways with him and decided on someone else to represent their organization as king. Elena was still banned from spending time with her son, but she was sneaking out to meet him anyway. Whole Foods sold some of the best cooked food that Jax had tasted, so they decided to dine there. He was pleasantly surprised when he spotted a very pregnant Royce at the desert counter. She looked beautiful standing there and Jax couldn't deny how much he still loved her.

Sadly, he would have to love her from afar. His time with Royce was yet another chapter in his book of life that was permanently closed.

***

"Let me get up out of here before your man comes in here fussing," Uri said when she walked into Royce's house behind her.

She sat Royce's bags on the kitchen counter and hurriedly left out the front door. She already knew how Caleb was. He would not only be fussing at Royce, but he would fuss at her too for picking her up. Uri only laughed at him because he was too overprotective. Royce put her ice cream in the freezer and opened the box that her cake was in.

"Your ass is lucky that you came back when you did. I was just about to walk out that door and come get you," Caleb fussed when he walked into the kitchen.

Royce laughed because she knew that he was serious. Caleb was in his boxers when she left, but he was dressed from head to toe now. He had his keys in his hand like he was about to walk out the door at any minute.

"Stop being so extra all the time Caleb. I wasn't even gone that long," Royce replied as she grabbed a fork.

"I don't care how long you were gone. You knew better than to leave at all," Caleb argued.

"Okay baby. I'm sorry about leaving and I promise that it won't happen again," Royce said with a roll of her eyes.

"Stop telling me shit just to shut me up," Caleb accused.

"Here, eat some cake and hush up," Royce said as she shoved a forkful of cake in his mouth.

"That shit taste good too," Caleb said, forgetting that he was even mad with her.

"I know." Royce smiled as she ate some and continued to feed him.

Caleb ate just as much as she did during her pregnancy, but he didn't gain any weight. Almost half the cake was gone already, and she hadn't even been home that long. Caleb grabbed some fruit punch from the fridge and they drunk it straight from the carton.

"Baby, guess who I ran into at the store?" Royce asked him as she shoveled some more cake into his mouth.

"Who?" Caleb mumbled with a mouthful of sweets.

"Jaxon," Royce answered. "He came up to me and asked if we could talk."

"Don't get that nigga fucked up," Caleb said seriously.

"No baby, it was nothing like that," Royce said, waving him off.

"What did he want then?" Caleb asked.

"He was on some ole apologetic bullshit. Talking about how it was him and not me that ruined our marriage. That part was never up for debate though."

"Fuck that nigga. No need to apologize now. He did us both a favor," Caleb replied.

"The entire Davenport family can kiss my ass," Royce said as she held her stomach.

"What's wrong?" Caleb asked concerned.

"Nothing, but I think I overdid it with the cake," she replied with a frown.

Caleb was about to reply until a small gush of fluid between Royce's legs startled them both. It felt like a water balloon popped to Royce, and her leggings were saturated.

"The fuck! I think your water just broke!" Caleb yelled nervously.

"No shit Caleb," Royce replied sarcastically.

"See, this is exactly why I told your ass not to go nowhere without me. What if this shit would have happened while you were out there running the streets with Uri?" Caleb argued.

"She would have known what to do. She has two kids of her own," Royce reminded him while walking down the hall to their bedroom.

"Where you going Royce? We need to get to the hospital!" Caleb yelled in a panic.

"I need to change clothes first Caleb. This is gross," Royce replied as she pointed to her soiled pants.

Caleb grabbed her a sundress from the closet and helped her out of her dirty clothes. He grabbed a soapy towel from the bathroom and helped her freshen up before she slipped it on. He grabbed the bags from the closet and took them to the car while Royce made some calls.

"Come on baby. What are you doing?" Caleb asked her when he saw Royce standing there talking on the phone.

"I was calling Uri and Brooklyn, so they can call everybody else," Royce answered.

"Okay good, now let's go," Caleb said while grabbing her hand.

"Baby, wait!" Royce yelled, stopping him from walking.

"What's wrong? Are you in pain? Can you walk?" Caleb asked, firing off a series of questions.

"I'm fine, but I want my cake," Royce replied.

"I know you ain't serious." Caleb frowned.

"I don't know when or if I'll be able to eat again Caleb. I want my cake," Royce repeated.

"Come on with your greedy ass," Caleb fussed while grabbing the cake box.

Royce's phone was blowing up and she tried to answer everyone's calls as Caleb sped to the hospital. She was excited and nervous, but she couldn't wait to meet her son. Caleb held her hand the entire time and that relaxed her a little. As nervous as she was, Royce couldn't see herself having her first child with anyone.

Chapter 44

"This is enough with the babies. Y'all ain't even giving me and my wife a chance to breath," Bryce Sr. said as he held the newest addition of his family.

After spending much of the day and most of the morning in labor, Royce finally gave birth to eight-pound, six-ounce Caleb Andrews Jr. She was sure that being shot felt better than labor and she would gladly take a bullet over that any day. Caleb was in tears when his first son entered the world and he loved Royce even more for making it happen.

"You act like I got a whole bunch of babies running around here. This is my first," Caleb laughed.

"That's why you get a pass. That and the fact that this lil nigga looks just like me," his father smiled proudly.

"You?" Caleb repeated. "That's all me right there."

"Dumb ass nigga, you look like me. Hell, all four of y'all do. Brook is the only one who looks like her mama," his father replied.

"I can't dispute that." Caleb shrugged, right as someone knocked on the door before opening it.

"Hey daddy," Royce said as she smiled brightly.

"Hey baby girl. Good evening everybody," Patrick waved and spoke.

Everybody smiled and spoke back, but the atmosphere changed the minute Sondra walked through the door behind him.

"Hello," Sondra said flatly as she looked around the room.

Everyone else had left, leaving Caleb's parents up there alone. Uri had gone to get them something to eat and she was coming right back. Sondra had been there earlier, but she left when Royce and Caleb wouldn't allow her to witness the baby's birth. It was already decided that Caleb was the only one who was going to be in the room during delivery. No one else had a problem with it, but Sondra was the exception. She called herself going off on Caleb, and Pam stepped in and let her have it. The tension was thick, and Patrick didn't want to ruin one of the happiest days of his daughter's life. Since he and Sondra rode together in the same car, he thought it was best if he took her home and returned once the baby was born. He was pissed, and he lit into her ass the entire ride home. He also made her call and apologize to everyone. He swore that he wasn't bringing her back up there if she didn't.

"Look at my handsome grandboy," Patrick said while smiling down at the baby.

"Have a seat so you can hold him," Bryce said as he stood up with the baby in his arms.

Patrick sanitized his hands and sat down in the huge rocking chair. He was all smiles when he was handed his first grandson and Royce was smiling too.

"You got two busy body cousins who are gonna be crazy about you," he said, referring to Uri's daughters.

"I heard they had you playing hairdresser yesterday. I can't wait to see the pictures that Uri was telling me about," Royce laughed.

"You know I'll do anything for my babies, but I hope that was a first and last time for that," Patrick replied.

"I hate to tell you, but that's only the beginning. My grandkids be having me into all kinds of crazy shit," Bryce laughed.

Sondra cringed when he referred to Uri's kids as her husband's grandkids. That's what they were to him, but it killed her to have to say it. Patrick loved them and always treated them as such and nothing had changed.

"I don't mind. I'll make a fool of myself for them any day." Patrick smiled.

"Don't you be in here trying to spoil my nephew uncle Pat. That's my job," Uri said when she walked back into the room with Royce and Caleb's food.

"You better get into the habit of sharing," Pat said as he received the kiss to the cheek that she gave him.

Uri kissed her auntie as well before she handed over the food. Sondra hated to hear Uri call her grandson her nephew, but that's who he was. She had no choice but to get over her feelings. Royce and Uri were still first cousins, but they liked the term sister better.

After having a talk with her aunt and uncle all those months ago, Uri decided to let go of her ill feelings. She didn't agree with the decision they made regarding her paternity, but holding a grudge wasn't going to change anything. She was thankful for the life that Patrick afforded her with because she didn't lack anything while growing up.

"We're about to go Caleb. We'll be back later tonight or in the morning. Call us if y'all need anything," Pam said as she kissed her son and Royce.

She was sure that Royce's parents wanted to spend some time with her and the baby and she didn't want to interfere. She could see that she was going to end up making Caleb's dream a reality and knock Sondra on her ass. She had Pam fucked up with trying to run everything and she had no problem letting her know it. She tried her best to be cordial, but her kindness wasn't reciprocated. When Sondra called herself going off on her son, Pam reached her breaking point sooner than she thought. Caleb was a grown ass man, but he was still her baby. Pam didn't give him a chance to defend himself before stepped in and said what was on her mind. She didn't give a damn about how Sondra felt after that.

"You wanna hold him honey?" Patrick asked while looking at his wife.

She seemed kind of distant around Caleb's parents, but she helped Royce get situated to eat her food as soon as they left. Pam had Sondra feeling like an unwanted visitor and she hated it.

"Of course, I do." Sondra smiled before sanitizing her hands.

She sat in the chair and held her first grandson for the very first time. It was love at first sight and she vowed to do anything in her power to always be a part of his life. If that meant getting along with Caleb and his family, then she would do it. If it meant holding her tongue even when she wanted to lash out, she would remain silent. If she had to change who she was to be in his presence, they could consider it done. Her handsome grandson was worth it all and more.

"He's so perfect." Sondra smiled as a tear escaped her eye.

Royce smiled at her mother bonding with her son. Sondra wore a genuine smile on her face and Royce hadn't seen that in a while.

"She looks kind of normal right now, huh?" Caleb whispered to her as he watched Sondra holding his son.

"Shut up Caleb," Royce laughed out loud.

"Before I go, let me show you these pictures," Uri said as she walked over to Royce's bed and pulled up her photo album.

"Oh God," Patrick groaned in embarrassment.

"Damn," Caleb laughed, as Uri scrolled through the pictures that showed Patrick wearing various wigs.

Uri let her daughter have all her old wigs and they loved to play beauty salon with them. Patrick never thought they would want him to play with them, but he became their favorite customer. They used his phone to take pictures and Uri sent them all to herself. Royce felt like her stiches were about to pop from laughing so hard. She loved the bond that her father had with them and she couldn't wait for her baby to get big enough to experience the same.

"This is Ashton, Uri," Royce said while handing her the phone.

Their entertainment was temporarily interrupted when Uri's husband called.

"Hey baby," Uri said when she answered for him.

"Hurry up and turn on channel four news baby!" Ashton yelled excitedly.

"Turn the tv to channel four news Royce. Hurry up," Uri said, just as adrenalized as he was.

She didn't know what was going on, but it had to be good for Ashton to be so worked up. Not much excited him, but whatever was on the news had piqued his interest.

"Oh, my Lord. What in the world did he do?" Sondra asked when she saw Silas being led from his home in handcuffs into an awaiting squad car.

"What happened Ashton?" Uri questioned, once the news had switched to something else.

They'd missed the entire story, but Ashton quickly filled them in.

"One of the neighbors called the police because they heard somebody screaming in the house. When the police came, they had to break the door down because they looked through the window and saw dude beating his wife up. By the time they got to her, she was unconscious, and they took her husband to jail," Ashton said, repeating what the news had reported.

"Oh, my God! Elena? He beat on her?" Sondra asked in shock.

"All the time, but she was good at hiding it. I tried to tell you that she was living a lie. I knew that it was only a matter of time before their secret was exposed. Jax told me about that a long time ago," Royce replied.

"But why? What did she do that was so bad?" Sondra wondered out loud.

"Silas is an asshole. I told you that the first day I met him. I've never met a man who hated women so much. I don't know what the hell you saw in those people." Patrick frowned.

"Now I see why she was always so nervous whenever she had to tell him anything. Poor thing was afraid," Sondra noted.

"That whole family is screwed up. I'm so happy that you're out of that mess," Uri said while referring to Royce.

"That makes two of us," Patrick co-signed.

"See what I saved you from baby. A pedophile sex offender and a woman beater. You wanted to fight me when we first met, but look at how things turned out," Caleb joked.

"I did not want to fight you. It wasn't under the best conditions, but I'm so thankful that we met," Royce said while smiling at him.

Sondra looked down at her sleeping grandson and smiled. She would never admit it out loud, but she was happy that they'd met too. No matter how she felt about him and his family, Caleb had helped to create one of the greatest gifts that she'd ever received.

Chapter 45

"**I** know I'm biased, but you are just the cutest baby that I've ever seen in my life," Sondra said as she looked down at her smiling grandson.

Six months had passed since Royce had him and Sondra fell in love every time she laid eyes on him. He was perfect, and he made everything that was wrong appear right again. He made Sondra see the world through brand new eyes and she just loved him to pieces.

"Auntie, can we go look in the toy department?" one of Uri's daughters asked with hopeful eyes.

Uri and Royce had gone to the hair salon and Sondra was honored when they asked her to babysit. Caleb's mother had the baby during the week, but Royce would let him stay the night with Sondra and Patrick sometimes on the weekend. Sondra never overstepped her boundaries, so she waited until she was asked. She didn't want to risk not seeing her grandson at all, so she played by Royce and Caleb's rules.

"Yes, but hold your sister's hand and don't go anywhere else. I have to get one more thing and I'll be right over there to get you. If you're good, I'll let you both pick out a toy," Sondra replied.

"Yay!" they yelled excitedly before holding hands and walking away.

Sondra needed a few things for her house, so they went to Target not long after Uri and Royce dropped the kids off. She was so busy looking at stuff in the baby section that she never did get what she went there for. It had been that way ever since her grandson entered the world. Sondra could never go anywhere without picking something up for him.

"These are just too cute to pass up. You're gonna take all your grandma's money," Sondra said as she put the pajamas that she'd been looking at in the basket.

She had a bunch of stuff in the basket for the kids and she swore that she wasn't buying anything else. She finally made her way to the home décor section to look at the throw pillows and rug that she'd originally gone there to get. As soon as she turned from one aisle to the next, Sondra was shocked to see a familiar face in her presence.

"Elena, how are you?" Sondra asked with a smile.

"Sondra! It's good to see you. I'm fine. How are you?" Elena asked, genuinely happy to see her.

It had been a while since the two women saw each other and the tension appeared to have dissipated over time. Elena seemed to have aged a bit over time or maybe it was stress. She didn't look like the same elegant beauty who Sondra had looked up to and once admired. She was dressed down in jeans and a sweater, and Sondra had never seen her without dress clothes on before. Maybe it was because she was no longer working and didn't feel the need to dress up anymore.

"I'm great." Sondra smiled as they embraced.

"And who is this handsome little fellow?" Elena smiled as she looked down at the baby.

"This is my grandson, Caleb, but we call him CJ," Sondra beamed proudly.

"Aww, he's adorable. I know you and Patrick are spoiling him rotten," Elena replied.

"Thank you and, yes, we are. It's almost impossible not to," Sondra noted.

"I know the feeling," Elena replied with a smile.

"How have you been Elena? I know that things have been hard, with all that's been going on with your family," Sondra said out of concern.

"We're fine honey. You know how the media is. They blow every little misunderstanding out of proportion," Elena said while flashing her signature smile.

"How is Jaxon? I saw that he had gotten into some trouble a little while ago too."

"Jaxon is fine. He's been going to counseling and it seems to be helping a lot," Elena replied.

"What about Silas? Is he going to counseling too?" Sondra asked as her eyes lingered on the cast that covered Elena's arm.

"Why would he? The media got everything all wrong. My husband is far from being an abuser," Elena said as she looked away in embarrassment.

She knew that she sounded like a fool and she felt like one too. Every news outlet and newspaper in New Orleans had reported what happened, so it was pointless to deny it. The day after Elena met Jax for lunch at Whole Foods was one of the worst days of her life. She had no idea that one of Silas' golf buddies was there and saw them dining together. Silas was furious when he found out and he made Elena pay dearly. She had no idea that one of the neighbors was out walking his dog and heard her screams of pain.

Elena was so embarrassed when her husband was arrested, but she denied everything when they asked her. She would never press charges on her husband, but she didn't have to. The state picked up the charges, since the nature of the crime was so severe. Elena was unconscious when they found her, and she had a long list of injuries. Things only seemed to get worse from there. Their daughter, who lost her house in the divorce settlement, ended up moving back in with them. She was having trouble finding a job that paid what she was used to, and she was always depressed. One of their other sons' wives finally got a backbone and left him when she got tired of the beatings, while the other son had fathered a child out of wedlock.

Jax, who was once labeled the black sheep of the family, seemed to be the only one who didn't have any problems. He was in counseling for his sexual addiction and he was still working at the gym. He had his kids over all the time and was building a better relationship with them. He hated that he had a degree that he could never use again, but he was content with the life that he now lived. Silas had loosened up a bit and allowed him to come around again, only because he saw that the rest of his kids were no better. He was still the same old tyrant that he'd always been, which explained the cast that Elena sported on her arm. Their finances were getting low and Silas didn't know how to handle it. Elena tried to always wear a smile, but she didn't know how much more she could take.

[373]

"You don't have to put on a front for me, Elena. We've both done that enough throughout the years. We didn't part ways amicably, but I still consider you a friend," Sondra said, switching Elena's thoughts from the past and back to the present.

"Thanks for your concern Sondra, but I'm fine, really. I need to get going. I have a few more stops to make. And congrats on becoming a new grandmother. That's one of the greatest feelings in the world," Elena said as she smiled uncomfortably.

"Thanks Elena. And just know that my number is the same if you ever need to talk," Sondra said, right before she watched her walk away.

For the first time ever, she felt sympathy for Elena. Sondra really thought that the other woman had it all together but, just like her, it was all a ruse. She knew what it was like pretending to be happy, but not knowing what happiness really was. Sondra had done that for years and it was stressful. It took Royce calling her out on it and staying away to make Sondra really see what she was doing wrong. She had to take a good look at herself and she hated what she saw. Hopefully, Elena wouldn't feel the need to hide behind an award-winning smile and be honest with herself one day too. It was one of the best feelings in the world and Sondra was a witness to that fact.

***

"What did your grandma say about me today bruh?" Caleb asked as he gave his son a bath.

CJ was all smiles as Caleb asked him questions that he would never be able to answer. Royce was still out with Uri, so Caleb picked his son up from Sondra and Patrick's house before he went home.

"You better not let her talk about your daddy. It's me and you against the world," Caleb said as he lifted him up from the water and carried him to the bedroom.

As soon as he laid him down, the phone rang, displaying Brooklyn's number.

"What happened? Where is Royce?" Brook asked excitedly as soon as he answered the phone for her.

"Calm your hyperactive ass down. She's not here yet," Caleb laughed.

"She told me that she was on her way home almost an hour ago. What's taking her so long?" Brook asked.

"She stopped to get something to eat and she had to bring Uri home. I'm happy that she took a while because I wasn't ready yet," Caleb said.

"Did you like what Co-Co did? That was so cute and different," Brooklyn replied.

"That nigga is always going overboard with shit. It's straight, but I got some words for his ass when I see him. My baby gon' have glitter all over him," Brian fussed.

"Stop complaining and be happy that we helped your ass. Tell Royce to call me. I don't care what time it is," Brooklyn demanded.

"She ain't calling nobody tonight. She bout to bust it wide open as soon as CJ goes to sleep," Caleb replied.

"Eww, that's entirely too much info," Brooklyn said before she hung up on him.

He had just finished dressing his son in a onesie and socks when Royce walked through the door.

"Perfect timing," Caleb said as he picked his son up and met her in the kitchen.

He was holding CJ backwards with the baby's back pressed against his front. When he saw Royce, he started kicking his legs excitedly.

"Hey baby. I missed you," Royce said as soon as she saw her son.

She gave Caleb a kiss before doing the same with her baby. She tried to take him out of Caleb's arms, but he wouldn't give him up.

"Boy, give me my baby. I haven't seen him since this morning. I know you see how happy he is to see me," Royce fussed.

"I got him, baby. Fix my food first," Caleb replied.

"How about you fix your own food and give me my baby?" Royce suggested.

"What kind of shit is that? You can't be my wife with that kind of attitude," Caleb argued.

"Okay Caleb. Don't even start the when we get married talk. I'm not in the mood to argue about something that will probably never happen," Royce said as she rolled her eyes.

She grabbed a plate and fixed Caleb some of the Chinese food that she had just picked up. Royce had a boot in her mouth, making him laugh at her sudden attitude.

[375]

"Thank you, baby," Caleb smiled when she sat the plate in front of him.

"You're welcome," Royce replied dryly.

"Stop looking so mean," Caleb smirked.

"I'm not," Royce denied.

"You know I love you, right?" Caleb asked, making her smile.

"I love you too baby," Royce blushed.

"Hold him until I eat," Caleb said while handing their son over to Royce.

She smiled as she picked him up and planted a kiss on his cheek. Caleb laughed as he watched Royce's face twist up in confusion.

"What the hell? Where is this glitter coming from?" she asked as she looked at her hand.

She looked at Caleb's shirt and it was covered in glitter as well. Royce turned her baby around to look at the back of his onesie and gasped.

"Yes! Oh, my God, Caleb! Yes! Yes!" Royce screamed as she ran over and jumped in his lap with their son still in her arms.

She was ready to fuss at Caleb about her baby being covered in glitter until she read the back of his jumper. "Will you marry me" was spelled out in gold glitter with the ring tied to a string. Caleb took the ring and placed it on her finger before planting a kiss on her lips.

"You were about to cuss me out, huh?" Caleb laughed.

"Hell yeah. Got all that damn glitter on my baby," Royce replied.

"Co-Co's ole extra ass did that. I asked for him and Brooklyn's help and he made the jumper."

"That was so cute." Royce smiled.

"Yeah, but now I gotta give my baby another bath," Caleb fussed.

"I'm so excited. I gotta call Uri and Brooklyn," Royce said as she jumped up.

"Tomorrow baby. We're celebrating by ourselves tonight as soon as CJ goes to sleep." Caleb winked.

"Say no more," Royce said as she got up and fixed her food.

She and Caleb talked about how they wanted their wedding to be as they ate their food. Royce had already had a big wedding, so she didn't want to have another one.

Caleb didn't care, and he was good either way. She did want another reception because the one that she had with Jax seemed more like a tea party. It was stuffy and boring, and she did not have a good time. She knew that with Caleb and his family, she would have the best time of her life.

"I'm going get all this glitter off him. Have him a bottle warmed, so I can put him to sleep," Caleb said while heading to the bathroom with CJ.

Royce cleaned up their mess right before warming CJ a bottle. Once Caleb put him to sleep, he and Royce took a shower and opened a bottle of champagne. Caleb refused to drink any of the fruity drink, so he chose to sip on Hennessey instead. Royce was all smiles as they laid around and talked about their future. She was happier than she'd ever been, and she didn't think she would ever get to that place. It felt good to really be happy and not just pretend to be. Who would have ever known that her husband cheating on her with his ex-wife would have led her to her soulmate?

EPILOGUE
(6 months later)

❝Congrats guys. Everything was beautiful," Sondra said as she greeted Royce, Caleb, and her grandson with a kiss.

Sondra still wasn't one of Caleb's favorite people, but he gave her credit for trying. She stayed in her place and that was all that he ever wanted.

"Yes, and the food is so good," Lydia said with a mouth full of pasta.

They were at Caleb and Royce's wedding reception and the newlyweds were walking around with their one-year old son, greeting their guests. Caleb and Royce rented a hall to do the ceremony and the reception was held right after. Royce had an event coordinator to decorate for her and she did a wonderful job.

"Thanks y'all. My event coordinator will be happy to hear that." Royce smiled.

"It does my heart good to see you happy and smiling all the time baby girl. I have you to thank for that," Patrick said as he shook Caleb's hand.

"I agree," Sondra said, shocking everybody with her admission.

As much as she didn't want to, she had to admit that meeting Caleb was one of the best things that ever happened to her daughter. She had never seen Royce so happy and that made her realize just how miserable she had to be with Jaxon. Sondra tried reaching out to Elena, but that was a waste. Silas forbid his wife from communicating with her and she blocked Sondra's number soon after. The Davenports made news once again when once of her sons was hit with a paternity suit. Sondra didn't realize how much she never knew about Elena, but it was all being made clear. She'd also heard from a mutual friend that they were going broke, but she didn't know how true that was.

"Did y'all need us to take CJ tonight or is your mother keeping him?" Patrick asked Caleb.

"We're taking him home tonight, so we can spend some time with him before we leave for our honeymoon," Caleb replied.

Royce had been dying to go to Paris and Caleb made her dream a reality. They were leaving in three days and she couldn't wait.

"I hope y'all are still letting us keep him for the week. We have so much planned for him," Sondra said excitedly.

"Yeah, he'll be there. We'll probably drop him off to y'all the night before we leave," Royce replied.

"Come on baby. We still have a few more people to see," Caleb said as he and Royce said their goodbyes to her parents and aunt.

They stopped and talked to a few of their co-workers before going over to say a few words to his parents. A few people wanted to take pictures with them and they happily agreed. It took about an hour before they had finally spoke to and seen everyone and they were ready to relax. Caleb's siblings, cousins, and friends were all at the table together, so they made that their last stop since, they knew that they would probably be sitting there with them for the rest of the night.

"Heeey Mrs. Andrews!" Shanti yelled, messing with Royce just how she used to mess with her when she and Brian first got married.

"You better know it," Royce blushed as she flashed her ring.

Caleb pulled out a chair for her to sit down as he sat down right next to her, holding their son on his lap.

"Baby, this food is everything. They can cater for me anytime," Co-Co said while stuffing his face with the plates that were in front of him and Dwight.

"Everything was so nice Royce," Kia spoke up.

"Thanks boo." Royce smiled. "The coordinator did a great job."

"You need to make Bryce go half on your reception. Him and Taylor seem to be having more fun than anybody," Brooklyn laughed, as Dominic rubbed her baby bump.

She swore that she was done having kids, but her husband had a way of changing her mind. She was five months pregnant with another girl and he was satisfied with four. Two boys and two girls was the perfect combination and he would be content with that.

"They remind you of the old people who stay on the dance floor until the DJ packs up his equipment," Candace laughed.

"Looking dumb as hell," David said while laughing with his wife.

Bryce and Taylor stayed on the dance floor, no matter if the song was fast or slow. Bryce closed the shop for the day and he was enjoying his day off. Uri and her husband were no better, and they were dancing the night away too. Once Caleb and Royce did their first dance as husband and wife, they hadn't been back on the dance floor since. Co-Co and Sweets only danced when some bounce music was played. They sat down and stuffed their faces any other time.

"That nigga is old. He's showing his age right now with those dance moves," Brian laughed as they watched their oldest brother doing the wop.

"The fuck are they doing now?" Caleb asked as he watched Bryce and Taylor doing a dance that he'd never seen before.

"Leave them alone y'all. They don't go out as much as they used to," Kia defended as she waved her hand in Jaden's face to get his attention.

Jaden was holding their granddaughter on his lap, but his eyes stayed trained on Jaylynn the entire night. Hayden was there with Sweets, and he and Jaylynn seemed to be at odds with each other. They had an argument earlier that day and Jaden was trying to make sure that his daughter was straight.

"I'm good baby. I'm trying to see why this lil nigga keeps following my baby around. He can fuck with me if he wants to. Harold gon' have three sons instead of four," Jaden swore, not caring that Sweets was sitting right there.

"She's not a baby anymore Jaden. She's a college student now and she knows how to handle herself," Kia assured him.

"She sure does honey. Jay gives that nigga the blues," Co-Co chimed in.

[381]

"Leave my nephew alone. He's just in love with his baby mama," Sweets defended.

"Fuck him. Lil nigga shouldn't have started nothing that he couldn't finish," Jaden fumed.

"And he wonders why Hayley be walking around our house cursing all the time," Kia argued.

"With her mean ass," Co-Co said as he looked over at her.

He tried to touch her hand and she pulled away and frowned. Between Hayden's parents and Jaden, she was spoiled rotten. Jaden used to always say that she didn't like anybody but him and that was proving to be true. If he was around, she didn't let nobody touch her or tell her anything and that included Jaylynn and Kia. She was almost two years old and her G-Pa, as she called Jaden, was all that she knew.

"My baby just don't be with the bullshit. Sometimes she have to say some shit to get her point across," Jaden said as he kissed Hayley's cheek.

"I'm so happy that this day came and I'm happy that it's over," Royce said as she tuned out the conversations around her and talked to her husband.

"Me too. I'm trying to make baby number two while we're in Paris." Caleb winked.

"And you know I'm ready," Royce replied with a smile as she laid her head on his shoulder.

She was content and that was one of the best feelings in the world. She and Caleb often laughed about how they met, but they were both grateful that they did. Royce remembered Uri telling her that no man was worth her tears, but she begged to differ. Caleb made her cry all the time, but they were always tears of joy.

Made in the USA
Monee, IL
13 September 2019